“The Veil Beyond The Grave”

By: Andru Hunter &Associat

Acknowledgements:

This book is a true story, seen through the perspective of several views. It is written from the perspective of the ghosts of the people who were killed in this awful incident. The story of the people who lived at the time is told as they saw the events unfold. We also presented a view of modern day investigators trying to finally get to the truth of this unsolved case. D&R Investigations who is comprised of, Andru Hunter (myself) and Denise Gowen Krueger, my very capable partner. We had many trials and tribulations in the investigation including threatening phone calls, telling or demanding that we leave it alone, and even one call was left with the ultimatum of “or else”!

Not shying away from such an obvious exciting case, we pressed on into a deeper abyss. Sifting through countless hours of trial transcripts; coroner’s reports; inquest reports; interviews with neighbors, friends, concerned citizens and the countless hours of paranormal investigations. We were trying to unravel all the half truths of more than a century, ending up with three gigs of information between hard drives, discs and flash drives. We left no stone unturned and the light of day became the conclusion. At the end it seemed so simple how could they have missed it back then? All the evidence was there for their interpretation. They started on a wrong assumption, as you shall see. Statements were made that should have tipped off investigators. You can also see from today back, that there was quite a bit of misinformation which may have been happenstance or intentionally planted. To this end today we may never know how this transpired. Wrestling with the paranormal encounters we had made us even more determined. For those of you who believe, I can tell you the fight at times was very fierce. Something beyond the grave did not want us to find out the truth. You will find in the book some of the nasty comments we received. Not all was told, like the night inside the barn when we were pelted with rocks from within the barn. I would like to call your attention to the picture on the back of the cover of this book. This appeared on the wall in the rain with water from outside. It is a caricature of a hangman. This came shortly after I had told the spirits of the accused that we had enough evidence to hang them by the neck until dead. Were they mock hanging me instead I will never know for sure. We are still searching, trying to figure out at the writing of this book who or what did not want us to find the truth and for what particular reason we cannot say.

People we would like to thank are the owners of the Crouch Property, JR and his wife. We will not tell you exactly in this book where the property is and would ask that you leave them alone to live in peace. Andru Hunter and Associates would also like to thank the Jackson County Court system for their search for evidence. The Jackson County Sheriff's Department, The Spring Arbor Township Board of Trustees, Ken Wright of the Jackson Citizen Patriot, Leanne Smith of the Jackson Citizen Patriot. All for following us throughout this investigation. Especially Leanne Smith who gave us not only her evidence but helping put us in touch with the right people. Thanks to The Jackson Carnegie Library and all the Librarians, especially Evan, for their tireless help and for putting up with us. Thanks to the Coldwater Library System, the Heritage Library in Hillsdale and the Historical Society of Union City.

Now I would like to take this time to thank a very important man who probably does not know how much he shaped my life and how much of a father figure he was to me at a time when in my young life I needed guidance. I always thought of him in tough times; learned the meaning of perseverance from him; as well as the fact that he always believed I could become anything I put my mind to. He of course has so far been correct. When life would come along and smack me, I always thought of him. I could see him standing there even when I was far away in another country. I know he is a voracious reader, a very educated man, kind and loving to his family. Thank you, Bob Lindquist! I sir, salute you!

It is always hard to thank the countless people who helped us investigate and if I left any of you out please accept my personal thanks. It was by omission only that this occurred.

Thanks To Dan Holroyd of SMP and with him Angie Berg, Manny Hernandez, Jason Snyder, and especially to our friend and colleague Frannie. A huge thanks to the current owners of the Crouch Property, John and Tracy. And the last but not least angel of all, Morgan. You know who you are baby and it was fun having you along. I hope we can have many adventures together.

This would not have been possible without the love, guidance and encouragement of three special women. First of all, I would like to thank my wife, Leslie, for putting up with the countless hours of solitude. She has endured me being locked up writing or out investigating. Thank you my dear for your love and understanding. Although she never went with me on investigations she would always make sure I had everything I needed to take along. I would also like to thank Denise Gowen Krueger, my partner in this and in D&R. She has stayed at my side through thick and thin; working countless hours on her own doing research; staying, as my wife did, by my side and not leaving me alone or in the lurch. She is truly a great friend and partner which none of this would have been possible without her tireless energy, love, input and dedication.

The third woman I have found over the years to be an intelligent vibrant woman who is very special to all who really know her. She started out as an investigator in this case. Then for personal reasons had to drop out. She stepped up at the end doing the editing of this book. Eight long weeks she struggled with it and came up with amazing insights on changes and technical questions. Without her this book would never be as good as it is. Thanks so much, words cannot express, to Amie Fournier-Flather.

You may wonder about Andru Hunter and Associates. We are a team of paranormal investigators, who look for the truth of the subject and not the ghost in the closet. With this I would like to give two Associates who helped when no one would. Going over countless hours of video and audio recordings. Helping with the digitization of written transcripts. Assisting with paranormal experiments in the cold late at night, travelling long distances, just because they are terrific friends and Associates to myself and Denise. Jon and Theresa Meyle. "We shall forge on into the future duck by our side to keep us centered and honest."

Chapter 1

Jackson County, Michigan, is located in the east central part of the state. The county was first the site of many prehistoric animals such as mastodons and was also a place of ancient gardens of the pre-Indian peoples who inhabited the area. The county is dotted with many lakes, rivers and springs.

Indian tribes met and fought early in this county as it was a great place for passing Indians on the trail from what we now know as Detroit to Chicago. It tied into the Sauk trail and moved beyond civilization in those days. Many were the battles here in this county between Pottawatomie, Kickapoo, Shawnee, Foxes, Sacs and some wondering Otchipiwas.

The first white man to settle in the Jackson County area may have been a Canadian fur trader by the name of Baptiste Boreaux. He probably started out by trading and married into the tribes around the year eighteen fifteen.

The settlers came from the east: Pennsylvania, New York, Vermont, and New Hampshire. They came west seeking, as all did during any westward migration to our nation, land that was free for the taking which brought with it new sound communities and prosperity. Amongst these early settlers was a man named Jacob Crouch who migrated from New York in the year of eighteen thirty three.

He cleared land for a farm in what is now known as Spring Arbor Township of Jackson County. He was able to build up his land interests to 500 acres and then beyond. He became one of the wealthiest men in the area and, quite possibly all of Michigan. In 1838, he met the young and beautiful Anna Busch. They were married in Washtenaw County that year. From that marriage grew the Crouch Children: Susan, Byron, Dayton, Ethel (who lived only to 4 years of age), Eunice, and at lastly Judson.

Judd was born in eighteen fifty nine. His mother in a hard labor at a late time in life unable to withstand the strain died 5 days after she gave birth. Judd was born a crippled child with one leg that was described in those days as "withered". Jacob after losing his wife, and the love of his life could not bear having the child around to remind him of her. Susan, just recently married and living just down the road, was given Judd to care for as her own. Along with the baby came a sufficient sum of money to care for and raise the child. Judd would be 11 years old before he realized that Susan and her husband, Daniel Holcomb, were not his parents. Receiving Judd to raise as their own was a welcome turn of events for Daniel because he and Susan had a child who had died at the age four of a fever. Both fussed and cared for Judd as he was their child. Daniel and Susan also had a daughter, Edith, who later became a central character in what was to happen and probably knew, or supposed, the truth of the matter.

Backtracking a bit, Susan Crouch had married one Daniel Holcomb, a local man who was regarded in the community quite highly. They lived on a farm just down the road from Jacob's House on Horton Road. That property does not seem to exist today. Daniel was a man who wanted money. He wanted it to be apparent he was a rich gentleman farmer, even though he was not. While Jacob worked his fingers to the bone to farm and run the operation, Daniel never quite understood what it meant to make money and save money. He was constantly being bailed out by Jacob over this or that, and it was said that if it were not for Jacob he would have never been able to keep the farm he was on. There also seemed to be an underlying problem between the two that maybe went deeper than just money. Reading between the lines today it is hard to say what that might have been. One gets the impression something happened between the two that caused a rift that was irreparable. Yet Jacob continued to step up and help Daniel whenever he could. Susan would also help with Jacob's farm books and expenses until Eunice arrived back from school.

Byron and Dayton Crouch were like any boys of the time, mischievous and in and out of trouble, but nothing really bad. When the Civil War began, both went to Illinois to join the Tenth Illinois Cavalry. Byron was 19 and Dayton was only fourteen, however he was big for his age. They took him along with Byron no questions asked. They both served in battle and were mustered out at the end of the war. Byron had achieved the rank of Captain and Dayton the rank of Sergeant. After the war, they returned home and talked Jacob into bankrolling them $70,000 to build a ranch near Seven Rivers, New Mexico. While in New Mexico they raised many sheep and made a decent living at it for a while. It was during this time that Dayton met his demise. It is hard to tell exactly what happened because there are not any records left from back then to help us gauge the truth. Dayton was killed by a shot in the head. We know not from what, a stray bullet, on purpose, in a gun fight, but the interesting part is that his obituary back home says he died of small pox. He was interred at Seven Rivers only to be dug up and moved to Frio County, Texas, where Byron had moved his ranching operations. Byron Crouch became a very wealthy cattle baron in his own right sending as many as three herds a year up the trail to the rail heads for shipment east. Byron sold the ranch in 1900 to the Halff Brothers who still own it to this day. It is still a working ranch of some nineteen thousand acres. Prior to the depression there was over One hundred thousand acres in full operation. Another interesting point is that according to the Halff Ranch, Byron stayed on the ranch until his death in 1924, but an obituary found for him showed that he actually died December 5 1920.

Eunice turned out to be Jacob's favorite child. She was the apple of her father's eye. He lavished upon her praise as well as money and love; something which he had not really shown the other children. She went on to school at Notre Dame and received a teaching degree. Returning from school, she set up house in her father's home and helped him take care of finances, bills and the running of the household. She met and married a younger man named Henry White who came from a prominent farm family in the area. Jacob took to him like a son from the first moment. Still, when Jacob announced to many after Eunice became pregnant that he intended to make sure that his last will would reflect that this child would be well taken care of. Others in the family were hurt and surprised that they would at least not get their fair share. Jacob went as far as to tell many neighbors in the area that when the child was born he would make sure that Henry White would no longer have a debt over his family or his farm. He was said by some to be almost childlike in telling this story.

Some say Eunice had the wool pulled over his eyes and he was dancing to her wishes. Others thought that maybe Byron, Daniel and Judd were stealing money from the old man. Jacob was a smart man but relied on Eunice to tally bills for him because his education was limited. While he did have bank accounts, it was believed at least by the general populace of the area that the vast amount of his fortune was there on the farm. The fact remained that he would put sums of money in protected spots around the farm but he may or may not know exactly how much was in the sums and it was easy for someone who found these sums to lift amounts from the stash. Unable to properly count it all, Jacob may or may not have known that he had less than he had originally put in there.

Jacob, while having a reputation as a stern man, was a dichotomy in the fact he would take in people who were down and out and needed help. Orphans or community people, who lost their homes, are examples of those who could find work and shelter with Jacob. No questions asked. Nothing in return but a good day’s work was all that was required.

In November of eighteen eighty three, the Crouch farm was ablaze with the end of fall colors and crops were nearing the end of harvest for the year. The cattle market was lucrative and Eunice was 9 months pregnant with her and Henry’s first child. Jacob was aglow with anticipation of a grandchild.

Thus the stage was set for the inevitable on the twenty first of November, eighteen eighty three. Oddly enough, it had been a very warm day for November and true to form for a day so hot, thunderstorms had come up as evening approached. The rumble of thunder was quite distinct in the west from late afternoon on as the storm front with the cool weather of fall behind it approached.

This night was special as Jacob and his live-in hired farmhand, young seventeen year old George Boles, walked up from the barn towards the house anticipating what Jacob had hoped would be a good helping of pork chops and mashed potatoes.

Chapter 2

1883

Jacob Crouch was a tall slender man with wide shoulders and a full beard and moustache that blended together making it a sea of black facial hair. He had a full head of hair that was still predominantly black but had some gray now showing. His eyes were dark and even at seventy one years of age were sharp and piercing as though he could look holes through you with just a glance. His voice booming, he was gruff but underneath it all beat the heart of a very kind man. He would take in anyone who was down on their luck, pay them a salary commensurate with their abilities and all he asked was that they follow orders and give him a good day's work for a good days pay. George Boles was one of these people. He had been found on the street of Jackson skinny from lack of good meals. Jacob found George to be a good kid at heart; he would work right along with Jacob all day long and not complain. He never caused any trouble and stayed around the farm. Jacob believed that George was pretty smart but for the lack of schooling George might go on to do great things in life. So education was something Jacob insisted on and had a tutor come in two nights a week to help teach George to read and write along with some basic arithmetic. This was something Jacob did not have, a formal education, and he realized his short comings were because of this. He wanted to make sure that George got a good start in life toward whatever he wanted. As it turned out, George did just that by becoming a prominent preacher in the Cincinnati area later in life.

"Storm coming up George, did you make sure all of the cattle were out of the north pasture and the gate closed so they could seek shelter in the barn and not the woods?"

"Yes sir, Mr. Crouch, just like you told me and I put Chloe and her calf in the barn and locked them in underneath so as to shelter them from the storm. I's also puts hay down for them hope it's enough until morning!"

Jacob smiled and patted George on the head, "Good boy son, now let's get us some supper I'm powerful hungry, Oh and right after supper I want you to go down in the basement for Mrs.
Reese and bring up some new fall apples and cider for later, My friend Moses Polley will be here tonight. He used to work for me just like you do now, he was a good boy, and then he moved east and got married. Now he not only has his own farm but he has come back to the area to buy cattle for farmers in his area for breeding stock. Smart lad him, just like you will be some day."

"Yes sir, Mr. Crouch, I is try sir."

"You have to learn to speak better George you should say I will try sir. Take out the is you ain't is nothing son."

"Yes sir!" said George smiling at being corrected. He loved Jacob, who had taken him in, gave him a roof over his head, food and work along with a good education. He would remember this man all of his life he was sure. "No is," he thought to himself. "I am."

Both men climbed wearily up on the porch where next to the door on a small table were a bowl and a pitcher of water. They washed their hands and faces, wiped with a towel and then entered the house. There at the table was his daughter, Eunice, and her husband, Henry. She stood to greet her father. He kissed her on the side of the cheek and then laid his hand on her enlarged belly. She was a diminutive woman full of spunk and a zest for life so great she nearly saved her own life later that night.

"When is that boy gonna get here?" asked Jacob patting her belly.

"When the good Lord decides it is time, father, and it may also not be a boy. It could be a girl."

"I know but I am sure it's gonna be a boy. Mrs. Swarmgern was by the other day and she said she felt as if it was going to be a boy and you know she is never wrong!" said Jacob smiling as he moved to the end of the table. That was his place at every meal. He stopped next to Henry White and patted him on the shoulder, "So did the horses get shoed ok?" he asked.

"Yes, all is done but I think the chestnut mare also has a loose shoe. She is shaking that foot sometimes; I will look at it tomorrow and if so will take her in to get fixed for the winter."

"Hmm... we should have had Willy Akers come out here to shoe them would have been faster. Maybe you better just set up a time for him to come and check everything including some of those wagon wheels. You know this weather is bound to turn one of these days and when it does I reckon its gonna be a cold snowy winter to make up for all those warm fall days we have had. Guess we need to get ready for it," said Jacob pulling up his chair at the head of the table and sitting.

George Boles waited with good manners until Jacob, the master of the house, was seated and then took his seat at the end of the table. Jacob's rules; he was fed first and then it was passed to Henry and then Eunice. Whatever was left over George could have, but one serving only. If there was none left then George would go hungry with what little he could scrape together. Jacob had taken Mrs. Reese, his housekeeper and cook, aside and told her to make sure there was plenty on the table so George could eat his fill. In his words, "George is a growing boy and is hungry. If there ain't enough at the meal then you make sure you have things for him to eat in the kitchen afterwards. I will not see the boy going hungry."

The meal was brought out by Mrs. Reese just as Jacob had hoped, pork chops with mashed potatoes and gravy and green beans. He forked chops and spooned potatoes and green beans onto his plate. Passing it on down to Henry and then onto Eunice, George patiently waited his turn and, to his excitement, there was quite a bit of everything left for him to put on his plate. He made sure that he did not take it all leaving more for Jacob and Henry should they want it. Mrs. Reese poked at him and smiled and whispered to him, "There is more in the kitchen George, take all ya want."

George looked down the table at Jacob who smiled as George forked a second chop before he set the plate down on the table.

Mostly the meal was quiet, which is the way Jacob wanted. "Eat in peace and quiet," was his motto. "Don't bring up subjects that would bring up indigestion later on," was his favorite saying.

They chatted, mostly small talk, about grain and animals between him and Henry while Eunice would chime in about community gossip that she had heard from women visiting her to see if she had the child yet. George kept quiet and listened taking it all in but using it as a way to learn things he did not know.

Mrs. Reese ate her food in the kitchen, which was customary, and was quick to bring out more coffee or tea for Eunice and anything else requested. She always got the cook's portion and Jacob was happy with that.

She was a comely woman, a bit on the portly side, but good natured. Jacob had also taken her in when he heard from a preacher's wife about her plight. She had been thrown out of her house, divorced by a good-for-nothing husband, and was living near a park in a small room when Jacob came looking for her. At only 22 years of age she was a bundle of energy. Working hard to keep the house in excellent condition and, at this point in time, checking on and waiting on Eunice hand and foot. She was glad for the job and she had her own little room just off the back of the kitchen. There was a bed, a nice comfortable easy chair, and a small fire place for the cold nights. George kept wood stocked in there for her. He slept upstairs in a room near the attic; a small bed and a trunk with a closet and another fireplace for winter. He was happy with what he had; it was home to him.

Yes, all was well in the Crouch house. They were warm, happy, and well-fed with a nice farm agribusiness to keep them prosperous. Although the winter would be cold, they would be well cared for. They were talking about Moses Polley when there was a knock on the door. Mrs. Reese came out of the kitchen to see to the door.

"Who in the hell disturbs a man during his supper?" growled Jacob sternly looking at the door.

Mrs. Reese opened the door to see Daniel Holcomb and Daniel's brother Henry.

"Could we speak to Jacob for a moment?" asked Daniel.

Daniel was a tall, thin man with spindly legs and a face that came to a point at mid-line like a hatchet. Henry was shorter than his brother with a round face and a permanent smirk that made people think he was a smart aleck even though he really was not. Daniel owned a nice farm just a mile down Horton Road towards Jackson. Married to Susan Jacob's first daughter, he seemed to be constantly in trouble handling money. Jacob, over the years, had put quite a bit of money into Daniel's farm. Daniel's farm was in constant money trouble and although his farm rivaled Jacob's he could not seem to make money at it. He always owed someone for something he could not pay. Jacob bristled but true to his underneath soul, he would pay for Daniel's mistakes and then complain about having to keep the young man afloat all his life.

"I suppose I may have to pay for this young man the rest of my life. I don't see how he is going to ever be any different with money than he has been. If not for me, he and my daughter would have been out in the street a long time ago," he would tell friends and neighbors.

"Just wait and I'll see," said Mrs. Reese not wanting to upset Jacob while he was eating.

"Who the devil is it Mrs. Reese?" bellowed Jacob as she returned to the room.

"It's Mr. Holcomb and his brother. They would like a word with you sir," said Mrs. Reese awaiting the tirade that was sure to follow.

"Damn impertinent son-in-law, if he needs money at least you would think the miserable whelp could wait until a man is done eating," said Jacob arising from his meal with a linen napkin still stuck in his shirt collar. He was still chewing a pork chop when he opened the door.

"Well, Daniel, what is it this time? Disturbing a man's meal you should know better than that at this time of night."

"I'm sorry Jacob but my brother, well, he wants some work and I was wondering you could find a position for him. He lives just to the east toward Horton on a small farm with his wife."

Jacob knew good and well who Henry was and all about him and his wife living on a farm, a small 5 acres that had been left to them by her father.

"Ack, I've nothing this time of year 'cept for George, myself and Eunice's husband till spring. You know that. Just let him stay with you for the winter. I am sure somehow I will be keeping him in some way or another before it is all said and done. Now I bid ya goodnight. I'm back to my supper." With that Jacob slammed the door in Daniel's face.

Chapter 3

Daniel balled up his hands into fists at his side as Henry put his hand on his shoulder.

"Don't worry all will work out, you will see. Now let us go home and not dwell on what is to be."

With that they turned and walked off the property and down the road. They passed a man with a backpack moving toward them. He tipped his hat and they bid him good evening. Had they paid some attention they would have realized that he turned into Jacob's farm. He was Moses Polley, a broad shouldered young man with a square chin, short hair, and a large black handlebar moustache. He was quite a striking young man. He had been around the area looking for cattle and now he had, at Jacob's insistence, come to stay the night. He had been in the area for several days seeing lots of people he knew and buying cattle. He carried with him a good sum of cash which he used to pay for the cattle as he bought them. He intended to hire a few men, transients mostly, to help drive the cattle back to Pennsylvania. He had just come from a pub on the outskirts of Horton where he had paid three men some in advance to start rounding up the cattle for him. He foolishly had flashed the money around the pub as he paid the three men.

He knocked at the door and it swung open with a force that made him take a step back. There stood Jacob expecting to see his son-in-law standing there still begging. His face changed from one of a threatening storm to a clam, as he recognized his old friend, Moses Polley. The thunder storm now was getting closer and the air was stifling outside. The wind had not picked up; you could not smell the rain as yet but you could smell the storm in the air and it was going to be a nasty one.

"Come on in Moses my friend," said Jacob extending his hand to the young man.

Moses shook the hand of the man and walked into the house. Jacob peered out for some reason although he did not know why just to see if anyone was there but the road was empty. He did not know why he did this, but he had the feeling that he was being watched. "Must be the storm has me on the jitters," he thought to himself.

"Come Moses my friend. Have ya eaten, lad?" asked Jacob.

"No, not as yet," said Moses.

"Good lad, I had Mrs. Reese make plenty extra in hopes you would be hungry when you got here. Mrs. Reese! Fetch more and a place setting for Moses here with some good strong coffee if ya would please," said Jacob.

Henry stood up and offered his hand to Moses, "Henry White, Eunice's husband," he said shaking the hand of Polley.

Moses recognized and gave back a good strong grip which was a sure sign of a good man with good character. He would have expected Eunice to marry someone just like that.

Eunice stood and, smiling at him, came around the table. Of course, Moses realized at once that she was great with child and he smiled at the fruit of the union.

"Eunice, you look exquisitely beautiful. It has been a long time," said Moses giving her a big hug as she eagerly gave one back to him. He did not realize it but at one time she was head over heels in love with him; wanted to marry him. Little did he know how close he was to being the heir apparent to the Crouch fortune.

Mrs. Reese brought him out a plate of pork chops with lots of mashed potatoes and gravy and a large portion of green beans. Moses sat down and dug into the food as the rest of them had finished theirs. They asked him questions about his farm and his wife; how they had met; and how he was coming along with the procurement of beef. He answered all the questions in between bites as he was hungry from walking all over this afternoon and then having a couple of drinks to seal the deal with the drovers he had hired.

The thunder increased to the west. Though the storm still was not upon them, it was now pitch dark outside as was the case this time of year. Moses Polley pushed back his plate and chair while rubbing his swollen stomach from the two helpings of potatoes and beans and the four chops he had eaten.

He took the last sip of coffee from his cup as George, on a wink from Jacob, moved from the table and toward the stairs to the basement. At that moment, a loud crack of thunder sounded and shook the house rattling the windows and some of the plates in the china cabinet.

"Gonna be quite a storm if it ever gets here," said Jacob smiling. "Let's retire to the parlor and savor some apples and cider for desert. George has gone to fetch them. Mrs. Reese, will you also please join us and bring some glasses for the cider please?"

With that they moved toward the parlor and all took seats. Jacob, who was keenly interested in politics, started grilling Moses on who people in his part of the country were saying would be the next president and why. He had his own convictions and he and Henry argued with one another on which the best candidate would be as Moses seemed to add fuel to the fire at times. Eunice had her own opinions and started at one time to express them when Henry shushed her; knowing that Jacob would not allow nor take any talk from a woman about politics. They had been there for quite some time as the lightning lit up the dim room that was only lit sparsely by two small lamps. Finally, after an hour or so, full with cider and apples they all decided to retire to their beds.

"Moses, as my guest tonight I would require that you sleep in my room on my bed. Some nights I take no pleasure in there, since my wife has passed and, well, I do sleep in the alcove under the stairs which there is always a day bed made up for me. I am sure I will sleep sounder there with the lightning storm we are having."

"Why thank you Jacob. That is quite nice of you but of course I will still try and seek the best possible deal on cattle that I can tomorrow," he said with a laugh patting Jacob on his back as he picked up his pack and moved to the assigned room.

Jacob let out a loud guffaw as he hugged Eunice goodnight. Then she and Henry headed for their room which was on the first floor next to Jacob's Room. Henry smiled and waved goodnight to Jacob not realizing this was the last time the two would see one another. Polley went into his room, stripped off his shirt and boots, and crawled into bed with his pants still on. He had pulled his suspenders down. He sat his wallet, fat with money, on the night stand next to the bed and curled up in anticipation of a symphony from Mother Nature in the key of a large thunderstorm that seemed to be upon them.

Henry closed the door and pulled on a night shirt as did Eunice. She sat on the bed combing her hair. A bit uncomfortable from all the food, she had used the chamber pot but now felt the urge to use it again. She wished that the baby would soon come as she was getting very uncomfortable being pregnant. Her husband pulled out some change and a wad of money and set it on the window sill. He then removed a ring and a watch setting it next to the money. As Henry blew out the light he thought he saw a face in the window as the rain started to hit the side of the house. The lightning was very loud and the thunder worse. He sat up on one elbow and looked through the window but saw nothing and marked it off as a glare from the storm. Soon they were sound asleep. Eunice turned toward the wall and Henry up tight against her backside with an arm over her. They were in deep sleep.

George Boles had gone up to bed. It was hot in the attic and he had a small window which he opened slightly as a small breeze came in. As luck would have it, the rain was from another direction. It felt good wafting over his bed. He pulled off his shirt, dropped his suspenders, kicked off his shoes and lay down for a good night's sleep. He was tired. It had been a hard day but he and Jacob had accomplished lots. He even got that old fence mended at the back of the house near the railroad tracks.

The Fort Wayne Jackson Saginaw railroad ran within less than one hundred feet of Jacob's house actually crossing over his property and splitting it just to the back of his home. There was also a stop in his back yard that he used to ship goods from the farm to Fort Wayne or Jackson and points south. This, of course, would be a crutch of controversy about what was to happen and actually added to the madness after the fact. George was almost asleep when he heard over the rain and storm the sound of the night train moving south.

The household asleep; it was after midnight and the house continued to shake with each flash and rumble of thunder and lightning. The storm even today some say was the likes that people would say they had never heard before.

Three men moved along the tracks in the back and then came up close to the back of the house; they slowly and cautiously moved off the tracks and toward the house. The wind whipped and lightning showed them but not their faces as they had hats pulled down close over their faces. One man, rather tall, wore a new pair of rubber boots. He seemed to be in charge and he said to the other two, "The time has come. If I know the old man, he is asleep under the stairs in the alcove. He can't live one way or the other; he has to die. Also, the papers have to be recovered and, if you can't, the little pregnant witch has to be put down. Also with the foul offspring she is carrying. The black boy upstairs will sleep through it."

"What about the housekeeper in the back?" asked the second man?

"Do what ya want with her but just make sure she can't or won't testify. They will never hear a thing in this storm so let's have at it before it subsides. I will keep watch through the parlor window for anyone escaping from the house out the front. You two go inside. I know the doors are never locked." He turned to the taller of the two men and said, "You go after the old man," and then he turned to the other man. "You get the papers; I know they are in a box on the floor under the what-not in the corner. Mind ya, if ya can't find the papers then you got to kill the pregnant bitch and her husband. Light a lantern if you have to and move stuff around. Anybody wakes up, kill 'em. I have had enough of him for one lifetime. Don't take anything that could be traced back to us. We will bury the papers."

With that the two men went to the east side of the house and moved quietly up on the porch with two handguns drawn. The third man moved to the west side of the house and down near the front where he could see in and also see the road and the lane into the house all in one. As he stepped in the mud, his left foot made a print in the mud so clear that you could immediately tell the manufacturer. The rain was pelting him hard and it was now turning cold but he held his ground as he saw the door open and the two men head in.

The first man headed towards where Jacob was resting as the other looked toward the two rooms on the left to make sure no one stirred from White's bedroom. He moved in slowly as Jacob snored; curled up in a fetal position facing the wall with his back to the man. Quiet in blissful sleep unaware of what was about to happen to him. The man moved the gun close to Jacob's head and pulled the trigger just as a clap of thunder and lightning boomed near the house. The man outside the window did not hear the shot but jumped at the retort of the storm wondering if his safety was in jeopardy.

Jacob had not made a sound only slumped in his sleep. A body or guttural noise that may have been omitted would have been covered by the thunder. The man turned and left Jacob lying in his position, moving out to the area next to the second man. Moses Polley must have heard the gun shot. The man outside saw him move to the open door of his room with both hands spread holding himself by the door frame. He tried to focus looking at the two intruders. A shot was fired his way and both men ran to the room to grab him in the doorway. They grabbed him and pulled him back toward the bed.

"Who in the hell is this?" said one man in a low voice.

"I don't know but shoot him again while I go kill the bitch and her husband before they come to and sound the alarm."

With that the man moved toward the other bedroom and opened the door. Henry White was setting up on one arm looking around in a stupor of sleep wondering what he had heard when the gun went off in Polley's room. The second man raised his gun and shot as Henry rolled off of the bed. He tried to get up as he was shot a second time. The first man entered from Polley's room and Eunice was now awake and trying in a pregnant state to rise and understand what the noise was. She raised her arm in defense of the shadow men and began to let out a cry as the thunder and lightning screamed across the sky shaking the house numerous times. Each man began shooting her and one had emptied his gun, dropped shells on the floor and reloaded as they pumped five shots into the woman. She finally fell back on the bed not moving; blood flowing everywhere.

She did not feel dead but she could not move. What was it that these men wanted? She knew in her mind that she had to stay awake for the baby; she could not succumb to death. If she lived the baby would live. She realized now she had been shot. She lay quite still on her back not able to move and unsure why. She lay looking at the ceiling.

"Let's pick up lover-boy and throw him back in the bed with the bitch," laughed one man. They did so and then went back out near the stairs to make sure George Boles had not awakened. The other man moved back toward the kitchen and to the door of Mrs. Reese' room. He opened the door and saw her in the lightning flash. He started to enter the room and then thought better of it. Gently, he closed the door and then rejoined the other man in Polley's room.

George Boles was awakened by a sound he was not sure what he had heard. Maybe it was a scream or sigh and maybe what he thought was a gun shot. Scared, he crept to his attic room door and looked down the stairs. He held the door slightly ajar; just enough to peek through. He saw the outline of a man carrying a lantern stop, look up toward his room, and then move on. Terrified, George ran around his room trying to figure out what to do. Would the men come for him? Were they killing people in the house or were they just robbers? Then he heard what he would later tell the sheriff what sounded like wheels squeaking and rolling carrying a load, like furniture was being removed. He stayed in his room till morning with the storm raging, and his heart pounding.

They tore through the drawers, moved furniture around and finally found the papers they wanted holding up a light to read them making sure. One smiled at the other and then put the guns up and left the house. They joined the third man. The rain had subsided but the storm blazed to the east and carried on its thunderous vengeance. All three moved slowly back to the railroad tracks and disappeared, two towards Jackson down the tracks; the third hopped the wall to the west of the house and moved out to the road quickly.

Eunice lay there in the wake of the attack thinking about her unborn child and then her husband, Henry. Was he shot? Was he dead? Why had he not come to her aid? She wondered if she was alive or dead. She heard no sounds of anyone or anything; surely her father would find her. Moses Polley, was he dead? Was he the man who shot her? It had all happened so fast that she could not remember the faces of the men in the muzzle flashes. How many times had they shot her? She closed her eyes to rest some; she knew she had to conserve her energy.

She drifted off and dreamed of a party where she was but a young girl of maybe fifteen or so. She was in a room with other young ladies and they were all dancing around a washtub full of apples and water. She laughed as she wondered who would miss the chair and have the first dunk for an apple. The music stopped and she sat down. It was Priscilla Moss. She held her hands to her face and then down on her knees with her hands behind her she tried desperately to get an apple. If she did, she was done and out of the game but if she could not then she would have to dance the circle again.

Priscilla was lucky. She got an apple on her first try and was dismissed to the chairs on the side that were not used. One chair each round was removed until two people and one chair remained. They would then circle around a chair until one of them could not sit. The first girl who lost the chair got an apple then the other had to do so to win or she would lose.

The music stopped and Eunice found herself without a chair. She did not want to go this early but she did not want to risk staying in the circle again. She was never very good at this game. Her mouth seemed too small to get a bite and she always ended with water up her nose. She bent down and went for an apple only to find a hand on her head as she was pushed under water. She fought flailing but to no avail. Quickly, the hand let off her head and she rose up to see her brother, Dayton, standing there laughing with all the other girls. She was coughing and spitting; she had swallowed water.

Eunice came to. How long had she been out? She could just move her hand and touched what she thought was Henry's body. Tears welled in her eyes as she realized what the cold body of her husband meant. Had everyone in the house been shot and killed by these fiends?

She stared at the dark ceiling again and thought she could feel her heart flutter. Please, dear God, have someone find me! Let my baby live! Take me if you want but please let my baby live! She wept in her mind at the thought of never seeing her child; she had so much wanted a child. She was hoping for a girl even though Jacob and Henry wanted a boy. She was ready to have several children. No sound as yet in the house. She moaned and suddenly she could see her father by her side.

Jacob was smiling and Henry was with him they were pulling at her to get up; she wanted to follow. Couldn't they see she was shot? Their eyes pleaded with her to come along and she couldn't.

She felt as if she was bound to the bed unable to move, unable to think. She felt the life ebbing from her so slowly. Jacob shook his head and looked at Henry. He put his arm around Henry's shoulder and steered him away from the bed and out of the bedroom.

She wept even harder inside. She wanted to scream to wake someone, anyone, even the neighbors. She thought now it was close to first light. Maybe she had made it through the night; she could not be sure. Now her heart slowed ever so much it struggled to pump in her chest. She tried to fight it. She heard a door open and a yelp. It sounded like George Boles. She tried to call but George did not hear or she could not make a sound. Someone had to come and save her. She stared at the ceiling as the room started to light. She could not move her eyes. Now her baby she was losing the fight and she knew it.

One last prayer and a final word passed her lips "Please" and her heart stopped. Eunice White and her unborn child were dead. She lay there with her eyes open. Suddenly she felt the urge to rise and did so with ease even though her belly was still large it had no weight or restricted her movements. She looked down at her lifeless body and realized what had happened. Where was she to go? Where did Jacob and Henry go? She was not sure.

Not wanting to stay in the bedroom with Henry's body, she made her way up the stairs and lay on George Bolles bed. It was softer than she had believed. She would wait here for Jacob and Henry to come back after her.

Chapter 4

George Boles sat in his chest with the fear of God in his mind. He hoped beyond all hopes that Mr. Crouch was all right. Maybe he was just seeing things. Maybe he had a bad dream. He was anxious for morning to come to talk to Jacob about what he had seen and heard

As the storms waned and sunrise came, he could see the smallest amount of light in the east through his window. He was still reluctant to move out of the protection of his chest. He was cramped and his body ached from being in there. Worst of all, he needed to urinate. The sun kept rising and became bolder; he was not sure what time it was. He heard the old rooster crow from behind the barn. He knew it was time to get up and go and get Mr. Crouch to explain things. The morning train rumbled past the house on its way south. Now he felt a new exuberance.

He moved toward the door to his room still with his shirt off and in his bare feet. Creeping down the stairs one step at a time he felt uneasy. At the bottom of the steps he stepped on something. He rubbed the spent cartridge off of the bottom of his foot, not realizing what it was, and moved on towards Jacob’s alcove.

Stopping in and looking at Jacob he thought he was asleep. When he touched Jacob to rouse him he realized Jacob was cold to the touch and he could see through the limited light that Jacob’s head was lying in a pool of blood.

George jumped back and ran towards Henry and Eunice's room. Opening the door he was greeted by more blood. Looking in on his way by Polley's room, he saw more blood and Polley lying askew on the corner of the bed with his eyes open.

George sprung from the house and flew out the door never touching the steps. Running at top speed he did not realize that he was barefoot or bare-chested. He ran as fast as he could to the nearest neighbor George Hutchins' home less than a half mile away. He was yelling at the top of his lungs as he went, "They has all been killed! They has had their throats cut! Help!"

He was yelling as he ran into the Hutchins' farmyard where he ran smack into and knocked down farmhand Dan Reardon. "They has all been killed at our house! They is dead!" yelled George shaking and now quivering on the ground. Reardon picked himself up and summoned another farmhand to help him with Boles. Charles Parks, helped get George up and on his feet. Turning toward the back porch, Dan went into house where Mr. Hutchins was talking with a neighbor while they ate breakfast. Hutchins could see the trouble in Dan's face and asked, "What is it?"

"George Boles is here from the Crouch farm and he is claiming that all up that way have been killed. Something about their throats being cut."

Hutchins and the neighbor sprang from the table and moved out the back door. He yelled at Charles Parks who was already moving toward the barn, "Saddle some horses! Reardon, go help him!"

He then turned to George lying on the ground shivering, his eyes wide open, "For God's sake, George, pull yourself together man and tell me. What has happened?" he asked, picking George up off of the ground.

"Theys all been killed Mr. Hutchins. Whitey and them all they has had their throats cut in their sleep."

About this time, Reardon and Parks came out of the barn leading horses. They threw George up on one and then they mounted one each of their own. They turned and moved at a fast pace out of the barnyard with dogs yelping after them as they moved and rode like the wind.

They swung into the farm lot, dismounting almost at the same time running up the steps at the back of the house and into the kitchen. Hutchins stopped as he entered the door. The smell of food was prevalent and there stood Julia Reese humming softly at the stove as she cooked.

"Who's been killed?" demanded Hutchins.

"Why no one that I know of, George" smiled Mrs. Reese with a blank expression on her face.

Hutchins and the men burst past her and into Jacob's alcove to find him dead with a bullet in his head. Next, they found Moses Polley shot in the chest and left ear. They then checked the bedroom of Henry and Eunice White. Henry had been shot in the head and the abdomen. Eunice had been shot five times. She obviously had been awakened and had tried to fight off her attackers.

George Boles was now behind them pulling on his boots and shirt.

Reardon turned to George and said, "Get on the horse and go fetch the sheriff. Now, boy! Move!"

George sprung out of the house again moving past a still-bewildered Mrs. Reese, jumped into the saddle of the horse he had been given, and moved off down Horton Road towards Jackson.

"I have no words," said Hutchins. Reardon moved out of the house, up on his horse and rode as quickly as he could to Daniel Holcomb's house. He jumped off and banged at the door with great urgency. Daniel came to the door followed by Judd and Susan.

"You gotta come to the Crouch home. They have all been shot and killed in the night. Jacob, Henry, Eunice, and some man we don't know who was spending the night. Hurry!"

With the news, Susan feinted dead away and Judd just managed to catch her before she hit the floor. A housekeeper came to help Judd get Susan to a chair. Smelling salts were called for and administered. Daniel said to Judd, "I will stay here and tend to her while you go to the farm."

Judd was not sure how he felt about this. His father who seemed to never love him was dead; a sister he knew but was never close to shot dead before she could have her child; and her husband, Henry White, whom Judd never liked but never spoke bad of, dead also. And who was the stranger that was killed? Was he one of the attackers? Had Henry or Jacob gotten off a shot before?

Word spread as George went to fetch Sheriff Eugene D Winney, sheriff of Jackson County. Farmhands moved across the local countryside going from house to house telling of the tragedy.

People in Horton and Spring Arbor knew of the killings before the sheriff. They all came to pay respects and some to see for themselves; most not believing until they had seen the crime scene.

Sheriff Winney sat in his office drinking a cup of coffee and finishing up a plate of eggs when the door burst open and a man stepped in. (Who the man was that summoned the alarm is not clear. Some accounts say it was George Boles himself and some say it was Hutchins and Daniel Holcomb. The exact truth of this has not nor may never be ascertained; even the court proceedings seem to be a bit murky on this account).

"Sheriff you gotta come quick, they has all been killed!"

Eugene Winney, a striking man of about six foot two and a large handlebar moustache. He sat behind his desk wiping his face with a napkin holding up his hand as two deputies came from the cell area behind him.

"Whoa there fella, let's start over again. Catch your breath and tell me what has happened," he said standing up and using all of his stature to quiet the man.

Chapter 5

September 2010

Sergeant Jack Monroe, 15 year veteran of the Jackson County Sheriff's Department, moved to the stop sign at the corner of Reynolds and Horton Road. He looked back over his shoulder to his right towards Reynolds Cemetery. He thought he had glimpsed something out of the corner of his eye. This cemetery was well lit due to the unusual amounts of vandalism there at night. His squad car pointed south at the intersection. He looked in his mirror and saw nothing coming behind him so he put the car in reverse, and backed the patrol car to his right off the road. He turned on his four-way flashers but not the light bar. He sat there studying the old graves and partly wondering about all the people buried there from times gone by. He did not think in his fifteen years of service he had known of anyone being buried there. He was almost certain that he had seen someone moving around the big headstone in the middle of the graveyard.

Stepping up out of his car, he pulled his flashlight out and put his baton in his belt. Then he walked cautiously toward the gate, unfastened the catch and walked in. He was not a bit afraid even if there was or was not anyone there. Maybe there was such a thing as ghosts but he was not sure and he only dealt with the here and now type people that were enough to worry anyone.

He stopped at the grave and shined his light at the tree line on the back fence.

There was no obvious breach in the fence nor did there appear to be anyone hiding back there which was good because if they were and they took off he did not want to have to scale the fence in pursuit. "Just getting too old for that shit," he thought to himself.

He looked at the headstone. It read Susan Holcomb. He wondered who she was; it was one of the nicer stones in the cemetery. There were maybe sixty graves in the small cemetery that he could see or recognize. He did realize there may be more there that were not marked or had the headstones removed by vandals.

Every year in November, there was the story of an anniversary about St. John's Cemetery in Jackson (the cemetery was about five miles as the crow flies from here). The story is told that a woman who is buried there rises from her grave and comes to the Reynolds Cemetery to find her father. He rises in a mist from his grave, they materialize, hug, and then she leaves as he returns to his grave. The man's name was Jacob Crouch; murdered not far from here in his sleep in 1883. His daughter, Eunice, who was killed in the house with him, was at the time nine months pregnant. She was the one buried in St John's!

Every year in November, people would show up in Reynolds Cemetery to see if this happened and it kept local law enforcement busy just keeping the people out and chasing them away!

He walked in the cemetery now just to ascertain that there was no one hiding behind a headstone or the one lone tree just off the middle. Finally, he was satisfied that he had done his duty and it was probably just a reflection. He pulled out a small note pad from his shirt pocket and noted the time, what he had seen, and a short note that he had gone in and checked it out.

He walked lazily back to his squad car, unlocked the door, took out his baton, placed it behind his seat, and set the flashlight over on the passenger's seat. Turning off the four-way flashers, he pulled out into the intersection and moved east on Horton at an easy clip. Keeping his eyes open at the homes, searching the shadows for anything that seemed out of place, he decided that he would have a cup of coffee. He smiled. He was coming up on the old abandoned farm. The original house had burned down in nineteen forty eight but a smaller one had been built in its place. At the moment, he knew the small home was under construction by the owner. The farm was once a large farm close to 2000 acres but now it was only a little over an acre.

He pulled into the driveway and up to an old tree. Swinging around the tree, he turned the car back into the driveway and sat there to observe traffic on Horton Road. Sometimes you could catch people speeding from this driveway. He knew he was just barely in Spring Arbor Township and the Spring Arbor Police loved to sit there and radar across that driveway.

Stepping out to the trunk of his car, he opened it and searched for a black backpack. He unzipped the pack, reached in for a thermos and a sandwich wrapped in a baggy. Reaching up to the microphone clipped to the epilate of his shirt he keyed the microphone. "Sixteen Twenty One to central."

"Central," came back the voice loud and clear.

"Show sixteen twenty one ten seven at eighteen five sixty two Horton Road."

"Ten four sixteen twenty one shows code seven at eighteen five sixty two Horton Road."

He closed the trunk and realized that the mosquitoes were now swarming him. It was the middle of September and there had not been any frost as yet to kill off the state bird of Michigan. "The *Cq. perturbans* and *Anopheles*, mosquitoes," he thought candidly. He stepped back into his car and poured himself out a measure of his homemade coffee. Inside the lunch pack was a chicken sandwich on white bread that Sally had made for him. Taking a bite he could tell it was just the way he liked it with mayonnaise. He had decided several years ago when the third child was born that he would start carrying his lunch saving an extra fifty a week he could save toward college for the kids. At first, he felt funny but when he watched the money roll into the account and start to accrue he was happy and hooked to do it. Now, he did not stop in anywhere except to check on things and there were a few places that offered free coffee to all police just so a presence was there all night long.

2010

Jacob Crouch awoke. He was stiff for just a moment and he had one of those terrible headaches he had been prone to recently. He reached for the pills the doctor had given him for this and a glass of water next to his little bed in the alcove. He downed the pills and the water. He pulled on his suspenders and stuck his feet into his boots. Looking at his watch and it said three AM. He stood. There had been lots of these nights lately. He would awake and move about the house in a stupor because the house after all of these years seemed foreign to him. It somehow looked and felt different. As usual, at night when he awoke with the headache, he would go out the door off the porch, pick up his lantern, light it and then head towards the barn. He sat there and rolled himself a smoke and struck a match to it as it glowed alight. He then got up; trudged out the door and, true to every other night, there on the tree stump just outside the door was the lantern. He raised it with one hand and then moved the glass up. He turned up the wick slightly and lit it with a match. It came to life. Jacob pushed down the glass and moved on toward the barn lighting his way.

Moving past the well house and the milk house; Jacob passed the silos and down a small incline next to the old windmill which was silent in the night with no breeze visible. He looked up into the night sky at all the stars and clusters above his head. This was truly a beautiful night. Walking to the back of the barn where he had a small chicken coop. All was quiet there so shuffling back south on the east side of the barn, he saw a flash of lighting. He jumped for a moment and let out a groan. "Lightning," he thought. Looking up in the sky he saw no signs of the storm that had been there and passed. He shrugged his shoulders and moved on.

Walking into the barn and down to the pen on the left at the far end was Chloe, one of his older milk cows who had a calf just recently. They had been penned up for the night due to the storm. As he stopped, Chloe came to him and nuzzled under his arm and the calf stuck its head under the second rail and tried to nibble at his pants. He patted Chloe on the head, grabbed a pitch fork and, reaching above his head, he pulled down several forks full of hay and tossed it into the pen.

Jacob caressed the calf's head; then he heard a noise and a rustle. Looking up he saw a strangely-garbed man at the south door and another at the east door with more standing behind. He raised his hand to order them off his property but suddenly they disappeared and he found himself returning to the house and his sleep.

2010

Sergeant Jack Monroe sat in his squad car listening to the light prattle on the radio as different squads called in for minor traffic citations, etc.; nothing eventful so far this night and he hoped it would stay that way. The last few nights had been filled with domestic fights bar fights, a stabbing, a wild party, and a huge barn fire on Route Sixty.

Jack now drifted off, staring into space of the field across the road, sipping his coffee and finishing his sandwich. Finally he released his gaze and glanced up in the mirror. The noise from behind made him jolt as he stared out into his mirrors. First his rear view, then each side mirror. He decided to investigate, stepped out of the squad car putting his baton in his carrier attached to his belt and grabbing his flashlight. He set the coffee on the dashboard and as he swung he saw a light.

The light had a strange glow to it but still it appeared to be moving by itself toward the barn. The night was clear but he could not see anyone carrying the light.

"What the fuck?" he said under his breath.

"Hey stop!" he yelled but the light continued at a slow pace to the back of the barn and disappeared around the corner on the east side of the structure.

He moved quietly and slowly toward the back of the barn; all of his senses now on guard.

Then there seemed like a flash of light and he ducked down waiting for the explosion report which never came. He reached up and keyed his radio.

"Sixteen twenty one to control take me off ten seven and be advised I have visual on prowler at eighteen five sixty two Horton Road, requesting back up code two."

"Ten four Sixteen twenty one, all units in the vicinity of eighteen five sixty two east Horton Rd unit sixteen twenty one requires assistance with possible ten seventy any units in the vicinity proceed code two."

Jack now moved up from where he was ducking down near the ground and moved slowly again towards the corner of the barn. He looked at the backside of the barn but could not see anything. He had shown his light around but it hit on nothing!

He turned and walked into Deputy Ed Dwyer, he jumped "Ah jeese Dwyer scared the livin' shit out of me," said Jack.

Dwyer laughed and said, "Well, you did call for back up didn't ya?"

"Maybe not that damn close God almighty!"

"So, Sarge, what ya doin' chasin ghosts?"

"Well, I saw someone with a light come down here and then," Dwyer put his hand up and said.

"I know there was a big flash behind the barn here but there aint nothin' here right?"

Jack looked at Dwyer and saw that there was not any trace of him joking around at all. He was dead serious and the hairs stood up on back of his neck.

"So what do you know about this?"

"I used to patrol this out here. What you saw was old Jacob Crouch getting' up to check his animals."

"Who the hell is Jacob Crouch?"

"He, his daughter, her husband and a visitor were all shot to death up there in the old house. The new one sits where the old one once was. It happened back in 1883."

"You trying to tell me I saw a ghost?"

"Well, I am guessing just like the rest of us you just saw the light. But now if you go around to that door and look in you will see Jacob in the barn feeding a cow and a calf. He will be taking down some hay from the loft above."

"Bullshit!"

"Suit yourself man, but I'm not pullin' your chain!"

Jack frowned a moment not sure what to make of this but Dwyer's face and eyes told him that he was not joking. Slowly he made his way to the side door. Finally, he turned and looked in with Dwyer on his back shoulder. There, just as Dwyer had said, was an old man with a black beard and messy hair pulling down hay with a fork and in front of him stood a cow and a calf.

"What are you doing here?" asked Jack.

The old man set down the hay fork, turned, extended his right arm pointing at Jack and said, "Where is she?"

With that he disappeared; like vanishing into thin air along with the cow and the calf.

Jack jumped; looking and now moving into the barn, "Where the fuck did he go?"

"Out here Jack," said Dwyer.

Jack came out of the barn and saw Dwyer pointing to a small light going up the hill toward the house and then disappearing into the night just before it got to the house.

"He does that all the time. I guess he is going back into the house and back to bed. I really don't think the old man knows he's dead."

"What do you mean?" asked Jack.

"Come on, Sarge. Let me buy you a cup of coffee."

"I got some in the trunk Dunkin Doughnuts Coffee. I got extra cups," said Jack tugging on Dwyer.

"You sure he did not go into the house?"

"Nah, we can go look if you want but that house is pretty torn up inside. It's being gutted and remodeled."

"Oh," said Jack opening his trunk and retrieving the canister of coffee. Then he remembered that he left it in the squad car. He grabbed a plastic cup he had in his pack and went up and filled his and Dwyer's cup up with coffee. He reached up, keyed the microphone and spit into it, "sixteen twenty one cancel the ten seventy."

"Ten four sixteen twenty one, ten seventy is cancelled."

"So how do you really know all about this?" asked Jack?

"This has happened to all of us at least once and maybe more who have patrolled this road over the years. I was almost sure what it was when I heard dispatch call in for backup. I am sure a few others surmised the same thing."

"So everybody will be laughing at me in the morning."

"No, maybe laughing with ya when you got a few hours to mull it over in your mind. Then you want to talk to everyone who has seen the same thing and compare notes. A lot of us have been there including Barry over in Spring Arbor. The neighbor on the hill has seen it from his kitchen several times also. Those of us who have seen it are in an elite club if you think about it."

Jack just shook his head and finished his coffee, a little more steady on his feet at this time.

"So who killed them?"

"Don't know. I have never read up on the case very much. Someone once said there was a trial for two guys who were found not guilty but don't know much more than that. I don't think it was ever solved. I think there was an article back in the 70's in The Jackson Citizen Patriot when I was a kid about the Crouch murders. I believe it was written by a man named Ken Wright."

"Well, let's clear and get back to patrol and let Jacob tend to his animals," smiled Jack as he stepped back into his squad car.

Chapter 6

1883

Sheriff Winney now had the story and was on his way west to Horton Road to investigate. He had taken two of his best detectives with him and he kept the carriage moving at a good speed all the way out of Jackson.

Of course, the word spread around Jackson like a wildfire in a mid-summer wheat field. The news traveled fast and people hitched, saddled, or got a train ticket west to see for themselves. Never had anything close to this happened in this community before. A lot of people knew the Crouch family, those that did not know them had at least heard of them. A lot of people knew the Crouch family and most had heard of them and knew of them.

Moving down the road a greater clip all the time they were closing in on the Horton Road address.

People now had come from near and far as quickly as they could. Call it morbid fascination or just complete utter disbelief, most of them had to see for themselves and now even the train stopped in the back yard letting more people disembark. Some now had become amateur detectives. They searched high and low for footprints trying to track anything; even the foxes of the area were not safe from accusation at this point.

People consoled Mrs. Reese as she sat in a shocked state trying to comprehend what had happened in the house where she had slept the night before. A lot of questions swam in her head like "How could I have not heard a thing?" and "Why did they spare my life?"

Cartridges were found on the floor, picked up, examined and either tossed back on the floor at random or kept for a souvenir. One man fingered the cartridge and then placed it on a small table just outside the room that Moses Polley had slept in. People tried to clean up Polley's room as things had been torn out of drawers and strewn about. There in the White's room Henry was resituated in his bed so he was close to Eunice' body. Blood on the floor was stepped in and tracked about. In moving Henry's body, some blood spatter occurred confusing the point later on in the investigation and subsequent trial. Men were combing the fields looking for tracks. Some thought they were hot on the trail down the tracks and, in their excitement to follow them; they subsequently lost the tracks and had obliterated any evidence of the tracks they had found.

As the sheriff approached he knew there would be the devil to pay. Almost a mile to the east of the Crouch home, buggies of all types as well as horses clogged the road. He had to stop and let the men with him move some of the rigs so they could get through. As if to mock him, several people walked by the stopped sheriff's buggy beating him to the crime scene.

As they tried to pull up to the house they finally gave up, stopped in the middle of the road, and finished the trek to the house by walking in. The front side and back of the house was filled with people meandering around and any number of saddled horses and conveyances.

The blood rushed to Winney's face as he realized any evidence of value was surely destroyed. He saw a few men that he knew, told them to round up a posse of about a dozen men and come back to him there in the front yard.

A man came up to the sheriff and said to him, "Got sumthin' you gotta see, sheriff."

Winney followed the man around to the west side of the house by a front window which looked directly into a parlor. There on the ground was a large wash tub turned upside down. The man lifted the tub and there in plain sight in the mud was a boot print staring at him with immaculate detail. The rest of the ground around the house had been churned up by people passing and coming and going at the scene so as no other track was found in the yard.

"Adams," he called to one of his young detectives, "Sketch out this print in every detail. You know what I mean? This actually may have been left by the killer."

"Ah, killers plural," said a man coming up to the sheriff.

"What?" said Winney turning.

"Ah yeah, sheriff, they is plenty of shells all over the house and from different guns. I knowed, my father was in the Civil War and he knew a lot about bullets," said the man handing Winney a spent cartridge.

Now Winney had enough and blew a cork. "I should arrest your dumb ass for messing with evidence! As a matter of fact, I should arrest the whole damn community! You people have no common sense what so ever. If there was any evidence worth using, it can't be now that you have all corrupted it."

He turned to see his posse forming. "I aint got badges for ya all but raise your right hands."

The men complied.

"Do you solemnly swear to act on the orders of the Sheriff of Jackson County, Michigan, as a deputy of a posse hereto with made up if so signify by saying I do? Oh and dummy here on the end it's your right had!" screamed Winney as the men cringed and they all looked to see which hand they had up.

"Well, do ya?" yelled Winney.

The men for the most part mumbled afraid to speak up now and there were but a few I do's that could be heard.

"All right. I want you all to split up in threes and I want everyone who does not live here or have something to contribute in the way of an eyewitness out of here. I want the goddamned road cleared of all the horses and conveyances."

"But most of all," he said smiling at the men. "I want it done in twenty minutes or I'm liable to start shootin' people!" screamed Winney yanking the hat off his head and crushing it with his bare hands in exasperation.

Adams had finished the sketching of the footprint. Winney looked over at the man who had showed it to him. "Get his name," he said, "and then if you would be so kind sir as to turn the wash tub over to cover the evidence you found and plop your nosey ass on it and don't move cause so help me God if you do, well, your life may depend on it."

He looked up as the deputies were doing a good job and people now had heard the threats from the big stalwart man and realized he might just start shooting at them. They orderly and with the help of the deputies left the property. The house emptied out and they were on their way.

He saw Mr. Hutchins starting to leave and he yelled, "Not you, Hutchins. I got questions for you and Reardon and where is that colored boy Boles? I got questions for him. Adams, I want Boles held for questioning. You understand? Find him and hold him along with that housekeeper. Round 'em up and set 'em down somewhere."

"Yes sir," said Adams, a man of average height with spindly legs and a small protruding stomach. His face was that of a pointy chin with long sideburns. The eyes were beady though piercing. He moved off on a mission turning his head this way then that.

The house finally cleared and Winney went in with two detectives to view the scene. There they found Jacob Crouch in the alcove under the stairs on his side facing the wall with a bullet in his head. He looked as though he was shot where he lay and was asleep at the time.

Next they went to Moses Polley's room. The drawers had all been ransacked in the room; clothes strewn on the floor, the bed and some on the body. It had appeared that someone had tried to hang some clothes and some had been folded and lay in a pile on the floor. Polley himself lay across the bed diagonally. Whether he was laying that way when he was shot was a matter of contention. There appeared some blood on the floor but it had been tracked about and trampled so much it was hard to tell if it was his or just tracked in on someone's shoe. There they found two shell casings on the floor; one in the doorway that had been stepped on and crushed. Just outside the doorway was a second casing, it was intact but it was hard to determine if that was the original resting place as another was found on a table just outside the door setting up with the empty end down as if someone had placed it that way.

Next they went to Henry and Eunice's room. There Henry lay next to his wife as if he had been staged that way. It was determined that someone had moved the body next to Eunice. It was not believed that the killers did this. Eunice lay there in her bed; eyes open looking up at the ceiling. Winney noted that even though she was dead, she had been alive for some time after the shooting because unlike the others rigor had not set in as yet and she was still warm to the touch. He felt a pang in his stomach. A woman pregnant; ready to have her first child; excited about the prospects of life.

He wondered had she seen the killers? Did she know them? What was it like for her to know she was dying and the baby dying with her, helpless? Nothing she could say or do but lay there and wait for the end. A tear came to the lawman's eye. He had seen some bad crime scenes in his life and many a mangled body but nothing stirred him inside quite the way this one did. He would remember the case for the rest of his life and work it and work it trying to come to a conclusion to it all.

"Where the goddamned doctor at? Get someone down the road and make sure they can get in."

A second deputy came up to the sheriff and whispered in his ear.

"Really then; let's see it," he said moving out to the west side of the house.

The two men walked toward a stone wall that was between the house and the railroad track. There at one juncture along the wall as a very good footprint in the mud as if someone had hoped the wall in the rain the night before.

"Does not look like the other boot print so best to sketch it. Probably will be hard to say if one of the killers made it or someone this morning just looking around?"

"There are some more tracks over across from the railroad tracks but they are not identifiable. It maybe whoever made this track was cutting across here moving west to some destination," pointed out the deputy.

"Yeah well, that sure could be so let's get a very good sketch detailed as much as possible. Measure it out real close and all and we shall see if something comes up that may point us back to this," said the sheriff walking back into the house.

He again was waylaid by another deputy escorting a man to him.

"Sheriff this man says he found tracks out in the field and he can identify who made them."

The sheriff looked at the man maybe in his fifties. He wore black pants, a long black coat, a broad-brimmed black hat and had a white thick moustache.

"That so and how is it that you can identify these tracks?" asked the sheriff pushing his full body at the man trying to see if he could intimidate him some. But the man to his credit did not wither. He looked straight in the sheriff's eyes and said.

"Cause I seen 'em many a time afore. No one can make that kind of track cept one man and that man is Judd Crouch. He's got that one bad leg that he wears that big iron brace on and it makes an odd track in the mud and that is there plain as day right behind the barn. So I'm thinking you may want to ask young Mr. Crouch some questions of why he was back there in that field. Maybe he has a good reason and maybe he was fleeing a murder scene?"

The sheriff now stepped back and thought about this for a moment. This man could have something there if we could tie that in. Killers could have gone across the fields in the back so as not to be seen walking down the road.

"Get his name and address and then sketch the tracks and make sure you write up a real good detail of how many there are and which way they is going, and follow them if you can," said the sheriff to the deputy. "Then report back to me here at the house and let me know what ya find."

Chapter 7

2010

Jack sat in his kitchen eating pancakes that his wife Sally had fixed for him. The children, Susie, Barry, and Clara were in the living room eating cereal and watching cartoons on TV. He looked over to make sure they were engaged and then started to tell Sally about his night. She knew after all these years that he rarely if ever brought his work home with him but when he did it was something he needed to talk about. She was amazed and very curious about his story.

Sally was a tall woman. Almost six feet tall, long dark hair and brown eyes; she had a shapely figure and nice legs. To Jack she was all he ever wanted and that was something she knew in her heart.

"Well Jack, I have been watching some shows with Susie at night. One is called The Atlantic Paranormal Society, or T.A.P.S. It comes on the Syfy channel on Wednesday night. It is not actors but a real-time show about ghost hunters and in the last year we have watched several shows. Also reruns of one on maybe Discovery called A Haunting about real stories of real people who experience paranormal activity in their homes or lives."

"Sally, that is all well and good but to what end is this story taking?"

"I have done some reading in the area at the library and we have real paranormal investigators in our area. Some groups are better and more equipped than others but the fact remains that they can sometimes get real answers in real time."

"Hmm… so you think I should contact one of these groups with my story?"

"Well, what could it hurt? It might be fun for you to do something outside of work; like work on this."

"Nah, if I told anyone about this they are on their own. I got lots of work coming up and if I ever expect to get that promotion and a bigger paycheck I got to go back to college and finish my degree this fall."

"Well, it is something to think about anyway."

"Yeah, I'll give ya that but unless there is a crime being committed you won't find me in that driveway at night anymore."

"I'm off to bed, hon. Will you go online and download the class schedule for me this fall so I can decide what to sign up for and when? The new list is to be online by 10am today."

"Yeah. Sleep well. I'm taking the kids out later for lunch and then some shopping at the mart. Do you need anything?"

"Toilet paper for the squad car if I have another night like that one," he chided.

Sally laughed, rubbed his head and gave him a big kiss.

Jack awoke at about five thirty PM and decided he would venture out to the library in downtown Jackson. He had read the note Sally had left him that she and the kids ate at Mickey D's and then went to her mother's to swim in the pool till dark. He hastily scribbled on the paper that he was headed downtown to the library. Jumping in his pickup truck, he sped off to his own destiny with Mickey D's and the library.

He parked across the street from the library and walked up the stone steps to the front door. As he entered, he saw the help desk.

"Where can I find information on maybe some murders from a long time ago?"

"The reference room is through those double doors. Just ask them and they will be glad to assist you."

Jack moved on and saw a young woman and man at the desk. He stopped and decided to play a trump card so he pulled out his badge and said. "Sheriff's Department, I would like some information on the Crouch case and also on ghosts."

The young man smiled and he rose. "I can help you deputy, would you like to read the paper about it? We can find some microfilm for you if you know the exact year and time."

Jack's memory now failed him and he could not remember the date or year.

"Uh… it happened about the turn of the century, nineteen hundred that is, not two thousand. The name was Crouch."

"Ah yes, then you would like to see our Crouch file. With that you will be able to ascertain the correct dates and then we can proceed to look at the newspapers of the day and find the story. Now, if you go up stairs on the next floor and talk to the lady at the help desk she will be able to locate ghost books for you. By the time you have a few of those to read; I will have the material here all set out for you."

"Uh, thanks uh," Jack took notice of the man's name badge. It simply said Evan. "Uh, Evan," he smiled and shook the young man's hand.

"Let's go this way and you can take the elevator up and look for your books. You can also copy any and all of the material here for ten cents a copy or, if you want, I have a key that can let you copy. It keeps count and then you can pay us when you are through."

"I think, Evan, I like the key as I am not sure how much I will be copying tonight. This is just a routine investigation of my own."

Jack pushed the elevator button and went on up. As the door opened, he went to the help desk on the second floor. Smiling at the young woman named Sandra he asked, "Can you help me find a book or maybe a directory for paranormal investigations or investigators?"

"Well yes, I think so," she said returning the smile.

"So are you looking for paranormal investigators in this area?"

"Yeah, or at least a list of them if possible. I really don't know what I mean by the area. I guess Ann Arbor or Detroit something like that."

"So have you had an experience?" She asked.

Jack began to spill his story to her. Why he felt compelled to do so he did not know, but she quickly became completely enthralled over the story to a point she stopped looking for the book. She stood very still at the end of a book aisle and listened intently.

"Wow, if that happened to me I would be so gone. I don't know what I would do," she laughed putting her hand to her mouth to stifle her laughter and amazement. "I think I have just the man for you. He has been in here before. Just go down and ask Evan for the business card for Hunter Ross. He is based out of Ann Arbor or something like that. He is a for real ghost hunter in the area and somewhat known by other police departments for helping on some cold cases I am told. My girlfriend met him in a pub just off campus at U of M and was completely taken by him."

"The books you want are here," she said. "I hope you find what you are looking for."

Jack did find a few books that were primers on paranormal investigations and found a web site for ghost hunting one-o-one by Jason Sullivan. He then proceeded back downstairs to see what Evan had found for him. He had it all laid out on a table in the back reference room. The Crouch File, a nice big manila folder.

"Here you are, sir, our file on the Crouch Murders. It took place on November twenty first or twenty second. Really they are not quite sure the time of day but sometime between ten PM and two AM. I will look in the card file we have here that is an index of articles on people in the paper and can copy from there articles on the microfilm. Now if you want, we can print those out also off of the microfilm or if you have a flash drive we can plug that in and load it."

"Thanks, I will just look through your files here and if I have any questions I will ask you," said Jack thinking as Evan started to walk away. "Oh Evan, there is one question. The lady upstairs said you might have a business card for a Hunter Ross? A paranormal investigator?"

"Ah yes, you think you may need his services?"

"Well I am not sure but she said you could tell me more about him."

"He is a very nice down to earth fellow, twenty years in the Marine Corps, recon division, retired a full bird colonel. He has a modest book store in Marshall, right downtown and he and his partner Victoria run the store. They are all quite a hoot. I love them just like family. Mr. Ross is a Forensic Paranormal Investigator. He has his own group of experts that work for him and back him on investigations. I will get the card; I have a few left. You can have one and get in touch with him."

Evan walked away with a slight rise in his gait as if he was excited to introduce Hunter Ross to anyone.

Jack opened the folder and the first paper in front of him was one from a newspaper article by Ken Wright, 1977. It was a picture of the Crouches, Jacob Crouch, Eunice White, Henry White, and Moses Polley! The headline at the top read "EVEN PINKERTON COULDN'T SOLVE THE CRIME". Between the pictures of the family was a photo of a house. It was two stories, looked nice and kept well. Not sure from what era but the caption underneath read "the Crouch Property".

Various other articles and type-written notes from other people adorned the thick folder. He found out that Jacob Crouch had two sons in Texas and that he also held ranch land down there; maybe as much as three hundred thirty thousand acres. This was a big ranch for Texas but not as big as some down that way. The article went on to say that Jacob was almost a self-made millionaire even in the monetary standard of eighteen eighty three.

He wondered if Jacob was robbed. He had read a small snippet that said that Jacob did not trust banks and was apt to carry large sums of money on him. Jack read on and absorbed as much as he could but at some point it all became muddled and confusing to him; too many twists and turns. He was not sure how to get through this and at least in this date and time there were no witnesses to find. He wondered if there were any living relatives and if the Mr. Ken Wright was still around to shed some light on the subject. Maybe he could go to the paper and get a copy of that article and read it to see what was said. He found it strange that there was not an article in the file to peruse. He looked at his watch and realized it was getting late and decided to call it a night. He had read all he needed to and next it was off to patrol for him. As he approached the desk, Evan was smiling again.

"Here is the card. I hope it helps and come back anytime. We are always anxious to help; that is what we get paid for."

Jack took the card and read in bold, simple black print on a brown card "D&R Investigations, Forensic Paranormal Investigations, Cold Case Files, Missing Persons, Paranormal Investigations of Home, Business, or Organizations, All confidential, licensed and bonded. Jack stuck the card into his pocket and continue on his way out of the library.

The man walked into his place of business, past the front counter and the back counter, into the back and then into an office. The room was about twenty feet by twenty feet. There were two desks; one at the front to your right as you went in and then one in the back left corner setting across the corner. In the corner behind the big black plush executive's chair was a corner shelf full of reference books on the paranormal. There was a black leather couch to one side and a black leather easy chair in front of his desk. At the first desk by the door, there were two more chairs upholstered red covering with wooden arm rests.

He was Hunter Ross; owner of this book store called the Hobbits Nook. There were several levels to one floor; as you went up a few steps to some shelves and then down a few to more shelves. Off to one side was a large couch and three easy chairs for people to sit, rest and just read if they wished. In the middle was a small island that had a small microwave along with Styrofoam cups and a large coffee pot with a white soapstone time marked on the side of it. In the center of the island was a small sink. If the coffee sat for more than twenty minutes it was dumped and a new pot was made.

Hunter went to the safe in the back of his office and spun the dial left then right then back left and opened the door. He had done this almost every morning now for the last ten years. Pulling out two large metal drawers he set them on his desk, and then closed the safe. Turning the locking handle he spun the combination cylinder. He picked up the two metal boxes and moved out to the counter at the front of the store. There he pushed eight six eight one on the register and it opened up the drawer which was empty.

At that point he opened the metal box and counted the money inside. It came up to two hundred dollars in small change. He dropped the box with the lid opened into the drawer and then closed the register. With a quick gait moving down some steps to a middle level of the first floor and to a second counter, there he did the same thing with the second box.

Hunter checked his watch. It was exactly eight fifty five AM just like every morning. He looked up to see Samantha unlock the front door with her key.

Samantha Flowers was a forty year old blonde with long hair that came down past her shoulders almost to her shoulder blades on her back. She was tall about five foot nine and maybe weighed close to one hundred and seventy pounds. She was a very beautiful woman with soft red lips and expressive hips as she walked. Today she wore the black high heels.

"I thought you swore off heels?"

"I had until my husband decided that I had to tag along to a party this weekend with his public relations firm. So I gotta stand for hours with a damn smile on my face in these black high heels and if I'm gonna suffer I am going to do it in here today and try to tone my legs up a little bit at a time."

She reached into a bag she had over her shoulder and pulled out a pair of Birkenstocks; soft brown made of Sumatra leather.

"This is what I put on when my feet ache and when they stop; back go the high heels."

The phone rang and Hunter, close to the counter, reached over and picked it up. "Good morning Hobbit Nook, may I help you? No, she has not. Uh yeah. I see. Ok, I will get a hold of her and let her know. Thank you for calling."

Hunter laughed, "Well, I'm gonna bet on which pair you wear the most. So this soiree is Saturday?" he asked as he pulled out his cell phone and punched in a number. Samantha stuck out her tongue and put her bag under the counter.

"Hey lady, where are you? Really! Well, the school just called. It seems that Amanda left her backpack including her lunch in the back of the van and the teacher wants to know if you can bring it back to the class room. Yeah, I know but this will have to come out of your pay. You know, missing hours just can't be tolerated here," he laughed, "Yeah well, the same to you." With that he hung up as Samantha giggled.

Then front door to the shop opened and in walked store associate Cheryl Treadway. She was a thirty-something lady with two kids and a husband who drove truck for a local excavating company. She had two boys; Tom who was 12 and Logan who was 11.

"Good morning, Miss Treadway hope we are well today," he said.

"Humph" was all he got from her. All three women had worked for him a long time. They all had fun together and if the truth be known, none of them wanted to leave for any reason. They all liked it here. They especially liked the aspect of Hunter being a ghost hunter or, as he was billed in many parts of the world, a Forensic Paranormal Investigator.

Hunter actually trusted all three of the women to run his business and always made sure they had nice bonuses at the end of the year commensurate with the profit the store turned.

He grabbed Cheryl and swung her around as if they were dancing; she led with him beautifully. She laughed as he swung her.

"What on earth are you doing, Hunter?" she laughed again as Samantha was now laughing

"I did what you told me not to. I went to the cemetery and danced with the devil and found her to be a beautiful woman in a very revealing red dress with jet black long hair. I just wanted to show you that I did do it," Hunter laughed.

Cheryl pushed away from him now and said, "Good for you. I'm just glad I was not there to see you make a fool of yourself."

"I'm just kidding. It was very quiet and it is really a nice place. I have secured the rights to go back there as often as I want. We will conduct experiments with our equipment there. Did not get much action but it was only the first time. Gonna go out there some on my own."

The door opened and in walked Victoria Carter, a 36 year old woman with long blond hair that flipped up at the shoulders. She had light blue eyes that jumped out of her face at you and endeared you to her. She was about 5'8" tall, slender at the hips with nice shapely legs and no blemishes. You could see that she had ample breasts that were kept in check with a very stringent push up bra.

"Thanks, sweetie, for calling me," she said giving Hunter a peck on the cheek as she walked by him.

"No problem, hon, I'll be back in the office in a minute," said Hunter turning to Samantha. "So, I have Jemma coming in about 10 to help you with restock. I have a shipment coming in this morning and I want them priced and up. Cheryl, let's change our window design just a little. You work your magic. You are so good at. I have an appointment to keep and maybe I will do it up in my apartment. There will be a deputy from Jackson County. His name is Jack Monroe. He may or may not be in uniform. So if someone comes looking for me you will know who he is."

Hunter turned and then went to the office in the back where Victoria and he worked side by side. Some thought that maybe they did more than that after work but nothing was ever admitted or proven. The girls in the store always had an eye on the place in the evenings and on the weekends.

"So how was your weekend, my dear?" asked Hunter as he passed her desk. She was standing unlocking the center drawer and she reached over and turned on her computer. Hunter now noticed she wore a dark red skirt about 3 inches above the knee and a matching jacket. Under the jacket she wore a white blouse with ruffles at the collar and on her sleeves as they protruded from under her jacket.

"Ah uneventful. Just me and the kids we went to the zoo Saturday. It was fun but they got tired before the day was over so we stopped for a bite to eat and some ice cream. I almost called you to see if you wanted to join us."

"Well, I would always be more than glad to accompany you and the children anywhere at any time. No plans I ever have are big enough to cancel that." He looked at her backside as she reached up on the book shelf next to her desk to put a book away. The skirt rose even further and he could not stop his glare. To say he found her irresistible after working with her the last ten years was an understatement.

She turned quickly and caught his glance and smiled at him. She knew of his interest in her for a long time and, to be quite frank, she was interested in him. She was just waiting for the right time and for him to realize that he had fallen in love with her a long time ago.

"So the kids are off to grandmas this weekend?" He asked coyly knowing the answer before it came.

"Yeah, they are. What did you have in mind?"

"I just wondered if you wanted to accompany me on an investigation if one turned up. You said you might if the time was right."

"Well, we shall see. Do you have anything in mind?"

"Couple of things… might just go with the group this weekend. I think they have something coming down the road. A warehouse or something like that."

"Well, when you get it all figured out let me know. Did you get Jemma to come in this morning to help with the books that should be here?"

"Yep. Told the girls about it and put Cheryl on redoing the window for some different aspect of interest."

"Hmm… that's good. She has a good eye for that."

"I also have a gentleman stopping in this morning from the Jackson County Sheriff's office. I am not sure about what but it has to do with a paranormal situation."

"Interesting; that should be very interesting."

"So, do you want me to fetch some coffee from down the street?"asked Victoria.

"Yeah, why don't ya get big cups and bring it back here? He reached into his pocket and handed her a fifty dollar bill.

She raised her eyebrows and said, "That's a nice tip but who is gonna pay for the coffee?"

"Yeah, get on out of here will ya," he laughed as the two women up front giggled.

Victoria left on her mission and Hunter returned to his desk. He sat and looked at his computer; same morning ritual. First the Wall Street Report, Financial News, New York Times, Yahoo Comics, and then he checked his email from the weekend and messages from his Facebook page. As he sat attentive of his computer, there was a small knock. He looked up to see a man in his early thirties, large black Polo shirt, khaki Dockers and suede shoes. He had short hair neatly trimmed.

"I'm sorry. May I help you? I was engrossed in the morning paper."

"Are you," the man stopped and looked at a business card he had in his hand, "Hunter Ross?"

"Yes, and you are?"

"Deputy Jack Monroe, Jackson County Sheriff's Department. I know I am a little early. The appointment was for ten and it's just nine forty five."

Hunter rose to meet the man and extended his hand in a greeting, "Ah Deputy Monroe, what a pleasure it is to meet you, sir. Please come in and sit down. That is what you want to be called Deputy Monroe or maybe Mr. Monroe?"

Jack found the man truly engaging and knew right away that he would get along well with him; there was just something about him that oozed confidence and intelligence.

"Call me Jack if you want Mr. Ross."

"Ha! Then you call me Hunter."

"Very well. Hunter it is," as he allowed himself to be shown in to the office and a chair in front of the desk.

"My secretary has gone out for coffee and sweet rolls but until she returns maybe you can tell me what brought you in search of me? Also, if there is a need for privacy we can use my apartment above."

"I am not sure there is any secret to this and it is possible that you already know about it but I am interested in getting some help to solve this old case."

"So then, we are talking of a cold case file?"

"I guess you could maybe call it that."

They were interrupted by Victoria entering the room. Jack stood up and smiled at her recognizing at once that she was a very beautiful woman.

"Jack Monroe, this is my assistant. Victoria Jameson. The apple of my eye and my undercova lova."

"You will have to excuse him, Mr. Monroe, he has these flights of fantasy all the time," smiled Victoria blushing and giving Hunter the "as if" look.

Jack laughed and decided he would like these two; and Hunter seemed to be well grounded. He was not sure what he was going to find a witch or warlock; some guy way out on the astral plane; or maybe some crazy meditative nutball. But he was pleased and pleasantly surprised.

"Victoria has our coffee. She can doctor it anyway you like, Jack, just tell her. I will, of course, take mine with three Sweet'N Low. You did get me an espresso shot in the coffee did you not?"

"Yes!"Said Victoria setting the plate of sweet rolls from Louie's bakery between them.

In Marshall, Michigan, Louie's always had the best fresh handmade sweet rolls from scratch and today she had brought some of the famous Nutty Rolls.

"Tori, sit down here with us. I think Mr. Monroe uh, Jack, has a case for us," said Hunter. He always used the name Tori as a term of endearment with her when he was serious.

Victoria responded to the nickname that Hunter had given her over the years and pulled up a second chair, sat down, crossed her legs and put a yellow legal pad on her lap. She reached over and grabbed a black ink pen from the top of Hunter's desk. Samantha walked past the door at that moment and Jack called to her.

"Sam, would you please close the door and as long as Mr. Monroe is here we do not want to be disturbed or take phone calls. Anyone wants Tori or myself tell them we are out or in a meeting please and thank you."

Samantha moved back to the door, looked right at Hunter and stuck her tongue out at him; a gesture that did not go unnoticed by Jack. He smiled and wondered about the work dynamics in such a place.

"Well, to begin again, I have stumbled across this case," began Jack, "Quite by accident and had I not have been in the right place at the right time, I still would be ignorant of it today," he laughed and said. "But quite a few of the deputies have had similar experiences over the years, talked among themselves but did not see any value in telling old Sarge here; only after he had the bejesus scared out of him."

"Not that old," thought Victoria, as she watched his face give off tell-tale signs of his story such as was it true, did he believe it, and was he alarmed by it? Hunter had taught her a lot about non-verbal communication over the years. She had been not only a good pupil but extremely interested on how the human body can tip things off even without conversation. She now could spot most lies a mile away; like the time her husband had declared that he was not seeing another woman. The head tilt gave him away.

She smiled as Jack continued on his story. He seemed sincere to her.

"Well, I don't know if either one of you have heard about the Crouch Murders. There were four people killed in a house in Spring Arbor Township in the year 1883. One woman was nine months pregnant. There were three men and one woman killed: the father, Jacob Crouch; his daughter, Eunice; her husband, Henry White; and a friend and visitor for the night, Moses Polley."

He stopped as both Hunter and Victoria were writing. Hunter looked up and said, "Oh, don't stop. Tori and I always do this when we are together. That way if one misses something the other may pick up on it and record it. Believe me we are listening."

"Oh Ok," said Jack."Jacob Crouch was a very rich man in his own right back in the days. Everything I have I derived from the Jackson library. The case is so famous that they have a file just for people to read about it. Of course, I can't attest to the truth behind this and that is why I wanted some help. Jacob was probably a millionaire even in the monetary system of 1883. He farmed maybe close to ten thousand acres and was a very successful cattle breeder and seller. He also owned what is purportedly a 330,000 acre ranch in Texas."

Hunter raised his head and his eyebrows. "Wow! That was quite a spread back in those days. Where was this ranch?"

"That I have not found out as yet and the articles I read in the file did not name a place in Texas. There were a few confusing references to a ranch also in New Mexico. The ranch was operated by two of his sons, one Byron and the other Dayton. There was a reference to Dayton having died but I could not come up with a cause for sure. One said he was killed in a gun fight in San Antonio; the other said he died from typhoid."

"Well, that may be hard to trace down but I have some connections with the Texas Rangers. Maybe they can help," said Hunter. Jack would learn as he got to know these two that Hunter was well connected in a lot of places. He had done extensive work with intelligence and the pentagon. He had become friends with a lot of important people over the years.

"Well, this case gets more complicated to a point I wonder if he was killed. According to a reliable witness during the trial, which we will get to later, an uncle got suspicious and had him exhumed when everyone thought he died from typhoid. They found the body had three bullet holes in it and, according to this testimony, the death certificate stated he died of typhoid also."

"Sounds like he died from lead poisoning," joked Hunter.

"Yeah," laughed Jack. "I have been on investigations in my career and I can tell you this is the most convoluted case you will ever have encountered. I don't know what is right or wrong; it takes twists and turns here and there. Just when you think you have it one way; something comes along to blow it all out of the water. Well anyway, to continue the synopsis, Jacob had another daughter, one Susan Crouch, who married a man by the name of Daniel Holcomb. They lived on a farm that was of very good size about a mile east of Jacob's. It is said that Jacob never liked Daniel but I really did not find out why. It seems strange to me."

"Why is that?" asked Hunter wanting to find out what the keen mind of a law enforcement officer thought about all of this.

"I really don't know. It's just something of an undertow to the story. Like he wanted her near but yet was mad she married this guy and I just don't know; something in-between the lines, I guess."

Hunter smiled. This man did not let much get by him. "So Jack, go on."

"Well, of course Jacob was married and the children were Susan, Byron, Dayton, Eunice and the last one, Judd. Judd was born in 1859. His mother was in labor with him for quite some time and it was reported as a very strenuous birth. His mother was not that young and, really, quite old for the time to be bearing children. She died 5 days after Judd was born. Judd was born with a bad leg that was described as withered back then. For some reason, and I can't be sure what, Jacob would not keep the child but rather gave him to Susan and Daniel to raise with a nice tidy sum of money. I read that it was around fifteen thousand dollars."

"Whew! That was a lot of money back in those days even for the life from birth to manhood. I wonder if that was to cover something up or keep quiet money?"

"I wondered that myself," said Jack thinking, "this guy is good. He knows his stuff when it comes to investigating and picking out potential clues."

"Anyway," continued Jack, "Judd was never told that Daniel and his wife Susan were not his mother and father. He found it out quite by accident at age 11."

"Wow that might piss ya off to find out your own father did not want ya and practically paid to have you taken away. That could be a strong motive for murder," said

Hunter leaning back in his chair to think about it.

"Well, it seems that Daniel and Susan were also being cut out of Jacob's will; can't really decide why. Eunice and her husband were going to inherit it all and or the unborn child it seems. Don't know how this set with the son in Texas and what the relationship was with the ranch; whether he got to keep that and it had nothing to do with the Michigan fortune or not."

"Hmm… he has been running the ranch as his own for how long we don't know but now some child is gonna come along and own all of it. That could be a motive for murder," pointed Hunter.

"Exactly what I thought, also," said Jack. "Well the murder scene, to continue, was abysmal at best. By the time the sheriff got there that morning, the whole scene was trampled by literally hundreds of people wanting to see for themselves; shell casings were picked up and moved or even kept. The bodies had been moved several times. To say the crime scene was ruined is an understatement. Living in the house was a stable hand named George Boles. He was seventeen and lived upstairs in a small room.

Everybody else lived on the ground floor. Also, living in a room of her own on the back of the house, was a domestic named Julia Reese. George says he thinks he heard the gun shots but she claims she did not. In response to that, the night of the murders there was one of the worst thunder storms of the century coming through. Everyone exclaimed on how loud the thunder and lightning were. Of course, George and Julia were arrested."

"Hmm… they would have been prime suspects at that point for sure even today."

"Well, they did arrest them both and they were in jail for a month or more. Can't tell ya much more than that at this time. Don't know where they went or what happened to them. If their motive was robbery, they did a lousy job of it and then why run and tell the neighbors? And, like, the housekeeper just be standing there when the first people come to check out the story cooking breakfast as if nothing had happened."

"Yeah, that makes some sense I guess but still, even today I would want to investigate them both closer. I like to know all I can know about everybody in a case," said Hunter.

"So, we have four murders and there are no clues to who did this. That is what you are saying?" asked Victoria.

"Well but wait; there's more," said Jack.

"Wait, I got a question that is burning in my head and I may be out of order of your story but you said something about a trial?" asked Hunter.

"Well yes, they finally, after a year, arrested Judd and Daniel for the murders and put them on trial. Now this was not just any trial. This trial was as big back then as the OJ trial was to us. Ann Arbor had no hotels as did Jackson at one point because of all the newspaper correspondents from all over the world were there to cover this. Once the story got out, as we say today it went viral or even crazier. Newspapers covered the trial every day in London, Paris, Rome, and Australia. Papers in the U.S. like the L.A. Times, the Detroit News, Boston Globe, New York Times, and Chicago Tribune. People were insatiable about news of the day from what was named 'The Great Trial.'"

"Wow, and I never heard of this."

"Yeah well, after Daniel and Judd were found not guilty it kind of died and interest waned. Daniel went on supposedly to Baraboo, Wisconsin and remarried; Judd stayed on Jacob's farm till around 1922, then he sold the farm and moved into Jackson. He finally married. He lived until 1946. The trial was so fierce that an ex-governor became the prosecutor. The original prosecutor had a heart attack arguing in session and died about two weeks into the trial. I think I read somewhere that the trial took almost seventy five days. I should also amend that they put Daniel on trial first and, when he was found not guilty, they just dropped the charges against Judd."

"Well you said there was more. Forget Hunter; I want the story," said Victoria.

"Ok. Then after the original four murders on January 2nd 1884, Susan Holcomb was found dead in her bed at ten AM naked, a sheet wrapped around her, a bottle of water in bed with her and a small bottle found on the window sill. The report I read stated the sheriff said she was force-fed rat poison but it was said to be a suicide by the coroner."

"Well, that is a nice dichotomy. How you can take a leap from one to the other. One does not force-feed oneself poison; you either take it or you don't. So, if she was force-fed poison then someone other than her had to jam it down her throat which does not make sense unto itself. I don't think rat poison would work very fast. That is something we may have to ask some toxicologists. Make a note, Tori, to find out what strength rat poison was back in those days or what it was made of; then we can find out how much it would take to kill a human and how fast," said Hunter.

"So, maybe someone killed her for what she knew but why naked at ten AM? Women did not do that kind of thing in those days," asked Victoria.

"Maybe she was waiting for someone to show up; like a lover? Maybe she was deep in this and there was an argument?" guessed Hunter.

"Well this is all very interesting. We need to do a lot of research on this," said Victoria.

"Ah, but wait folks. There's more," said Jack grinning.

"More?" questioned Victoria.

"Yep, a month after Susan died a farmhand on Jacob's farm committed suicide! His name was James Foy and he had been a hired hand for some time. That is all I can tell you about him, not much written."

"Hmm… maybe he was blackmailing someone or was being blackmailed. Maybe he was the lover or consort of Susan's. He also might have been killed for what he knew," said Victoria.

"Wow, this is deep and convoluted," said Hunter.

Jack laughed and coughed smiling at the enthusiasm that these two seemed to have for this as he had read it he also was bitten by the bug. "But wait there is more," he chuckled. "The Pinkerton Detective agency was called in and they could not solve it so the Governor in response had appointed a detective from Battle Creek by the name of Galen Brown. Mr. Brown set up camp in Horton and moved throughout the community asking questions about the murders. He even interviewed Judd and Daniel. After being there over a week, he was walking back down Horton Road to his hotel in Horton when a buggy drove up with two men in it and asked him if he was Detective Brown. He answered yes. They shot him, drove away, left him for dead in the road but he survived. Did not read much more about his involvement so he may have been hurt so bad he could not continue on. In those days a bad wound would take a long time to heal."

"So did he know who shot him?" asked Hunter.

"He swore it was Judd Crouch and the sheriff went and arrested him for it; took him in for questioning. I don't know why but they released him. No one that I can see was ever charged with the attack."

"Boy, it sure sounds like maybe someone in the background was throwing money around to keep this quiet. The whole thing, I mean. The son in Texas would have had that kind of money. Maybe Mr. Holcomb himself if he had money and also he could have been guilty of killing his wife. I wonder what his alibi was that morning?" questioned Hunter.

"Well now, that is the entire story in a nut shell. This may be the coolest crime I have ever encountered in my career," said Jack.

"I agree and what is it you want us to do?" asked Hunter. "I can't do this alone and, as you know, there are not any witnesses alive to question. Very little if any evidence, not much in the way of anything for DNA, etc. So I asked and quite by accident a young man named Evan spoke highly of you."

"Ah yes, Evan. We have used his help before in looking things up. I think he is a very interested in all of this also."

"Yeah, and he seemed to know where everything was. I was still not sure how to proceed with this even after he had given me your name. That is when my wife made me sit down and watch a few episodes of T.A.P.S. and some nervous guy named Zach."

"Yeah, those are good shows; better than most and very close to real life investigations. I must say, I have always been impressed with them both. Now there are several on that are a bunch of hogwash. If you just stick to those two you will be well informed. Do you want to have us do this or do you want to be in on it? I don't think it matters to me or Tori. She assists me on investigations. We make a good team and we have others we can call in on a moment's notice to help."

"I would very much like to do some investigating with you. I had an experience out at the Crouch property and did not even know what it was until later. I guess you would have called it an intelligent full body apparition. I found out later that a lot of my guys over the years have had the same thing."

Jack sat and told his story of the night in between drinks of coffee and questions from Hunter.

"Well, that is all quite interesting. We will try and find the property owners because we do not do anything without permission. We need to start with any basics you can get. Would there be any notes left in a file anywhere by the sheriff back then and, if so, could we read them without a court order? Next, if we could get a peak at the trial transcripts as well as the inquest reports for the original four murders and Susan's death and that of Foy it would be of great interest," stated Hunter.

"I think, if I remember correctly, the Smithsonian has all the records and notes that used to belong to the Pinkerton's and if so maybe we can pay to get some copies of those," added Jack.

"So what we will have to do is have a meeting about every ten days to find out where we are with the case and where we are going. After being dead this long they may not be around to contact; we are on the envelope for most spirits I think here. I have read some on that and there are a lot of different theories but nothing any one can support with evidence. That is one thing we want to do is have good evidence to support what we say. You know there just might be a book in this. I have a friend, Andru Hunter. He is an author and he may be interested in writing this for us. I think it would be a big book if it is advertised correctly."

"Well, here is my card. You can get in touch with me at anytime; on the cell that I carry for the sheriff and also carry my own that number is on the back," said Jack standing and handing the card to Hunter. Hunter reached down into a box on a shelf behind his desk and gave a card to Jack, it said, "D&R Investigations."

"That is my cell phone and you can get Tori here any time Monday through Friday. Just leave a message and we will get back to ya.

This is Monday so let's say we meet a week from Tuesday to compare notes and see where we are at with this. Here, let me put my email address on the back of my card, if you will, that way it is another way to get in touch with me."

Jack smiled and shook Hunter's hand and turned to Victoria and shook her hand thanking them both. He waved as he walked out of the office, into the store and out onto the bright sunny street of Marshall.

"Well, this could be real fun. Don't you think?" said Victoria.

"It will be a real challenge before it is over. I do believe we really may have to think outside the box on this one."

Chapter 8

1883: Sheriff's jail in Jackson

"Well, we need to get a confession out of these two before the inquest. They have to be in on this. How can there be no evidence on them?" said Sheriff Winney as he continued, "The Pinkerton's will be here tomorrow. They have been summoned by Byron Crouch. Maybe they will have an idea how to pry a confession out of these two. Let's move blacky back to the cold cell and see how he fares back there. Keep it nice and dark; only one blanket, mind ya, and make it a skimpy one at that. He will either talk or die. Those two just have to be in cahoots in this somehow. There is no way they were left alive and she heard nothing. Hmph, don't believe that for a minute. And he says he climbed in the trunk but all his clothes were on the top just like he left them the night before not dumped on the floor. I am willing to bet he can't even get in that damn trunk," the sheriff looked down as the door to the office opened.

A man and woman nicely dressed entered the office and moved toward the sheriff. The man took off his hat. He had a round face with a handlebar moustache and red hair. He was of slight build. He wore a striped grey and black suit and black shoes with pointed toes. The woman was of average height and looked to be in her late twenties.

"I am John Carmone with Pinkerton Detection agency," he said sticking out his hand and a dropping a card on the sheriff's desk.

Winney shook his hand and looked at the woman. He realized that he only had on his undershirt and quickly pulled up the suspenders on his pants. "I am sorry, sir. I do not mean to offend your wife. I am Sheriff Winney."

The man laughed a small laugh and said, "Oh, Milly here is not my wife. She too is a detective with the agency. She and I have worked together on many cases. She can be invaluable and is quite the little actress."

"A pleasure to meet you, Sheriff," she did a little curtsey and stuck out her hand in lady style toward him. Not knowing what to do exactly Winney cracked a sheepish grin.

"We will start tomorrow by introducing Milly here as an imposter Christian woman who will visit Julia Reese. We will probably be able to wrap this up quickly; I think a confession is forth coming."

"Well I sure would like to round this one up and be done with it. I don't mind tellin ya I got a lot of pressure on me to get this thing solved by more than one camp. This is a hot case politically let me tell ya."

"Well, if I might, concerning the young black gentleman Mr. Boles, you should take a snitch or an officer, black preferably, and stick them in the cell with him and see if we can get a confession that way. My supposition is that he is uneducated and won't know one way or another, what is legal."

"Well, we put him in a back cell separating him from the others in hopes he might crack but so far not a peep out of him," said the sheriff.

"Try the snitch and then play some hardball with the woman does not matter which one confesses as long as he or she implicates the other one it is over."

Sheriff Winney asked the jailer to come up and then go out and find Pierce and Sheppard and bring them back here. The man left going out the door.

"We will interrogate her good tonight and make sure she does not get much sleep so as to help Milly here gain her confidence in the morning. Make sure, Milly, that you complain about the way we are treating her."

"Ok then, we are off to the hotel for a night's rest Tomorrow I shall go over the notes with you so I can make my report to the home office at the end of the week." With that John and Milly walked out of the sheriff's office to be met at the door by the two detectives, Pierce and Sheppard.

"Good. Lads, I have a job for you tonight and I know it will be hard but I want a confession out of Mrs. Reese. So into there and talk to her and see if she will tell us all about this. Press her and press her hard; don't let up. Keep asking the same questions over and over again. Wear her down. I don't want her to get much sleep tonight," coached the sheriff.

"Ok!" said Pierce. He was tall with hair to his ears, a beard neatly trimmed and a handlebar moustache. Sheppard was a shorter, stout man with a small protruding stomach. He was balding on top and had long sideburns. Both men were crack investigators for the department and they had a good background in getting confessions. They moved back to the cell that held Julia Reese and had the jailer open the door.

"Mrs. Reese?" asked Pierce tipping his hat to her cordially.

"Yes."

"I am sorry, ma'am, but I would like you to accompany us to another room where we can sit down and discuss this case in hopes that we may be able to bring it to an end."

"Oh, thank goodness! I so much want to leave this dreadful place. I have been here for weeks without much of anyone paying attention to me. Can you tell me what is to become of me?"

"Well, that will depend on you and what we can discuss, Mrs. Reese. Now if you will follow me?" Pierce and Sheppard took the woman to another room in the jail. It was a bleak room with a small square table in the middle and three chairs; hard- backed, uncomfortable chairs. In the center of the table was a small coal oil lamp that flickered and licked at the shadows of the wall. Except for the table where she sat, the room was dark and the two detectives could move toward the table and be seen then step back into the dark to watch the reaction on her face to a question.

"Well, Mrs. Reese, we have a few questions about the Crouch murders and we would like you to see if you can supply some answers for us."

"Well, I will try but it is like I have told them already; I really don't know anything."

"So it was a stormy night, I understand. Is that correct?"

"Yes, it was and I did not feel well so I went to the cellar and took a small nip of hard cider to help me sleep."

"Can you explain to me something I am having a hard time with? How is it you can sleep in a house where four people are brutally murdered with pistols by two different individuals and not awake to the sounds of the guns, the struggles, and what surely would have been Mrs. White's screams?"

"Well, no, except I am a sound sleeper and that night after my small nip I did sleep well and went right to sleep. Surely you don't think I had anything to do with this, do you?" Mrs. Reese looked into Pierce's face and knew the answer as the corners of his mouth turned up. He slammed his fist into the tabletop making her jump.

"By God, I'll tell you what I think, Mrs. Reese. I think you and young Boles saw your chance and took it to rob Mr. Crouch of all of his money, valuables, and the pot was sweetened that night by Mr. Polley and all the money he had on him. So how was it done? Tell us. You don't have to cover for Boles. We know he did the killing. Did he have one or two guns, Mrs. Reese?"

"I don't know. I mean, I was not part of this or rather I didn't do anything. I was asleep that night. I heard nothing and knew nothing was wrong until the next morning when the neighbors came into the kitchen."

"How can you calmly cook breakfast with four dead people in the house? That is so cold, Mrs. Reese. I can scarcely believe such a thing in all my years of police work."

"Don't you call them to breakfast, Mrs. Reese, when you get up in the morning?" asked Sheppard.

"No, that is George's job to get Mr. Crouch out of bed and going. A lot of mornings they go to the barn to look after the stock before breakfast; especially in the aftermath of a storm. So not seeing them I really did not think anything about it."

"Did someone pay you two to do this? What was their motive?"

"No motive, sir. I mean, that, well… there was not motive because I had nothing to do with it."

"Can you explain why those people were killed and you and Bolles were spared? They just walked in and said 'well we don't need to kill the housekeeper that would not be right and the young blacky upstairs; we feel sorry for him but we are gonna blow the pregnant lady who is ready to give birth away. Come on, Mrs. Reese!"

Sheppard stepped in as Pierce walked away. He put up his hand and waved it at Pierce as if dismissing him. Julia Reese was now welling up with tears and wondering what it was that she could do to prove her innocence. How could they believe she was even capable of such an act?

"Now Mrs. Reese, please try not to cry ma'am. Mr. Pierce is a bit tired and he is kind of cranky. The sheriff what being down on us both cause he is getting yelled at to solve this crime. If there is anything you can tell me about that night or the next morning… please, let's go over it again."

The questioning went on for three more hours. Mrs. Reese was exhausted but stuck to her story. Most of the time when asked she would say, "It was just like I said before; I heard nothing."

George Boles lay on the bed in his cell covered up in a small, threadbare wool blanket trying to sleep. The cell was cold and he had a headache from the cold. They did not bring him any supper this night and his stomach was plenty empty. He asked the jailer about this, he was told he knew nothing about it and now it was too late to do anything anyway. He was sorry that Mr. Crouch was dead. He wished he could ask him what to do. He had prayed to God to get him out of this. How could they believe he had done this? Why would they think he would do this and then go and tell people they are dead instead of running? The questions stirred in his head as he finally slipped off to sleep.

Morning came early for Mrs. Reese as she was poked and questioned until almost four in the morning then returned to her cell. She had not been given water the whole time nor allowed bathroom privileges. Her breakfast was notably cold as if it was left outside in the winter weather on purpose. She pulled the shawl closer around her neck and the blanket from her bed over her head. She nibbled on the toast which was hard and cold she could hardly bite it. She heard the footsteps but did not look up. It was the jailer for the day shift.

"Mrs. Reese, you have a visitor," said the man.

She could see a woman in a long, floor length dress with button-up collar. She had on a long winter coat, mittens and a large hat on top of a bonnet. The door opened and the woman popped in.

"Heavens, Julia! I am so sorry to hear of your plight! Why when I get out of here I am going to give them a piece of my mind; treating a woman this way why it's shameful." Milly could feel how cold Julia was under the blanket as she hugged her. She thought they may have gone too far. She yelled at the jailer.

"You bring this woman some decent food and warm tea immediately or I shall have more than a word with your sheriff; then on to find a lawyer and a judge to straighten this out; and put coal in that stove. Warm it up. This woman is nye on death in here. Now, you just sit down, dear. I will make sure they take better care of you, poor thing."

Julia looked at the woman and said, "I'm sorry and thank you for your concern but do I know you?"

"Oh lands, Julia! It's me, Sally Timmons! I know you have not seen me for many years back in school. Surely you must remember?"

Julia could not remember but she smiled as if she did. Right now a kind voice and a sweet face was all she needed and maybe, just maybe, this woman would be the key to her getting out of here. It was not long before the jailer had shown up with a warm breakfast.

"Mrs. Reese, the Sheriff says you can go across to Kate Belling's boarding house with me so you can have a bath when you are finished with breakfast."

"You tell the sheriff that she will be glad to go and to give her word she will not try and escape, but I shall accompany her to make sure she has what is needed and that she is not disturbed. You can guard her door from the outside."

"I am sure, Mrs. Timmons, that he will be more than glad to let you come along," said the jailer smiling.

Well, whoever this woman is she sure was able to put a burr under the sheriff's saddle. Julia longed for a bath and she wished for a change of clothes.

"I don't know where my clothes or belongings from the Crouch house went to. I would like a change of clothes."

"Don't worry, my dear. I shall get you some fresh clothes," said Sally Timmons patting her on the hand.

Chapter 9

2010

The black 2009 Dodge Charger bolted from the parking lot behind the Hobbit Nook, out to Michigan Avenue and east toward I-94. Hunter drove as Victoria sorted through a small pile of papers from a file; mostly Internet printed material.

"So, gorgeous, what did you find?" asked Hunter.

"Why do you always call mom gorgeous?" came a small voice from the back of the car. The voice belonged to Victoria's 11 year old daughter Amanda. Victoria and Hunter had talked over the fact that Amanda was very interested in what they do and was a very good student in school. She applied herself well to math and the sciences and had spoken already of doing maybe Astronomy or Veterinary Medicine. Victoria smiled in the passenger seat; still reading but eager to hear the answer to this. She knew Hunter would find something to say.

"Well, I don't always call her gorgeous. Sometimes I call her Tori or Victoria, but you know she is gorgeous and I just want to make sure that she remembers that she is."

"She is pretty. Terry Marks said you were mom. He said you were hot."

"Who is Terry Marks?" asked Hunter now distracted from the conversation. "And does he call her anything else?"

"He calls her Mrs. Carson when she can hear him."

"Who is this Mr. Marks?" asked Hunter with a smirk but trying to look concerned and jealous at the same time.

"Oh Hunter, that is just one of her friends that she plays with. Can you think that there would be anyone else but you, my darling?" With that Victoria batted her eyelashes at Hunter.

"Aw jees… that was frightening," said Hunter playfully as she punched him in the shoulder.

"Mr. Marks, huh!" exclaimed Hunter with a put on serious face now looking into the rearview mirror at Amanda.

"Hmm… I can see I am gonna have to keep an eye on you Tori, and I want you, little missy, to keep an eye on her when I am not around if you please. You can report to me," said Hunter looking at Victoria as she smiled at him and he winked at her.

"OK! How much does it pay," asked Amanda?

"About a dollar two ninety eight," said Hunter

"Listen, I will tell you what I have found out so far and we can go from there today," said Victoria colleting her pile of papers in order.

"You gonna take notes, sweetie?" asked Hunter looking back at Amanda.

Amanda sat up, grabbed a spiral note book and a pen she had and opened it up writing "The Crouch Investigation," on the top line.

"I have found something really strange about all this. You know that I told you I was going to do an ancestry check on ancestry dot com?"

"Yeah, did you find any present day people related to them?"

"No, but in 1675 I found I had a relative that was on their family tree as the same person so I am related to them!"

Hunter stared ahead for a moment and then looked at Victoria. Her face was very solemn and her eyes were filled with doubt and disbelief.

"So, you are sure of this?"

She hung her head looking down at the file and shook her head, "Yeah, I went over and over it. Amanda and I are relatives."

A smile formed slowly on Hunter's face and his eyes lit up.

"So maybe this is a paranormal thing. Are they reaching out from the grave to you?"

"I don't know for sure but, well, I guess maybe I feel more compelled than ever to get to the bottom of this horrible crime. It seems to me, on the outside this was all about Jacob's money and his land. They got to arguing over this and then started killing one another off until the last one standing got everything; which seems to me to be Byron."

"What happened to Judd?"

"I am not sure. We will have to research that. All I could find was that he died in 1946 and the house burned down sometime in the 40's also maybe it was 1948."

"So, the house that is there is not the original home?"

"Yep!"

"Well, that may make the whole thing harder if there is not any of the farm buildings left. I wonder if the barn is the same?"

"Well, Jack said that they see Jacob or what they feel is Jacob in the barn feeding the animals and the animals are there with

him so that means they must be on the property."

"Did you ever wonder if there is a life expectancy for spirits? I don't know how to say this. Maybe they are in limbo or in heaven and then are reincarnated or pass on to another world another realm. Maybe we are pushing the envelope on this."

"No, I guess that maybe I think they remain on and on in limbo or heaven or where ever they are until, as the Bible says, till Judgment Day."

"The ancient Egyptians believed that there were three souls or the soul was made up of three parts: Ba, Ka, and Akh. If one would die; they all would die. That is why they mummified the body. According to their beliefs, it was to keep all of the souls together and intact," commented Hunter.

"I think that Ba was like a bird with a human head. It was the character of the deceased. Ba lived inside the tomb with the body but it was allowed to come and go to the living world at will.

"Ka was like a doppelganger of the dead person. I think all it was, as it is told, is a pair of raised arms. The great Creator, Kuhmmmm, created Ka at the time of inception I believe and it represented the exact physical and emotional replica of the original. During life, it lived imprisoned in the human heart. Ka it was believed that it could not live without the body being preserved. The only caveat to this was if the body could not have been preserved for some reason. Then an exact replica of the living form was painted on the wall inside the tomb and Ka could live inside the painting. Ka was the reason they left food items, water, gold, etc. in the tomb. So Ka could live he needed real lifetime nourishment and he could procure this on the outside with the gold that was left behind."

"You mean he could trade a gold bar for a loaf of bread?" asked Amanda in a serious tone.

"Well, this is what they believed, honey. It does not mean that is how it really worked. And at some time towards eternity you would think that he would have run out of gold and had to get a job in a convenience store or something," smiled Hunter looking in the mirror to see Amanda rolling her eyes in disbelief. Victoria chuckled.

The last one, Akh, was said to represent the immortality of the dead person. When he was drawn he was usually depicted as a bird. This part of the soul is the one that made the trip to the underworld and takes its place in the afterlife.

"So, the gist of all of this is that if anyone of these souls failed to exist; the others also died. Therefore, at that point the spirit was non-existent and could not haunt anymore. One of these dying, especially one of the first two, was inevitable. So, therefore Egyptian spirits could only maybe hold out for a century or so. Then I guess - poof."

"Well, all of that is good but we don't know if that is how it really works. So I say we try and contact. We have had visuals."

"Did you find out who owns the property?" asked Hunter.

"No, but Jack is working on it. He said he could find out quicker and keep me from making a trip to the township hall and looking at the tax records."

"We never did get an exact address nor directions to this property did we?"

"No!"

Hunter, now east of Spring Arbor Michigan on M-60, was approaching Reynolds Road. He swung the car into the far right lane with the right turn signal on, stopped for the red and made the turn heading south on Reynolds Road.

"The cemetery is on the corner of Reynolds and Horton, I think, which is a few miles up here. I looked it up on Google Maps. There really is a church on the corner, then the cemetery but, from what I have read, it does not belong to the church but to Spring Arbor Township. It is also known as the Crouch cemetery," said Hunter.

The Dodge driving up a hill came to the cemetery. It was completely fenced in with very good fencing. It had been kept well, trimmed and mowed just recently for the fall. All the leaves had been cleaned up. It was smaller than a football field and had some empty areas where there were no headstones. Hunter wondered, as he got out of the car and helped Amanda out of the back, if it was because of indigent people being buried there.

He led Amanda and Victoria followed as she watched Amanda take Hunter's hand as he opened the gate.

"Honey, you either go with me or your mom. This is small; still don't stray too far away from us and be careful where you step. It can be easy to trip and hit your head in these places. Sometimes headstones have been knocked over and you can't see them till you trip."

"Ok!" she said as she skipped off pulling her digital camera out and snapping a picture. Victoria came to his side, put a hand in the middle of his back and gave him a caress.

He jumped, "What!"

Victoria smiled at him and with warm eyes said "Nothing, can't a woman pat her friend on the back?"

She moved off to catch up with Amanda and handed her a small device called a ghost meter, which had a small scale and a red light on the top that flashed if you got any kind of increase in EMF (electro magnetic force). Hunter smiled and moved toward the other end of the cemetery. He had a black tactical assault jacket that he slipped over his shoulders and zipped it in the front. He was ready for action. Under his left arm was a Smith & Wesson 380 chrome-plated revolver with a six inch barrel. He had stashed in his vest several revolver drum reloads. In the right side under his right arm, was a small pocket that held an assault knife and he had a four million volt stun gun tucked in another pocket. He put the lanyard around his neck which had his identification on it. In other strategic pockets he had an induction probe for testing for lines in walls and could also be used to tap into a phone line, and a MEL-meter which had two functions: an EMF detector and a temperature probe that stuck out of the top. Also, there was a small red light on the top that acted as a flashlight at night. He had his cell phone clipped to his right shoulder and hanging from the bottom right of the jacket was a metal-cased flashlight that served not only as a light but was also a stun baton. He had extra batteries and three audio recorders as well as an infrared temp gun.

He moved down to the end stopping and taking pictures of every headstone in order to assure he would have a record of them if he needed to look for another name some day. He met Amanda in the middle next to a large plot that said "Holcomb". He realized at once as Amanda snapped a picture that it was Susan Holcomb's grave. He wanted a few minutes alone at the grave without Victoria or Amanda there.

Amanda, with her back turned to him, did not see him motion Victoria. She knew he wanted Amanda to come down to where she was. Victoria sat down on the ground and called Amanda who went running over and sat next to her on the ground.

"Let's just sit here and see if we feel see or hear anything. Do you have your recorder on, sweetie?"

Hunter turned toward the marker that said "Susan Holcomb."

"Hello, Susan. If you are here; I would like to talk to you for a moment."

Hunter reached into his vest and pulled out an audio recorder, turned it on and set it to record. He placed that on the top of the plot marker. He then pulled out a second one, moved back to the far corner of the plot and on a small stone that said "Susan" which marked her grave in the plot. He placed that recorder there after hitting record and watching the red light come on. He then pulled out a third recorder and did the same thing pushing record. Moving back towards the center of the plot in front of the stone, he pulled out his induction probe and got a distinct hum toward what appeared to be large power lines behind the back fence of the cemetery. Moving it in different directions quieted it down.

"Susan Holcomb, my name is Hunter Ross," he began. "I would like to talk to you if I could. I am studying the case of the murders of your father Jacob, your sister Eunice, the mysterious death of your brother Dayton, and the circumstances of your own death."

Hunter could feel an electric-like charge drift over his body causing the hair on his arms to stand on end. A chill shivering down his spine simultaneously causing an outbreak of goose bumps.

"Well, someone is here. Whoever you are, if that's you Susan, you can talk into any of these little black boxes here with the red light on them. I can listen to them later and they will record what you say. Tell me about yourself and your family. Tell me about Judd. Was he a good boy, Susan? Or was he a psychopathic killer? Did he have anything to do with Jacob's death? So far from what I have read, Susan, it seems he was deep into this with maybe your husband Daniel. Can you tell me; is that true? I also read that the sheriff said you were force-fed rat poison. Lots of stories and they get wilder every year on this anniversary. You can tell me the truth or put me on a track to find it. I am going to solve this Susan. It has been 127 years and it has gone on fucking long enough. It's time to tell who did this, put it to rest and get some kind of goddamn justice for you your family and whoever else was a victim of the greed that seemed to permeate your family. I am going to dump it all over them before I am done, Susan. I need the truth. Let's stop the lies and the massive amounts of innuendos that have been circulating around all of these years. I am not going to go away, I will be back and back and back until this is solved with or without your help. And if your precious little Judd was guilty I'm gonna fry his ass. You can't protect him! Maybe you can help him. If he is innocent; show me the proof."

Victoria and Amanda walked up now to the grave.

"Susan, this is Victoria and her daughter Amanda. They are related to you."

"Hello!" said Victoria. "I looked it up and it's true. We are related. Amanda, go to the car and on the back floor is a windshield snow brush. Bring it here. I want to clean off this marker for Susan."

With that, Amanda ran to the gate out and to the Charger as Hunter reached up with his keys and hit the unlock function.

"I hope that you can help us solve this after all these years and then, dear, you can rest in peace. No more people out here asking questions; walking over your grave. The world will know the truth and that is all we are looking for. It will do no good to hide this anymore. After all this time, let the story be told, dear. You can talk into my device here if you have any messages for me."

Amanda came back with the brush and Victoria commenced brushing off some of the mold and the dust that had encrusted the stone. "This is Amanda. She is my daughter. She wanted to come here and meet you. She is very excited about us being related. That is really cool, I think. Did someone reach out to me from beyond to help solve this and finish up the case? I know this all can be painful for you but maybe one last time and, like Hunter said, it will be over for eternity."

"Did you see Jacob's grave?" Hunter asked Victoria.

"No, did you?"

"No. Susan, where is your father buried? I would like to find him and talk with him. Is he here? Tell him to come and talk to me. Jacob Crouch, if you are here, come and talk to me. Speak into one of the many red lights here. Where is your grave, Jacob? Do you know you are dead, Jacob? You were shot in your sleep. Susan here knows all about it. Moses Polley, your friend, was shot and killed the same night as was Eunice and her husband Henry. I know you don't remember it. You were asleep when it happened but I am here to solve it. The murderers have never been brought to trial."

"Jacob, we really need your help. If you could just point out to us somehow where your grave is and we need to find your farm," said Victoria.

Hunter picked up the recorders one by one and turned them off but he kept the one in his hand recording as they exited the cemetery. He had gotten many voices this way and was always keen to see what was being said all the way up to his vehicle. This later would prove to be a vital link in communicating to a spirit in this tough case.

As the Dodge Charger pulled up to the corner and made a left turn onto Horton road, a figure stood at the back of the cemetery and watched as it sped away. It was the figure of a man, Jacob Crouch. His wife, Anna, came to his side. She smiled and he said, "I think, Anna, this one just might pull it off and then we can all get some rest. I'm going out to the farm and try to keep him on the right track." With that he disappeared.

Slowly, they drove down Horton Road looking to both sides trying to see anything that would give them a clue. There were several old houses that could have been it. Victoria had a plot of the historic sites of Spring Arbor Township and this one was marked. Jacob stood in the bottom of the barn looking out at the road waiting for the Charger to drive by. Shortly he saw it but it did not slowdown. Instead, it kept going on down the road to the east. Jacob moved out to the edge of the road and waited there until the car came back a second time.

"Well, shit. We may strike out Tori. I can't see anything like it shows on the Internet."As he passed the house a second time, he was looking down the road when something caught his attention out of the corner of his eye. He looked at the house to his right noticing that there was a barn behind it. The house looked somewhat new but the barn looked old. "That's it!" shouted Hunter making Amanda jump in the back of the car.

"Sorry, Amanda honey. I did not mean to scare you."

Amanda smiled and looked out of the window. "Do you really think that was it, Hunter?" asked Amanda.

"We shall see, my dear," smiled Hunter as he turned the car around and headed cautiously back toward the house. At just normal speed on Horton Road he could see why it was hard to find and why, with radar running, the sheriff's liked parking there. Both directions were blind and it would be hard to see them until you were on the radar good. Cautiously, he pulled into a dirt driveway and crept up toward the house.

"Hmm… looks like someone is fixing up the house. That is definitely a new roof," said Hunter. He had noticed that at least one window had been removed in the front of the house. He reached into the car and pulled his vest on. Taking out his identification, he hung it over his neck. Amanda came out of the car on his side like a shot in the night. Victoria came around his side of the car and stopped as he reached out and firmly grasped Amanda's arm to impede her progress.

"Hold on there, kiddo. We don't know what is here. You stick close to me and mind where you step. There could be an old well here and who knows what might be lurking in that barn or house from the real world. Stick to me like glue, baby," said Hunter as he pulled Amanda closer to him with a hug around her shoulders. He felt her stop, consider what he said and then grab the back of his vest.

"I'm going out front to look around," said Victoria. She reached over and pulled Hunter's assault knife out of his vest. She would use this to cut branches and weeds in search of the marker.

Amanda grabbed Hunter's hand. They moved down the drive, past the house, and toward the barn.

"This is a really old barn, Amanda. You can tell by the way it is built."

The top of the barn of first floor had a huge barn door that moved in on the level to a floor. There was an opening in the floor to allow you egress to the basement. A place to throw down feed and hay stored on the first floor. The bottom part of the barn was built up with cobble stones for a foundation. The basement had been dug into a small hill so as one side was below the first floor and had the hill for protection to the west. The east side came out on level ground with several doors opening out of the bottom," schooled Hunter.

"See hon, back in those days they had no way to heat the barn and keep the animals warm in the winter. So they would dig it into the ground and protect it with walls and dirt on the west and north side. When they closed the doors below and stuck the animals in their pens then it would stay nice and warm down here from the heat of the animals themselves. It was safe and secure from the wind and there would be lots of hay above for insulation."

"Wow that is cool! What did you do back in those days?"

Hunter winced and then smiled at her as she giggled. They moved up out of the bottom of the barn toward the house. The back had an all-season porch that was in somewhat disrepair. Another window was missing on the back side as Hunter stopped and looked inside. A few new kitchen cabinets had been set. Lots of wallboard in the family room as well as the living room area had been pulled off the walls and left in piles. There were several McDonald's drink cups in various places as well as several water bottles in the debris piles. They moved around the west side of the house to the front and came to the main door. It was a solid white door metal and wood. There was a padlock on the front of it and no latch mechanism. Hunter reached into his vest and pulled out a business card. He took out a pen and wrote on the back "Please get in touch with me as soon as possible. Thank you, Hunter Ross."

Suddenly, he could hear Victoria yelling behind him. He turned to see her near the ditch in the road beckoning to him and Amanda. He quickly walked toward her and the road. She had cleared some weeds in the front and had found the kicker to the whole puzzle a historical marker for Spring Arbor Township marked twenty three.

"Hey sweetheart, here it is and I found it," she said snapping a picture of it and then doing a little victory dance. Hunter smiled and Amanda rolled her eyes hoping nobody had seen her mom doing that and also hoping, if they did, they would not associate the two of them as being related.

"Hmm… so this is not the original house? Did we read that it had burnt down or did you tell me that?"

"Yeah, remember I said it had maybe in 1948!"

"Oh yeah, that's right. Well, I left a message for the owners here on the door so we shall see if they get in touch with us."

The three headed back towards the Charger, Hunter taking one last look at the house and unable to shake the feeling that someone or something was watching them.

Jacob stood smiling as the black car pulled out of the driveway and headed east toward Jackson. He disappeared as quickly as he had appeared. Another, however, watched from the top of the house on the second floor; one that would have a profound ending for this case.

Chapter 10

1883

Kate Belling helped Julia Reese up the stairs in the boarding house to the bath at the top of the stairs.

"Land-a-goshen, dear! They have not been treating you well at all over there. You need some nourishment. I will talk to Mr. Baker and have him consult with you. He is a lawyer friend and I think he will represent you. Have they even given you a bail hearing yet, dear? Mrs. Frink, the Reverend Frink's wife, was asking about you the other day. She said if they let you out soon and a lot of us think they must as a matter of fact we are going to make a point of it at the inquest that they do so. There is absolutely not a shred of evidence against you or George Boles."

"Thank you, Mrs. Belling, and I am not sure but I had a strange visit from a woman who helped me immensely today. She says she is an old school friend of mine but I can't place her. But she did raise a fuss an' all with the sheriff and get me a hot breakfast with some coffee and a chance to take this bath. Please, Mrs. Belling, don't let them send me to prison. I did nothing and I don't know how to prove my innocence."

"Cooler heads will prevail at the inquest. I will have Mr. Baker speak for you and George Boles. He will take care of everything; I am sure. I will keep you posted. From now on I am going to bring you meals from here just to make sure they are treating you well and that way I know you are getting good food and on a regular basis. Don't you dare admit to nothing, you hear me? Just say the same thing over and over. I don't know anything about the murders; I slept through it."

"Yes, Mrs. Belling. I will, ma'am."

With her bath finished, she walked back down the stairs to a waiting Sally Timmons and the jailer. Mrs. Belling had given her some warmer clothes to put on.

"My, you look so good. Let's get you back now, my dear, and thank you, Mrs. Belling," said Sally Timmons. Taking Julia's arm, they preceded the jailer out of the door and went across the street.

George Boles lay in his cell cold now and he heard a scuffle of feet outside his door. Rolling over and looking up, he saw a deputy with a new prisoner. He was a black man about six feet four inches tall; maybe two hundred and twenty pounds. The deputy unlocked the door and pushed the man in with George.

"Sorry, George, but we is full up and well, you gotta stay with this guy for a while. You two gotta share the bed and all but back here that will be warmer anyway," said the deputy slamming the door and walking away.

The new prisoner turned his back on George and looked out of the bars helplessly.

"Damn, I's in trouble now. No tellin' if'n I ever gets outta here," he said with a touch of anger in his voice.

George just rolled over in his bed and closed his eyes against the cold.

"They do feed ya don't they around here? I ain't had nuttin' good since last night. My belly is roarin'."

The man looked at George and just shook his head. "I was set up, ya know? They is usin' me fo' a patsy. They say I stole some money from this man and I did but they is goin' on like I was some kind of criminal or sumthin'."

At that point the jailer and a detective named Harris came back to the cell, "Hey George, I just came back to see if you had anything to say. You know, you will feel better if you get this off your chest. I am sure even Jacob would have wanted you to tell the truth. He is setting up there with God right now saying 'He was a good boy. You wait and see, God, he will tell the truth and tell us all what got in him that night that made him do such a thing. Can't you picture that, George?" prodded Harris.

George laid there looking up at Harris from the bunk with wide eyes. "Did not shoot Mr. Crouch and all dem people. I was hidin' upstairs," said George.

"George, who do you think is going to believe that you hid in that trunk? Why, you can't even fit into it. Besides, the clothes were still on the top of it when I investigated the day of the murder. You're telling me you took them out to lay down in the trunk and then made sure before you went downstairs to check for what you were sure were murdered bodies you took the time to fold the clothes back up and put it on the chest but you did not have time to put your shoes or a shirt on?"

"I never says that. You is puttin' words in my mouth. I did not have nothin' to do with shootin' them peoples."

"Do you know what an inquest is, George?"

"No, sir."

"It is like a trial before a trial to see if they have enough evidence to hold you and charge you with murder and try you, George, for murder."

"Yes, sir."

"George, I got enough evidence here right now to win the inquest and have you held over for a trial for murder. Folks ain't gonna take too kindly to you shooting Ms. Eunice."

"No, sir, but I did not shoot her, sir. I don't even owns a gun, sir."

"Got a man says you talked to him about buying a pistol when he was at mister Crouch's. He said you told him you would love to have a gun but that Mr. Crouch would not allow it. Is that true, George?"

"Yes, sir, I mean no, sir. You is confusin' me now, sir. I wanted to buy a gun so I could have it to shoot at varmints around the farm and such. Mr. Crouch said he thought that was a good idea but said I would have to work and save money of my own to buy it 'cause he was not going to be responsible for puttin' no gun in my hands."

"Really? Why was that, George? Was he afraid that you might turn and use it on his family?"

"No, sir. I means, I don't rightly knows, sir."

"Shit, George, seems to me you don't know nuttin' and that, George, is gonna get you hung by the neck," Harris pulled his left hand up above his head and dropped his chin as if he was being hung. This made George squirm in the bed and move back closer to the wall. His eyes got bigger and it was like he could feel the rope closing around his neck. How could they think he would do such a thing? Harris shook his head and moved away from the cell.

"You is dat George Boles dey is talkin' about, ain'ts you? Whooee! Boy, you is in trouble! I hear they gonna hang you, boy, for killin' all dem people and for what? A few dollars? I don't gets it. Why you don't run, boy, instead of bringin' the law down on ya that way?"

"I tell them the truth. I hid in dat trunk and I did not kill nobody. That is why I don't run but they don't believe me. I'm gonna swing for it; for sure I is."

Oscar came over and sat down next to George on the bed. "You see, I did take dat money like they said I did but not sure dey can prove it. Me, I know I'm guilty and at the most I gotta do some years in prison cutting wood, most likely, but you is gonna lose your life over dis boy. I had a friend of mine one time he got in dis fight with anudder man and he stab dis guy see and he die. Well, dey catch up with him, takes him back to jail and he is given a lawyer. Well, dis lawyer says they got ten witnesses in dat bar what saw you do dis. Dey is gonna tell at the trial and dey is gonna hang you for sure and there ain't nuttin' we can did about it. Well, my friend he started to cry 'cause he don't wanna die and the lawyer he set there thinkin'. He say 'Hold dem tears, boy. There might be one way out of this and one way only and dat be you tell them you will say swear to it that you is guilty if they change the sentence to life in prison or maybe even thirty years it's better than bein hung. Know what? That is what he did and they did give him thirty years and no trial was had. Now that lawyer, he pretty smart. He was. Maybe you need a smart lawyer like that."

George sunk back on the bed. He thought about this but he was not guilty. "Surely, when they have that first trial they will realize I am not guilty," he thought.

Chapter 11

2010

The Charger had been making laps around St. John Cemetery in Jackson, Michigan. They were looking for the gravesite of Henry and Eunice White. Jackson has a unique cemetery situation in and of that St. John and Woodlawn cemeteries are combined. One is on the east side and the other is on the west side of a fairly large plot of land. They interconnect with one another through small gates in a fence that separates them.

Victoria pulled out her notebook and caught an Internet signal. She then typed in "grave registration" for the county and found exactly, by a picture online, what the gravestone looked like. She showed it to Hunter and they continued on over into Woodlawn from St. John. "Wait!" she screamed as Hunter brought the car to a screeching halt. Dressed in her tight-fit jeans and a sweatshirt, she bounded out of the car before it stopped and, running down a side road, she stopped and snapped a picture. Hunter shut off the car. He and Amanda took up chase thinking that she had spotted it. Hunter stopped and looked at the headstone realizing that it was nothing like the one they were looking for.

"What the heck are you doing?" asked Hunter as they caught up with her.

"Look at the size of that angel," she said pointing to a large tombstone adorned on the top by an angel that must have been eight feet of what looked like white marble.

"I am sorry. I thought that you saw the one we were looking for," said Hunter in an off-handed way.

"Oh you, shush. I want to take some pictures while we are here. Someday, I am going to write a book about head stones and if I see something unique like this I want a set of photos on it so I can easily describe it and at the same time tell all where I saw it. You go look around and see what is where and I will meet you back at the car. There are a few more around here I want pictures of."

Hunter smiled and walked off. When she was like this there was no stopping her and, he had to admit, she had a great eye for some fantastic photos. Many times she had taken pictures of something and he had thought "What is so special about that?" Until she showed them to him. Her eye for light and dark were especially keen and the photos always presented a look that was not seen by his eyes at the time. He really loved looking at her photos but most of all; he thought as he glanced at her back over his shoulder, "I just like looking at her."He smiled to himself as he climbed a hill looking at headstones and thinking about dates.

He loved pouring over cemeteries just like Victoria. As he said, it always told a story. It told a story of the community; all the trials and tribulations that it had undergone through sickness as well as health. Veterans who served from the community: some lived to come home and tell the story, some did not. Even those that did not return also told a story.

There were mysteries also within the graves, such as the time he read the head stone "Joe Slocum erected by his family, may God have mercy on his soul." At first, he laughed when he saw that. Then, reading between the lines, he decided that the family thought he was an evil S.O.B. and they really did not want him to go to hell for all his earthly transgressions.

He moved back toward the Charger as he could see from his vantage point at the top of the hill that she was walking back up toward the Charger. She was beautiful in the sunlight. The breeze was cool but not cold and it was like she radiated toward him.

"So, did you get what ya wanted?" he asked getting into the car. She handed him her camera and he pressed the pic button to see what she had taken.

"Wow, dear these are good," Hunter said smiling at her.

"I want to go over there. I think I saw a mausoleum and I would like to see if it has any kind of architecture to it at all."

Hunter put the Charger in gear. They moved along the road in the cemetery creeping along at a snail's pace, still looking to see if they could find the final resting place of Eunice and Henry White.

They stopped near a round edifice that looked like a circle on top of a square stone. It was white but the bottom square was black. Inside the ring was the inscription, "Lewis and Dorothy Hartley bonded together in love united in death."

"Hmm… that is different," thought Hunter. "It is as if one of them wanted the other to not get away; like stalking after death. That might be an interesting couple to contact to see what they say," he mentioned to Victoria.

"Oh you, don't you have a romantic bone in your body?" she chided "I think it's sweet."

"What? That I don't have a romantic bone?" he looked around and saw that Amanda was out of earshot looking at another headstone. "Come back here tonight, baby, and I'll show you a romantic…"

He was stopped short as she turned smirking, waving her finger at him and laughing, "Woo-hoo! What time, baby?"

He smiled at her and then seriously looked again at their surroundings. "You know, unlike Reynolds, I don't feel anything here. It is like something is missing or someone is looking for somebody. I don't know. Something about this spot. Like something is screaming out. It's not right."

Victoria lovingly put her arm around Hunter's waist and hugged him trying to decipher what he felt. "I don't know, sweetie. It's just very peaceful here to me which is real strange."

"Yeah, maybe. No, I don't get that at all. It's like something is watching me or tugging at me," said Hunter.

Hunter and Victoria walked hand in hand toward the large mausoleum. Amanda was at the front already looking through the glass double-doors. Peering inside, it looked like some huge Roman edifice inside.

"It would be nice to spend the night in there doing an investigation just to see what we get," said Hunter.

Victoria took several pictures through the glass and around the outside. They moved back to the car and once more continued on their way criss-crossing as the sun hung toward the end of the day in the sky.

Suddenly, Hunter let out a yell and jammed the car into park. "There it is," he said, pointing to a large white stone on top of a small hill. It was near some trees. Hunter jumped out and moved toward it with Amanda and Victoria in tow. Amanda moved off to the right looking at another odd stone and some names.

"Amanda, come on over here, honey. We are going to do an EVP session and I want you sitting down and being quiet," said Victoria.

Hunter popped open several pockets on his vest and pulled out audio recorders. He handed one to Amanda. "Ok, hon, try and hold this real still and not move it around or just put it down on your lap. Any movement could make a sound like a voice or maybe muffle something that is there." He pushed her record button saying, "Amanda's recorder at White's gravesite."

He then quietly moved to the grave marker, pushed the record button and whispered into it, "Graveside recorder White graveside Woodlawn Cemetery with Victoria, Amanda and Hunter." He then set the recorder down and pulled out number three which he velcroed to the back of his right wrist. He then whispered into it, "Personal recorder in Woodlawn cemetery at White grave site." He then nodded at Victoria.

"Henry or Eunice White, are you here with us?" she asked. "We would like to speak to you. What happened to you is very sad. I am so sorry for the loss of your lives and the prospect of living many years in bliss together. The loss of not having your first child; do you know what happened to you?"

"I feel that whoever is here with us, whether it's Henry or Eunice, you know what happened. Maybe you know who and why. If you can tell us that I would appreciate it. We are detectives and, once again, even though it's the year 2010 we can employ investigative techniques today to your case that were not available back then. But you still will have to give us some clue or lead us in a direction," said Hunter.

"I found out, Eunice, that you and I are related way back. I am sorry for what happened to you, sweetie, but you can come and talk to me anytime you want. Tell me what happened. You can talk into this red light and I will be able to hear you when I get home on this device."

"You were both murdered in your sleep a long time ago. Maybe you know that and maybe not, but do you have any idea who might have done this to you and Jacob and Moses Polley? Or why they did it?" asked Hunter.

"We will not rest until we figure this all out. We are not going to give up until we have leads and solid evidence to close this case; you have my solemn word on this. No more stupid people asking stupid questions; people who don't have a clue. This is what Tori and I do and we will finish it for good so you can both have some sense of justice and eternal peace. At least, it will stop a lot of people from coming here and bothering you."

"Ok we are going to go now so you think about it and we will be back to ask more questions," said Victoria.

With that Hunter turned off the recorders first saying "end session" into each of them. He did keep the one on his arm running all the way back to the car. He opened the trunk of the Charger; put the 380 into a box and locked it; laying his vest down, he grabbed the stun flashlight and the stun gun; put them in a special box and locked it. He then said "end session" into the recorder, turned it off and put it into his vest.

The sun was starting to set as he got in the car. He said, "Ok, let's go pick up your brother and sister and go get some supper at maybe Mickey D's."

Chapter 12

1883

George Boles had been locked up for the afternoon listening to new a cellmate tell about all the crimes he had committed; some he had gotten away with and some he had not.

"Ya know, boy, I ain't sure that blanket is gonna be big enough to keep us both warm tonight. Maybe I ask jailer for a nudder."

George now had enough and yelled and carried on through the bars so much that finally the jailer and sheriff came back to see what was the matter.

"Dere ain't no way I'm stayin' another minute in this cell with this bad man! I ain't done nuttin' to deserve this! Do what you wants with me but I want outta this cell now! I just keep screamin' till you does something about it!" With that, George let out another blood-curdling scream at the top of his lungs.

The door was opened and two more deputies came back. George was cuffed around, his shirt stripped from his top, shoes and socks taken, and he was thrown into a bull cell. He had gotten his wish for a bull cell in those days was a cell devoid of anything but a chamber pot. No bed, no blanket, no windows, no bars and a solid iron door that slammed shut with finality. George stood and shuddered in the cold cell. "Lord, what I has got me into now," he said.

Julia Reese heard the screaming and knew it was George. She was terrified that they were somehow hurting him. Was it other prisoners or was it the deputies that came running?

Suddenly, her cell door opened and she was confronted by two detectives.

"Good afternoon, Mrs. Reese. We would like to ask you a few questions," said the first man taking off his coat and hat and rolling up the sleeves of his shirt. He was of medium build, sandy blond thick hair and a darker moustache. His blue eyes complimented a really nice smile. The second man lit up a large cigar and puffed at it wildly making sure some of the smoke went her way as an irritant. He was shorter and quite a bit stockier. He had on a black and gray striped suit, matching pants, and coat with a vest. Also, under his round, fat face was a beard and a moustache. His eyes were dark but of non-descript color. They seemingly darted to and fro as he talked. Adding to the mystique, he never once looked her in the eye. She remembered that her grandmother had once told her that you can't trust people who don't look you in the eye when speaking to you. She would remember this about this detective and it would help her keep her sanity.

"George, for God's sake, do you have to smoke that thing in here in the presence of this lady?" asked the blond detective.

"Listen, Larry, the sheriff said come back here and talk some sense into this lady and get her story down and straight for the judge so I will smoke if I want to. I was ready to go home to a nice fire, my chair, the paper, and a hot supper my wife had cooked. And now I gotta spend time with you back here coddling some lady who shot four people while they slept. It's an open and shut case. She has no alibi. What was it you said? Ah, yes, I slept through it all. Ten shots in one house by two different guns and you slept through it? I don't believe that story for a minute, young lady."

"George, be quiet so I can think and the lady can help us understand her story. I don't for a minute believe that she shot four people. I am sure she can explain to us how she slept through those shots; maybe it was possible. Did you have too much to drink, Mrs. Reese, and you passed out?"

"No, I don't drink detective."

Larry reached into his jacket pocket and pulled out a small note book and pencil. He loosened his tie and flipped through the pages.

"Maybe we got something wrong here, ma'am, cause it says here that you sat and drank hard cider before you went to bed?"

"Hard Cider, Mrs. Reese, did you drink too much? Out of control and mad at the Crouches for something so you just went out of your mind on hard cider and shot them all? Bang! Bang! Bang!"

With each bang, Mrs. Reese jumped and put her hand over her mouth as if she could see the people being killed.

"No, it was not that way. I did have some cider but only half a glass. I had to go out and do the dishes from the evening meal so I did not stay long for the conversation. The cider was not hard; I am sure it was fresh from being squeezed in October."

"Could have been last years and maybe it had a nice bite to it so you just downed more of it while you did the dishes," said George pointing his finger at her with a wry grin and the cigar in the other hand.

"You know, that would have really made me mad. I know how you felt missing out on all the fun and gaiety because you had to clean up after them. No offer of help, no extra pay, etc. just go do the dishes, Mrs. Reese. George got to stay, did he not?" asked Larry.

"Yes, but no, that is not how I felt. It was my job to get those done and I was tired and wanted to be done with my work so I could go to bed."

"You did not want to hear Mr. Polley's stories from back east. How could you not want that? I know I certainly would have," said Larry.

"Yes, oh, very much wanted to hear them," said Mrs. Reese.

"So you got the short end of the deal all the time huh, Mrs. Reese? Like the hired man who was takin' a shine to ya and Mr. Crouch sent him on his way sayin' he was getting a bit too friendly with ya."

Mrs. Reese shook her head and lowered it looking at the floor. Tears were starting to flow down her cheeks. They had this all wrong but from her perspective she knew this looked bad.

Larry reached out and pulled up her chin. Looking into the teary eyes he handed her a handkerchief.

"Bah!" yelled George as he waved his hand in disgust at her and puffed harder on the cigar. The smoke was now filling up the cell and her sinuses were screaming for some relief.

"Mrs. Reese, did you love this man? Were you sorry to see him go? I bet you were more than a little mad at Mr. Crouch. Taking a man away from you like that; he had no right to do that. I must say, that was a shameful thing to have done," coaxed Larry, thinking that maybe he had hit it on the head.

"What's this boyfriend's name and we can have a talk with him? Maybe he was the one who did it and you are coverin' up for him?" asked George

"Mrs. Reese, it will do no good to hide him. We can find out. Just make it easy on us and we will let you have some rest. Just tell us why you wanted them dead; especially Eunice."

Julia Reese was crying now head bent low. "It's gonna come out any time now," thought Larry and George must have had the same idea as he eagerly leaned over to hear even the slightest of whispers. He put his hand on Larry's shoulder.

She stood up and pushed back so hard on Larry that he was surprised and almost came off the chair he was sitting on.

"I did nothing. I don't know anything. I will never know anything. And I will not confess to something I did not do so you are wasting your time, gentlemen." She dried the tears on her face, threw the handkerchief at Larry, then went over on the cot and lay down for the night.

"Maybe come morning you will remember something that can be of help, Mrs. Reese. We shall be back bright and early to see if a little sleep has cleared your head," said Larry.

He then turned, moved out of the jail cell and the door clanged shut with a final resolution. She laid there for the longest time staring at the wall. She had done nothing; she did not understand how they could hold her like this. No trial, no lawyer but, then again, it was not like she could afford one. She did not know what to do or who to turn to. She thought about Sally Timmons but there was something about the woman that made her uneasy; a certain something that was not right about her. She could not pick it out but she knew she dared not trust her no matter what.

It was cold and George sneezed as he sat on the cold floor. No shirt. No shoes. He huddled raising his knees to his chin and locking himself in with his own warmth. The jail cell door opened and in walked the jailor. He set down a small tin cup of water and two slices of bread.

"'Cause of all the trouble, George, the Sheriff says all you get for a while is bread and water."

"Can I at least have a blanket?" asked George

"Nah, lad, I'm afraid not. The sheriff, he is in a foul mood because of you. He says you won't tell what happened when ya knows and he says you can rot in here till ya die for all he cares. I empties the chamber pot once daily lad, so make good use of it. If you spill it, you wears it and sleeps in it," said the jailor leaving George to fend on his own.

The door shut quietly and the lock turned from the outside with a loud and distinct click. George had never felt this alone before; there was no one to turn to. Maybe he should just confess. *It* seemed like they would most likely try and convict him anyway. They were dead certain that he was guilty.

"What I do, Mister Crouch? What I do, sir? You always had the answers for me. Who dat want you dead and to kill Ms. Eunice and her husband dat way? I don't know whats I should do, Lord, has Mr. Crouch to help me please."

Chapter 13

2010-1883

Eunice moved about in the house. She could not understand why it was such a mess. Walls were torn down; it looked different to her but still it felt like home. Where had everyone else gone? She was alone; ready to have the baby. She tried to go out to the road but never made it all the way before she had to turn around and come back. Father would surely have to come and take care of the animals soon.

She walked out of the back kitchen door to the raised porch and down past the pitcher pump set in the ground. Moving down toward the end of the barn, she could hear the animals but not see them. She walked through the back door and there was Missy and her piglets along with Chloe at the far end and her calf. She could not tell but thought that Chloe should have some hay. She grabbed a pitch fork and brought some down from above into the pen. She also brought down with her some hay that went into her hair. Not noticing she walked up the incline from the barn back into the house and onto her bed where she lay down resting till someone returned home. She closed her eyes and was off to sleep. She was awakened some time later. It was night. She thought she heard a noise and listened but all she could hear was the peaceful breathing of her husband next to her sound asleep. She wondered if she slept through supper but realized she was in her night dress. She fell back asleep only to be rudely awakened by the sound of two loud cracks and a moan.

She could smell gunpowder and saw two shadows closing in on her bed. Henry lay beside her shot. As she started to scream the guns went off; two from one and three from the other. She tried to put her hands up. Her baby was in danger. How could they be shooting her and the baby? Then she fell back looking up at the ceiling.

2010

"Thanks for buying us supper. It was not necessary," said Victoria walking back into her living room where Hunter was now slouched on a couch; boots off and feet up on an ottoman. He was engrossed in files that she had amassed on the Crouches.

"That's ok. It was a lot more fun than eating a TV dinner at home by myself," said Hunter not looking up.

Victoria shook her head and said, "I will take that as a compliment," smirking at him.

Hunter raised his head for a second trying to figure out what she was talking about. "Huh?" he said shaking his head, trying to get his brain out of the papers and back to the present.

"Oh, never mind, Hunter Ross," said Victoria in exasperation. She knew when he was thinking about a case there was no use in discussing anything current with him. She was almost sure that they would never be romantically linked.

He and Victoria had worked together now for some years and had become good friends. Nothing more than that but, some thought, maybe more went on between them.

"Well, I have Billy in bed and Sherry is in the bath. Amanda is supposed to be finishing up her homework. Tomorrow is another day of school," said Victoria a bit frazzled.

"Tori really I don't know how you do it. Working, taking care of three children, and making ends meet. My hat, my dear, is off to you for a fine job," said Hunter.

"You really think I am doing a good job with them? Sometimes I wonder!" she sighed plopping down next to Hunter.

He reached up and put his right arm around her shoulders. As he pulled her to him, she laid her head on his shoulder with a dream-like look in her eyes. She stared out her window at the night and suburbia.

"You, my dear, are not only a perfect mother to these children but a great partner to me. As we do business together and investigate things in the coming years, I want your promise that if it becomes too much that you will tell me and stop. The children are far too important to let them slide to the side. I don't want you stressed because you can't keep up. Also, remember that I am here to help you anytime you need it."

Victoria shook her head and resigned to the fact that maybe there would never be any romance between them. Maybe he would always think that she was his business partner only.

"How many years have you known me; or worked with me and for me?

"It's been close to four years now since Jeffery left with, uh, that woman to parts unknown."

Her husband, Jeffery Carson, went out for milk one day and kept going with the woman who worked down at the local Mini Mart. They had moved to Idaho and started a potato farm leaving behind his dentistry practice. He had written Victoria a letter telling her to sell the practice, the motor home, the boat and anything else that was his. He said that he felt encumbered.

She sued for and won some child support; but it was slow in coming and always short of money when she got it.

"Mom, I need help getting dry. I'm done," yelled Sherry.

"Ok, coming," said Victoria smiling and caressing Hunter's face as she got up.

Finally, with Sherry in bed, she came out with a large glass of iced tea for Hunter and again sat down beside him.

"The problem I can see with this case is that none of it makes any sense. We have way too many conflicting stories. Which ones are we to believe? One paper writes one thing and another says something else."

Hunter's cell phone rang and he answered.

"Yeah? Let me write that down. Ok. Uh huh. Yeah. Hmm… well, it is nice to meet you. Would it be possible to have dinner Friday night? At, say, Marino's in Spring Arbor? It's on me. I think it is best we do a face to face. Ok, how about seven PM or is that too late? Great! Seven it is and thanks for getting back to me."

Hunter hung up the phone and looked at Victoria, "That was Mr. Spector. He is the current owner of the Crouch property, and I have a dinner engagement Friday night with them. Wanna come?"

"Well, don't forget you have lunch with Ken tomorrow and we have the Spring Arbor Township meeting tomorrow night.

"Oh yeah, that's right! So are you in for all of that or not?"

"Sure, but what will I do with the kids?

"How about your mother? Ask her over for a few days and maybe on Tuesday or Wednesday we can go to the library in Jackson and spend the day. I'll give ya money for Mom if ya wanna go play with me little girl," said Hunter winking.

"Well, if you leave forty for Momma what will be left for baby?" she said pouting then laughing.

"I got plenty left for baby. You know, sweetheart, whatever baby wants; baby gets," said Hunter in a corny Bogart voice.

"Well, hon, it's time for me to go. Need to get home, rest a little and then hit the hay."

"Mmm!" said Victoria, as she rose to kiss him on the cheek.

"See ya tomorrow, sweetie! Love ya!"She said as Hunter pulled on his boots and headed for the door. He stopped, went back and gave her a peck on the cheek saying "Yeah, gorgeous, love ya, too. More than you know."

He grabbed his file folder and went out the door. Stopping he had a thought, "Maybe this is a good time to get Jemma involved. She has asked several times. It would be good for her to go to lunch tomorrow and then out to Reynolds's Cemetery. She can accompany us to the meeting afterwards."

"Sure. I will call her right away and have her come in tomorrow morning. I need to stay and do invoices and some bills anyway. She can accompany you to lunch tomorrow."

The Charger sped across Marshall and he pulled into a small parking lot behind the book store. He put a placard in his window that identified his vehicle for the police as designated to park there at night. He walked to the back of the Charger, picked up his vest and put it on, then picked up the weapons boxes and closed the trunk moving toward the back door of the book store. He reached up, pressed in a code, waited for a response and pressed in a second code as the latch on the commercial steel door opened. Stepping in, he closed the door and set the alarm. He looked briefly into the back of the store then made a left turn and climbed the stairs to his apartment. The hallway to his door was curved and trimmed out in expensive molding. The hardwood floor under his feet had been nicely restored. He stopped at his door and slid a key into the deadbolt. The door opened and he walked in. He looked back down the hall to the ceiling at the security camera and motion detector. He stopped at the door, put a code in and pressed the button labeled "arm" as the motion detector and camera lit up in service. He closed the door as the alarm beeped to warn of the setting in the hall being activated.

He dropped his keys on a small telephone table at the door, pulled off his boots, and dropped them on a special Rubbermaid tray on the floor. The living room spread out before him thirty feet by thirty feet, twelve foot ceilings; the windows to the left looked out over Main Street in Marshall. These windows directly faced the north and his east window looked out over the building tops. The apartment was richly appointed with a few winged easy chairs, a large black leather couch and two recliners all facing the west wall where he had a giant screen TV. To his right were two doors; one went to the kitchen, which was a small kitchen with all stainless steel appliances in it and a nice ceramic tile floor. There was a door beyond that opened up to a small dining room with a table that could expand to seat eight. The other door in the living room went into a hallway that had a small bedroom on the left and a guest bathroom on the right. At the end of the hallway was another door that opened up into his master bedroom, twenty by twenty. Just off to one side was a master bath with a fifty six inch by fifty six inch shower stall with three shower heads, one in each wall, and then a head in the ceiling to simulate rain. There was as small light, a fan in the ceiling of the shower and a door that closed tightly. There was no edge; the floor of the shower water ran into a back corner to drain.

Hunter moved over to his computer and clicked it on. The big screen monitor came alive as the hard drive whirled. Hanging up his vest in a closet, he also put his pistol box and stun weapons up on the shelf. He then walked back to his bedroom taking off his clothes and throwing them in a pile. He stopped and looked at himself in the mirror.

He was proud of the fact that he still maintained the same thirty six inch waist line he had in the military. However the six pack abs had turned into border-line cheese logs. He laughed as he patted his stomach and put on an old t-shirt. He reached into the second drawer of his dresser and pulled out a pair of navy blue sweat pants. He pulled them on and took off his socks slipping his feet into a lined pair of real leather moccasins.

Shuffling back toward the computer, he hit a button which tied him in with the store's server below. He then walked to the kitchen, grabbed a bottle of water from the refrigerator, and then moved back to his vest. He pulled out the audio recorders. Sitting down at the computer, he took the first recorder, pushed a button on the back and a USB connector came out of the device. He plugged the whole thing into a USB port on the front of his tower. He downloaded the days audio sessions onto the computer then he erased the audio device. Bringing up a program called EXP Studio he was able to pull up each individual session and listen to see if he could hear any voices other than Victoria Amanda or himself. He put on the Koss headphones and leaned back in his high back black leather office chair watching the voice imprint on the studio play. Suddenly, he heard something in the background behind his voice.

He stopped, marked the selection, noted the interval in which it started and when it stopped then highlighted that section, called up a second application of EXP Studio and downloaded the copied portion that was only eight seconds long.

The snippet played like this:

Hunter: "Susan, if you are here I would like to talk to you for a moment."

Then at the very end, ever-so-slight, on the first track but stretched out to the second track was the obvious voice of a woman that said clearly, "No! Don't!"

He played it over and over then made a copy of it for later on a CD. Hunter went back to the original track where he had left off and continued to listen. At one point he noted that he felt someone was there with him and he remembered he had goose bumps for no particular reason.

Hunter: "Well, someone is here. Whoever you are, if that is you Susan, you can talk into any of these little black boxes here with the red light on them."

Again, just after that, Hunter heard a noise not consistent with the background. He again marked then copied the interval and put it on the second studio application then elongated it. When he did this he heard, "Help!" in a woman's voice.

He copied this down and kept reviewing the tape. At one point, he had swore while asking questions saying "Goddamned" and a male voice came back that said, "Don't swear."

Later in the session an answer to one of Victoria's questions about being related. At the end of it a gruff male voice said, "Go Away!"

Another time he had a whisper that was hard to make out. It might have said "cover" or "corner". He was not sure but made a record of this.

The last one was a complete surprise but it was also why he kept one recorder running until he was ready to get into the vehicle. He had closed the trunk, his vest still on, and he was walking to the car just before he ended that recorder's run. He got a voice, male and gruff, unlike any of the others. Raspy and very commanding this voice said "Leave Us!"

He wondered if the last one was old Jacob himself who did not want to be disturbed.

Chapter 14

1883

The door opened to Julia's cell. It was early morning. As on cue, her new found friend Sally entered. Today she had a Bible with her.

"Did you get a good breakfast, my dear?" she asked.

Julia just shook her head and stared at the floor. "I don't know, Sally. I am tired of all this day in and day out. Some days I would just like to say 'Yeah, I did it now leave me alone' but I know that is what they want. I am not sure what it is that I am supposed to do. I did nothing. Why can't people understand that?"

"Sometimes it is best to just pray and wait for the answer. I brought you this Bible. Just use it for solace and comfort. Get down on your knees to God, Julia, and pray. Ask him for answers to all of this. He will help you. Pray to Him; cleanse your soul. Pray to Him; confess and confide in Him. It is the one thing that will make you feel better. Confession, they say, is good for the soul."

Julia sat there for quite a while her hands clasped together asking god what she should do. She got an answer, finally, but it was not the one that Sally was hoping for.

"You are right, Sally, and now I do have inner strength. I am ready to face whatever it is that they will throw at me. God knows I am innocent. He will protect me, care for me and make sure that I am not unjustly harmed." At that moment, a man with a tall stove-pipe hat and a coat with tails appeared at the door of the cell as if out of nowhere. He had the jailer in tow to open the door.

"I wonder if I could have a word with you, just the two of us, Mrs. Reese?" said the man smiling. He was carrying some kind of small package.

"That's ok, Julia, I will be back later. I may have a plan to help this situation along." As she walked out, she gave the new man a harsh long stare as if to say don't mess with this person; she is mine to protect.

The door closed and the man sat down next to Julia. He patted her on the back. He reached into his pocket and pulled out three handkerchiefs and laid them on her bed telling her, "Just in case you need some, I will leave these with you. My wife suggested I bring them to you. I can see that you are being treated in a rather Spartan way. I shall have a word with the Sheriff about this and I am sure it can be fixed."

"I'm sorry, but if you are here to do me good just like the others who come around here and promise all just like the lady across the street who promises me meals that I never see; my faith today is at an all time low. I am ready to confess to this whole thing and just be done with it. I would rather live in prison the rest of my life in peace than be hounded as I have these last few weeks. And poor George, I don't know what they did with him. He screamed and yelled once. A bunch of deputies came running and I have not seen him since. I fear that he may be dead or in grievous condition."

With that Julia lowered her head and started to cry again. She reached over for one of the handkerchiefs and dried her tears. "I am sorry, what is your name?"

"I, my dear, am Mr. Parkinson of the law firm Parkinson and Hewitt. My partner and I have been engaged by concerned citizens of the community to represent you and to make sure you are taken care of. I and my partner, dear, are your new legal representation."

She looked up in his face and her eyes got wide as he featured a grin from ear to ear.

"Now, my dear, if you need anything, you just let me know and I shall make sure that you get it." He smiled at her and she knew she could, for the first time, trust someone. His smile was infectious. "I will indeed make sure Mrs. Belling is allowed to bring you meals. I can assure you that it will be much better fare than you have had these last weeks."

"George," she blurted out, "Will you check on him? I am sure something has happened to him. He was only a 17 year old boy. He and Mr. Crouch, they had a real good relationship. I know George liked it there on the farm and he would have never done anything to hurt Mr. Crouch."

"Yes, dear, I will so inquire but another man, a very prominent man, has been hired to represent Mr. Boles; the Honorable S.M. Cutcheon of Ann Arbor. He is a very good barrister and I am sure will take very good care of Mr. Boles' needs."

"Thank you!" was all that Julia could say.

"Starting now and until you are released - and, my dear, you will be released - you do not talk to anyone about anything unless I am with you. Answer no questions unless I am there during the questioning. If they must question you, then they must send for me and they know this. Tell them nothing! Regardless of what you may have said; tell them nothing. I will work on getting you released or at least out on bail. They will be starting a proceeding tomorrow called an Inquest. It is held by the coroner to certify the death, time of death and means of death of Mr. Crouch, Eunice, Henry White, and Moses Polley. They may want you to take the stand and tell them your story. Just stick to your story; do not add anything no matter how trivial it may seem to you. Answer politely all questions yes or no or to the best of your ability and recollection. No one needs a slip of the tongue from you that may send the sheriff off in a direction that will eventually get you indicted for murder. As it stands, they do not and cannot hold you past the inquest and must release you. Do you understand this, my dear?"

With that Julia smiled and nodded her head yes.

The lawyer stood and said, "I shall be back after supper tonight to check to make sure you have had Mrs. Belling's meal." With that, he tipped his hat to her and she rose, rushed to him and gave him a big hug and a small kiss on the cheek which made him blush and laugh.

"Good day to you, ma'am," he said turning and yelling for the jailer to let him out. He walked out and left moving back in towards the sheriff's office. "We need to have that a little warmer back there, Sheriff, and she needs another blanket for night. Mrs. Belling will be here with meals. I had Judge Samuels sign this court order addressing the treatment of the two prisoners in question and he has, as you can see, mandated that Mrs. Belling be allowed to not only bring meals to Mrs. Reese, but to also allow her a space with table and chair in which to eat this meal. She also now knows that you must send for me first before she can be questioned. So no more late nights with detectives in a lady's cell pressing her. I hope this is understood?"

"Yeah," said Winney, "I understand but one more day or so and I think we would have gotten a confession out of her."

"But the question would remain was she coerced into making that statement so the treatment would get better? Or was she guilty? And maybe, sir, it made very little difference to you but I can tell you now that Cutcheon is coming tomorrow to represent Mr. Boles and he also will have with him a writ. And he is ready to lodge any complaints against the sheriff's department for mistreatment of Mr. Boles."

Winney winced a little bit. He knew of Cutcheon. Once a very well-liked judge with a great legal mind, he had decided that he would forsake the bench in pursuit of a career defending and helping those in need and stepped down surprising everyone. Winney knew he could be big trouble as he watched Parkinson leave. When the door closed, he slammed his fist on the desk. Looking at his deputy, he said, "Reckon who hired all these high-priced mouth pieces to represent these people?"

The detective shook his head and looked out into the night from the window as snow started to drift down in the street.

"Find out. I am curious as to why someone would pay all that money. We actually may have a lead in there somewhere."

The deputy scurried out of the building as if in a rush to make a contact.

George Boles lay on the floor in a fetal position. It was the last of any defensive modes he had. His mind was numb from a week on bread and water. He had missed the chamber pot a few times and messed himself; a condition the jailer refused to remedy. He had no shirt, shoes, and no blanket. Just the hard cold floor to lie on. His head hurt tremendously. His stomach now gurgled and he was afraid he was going to be sick again. He tried to take a deep breath but his chest was so congested that he let out a big cough with a huge rattle on the end of it. That had hurt his chest and he rolled over looking up at the ceiling. That cough was now becoming more consistent. He was dizzy from lack of food and very cold. His body shook involuntarily from the cold. He barely heard the jail cell door open. All he knew was that two arms had grabbed him and pulled him to his feet.

"Get him cleaned up and over to Mrs. Belling's. I want him shaved, bathed, fed and in a proper cell with a bed and warmth before his lawyer gets here in the morning," said a voice. The voice was that of Sheriff Winney.

The deputies did as they were told and soon George was back in a warm cell with blankets, food, water, hot coffee, and a doctor there putting a poultice on his chest.

"That should get the congestion out of there in no time, George. I know it's a little hot and it burns but it can't be helped." He turned to the jailer, "If he starts coughing, I want you to come back here and give him a spoonful of this."

"Aw, doc, I ain't no nursemaid,"

"Sheriff's orders. He says get him cleaned and well. He has to go to the inquest tomorrow."

"Well, ok," muttered the man as he closed the jail cell.

George could not believe his luck. He ate the bowl of soup provided for him and drank the large cup of coffee they gave him. He rolled over on the cot, pulled the warm blanket around him and went to sleep confident that his nightmare would soon be over.

"Please, God, Mr. Crouch, help me. I needs you now. Please, Lord, help me," he said over and over in his mind.

Morning came with a bright cold sunshine just like a lot of Michigan mornings in the winter. The air was crisp and a light snow had fallen the night before. It had a cold crunch to it under your feet when you walked.

Julia Reese sat on her bed with a warm shawl over her shoulders enjoying a cup of tea after her breakfast. She was reading a Bible just like Sally had urged her to do. Funny, she still had this feeling about Sally. She did not remember her from school and how did she know all the way from Chicago that Julia was in jail? Something did not add up for her. As she sat pondering, the jailer came, opened the door and let Sally in. She waited until he was out of sight and then opened up her jacket, took off her bonnet, and sat it on the bed next to Julia.

"Ok, this is a good morning. There was no one out front and the jailer just took me back. I had planned it this way. You have got to get out of here and get away or for sure they are going to convict you. There is no one in the jail but the jailer and he is busy reading the morning paper. You should be able to just walk by him. I managed to get the key from his pocket."

She went over to the cell door and produced a key ring and gently unlocked the door holding it so it would not swing open.

"We have to hurry if you are to get away. The train will be leaving in less than a half an hour." She stuck a folded piece of paper in the front pocket of Julia's dress and then moved across the cell looking as best she could down the aisle. The coast seemed clear.

"What train?" asked Julia surprised while trying to take this all in.

"The next train to Detroit. You can get off there and make your way across the bridge to Canada and you will be safe there. When you cross the bridge, there will be a man named Wilbur. He is my cousin and he will have a horse and buggy waiting. You can't miss him." With that, she pulled out two small revolvers and handed them to Julia. "If the jailer gets up and notices you, just shove the pistol in his chest and pull the trigger. Then just keep going. But dressed in my clothes, I am sure he will not notice. If he asks any questions, just say yes or no or whatever but keep going. They never ask me anything on the way out."

Julia looked at the pistols. She had never fired one before and they felt strange in her hands. Sally now was busy putting on the coat and bonnet that she had worn into the jail. Julia felt funny about this. "I can't do this, Sally. I am not a criminal and I could never shoot another person no matter what."

Sally pushed over towards the cell door forcing her out into the aisle. Julia retreated and dropped the pistols on the bed. Again, Sally tugged at her and had her partway out of the cell. This time Julia could see Detective Harris from a hidden vantage point down at the end watching all of this. Suddenly, it sank into her that they were setting her up. She guessed even the pistols were empty. Stronger than Sally, she pushed her way back into the cell, took off the garments and threw them out the door along with the pistols.

"Now, I want you out of my cell to never return, whoever you are! I saw Harris and I know the trick. Get out! I have a lawyer now to take care of me. In fact, I have an entire law firm to help me. I shall wait for the law to clear me and they will because I have done nothing wrong and there is no proof that I did anything wrong."

With a final push she shoved Sally out into the aisle, slammed the jail door shut and locked it with the key. Then she threw the key down the aisle listening to it clatter all the way down. It slid and came to a rest. True to form, out stepped Harris and picked it up. He started twirling it on his index finger and smiling.

"Stupid little fool, you could have been free. I have come here every day to help you and this is all the thanks I get."

With that, Sally picked up the things on the floor, held her head high and huffed out of the jail to the main office. As she came through the door, she was greeted by Carmone the Pinkerton Detective, the sheriff and two deputies. She was also followed by Detective Harris.

"Well, I can see that did not work. We have no choice but to go to the inquest and there is no doubt in my mind that she and Boles will be released."

"So, do you still think they are guilty?" asked Carmone.

"I am not as sure as I was at the beginning of this. The boy I think just got excited and told some whoppers that hurt him. Hell, he could not fit in that trunk and none of the stuff was taken out of it nor the clothes on top of it pushed onto the floor. Still, he did not run nor she. If they were after the money, they could have been long gone west or somewhere and we would have never found them. The stories they tell are just crazy enough to be correct so I guess I won't feel bad about letting them go. In a case where someone is in a place and is the only one not killed, you have to take a hard look at 'em. Shit, that's what we get paid for, ain't it?" said Winney.

"I guess we got to open this thing up and hope that the inquest sheds some light on the case."

"Well, Sally, you head back to the main office tomorrow and thanks for all ya did. Tell Wordell that I am going to stay around here and if he has any other operatives that he can send out I would appreciate the help. I really don't want to give up on this right now."

"Yeah, I'll give 'em your best, I will," said Sally kissing Carmone lightly on the cheek as she passed out of the door and down the boardwalk to the hotel.

Chapter 15

2010

Hunter moved across the office and out to the cash registers with his morning routine. Jemma came in, a short diminutive young lady with jet black hair that had fire engine red highlights. The hair was short; above her shoulders and combed to one side. She had on black make-up and a ring in her nose. Her nail polish was royal blue and she was wearing a plaid skirt with a big golden safety pin in the front holding it together. On top, she had a white short-sleeved blouse and a black sweater that buttoned up the front but it was open.

"Well, good morning Cruella," said Hunter poking fun at her. He liked Jemma. She was twenty-some years old and lived across the street with a boyfriend who was painfully thin. Hunter always wondered if he was a heroin addict; he at least had the look. As far as he knew, the kid never had a job but seemed to have money enough to pay the bills and keep the two of them.

Jemma stopped and stuck her tongue out at Hunter which revealed that she now had two tongue rings.

"And, young lady, what does a second tongue ring do that one can't?" asked Hunter half poking fun at her.

"I drives dicky wild!" she said with her head slightly bent in a naughty pout.

"Ah Jesus, Jemma, that is too much information this early in the damn morning. Now I will have that image burning in my brain all day."

She laughed at him as he put up a hand and waved it at her. "You have ruined my Girl Scout image of you now and forever," said Hunter.

"Naked or clothed," smiled Jemma as Samantha and Cheryl came through the door. Samantha took one look at Hunter's red face and said, "Ok, what have you two been up to now?"

"Nothing. It's just sometimes she can be a real tease when she wants to be," said Hunter moving back to the office.

Cheryl looked over at Jemma who had an impish look about her.

"I think it's best we just get to work, ladies, and I can use some of that coffee down there," said Samantha moving down to the second tier coffee bar.

Victoria walked in wearing a black pair of pants and a blue top with a gray sweater that buttoned up the top. She was carrying her coffee from Mickey D's topped with lots of whip cream and chocolate swirls. In her other hand, she had Hunter's coffee which consisted of one large coffee with an espresso shot and four Splenda.

She walked into the office, set down the coffees and took off her sweater. She gave Hunter a peck on the cheek and said, "Good morning, hon."

Picking up a notebook from her desk she said, "So, today is the day we go to Spring Arbor and ask permission to do an investigation on the night of November 21st, the anniversary of the murders."

"Yeah, seven pm correct?" asked Hunter, not looking up from bill of ladings on his desk for the book order.

"Ok, and mom is all set to watch the children. Anything else except business today?"

"No, except once you get the kids settled I would like to hotfoot it over to the cemetery and do some more checking and answer some questions."

"Sure, no problem. As soon as I get supper started then we can leave."

The phone rang and Victoria answered it. "Hey, stud, it's for you. A Mr. Ken Wyatt from the Jackson Citizen Patriot," she said raising her eyebrows. Hunter picked up the phone.

"Hello? This is Hunter Ross. How may I help you?" he said coyly.

"Ah, yes, Mr. Wyatt. How are you today sir? Well that is good. I was wondering if I could meet you for lunch today. I would like to ask you some questions about the Crouch murders. I understand that you wrote an article in 1977 about this. Sure, 1 pm at Gaston's. Yeah, I know it. Well, we shall see you there and have a nice day," said Hunter hanging up the phone. "That should put me back here sometime after school."

"How about me drive over there and meet you at the cemetery and we can drive on into Spring Arbor together?" asked Victoria.

"Sure, that could work. So, if your mother is babysitting tonight, is this a good time to take Jemma? She says the crack addict is in Detroit. Probably making a new score," said Hunter.

"Hmm… well, that way she will feel like part of the team. I think she will make a good member and, who knows, maybe we can get her away from freak boy some day," said Victoria.

"All right, it is settled. We shall meet there and then a quick bite to eat and then home," said Hunter picking up some books and moving out into the store. He walked toward Jemma and she eyed him suspiciously. "I was wondering if," Hunter was cut short.

"You were wondering if I would like to go with you tonight to the cemetery and all, correct."

"Uh, well, yeah," said Hunter very puzzled. He halfway turned and looked back in the office. Victoria was standing in the doorway sipping coffee leaning against the doorjamb and smiling. "How did you know that, young lady?"

"Remember I have these special powers but when I am around Kryptonite, they fade away," she said smiling. Hunter just shook his head and took the books across the shop to shelve them. "And, yes, I will have lunch with you today," she said laughing as Victoria choked on her coffee trying to stifle a laugh. Hunter stopped, turned and, for the first time in a long time, he saw a smile on Jemma's face.

The afternoon sun was warm for November and the farmers were out in force picking corn trying to get the crop in before the first real snow would hit. Usually, sometime after the fifteenth of November, deer hunters would be graced with one good morning of an inch or so to help track the deer. Then, after that, even though it was not winter the weather turned quite cold and snowy for many months with but little break. The leaves had crashed down to the ground adorning mother earth with the entire red and golden splendor; a nice new carpet awaited the ground to keep it warm for the winter. The Charger purred along and Jemma sat back looking out of the window at the beautiful sight fall had to offer. She felt warm, alive and really wanted - unlike with Kyle her live-in boyfriend. She was head-over-heels in love with him at one time but she knew that it would not last much longer.

He was off in a different direction and she did not want to leave Marshall quite yet.

"Have you ever been in love, Hunter?" she asked.

"Sure, actually at my age quite a few times. Just never hooked up with any of them for a variety of reasons."

"It's just… Kyle and I… we seem to be drifting apart and I am not sure what I want."

"Well, it probably means he is not the one. You can fall in and out of love for various reasons and each time I have noted it seems to be with someone different. Love can be an adventure and I think when you finally pick someone you know it is that one and, well, that is when the lifelong adventure begins into the good and bad things all rolled into one as you travel down life's highway."

"Hmm… that is pretty profound. I guess that makes things look a lot different coming from someone as old as you. I guess you have seen it all."

Hunter could not stifle the laugh. "Well, I hope this old man is around a long time before they throw dirt in his face. I got a few things I would like to do yet and one of them is to solve this case. So, are you interested in joining Victoria and me in the quest for the unknown?"

"Sure, I think so. You know, I have these premonitions but really can't tell you much more than that."

"Well, I am no expert but I think what you need to do is to exercise your mind. First, you need to find a good book about being a psychic. Look through them and take one that you like; one that draws you. It should keep you interested all the way through. Also, pick out one on the Zen Mind. Just read and let your mind flow. I think you will find the inner talent that you have and it may be much stronger than you think. Remember, I am always across the street if you need me," Hunter reached over and lightly patted her on the shoulder.

She smiled back at him and said, "Thanks, I will get the books and I will remember where I have a friend if I need one."

The Charger pulled into the small steak house and they got out. Hunter set the car alarm with a beep. Jemma smiled and took his arm walking in side-by-side with him. As they came in the door, Hunter made eye contact with Ken and he stood to shake hands. "Mr. Wyatt, this is an associate and employee of mine, Jemma Choun. She works with us from time to time and will be assisting us on the case. Besides, she is beautiful and old men like me love to be seen in public with beautiful young girls." He paused, leaned into Ken a bit and said, "Makes the old fogies think something is afoot eh, Holmes?"

Ken laughed and patted Hunter on the back. He knew right away he would like this man. He was not sure what to expect in a ghost hunter. He had snickered a little but what the heck, it's a free lunch and he was one never to turn that down. Especially not at such a nice place. The Maitre d' came and asked them for a table. Hunter flipped a twenty dollar bill out of his hand if as by magic and said, "Nice table for three if you would, sir, and we would like one where we can talk in confidence without interruption if you would, please."

"Right this way, sir," said the man smiling and motioning with his hand. He took them to a back corner; a nice round table and no one was dining near them. A lady walked up, "Petite and blonde, she looks to be close to thirty," thought Hunter.

"Hello. My name is Marie and I will be your server today!"

Again Hunter, with the surprise twenty out of nowhere, flipped it up and stuck it lightly in her apron front, "That is for you, my dear. No sharing that. I will leave a tip you can share later. Just keep the drinks coming. We may be here a while talking past the end of our meal."

"Thank you, sir, and what may I start you out with?" She took the orders and moved from the table as Ken struck up the conversation.

"So, why is it you are so interested in these murders?" he asked.

"Well, my partner Victoria, who could not make it today, and I are Forensic Paranormal Investigators and we would like to take a crack at solving the Crouch case. We know something of it but probably not as much as you and, well, I was wondering if I could at least be allowed to peruse your notes in hopes that something may jump out at me?"

"Well, I have no problem with that, young man, but my notes are no longer around on that old article, I am afraid. I looked at the paper before coming in and I emailed you as best I could some pictures of the article. I don't know if they will be of any use to you or not. The paper is very old and we actually had to use white cotton gloves."

"We shall see if we can enhance it enough to read it. Does the newspaper have archives and, if so, is anyone allowed admittance to read and study them?"

"No. If you want back articles you will have to go to the library downtown. You know the Carnegie? And they have it all on microfilm. I am sure you can find my article down there. You know, that was a long time ago and I can remember some of it but there have been a lot of articles over my desk in that period of time. I shall see what I can dig up and what I can recollect. I doubt if there are any family members around anymore. It strikes me as most that were here in nineteen seventy seven were fairly old and if you did find them today they may not be able to tell you very much."

"We are going to the Spring Arbor Township meeting tonight and see if we can get them to grant us permission to go to Reynolds Cemetery on the night of the anniversary to watch to see what happens. I really think I know what will happen," said Hunter.

"You mean the tale about Eunice rising from her grave in Woodlawn and in mist form moves to Reynolds to the grave of her father? And he then arises from the grave, they materialize, hug one another and then he goes back in the ground and she's back to her grave in Woodlawn?" asked Ken.

"Well, so some have told it that way, yes," smiled Hunter.

"You say you know what will happen. Can you tell me what that is?

"Yep. My guess is nothing," smiled Hunter.

Ken let out a small laugh as the girl was setting down the

drinks, "Are we ready to order yet?"she asked.

"I think so. Go ahead, Jemma. Ladies first," smiled Hunter

They ordered their meals and Ken began to smile.

"You know, they have a big problem over there with people

showing up on that night and it keeps the police very busy."

"So, do you think they will let us in or not?"

"If I'm a betting man, and I'm not, I would say yes but as you said, we shall see," smiled Ken.

The conversation moved from the Crouch murders on to other topics of interest between the two. The three talked for over two hours.

As the bill came Ken said. "I will be at the township meeting covering for a reporter tonight. I'll see you there and good luck." He stood with Hunter, they smiled and shook hands. Jemma shook his hand and smiled at him. The gesture was not lost on Hunter.

As the black Charger leaped out of the parking lot, he swung out to the west and BL-94. This took him to Rte. sixty and eventually the intersection of Reynolds Road. "You should have given him a business card you know," muttered Jemma.

"Huh!" said Hunter lost in thought.

"Mr. Wyatt… you did not give him a business card. Should you not have?" she asked perplexed with one eye askew.

Hunter laughed and patted her on the hand, "You, my dear, are full of surprises."

She stared at him for a moment as if she was lost in time. He looked back into her the dark eyes that were so haunting behind what he thought was really a very pretty face.

"We are here at the cemetery. It looks as if Victoria is not here yet. Let's get out and traverse around some." She got out still looking at him as he pulled out the three eighty and shoved it into the tactical vest. Next went the stun gun and then on with the vest.

They moved through the gate and he started down the row with the Mel-meter in his right hand. Suddenly he could feel her hand in his left hand. He looked at her and she smiled at him; something he did not normally see on her face had happened twice in one day.

"This is called a Mel-meter. It measures the electro-magnetic field or, as you will hear it called in the paranormal parapsychology world, EMF. Lots of things put off a field around objects that can and do generate electricity. Take those wires over there for instance. If we could get up close enough to them we would detect a magnetic field that also has some electrical properties. We think that when spirits are near us, or nearby maybe trying to manifest themselves, they will give off EMF. Of course, there are other things that can do the same thing such as wiring, common appliances, cell phones, walkie-talkies and probably any kind of common electrical device. This is called a K-2 Meter and it does the same just not quite as finite a measurement."

Hunter handed the K-2 meter to her. "It's on. Just watch for the lights to light up from yellow all the way to orange or red. The more they light up the larger the field. I think some EMF can actually occur in certain substances and maybe even some in and around these grave markers. See, small amounts of minerals can be found inside most rocks or stones. Some so very minute that they are barely a trace amount. But when you put several trace amounts of these things together you will come up with possibly a small energy. When we talk about haunting later I will show you some different types and then we can pull this all together."

They walked on and finally came around to Susan's grave again. Hunter withdrew his usual three audio recorders and laid them out around the plot.

"Hi Susan, it's me Hunter. I told you I would be back. You did not give me much evidence before. I know you are there; you can hear me. Maybe they were right. Did Judd hate his real daddy and then shot him in the head? Is that how it went down? Because I will find out Susan. Tell me what you know or give me something to work on if it was not Judd. Right now, it all points to him and Byron as the two to gain of this. Do you want Judd's name drug through the mud?"

Jemma put her hand on his arm and said in a low voice, "Not so gruff. You are scaring her!"

Hunter paced around the plot looking back at the grave marker as he had on previous visits.

"I have ways to figure this out with science today that you could not even understand back then. It may not always be right so if you don't tell me I might get it wrong by accident. Did you have something to do with this, Susan? Was Judd protecting you or Daniel? You died from this Susan. Maybe you were poisoned. Were you force-fed rat poison like the sheriff said in some paper interviews of the day? The coroner said you committed suicide and your family doctor said you died of natural causes. Who was right, Susan? Why is it someone does not want us to know? Why are all the trial transcripts missing?"

Hunter moved again with his hands on his hips looking up to the sky."From what I am reading about your husband, it sounds like he was a real piece of shit. Susan, what do you say about that? Did the stress of knowing about this entire mess kill you? Did someone kill you to shut you up or did you just kill yourself because you did not want to have to testify about what your husband and Judd did?

xWho was it, Susan? You took it to the grave with you and you know it's been 127 years of bull shit, Susan."

Hunter kicked at the grass and looked at Jemma who was quite enthralled with him and his questioning. He kicked at the grass beside the marker as if in disgust.

"So, you would sit there in silence and not let out a word about the truth and just let people think bad things about those who did not do it and good things about those who had a hand in it?"

Hunter and Jemma looked up to see Victoria pulling up behind Hunter's vehicle. She got out and as she walked toward the grave Hunter finished his dissertation.

"Speak up into one of these devices, Susan, and I will be able to hear your voice. Give me a word, a phrase, anything that will lead me to the truth. For God sakes, they killed your sister, Susan! Doesn't that bother you in the least? She was pregnant with a child; ready to give birth. Are you not the very least upset mad about that? I would think if Judd or your husband had anything to do with it you would at least want your father's and sister's killers brought to justice. What about poor Moses Polley? He left a family behind without support. They had to live on hard times back then, not much food, probably lost their farm. How can you justify covering up for someone who would do all that and for what? Some Goddamn money! Some land, a few head of cattle, is that what the price of an old man and a young woman about to give birth to the world are worth? And a father and husband of a family who loved him and needed him to take care of them? You are protecting these God awful men. I'm gonna leave you now, Susan, and I will be back. You think about this. I might be the last chance to get any of this right. All I am asking, if it is hard to communicate, is for a name, a phrase, anything that will lead me to the truth of the matter. Think it over, Susan. I will be back. I am not going away and the only way you can get rid of me is to tell me the truth or help me find out what the truth is. I am here to stay until this is over. You will get no peace until I do. I will keep coming back and back and back until you can't stand it anymore. No need to try and scare me. I don't scare and I think you know that."

Hunter looked down at the ground as Jemma moved next to him and grabbed his hand. Victoria came from the other side put her arm around him and rubbed his back.

"Jacob, if you are here don't threaten me and tell me to leave it alone because I am not. It is time, all of you, to finish this chapter up. This is the time now and people will stop coming, no more questions and you can all rest in peace."

With that Hunter walked away and out of the cemetery as Victoria and Jemma stood there while Victoria spoke her piece.

"Hi, Susan. It's me, Victoria. All he wants to do is find the truth and let everyone know what happened here and who it was that did this to your family. I want to know; it was my family also. I'm sorry and I know it's hard but you have to stop grieving and crying in the grave and step up and help finish this. You know so much about all of this and I think you know the truth," said Victoria placing her hand lovingly on the head stone.

"The next time I come out here, Susan, I will bring some flowers to brighten up the grave area. This is a very nice final resting place. I know Jacob has to be buried here close by and it must be a comfort. Please, sweetheart, step up and do what's right. Don't let any of the others push you around. Come and tell us. Jacob, you can help too I think. Maybe you are not sure what happened to you but you were shot in the head while sleeping. Some say Judd and Daniel did it. We want to find the truth and if they did not then we want to find out who did. We will publish it all in a book for all to read and understand and it will stand forever as a document showing what really happened. The crime that the Pinkerton's could not solve."

She and Jemma stood there holding hands with heads bowed as the sun lowered in the west making its final appearance for the day. Hunter had removed his vest and put it in the trunk with his pistol and stun gun. Victoria and Jemma, after several minutes of quiet, picked up the recorders and shut them off one by one and walked out of the cemetery to the cars. Victoria handed the recorders to Hunter and he stowed them in the trunk in his vest where they belonged.

"Well, off to Spring Arbor to see if we can get permission to investigate here at night," said Hunter as he and Jemma climbed into the Charger and Victoria into her van. Hunter pulled around the corner to the west on Horton Road into the corner church parking lot. As he turned he looked up at the sign in front of the church. It read, "Sunlight Church, Pastor David Channel."

Hunter wrote that down on a piece of paper, and then turned the car left around the corner and back down Reynolds Road toward Spring Arbor.

They pulled into the Teft Road address; a nice modern building right in the middle of Spring Arbor on the south side of the Main Street or Rte 60. Spring Arbor College was right across the street. The three moved into the building, down a small hall and through a door where the meeting room was. Hunter saw Ken immediately and motioned Jemma and Victoria to follow him. He stopped and Ken stood up.

"Ken Wyatt, this is my partner, Victoria Carson, and my partner in D & R Investigations."

Ken shook Victoria's hand and said, "Nice to meet you, Victoria, and hello Jemma."

Jemma, Victoria and Hunter sat down next to Ken who leaned over quietly and said to Hunter, "You are not on the agenda." He handed a printed sheet of paper showing what the agenda of the meeting was.

"I talked to the township clerk and she said I was to just stand up when it was time for citizen's comment, ask my questions then and present what we have. I have some sheets explaining what it is we are doing, out there."

The President, a tall man in his late forties, stood with the other board members and said, "Please stand and let's recite the Pledge of Allegiance."

The small crowd of six people plus the five board members droned out the pledge; all covering their hearts with their hands.

"I will call this meeting to order, and I know Mr. Ross you would love to approach the board with a question. You may do so but first, is there any comment by the citizens?"

People looked around and none stood nor raised a hand.

"Very well, Mr. Ross, we are going to consider you our first point of business tonight. Please rise and state your request."

Hunter and Victoria both stood.

"I would like to present to the board a copy of a statement made by myself and my partner, Victoria Carson," he said pointing to Victoria and walking to the table to hand out the pages to each board member. He stood silent for just a moment allowing them to read the paper he had passed to them.

"My name is Hunter Ross, and I am a Forensic Paranormal Investigator. My partner and I, on our own initiative, have opened the old Crouch murder case to see if we can use modern day forensics as well as up-to-date detection methods to determine once and for all who the murderers are. As you can see, we have listed the types of equipment that we use. We are not psychics or mediums. We don't pretend to converse with the dead although we do get answers on digital recorders sometimes to questions. We are not sure exactly scientifically what these voices are but assume they are, for the want of a better word, from the other side."

Victoria took over for a moment continuing the discussion to show that she was equally adept at using the detection methods.

"We use EMF meters as well as infrared and full spectrum cameras, temperature laser detectors and different arrays of communication devices. With these we hope to get maybe some answers beyond the grave to some of the burning questions in this case."

Hunter continued, "We saw the sign at the Reynolds Cemetery as to the warning about no one allowed in after sunset. We have, in the past, investigated cemeteries with the permission of the governing body's approval and we never go anywhere unless we have permission to be there. Should you decide against our request, we will honor it by not crossing into the grounds at night. We would like permission to set up equipment and run a short investigation on the night of the anniversary of the murders. That would be November 21st night into early morning of the 22nd."

The members paid close attention to his speech and to the papers handed them. The president spoke up at first and said to the village police chief who was in the office.

"Dale, what is our legal stance on letting them do this? Do you know what the law says in our codification exactly? Do we, as the board, even have the right to grant this if we should so desire?"

An older man in his mid-fifties stood up in the back of the room. He had on a flannel shirt and a pair of Dockers. "I don't know, Wes, without looking at the cemetery ordinance."

"Well, Mr. Ross, we won't say yes or no at this time but we will take a short adjournment to take your request under consideration and to give us a few minutes to read up on the ordinances." With that he stood, rapped a gavel on the table and said, "we are going to take a short ten minute recess at this time."

The president and the police chief walked out of the door, down the hall and into an office. Hunter and Victoria went back and took their seats.

True to their word they came back in about ten minutes. The president huddled for a few moments with the board members and then called the meeting to order.

"Mr. Ross, we have examined the request and found that we do indeed have the power to grant the request. But in this case, we have decided as a board not to do so at this time. I would invite you back next year to reapply if you so desire. We will, at that time, send out letters to the adjacent homeowners and have them answer as to whether they want you out there at night. While I am sure you will be peaceable, we have to take in consideration what kind of crowd you may draw and how much noise and confusion they may cause along with damage to the property. Then there is the chance that we set a precedent which would dictate that later we may have to let others in to do the same thing and we have been adamant about keeping people out there at night. Of course, on the anniversary the police department as well as the county sheriff and the state police have problems trying to keep lookers out. So, after weighing all of this, as I said we regretfully feel we have to decline your request. We do, however, applaud the fact that you came to us to ask the permission. We, of course, invite you anytime during the day to investigate all you want and if the township clerk can be of any help historically for records, please feel free to ask."

Hunter rose to address the board. "I would like to thank the board for taking in consideration of our request on such a short notice and for at least debating the idea of granting to us. We do recognize the plight of the township in this matter and, rest assured, we will honor your wishes and not trespass after dark that night or any night for that matter after the sun has set. Thank you very much."With that, Jemma and Victoria stood and they walked out of the board room followed by Ken Wyatt.

"I am sorry but I guess they do have a point I will put a small story about this in the paper and, well, if there is anything else I can do for you let me know. And also feel free to call me anytime. Keep me posted as you investigate because I am interested."

Jemma at that point jabbed Hunter in the ribs with her elbow, "Cards to him," she said in a low voice.

Victoria heard and realized that Jemma was correct and pulled out two cards one for her and one for Hunter. "This is a good way to keep in touch with us should you wish, Mr. Wyatt, and thank you so much for your help."

Ken stuck out his hand taking each of the three and shaking them, "Good evening to all," he said turning and going back into the meeting room.

Chapter 16

Hunter came down to the office a little late the next morning. Jemma was already there with coffee in hand for him.

"Sleep well, dude?" She smiled as she handed him the coffee. "Just like you want it: large coffee with an espresso shot and four Splenda, that should jump start you."

"Ha! Thanks, I wanted to punch that alarm clock this morning. So much on my mind last night; I just sat there in my easy chair looking out on Main Street trying to figure some of this out. It seems when you get to one thing something else tells you no or it does not fit nor make sense."

"Hmm… don't worry. It will come. There are lots of answers to be gotten in this case," assured Jemma.

Victoria came in the office on a fly, "Hunter have you seen the Jackson paper this morning? Seems like Ken gave us a write up and I am told by someone that it is on MLive.com."

Hunter spun in his chair to his left and pressed the "on" button to his Dell tower. As he watched it boot up and come to life, he wondered what Ken had said. He hoped it was something good about them and not bad. He still did not have a good handle on what Ken thought of them and their venture.

He clicked to the Internet after boot up and went directly to the MLive.com page. There, after a little searching, was the article and it read:

There will be no township-sanctioned "Ghostbusters" probe at the old Crouch Cemetery later this month. Monday night the Spring Arbor Township Board denied a Marshall man's request to spend the night of Nov. 21-22 in the cemetery doing a paranormal investigation into the 1883 Crouch murders.

Hunter Ross wanted permission to spend from 10 p.m. Nov. 21 until 3 a.m. Nov. 22 in the old cemetery, at Reynolds and Horton roads. He and his partner, Victoria Carson, run D&R Investigations, billing themselves as "forensic paranormal investigators" into unsolved murders and missing-person cases.

However, the board, after consulting police and ordinances, denied the request because of past neighbor complaints. Those included parking issues, noise and what board -chair Wes Caldwell termed "inappropriate behavior."

The Reynolds, or Crouch, Cemetery contains the remains of Jacob Crouch. He was the central figure in a murder case that has excited interest for decades and is a subject of multiple Web sites.

The cemetery is posted as being open from dawn until dusk. Ross saw the sign, and told the board, "We don't go anywhere without asking permission."

The Crouch murders took place during a stormy night between dusk Nov. 21 and dawn Nov. 22 in 1883. Four persons were shot in their sleep — the 74-year-old widower Jacob Crouch; a daughter, Eunice, and her husband, Henry White; and Moses Polley, a Pennsylvania cattle-buyer who was spending the night.

Other mysterious deaths occurred in the months after the murders. Several men were charged and tried — including Judd Crouch, one of the old man's sons, who lived in Jackson. However, there never were any convictions. The murders have remained unsolved — Jackson County's most notorious "cold case."

Hunter Ross and Victoria Carson had planned to use a variety of instruments in their probe, including infrared cameras, electromagnetic meters and digital voice recorders.

"We are after scientific facts that can be measured and applied to paranormal activities," Ross said.

Though denied nocturnal access, Ross said they plan to seek consent to conduct an investigation on the old Crouch farm, about a mile east of the cemetery on Horton Road.

"Well, that was short and at least to the point. Nothing bad to say about us," said Hunter.

"So now we try and gain access to the property and go from there?" asked Victoria.

Hunter picked up the phone and called the Jackson County Courthouse. He asked for someone who could help him locate trial transcripts. A ladies voice came on the phone, "Mrs. Dawes, how may I help you?"

"My name is Hunter Ross and I am a private investigator. We are looking into a cold case file that happened a long time ago in Jackson County. Do you have records back to 1884?"

"Oh yes, Mr. Ross, and even further. What case are you looking for?"

"Jacob Crouch, murder. There was a trial of a Mr. Daniel Holcomb and one Judd Crouch toward the end of 1884. It was a big trial with lots of witnesses and quite a bit of detail. I know I can't have the records and to try and copy them would be futile but I have a friend who is a top-rate photographer and he would be more than happy to spend some time photographing these records so we could read them. Would that be all right with you?"

"Well, certainly we can try and see what we can find but I must tell you, there is a twenty dollar an hour fee for employees to do that payable in advance of any paperwork we would turn over to you. And in this case, before you would be able to photograph it."

"Not a problem with that. I am also interested in the inquest reports from December 1883 on the Crouch murders, the inquest reports of Susan Holcomb January 1884, and one James Foy January 1884."

"For that you would have to call the coroner's office."

"Would you happen to have that number for me?"

Hunter sat attentively writing down the number and handed it to Victoria who then went to her phone to make the call.

"Give us a week or so and then we will call you and let you know when you can research all of the court transcripts. I also might suggest that you try the Carnegie library downtown. They have an extensive microfilm section that may also hold records you are seeking."

"Yeah, I know them. Have used them on several occasions. Thanks, and thank you so much and thanks for helping."

"No problem and good luck. I hope you solve your case."

Victoria moved back across the room hanging up her phone at the same time Hunter did. "Well, no soap. They suggest the newspaper of the day probably had the inquest results. They do not have complete records before 1900. Also, yesterday I called the township office to see about who might have owned that property after Jacob was killed. They could not find records for the year 1884 but they suggested looking at some microfilm documents in the library and some census books to see who lived there. Also, I had no luck finding anything out about a Will he may have left."

"Great, then we are underway and I guess our next trip is to the library so we can see that Crouch file for ourselves," said Hunter.

"So, we go back to the cemetery and ask more questions, do some hack box everywhere and see what goes bump in the night. Then we need to head to the library and see what we can dig up. The Citizen Patriot does not have archives but it is supposedly on microfilm in the library. So maybe, if we are lucky, the Jackson paper sent reporters to cover the trial. There might have been inquest reports also along with obituaries and maybe even some interviews and articles that might shed the light on the case," stated Victoria.

At that moment the phone rang and Victoria picked it up.

"Why yes, he is right here," said Victoria pressing hold and hanging up the phone. "A Mr. Stauffer for you, sweets," said Victoria smiling at Hunter.

"Hello. Hunter Ross here, how may I help you?"

"Mr. Ross, I think you are looking for me. At least, that is what your card said and also what Ken Wyatt said. I am Clark Stauffer and myself and my wife own the Crouch farm or at least what little is left of it."

"Ah, yes, we were there the other day and I left a card on your door. My partner and I would like to sit down and talk with you and your wife if you don't mind, Mr. Stauffer."

"Call me Clark and I am sure we would love to. Just so happens that we both took a day off to do some things and it is hard to catch us during the week with work and all."

"Well, how about Spring Arbor for lunch? Say, Marino's Pizza about noon? Myself and my partner, Victoria, will be there to meet you."

"That is fine, Mr. Ross."

"I must insist on one thing, though. If I am to call you Clark then you can call me Hunter."

The man laughed a good-natured laugh and it made Hunter smile.

"Ok. Hunter it is then. Say noon at Marino's."

"Very good, Clark. We will be looking forward to it." With that Hunter hung up the phone. "Well, Tori. Looks like you and I have a lunch date." He turned and looked at Jemma and said "Does Motel 6 have hourly rates?"

Jemma blushed and turned away giggling to herself.

"Yeah, as if mister! You can wait on that, big boy," said Victoria pinching his cheek hard between her fingers as she walked by.

"I am Marriot or Hilton material and don't you forget that." With that Hunter just shook his head and watched her walk away, something that was not lost on her as she looked over her shoulder to make sure he was still looking.

They sat in Marino's watching the college kids come and go for their early lunches as a small blue car drove into the drive way. A man in his forties climbed out of the car and a woman of similar age did the same on the other side. Hunter smiled as they grasped hands and held hands coming toward the door. He knew instinctively as he watched them enter that they were the Stauffers. He rose, waving his hand as they noticed him and Victoria. They smiled and moved toward the table.

"Clark, I presume?" asked Hunter

"Hunter, yes, and this is my wife Julia," said Clark as Hunter took her hand and shook it.

"May I present my partner in crime, Victoria." Both people shook her hand and, with the introductions over, they all sat down.

Hunter had taken them in as they had walked across the restaurant. He was about 5′9″ tall with a slightly rounding face, blue eyes that were alive and you could tell by them he was a fun-loving man. He had a goatee neatly trimmed and short hair with a somewhat receding hairline on the front. She was about the same height with a nice smile and brown eyes. She had chestnut colored hair that was styled and combed nicely. She walked lightly on her toes and Hunter thought immediately that she would make a wonderful dance partner.

"So, you are a ghost investigator then, Hunter," said Clark.

"Actually, Victoria and I are a rare breed and a new type of investigator," said Hunter.

"We like to call ourselves Forensic Paranormal Investigators. We like to churn old murder and cold case files looking to see if today's forensics can offer any answers to the past," commented Victoria.

"That is what has brought us to your farm. I see it is under construction," said Hunter.

"Not much has been done since we bought it. We did not know until after we had purchased it that it was such a famous place. The minute I saw that marker out front and looked it up I was like, Oh my!" said Julia.

"We are not sure what we want to do with it. We kind of thought that it might become our retirement home but now with all we have found out about it and all the people calling us about doing investigations there… well, it's just at times too much," said Clark.

"We don't mean to be one of those that bugs you and I must tell you we set up all sorts of technical equipment. All that we do is very scientific. We do not use mediums, psychics or anything like that. We want good measurable contact with anything that will speak to us or leave us a sign or any kind of communication. What we are looking for is a word, a phrase, anything like that to lead us in an investigative direction to maybe finally help solve the crime. We would also like to debunk the spirit from Woodlawn rising up and moving to Jacob's grave just to hug him on the anniversary of the murders. I am sorry but that is the dumbest story I have ever heard."

"Well, I agree with you there but many around here still show up I guess on that night to take a look and see what happens."

"Do you know the pastor of the church next to Reynolds Cemetery?" asked Victoria.

"I can't say as I remember but I think I met him at the school once for some reason or another."

"We did not get permission last night to investigate the cemetery. We thought we might next ask the church if we could investigate from their property across the fence."

"Yeah, I saw that in the paper this morning. Ken's piece. Stupid people, what do they know? It really could not have hurt a thing. It's just some people just don't understand what you are doing or trying to do."

"Well, in my opinion they had a good point and I don't know if that is why but I think if they would have let us in they would have to let anyone in at anytime and every year. There would be a bunch of people soliciting them trying to get into there to see Jacob and his daughter embrace."

"So, do you think our place is haunted?" asked Julia.

"I am not sure. We stopped long enough to just look around and leave you a note. We took some pictures for our file."

"There seems to be a great deal of controversy on where the old house sat," said Clark.

"Your house now sits right on top of the whole schabang. You can tell by the way it slopes away from your house and if you pick around in the soil some there you will find cobblestones the type used for foundations back in the day," said Hunter.

"So, you would like to do an investigation of our property then?" asked Clark.

"Yes, if we could on the night of the anniversary just to see what happens," said Hunter.

"I guess that can be arranged. We have already planned a bonfire party for the night in question that way it would keep people off the property. So you are invited to visit and set up your equipment for the night if you wish."

"We will be there maybe only six hours or less. I think we might start at around nine thirty and go to two AM or so."

"We would like to have some copies, if it is possible, of your research so that we could make up a scrapbook. We have some things we have found on our own but I am sure we don't have all of it by any means," said Julia.

"Not a problem. We would be more than happy to share anything we get with you. Have you had any experiences there that would be classified as strange or out of the ordinary?" asked Hunter.

"No, not really," said Clark.

"I guess I get the feeling sometimes I am being watched but other than that, no, we have not really seen or heard anything," said Julia.

"We will come out and investigate but whether we find anything is another story. I guess we will wait and see what comes. I think we should eat and then, if you don't mind, Victoria and I would like to take a look around the property."

"No, not at all! Help yourself," said Clark.

"Also, lunch is on me so help yourselves," laughed Hunter.

The Charger started down Reynolds Road toward the cemetery. "That was a nice lunch and I like them. They are a neat couple," said Victoria. "Marriage can be fun and wonderful," she smiled coyly and looked at Hunter, "Don't you agree?"

"Yeah, I suppose so. You know, I can't figure this out. Every time you try to get close to the story and the motive it just seems to slip away. I can't wait until December when we can get all of our material from the library. I am willing to bet that it is all in there: the inquests, the trial transcripts, all we gotta do is look."

"Why would someone purposely set out on such an old case to destroy any mention of it forevermore?" asked Victoria.

"It may be, my dear, when we find the answer to that question we will find the answer to the whole puzzle."

"You would think that trying to shoot that detective in broad daylight would backfire on you and yet they did not keep Judd in jail after they questioned him. I wonder why?"

"More questions that when solved, my dear, may give us volumes of answers."

They pulled up to the cemetery and off the road as they had done before. As Hunter stepped out of the car, he noticed that there was a small nip in the air and Victoria had on a beautiful pull-over white angora sweater with a high neck, black slacks with pink tennis shoes on. Hunter had on a polo shirt with a flannel shirt over top but open on the front and worn like a jacket. He opened the trunk, pulled out the three eighty and shoved it in the holster of his tactical vest. Pulling open a box, he shoved the stun gun in a holster under his left shoulder and pulled on the tactical vest. He grabbed a dark blue all-cotton ball cap and put it on his head. Slamming the trunk, he smiled at Victoria who grasped his hand and hand-in-hand they walked through the gate to Susan Holcomb's headstone.

"Hello, Susan. This is Hunter Ross again. I told you we would be back."

From the back corner of the cemetery unseen by human eyes stood a man in blue bib-overalls and a wide black hat. He had a dark beard and piercing eyes. He stood there with his hands in his front pockets just looking on at Victoria and Hunter. A woman with gray hair in a bun stood next to him. She had on a long print dress with an apron over the front. The man spoke to her not in a hushed tone but in a regular voice as if he was not worried about being heard by Victoria or Hunter.

"Yeah, Ma, after all those years and all the fools I get the sense he is the one. He will unravel this mystery for us and then we can have some peace."

"Heavens to Betsy, dear, go on over and make an acquaintance with him and I shall go and listen to the pretty lady. I really like the trust and strength in her face."

The couple moved across the cemetery walking almost in a flowing action as they came up to Susan's headstone.

The old man moved up close to Hunter. Hunter shivered involuntarily as if a chill had descended on him and the hair on his arms rose. He could feel tightness in his chest and he pulled out the MEL-meter, flipped it on and took a reading of 3.6. He checked again and got the same reading to his left but to the right it was zero. Without electricity, it should have been that all along. He was puzzled.

"Is there someone here with us? It's all right. We mean you no harm. We just want to talk and maybe ask some questions. Questions that maybe you can answer and maybe you can't."

Jacob moved as close as he could and whispered in Hunter's ear, "Jacob is here!"

Hunter oblivious to the statement pulled two audio recorders out of his vest and sat one down on the top of Susan's headstone, the other on the Holcomb plot stone.

"These devices will help us hear you when we get back home tonight. We can play them back and find out what you said."

Jacob moved toward Susan's stone. "Rise daughter," was all he said. Materializing out of air was another woman with dark hair. She had a pointy chin and her face was gaunt and drawn. She had the expression that the problems of the whole world were upon her. Tears ran down her cheeks as she looked upon Hunter and Victoria for the first time. "How oddly they are dressed," she thought.

"Who is here with us?" asked Hunter.

He waited for a response and then said, "Jacob Crouch, are you here? If so, how old are you, Jacob?"

"Yes!" came the answer but Hunter did not hear it. Hunter waited a short bit and another answer came, "74!"

"Susan, are you hear?" asked Victoria.

Susan stood still. Tears now starting to flow, she kept looking back to the southwest corner of the cemetery looking for something that was not there or for something to come. She trembled and started crying harder until she was almost wailing.

She moved closer to Victoria. "A relative, a friend, maybe she could help? She must know. She must understand," thought Susan. "How can they not see me nor hear me?" She looked around and saw her mother at the northwest corner of the cemetery but could not see her father although she knew he was there.

"Questions to answer, people. If not now, later. I want to know who is responsible for what. Jacob, you and your wife may not know. I don't understand your side but, Susan, you died because of what you knew. Did someone poison you, Susan? The sheriff says you were force-fed rat poison. Is that true? You don't do things like that to yourself. Who was responsible, Susan? A name, all we need is a name into one of the red lights."

Susan moved next to the light but all she could think to say was not and then she broke into sobs.

"Susan, I am not going to give up. I will keep coming back and back and back and we can go over the same old questions again and again. Were Judd and Daniel both in on this? I know he is your brother surrogate son, but if Judd is guilty I am going to find out and I will dump this over whoever is guilty and then force-feed it down their throats. Daniel and Judd, were they mad at Jacob for some reason?"

The dark mass had now accumulated at the southwest corner of the cemetery and was moving toward the middle and the Holcomb plot. Susan, in fear, reached out and touched Victoria lightly on the shoulder.

"Oh my God!" screamed Victoria as she staggered forward falling toward the headstone. Hunter was quick enough to catch her in mid-fall just before she banged her head on the stone. Susan disappeared as did the dark mass. Jacob shook his head looking at Victoria and he said "Grab her!" in a quick voice.

Chapter 17

Hunter had Victoria upright but she was woozy on her feet. He started to lead her out of the cemetery but she could not walk. He then reached down and picked her up. She instinctively put her hands around his neck and buried her head in his shoulder as he carried her out to the car. He sat her down on the hood of the car and kept his hands on her to steady her. She was looking down and smiled mouthing, "I'm ok," as she put her hands down on the hood to steady herself.

"Can you steady yourself while I get you a drink?" asked Hunter. She quickly and quietly said yes.

He went back to the trunk of the car and opened up a small locked box in the back. Pulling out a bottle of Canadian Mist, he started back toward Victoria. As he got there she started to tip forward and he caught her again and pushed her back up.

"Come on, sweetie, snap out of it," said Hunter. He opened the cap on the top of the bottle and held it to her mouth and said, "A sip, honey, just a sip."

She took a drink and recoiled from the sharp taste and then coughed as she swallowed.

"My God! Are you trying to kill me?" she asked.

"Nah, just get you drunk so I can take advantage of you," said Hunter smiling.

She reached up with both hands and pulled his face to hers embracing him in a kiss. He could not believe this was happening. He had wanted to kiss her for years but he just never got the nerve to do so. He had feelings for her and the children. They were the perfect ready-made family for him. The kiss lingered and became more passionate as it went on. Finally, he broke away from her. Still holding the bottle, she looked down at the ground smiling and he took his index finger under her chin raising her head to look into her eyes.

"You want another drink?" he asked.

She nodded yes and took the bottle from his hand, took a large swig and then coughed. She set the bottle down on the hood of the car as she slid off. Starting to list to the right, he caught her around the waist and instinctively pulled her toward him. She raised her arms as he bent to kiss her again. This time both bodies were entwined in a long, passionate kiss. So long, in fact, they did not notice the Spring Arbor Police car pull up behind them until the flashing light got Hunter's attention. By that time, the patrolman was next to them smiling and looking at the open bottle of whiskey on the hood of the car. Hunter jumped back almost knocking Victoria over.

"Good day, sir. What a.. is going on here?" asked the officer looking at the tactical vest and the handle of the pistol protruding from one side. He instinctively put his hand on the butt of his pistol.

"I'm going to ask you to place your hands on the car if you would, sir, with your feet back. And, ma'am, would you please step to the back of the car and place your hands on the trunk and keep them there in plain sight?"

Hunter did not argue but complied calmly as the officer unbuttoned the gun flap on the vest and pulled out the silver-plated .380.

"Quite a weapon you got there, sir. Are there anymore I should be aware of?"

"Inside the vest in the left side I have a stun gun and there is a large knife in the bottom right pocket of the vest. The rest is just equipment."

"2712, request back up Reynolds Cemetery on the corner of Reynolds Road and Horton Road." The radio snapped back the acknowledgement and sent out a call for assistance. A quick answer came back from the Jackson County Sheriff.

"Now, sir, if you would put your hands on top of your head."

Hunter knew the drill and put his hands on top of his head interlacing his fingers. The patrolman was taken aback but said, "I am placing cuffs on you for your protection and mine."

"I think that is an excellent idea, officer, and you will get no argument from me."

The patrolman put the cuffs on and then spun Hunter around. He reached up inside as Hunter had told him and removed the stun gun placing it on the hood. He then went through Hunter's pockets in the vest taking out all the equipment and knives in his vest and spreading them out on the hood. At that time, a county sheriff unit pulled up in front of them. The deputy crawled out of the car and moved toward the patrolman who seemed eager to show what he had caught.

"What's up, Roy?" asked the deputy.

"I caught these two engaged in a lip-lock outside the car. He was carrying and had an open bottle on the hood of the car," said the patrolman.

"Nice pistol. Do you have a permit for that?" asked the deputy.

"Ah, yes officer, in my wallet if you would and also a CCW permit to carry it and the stun gun as well along with the knife."

The patrolman looked perturbed at the fact that the gun may not be illegal.

"Mr. Ross is it?" asked the deputy.

"Yes, sir. I am sure if there is any problem that Sergeant Monroe will vouch for me, if he is available."

The deputy keyed his mic and called central dispatch to patch him through to Deputy Sergeant Monroe.

Soon, a familiar voice was heard on the radio and the deputy turned and said something hidden into his mic from Hunter.

"Ok, Roy, turn him loose. He has a permit and a CCW for the pistol and all the stuff he has. Sarge says he is a FOS and working on a case for the department."

"I am sorry, Mr. Ross, I did not know. Of course, you can understand," he was cut short by Hunter.

"Officer, there is no need to apologize. I would have done the same thing you did and you should be commended on the way with which you handled a potentially dangerous situation without help." Hunter reached out and patted the young man on the back. "I would have told you the whole story but I would not have believed it either."He reached for a small rectangular thin silver object on the hood of the car. He popped open the lid and pulled out a card that read D & R Investigations, Forensic Paranormal Investigator: Hunter Ross. He handed a card to both the patrolman and to the deputy.

"Oh, you are that ghost hunter guy from the meeting the other night who was denied access after dark here, correct?" said the patrolman.

"Yeah, that's me. You will see us here and at the old Crouch property quite a bit from now on. Usually this Charger will be in the area."

"Can I take my hands off the trunk now, boys?" asked Victoria.

"Oh yes, ma'am, you sure can," said the patrolman smiling and a bit red-faced. The deputy chuckled to himself.

"Well, we all at the department think they should have given you the chance to investigate. I mean, you did ask in a very polite manor. Do you think this cemetery is haunted?" asked the patrolman.

"I would have said before now that I thought it was not but Victoria just had an incident out there. She nearly fainted and hit her head on a gravestone. Something did that to her. I don't know what so I guess it bears more investigation. Now do I believe what the Internet says? That Eunice rises from her grave on the anniversary night and comes here to embrace her father? No, I don't believe that and if she did no one would see or know it. I can tell you."

The Deputy stepped forward and extended his hand as Hunter took off his vest to replace all the items in it. "Deputy Carl Place, nice to make your acquaintance. I'll make sure that Monroe puts out the scoop about you to the rest of us and, also, I am sure he will contact Spring Arbor about the same so you don't have to go through this all the time."

"Thanks!" said Hunter smiling back at the man.

"I get it now. The whiskey was for her but the kiss… well, maybe I don't understand," said the patrolman.

Victoria had now sat down in the car with her legs out on the ground and she smoked a cigarette to calm her nerves. She had been trying to quit and actually had quite a few times but not for long.

Hunter leaned over to the patrolman and said, "Don't worry. I don't know what happened or why either," as he winked at the young man.

As the deputy made his way back to his car, the patrolman decided to make his hasty retreat also. He stuck out his hand to Hunter and said, "Patrolman Jack Snyder. If there is anything you need, just come to the township hall and ask for us. We are in the back. Good luck on your investigations!" he said with a wink walking away. "And good night, ma'am. Have a good evening."

Hunter now had capped the bottle and picked up his vest. He moved back to the trunk, opened it and secured it all. He then walked away into the cemetery. Retrieving the recorders, he returned them to the vest and closed the trunk.

He got back in the Charger and they pulled out to the stop sign as Victoria was fastening her seat belt. She leaned over and kissed him lightly on the cheek with a coy smile and buckled up. Surprised, he turned and looked at her staring into her eyes. Suddenly, they were jolted to life by a car horn from a pickup truck behind them. Hunter made the left turn and drove down the road toward the Crouch farm.

Pulling in the drive, he set the brake and as Victoria went to unbuckle her seatbelt he put his hand on hers. "Are you sure you are ok to go on now?" he asked.

"Yeah, wherever you go, baby cakes, I will follow," she said.

He smiled and opened the door. Going back to the trunk, he took everything out and put on the vest just as before. Victoria reached in the back of the car and pulled out a varsity jacket; black with gold and orange piping. In big red letters on the back it said "Forensics" at the top and underneath "D & R Investigations" in forest green. Her name was on the front of the jacket. Hunter came around the car, handed her a flashlight and pulled one from his vest. He looked up at the sky and said, "Reckon we don't have much time, ma'am, afore it gits dark, I mean."

Victoria gave him a light tap on the shoulder as he howled.

"You got your camera, woman?" he asked.

"Yeah," she said grabbing his free hand as they walked toward the barn, "and I got a good friend in you."

"Best of friends I hope, always, my dear!" he said.

They walked toward the old barn. It had partially been dug back into a hill. Outside on the south side of the barn they were approaching stood a modern-day silo. They walked down a small incline to an open doorway that lead to a concrete floor. One side the cobblestone foundation had been parged over with concrete. Hunter turned on his flashlight and, with the MEL-meter on, he started walking around the bottom of the barn checking for any EMF fluctuations or any reading at all. It did appear to him that the barn may never have had electricity. Victoria started snapping pictures, setting out three different audio recorders, turning them on and recording the date, time and place on each one.

Unable to find anything with the meter, Hunter put it away. He pulled out his own recording device and turned it on.

"Hi, my name is Hunter and I mean no one any harm. I am just here to make contact with you. These devices will not harm you. Step up and talk into any of them where you see the red lights and we will be able to hear what you said when we play them back later."

"I'm Victoria and this is my good friend, Hunter. If there is anyone here, could you tell us your name?"

Silence ensued. They knew from experience just because they could not hear anything it did not mean there would not be responses on the recorders later.

"How many of you are there, can you tell us?" asked Hunter

Silence again. Hunter pulled out his laser thermometer and shot it around the barn in various places; the average was between 43 and 43.5 degrees Fahrenheit.

Out of the corner of his left eye, Hunter saw a shadow move in the northwest corner of the bottom of the barn. As he had done in the past, he did not turn in surprise but simply reached to his belt easily and slowly grabbed at his small digital camera attached to it, pulled it off, pressed the "on" button with one hand and pressed down on the shutter button as it went off in that direction in rapid succession. Victoria jumped in surprise and turned in that direction but kept on with her questions as if nothing had happened. Hunter now turned and continued to snap pictures in all directions above, below, to the right, to the left, all at random. He finally had enough as Victoria ended up her questions.

"Did you live here on this farm?"

"If you did live here, were you happy here?" asked Hunter. "Can you tell us what you liked most about the farm and what you did on the farm? If you are a man, did you, can you tell us if you owned the farm and, if you have not, tell us your name? We are very pleased to meet you and make your acquaintance."

Victoria was getting some spikes in the center of the barn basement with her K-2 meter. "Are you making this go off? If so, make it blink once for yes and twice for no?"

The meter continued to show some type of EMF in the center of the barn floor but the flashes were random and had nothing to do with an entity in the area. Puzzled, Hunter took out his MEL-meter and found the spot where the K-2 had been blinking. He moved around the barn. They had come in the south main doorway and now he was heading to an east doorway that had no door either. His meter fluctuated between 2.4 to 3.1. He moved out of the barn and if he went just a little to the left or the right he would lose the reading. He moved until he was heading straight east toward a cornfield. Victoria had followed him out of the barn and in that direction. He stopped at the cornfield.

"What is it?" she asked.

"Hmm… not sure, hon. Maybe, well, I don't know for sure. I will have to ask but it might be a ley line. I have really never searched for one before and I have read that they can occur almost anywhere in conjunction with the earth's gravity if the atmosphere is right. Cool tonight and the air is dry which bodes well for static electricity. We might not really have found that on a different type of night; especially a rainy one or a damp one."

As they turned to walk back to the barn, in a window to Hunter's right something flickered. It was a black outline of what looked to be a man with a broad brimmed hat. Victoria, not taking her eyes off of it, tapped Hunter on the arm. "Hon, hon, sweetie, look in that window," she said.

The shadow moved quickly and Hunter smiled to himself, "Yes dear, it's ok. I saw. It was in the back of the barn earlier; that's why I was snapping pictures. Someone or something is curious," he smiled and grabbed Victoria's hand as they moved back to the door in the barn.

Walking in the barn Hunter pulled a small infrared camera out of his pocket and started taking video. "You don't have to be scared and if you have something to say to us; come on out," said Victoria.

"We don't mean you any harm. All we would like to do is get to know you; that is why we are here. We will be back many times in the near future so; you can feel free at anytime to step out and say hello, smile, shake my hand or Victoria's, maybe even manipulate our equipment so we can have a conversation."

The barn lengthwise was split down the middle in the bottom with stalls on both sides as if they may have even milked cows and kept pigs in there. Not all of it was old. The floor was concrete with a drain. There was a walkway about three feet wide down the middle clear to the end. Different stalls left and right existed.

"Go to the first stall and put a MEL-meter up on the post. There is a nail there and turn it on," Hunter instructed Victoria.

She started forward with a little hesitation and Hunter turned on his 12 L.E.D. flashlight that lit up the area sufficiently. "You ok?" he asked her.

"Yeah, just a little shy after that experience. Never had anything like that happen to me before."

"Me neither. If you want to quit and go home, we can."

"No, we have come this far. Let's finish." She hung the Mel-meter up and it read a steady 0.00.

"Ok, let's set up a few K2's between the MEL-meter and the back in a similar fashion. Now, if anything moves in here we should know it for sure. I am putting my K2 at the door here and we will mount a small camera up to check for anything that moves from the other door. While you are down there in the back, set out a couple of digital recorders. That way if we can pick up anything we will know if it said anything."

With that, Hunter went to the center of the walkway and moved a small aluminum ladder that was there so he could climb up in the top of the barn. He then went back to a small workbench and set another case up. Opening it, he pulled out another infrared camera. He checked the batteries; they were fully charged. He then mounted a tripod on the bottom of camera and extended it up three feet high. Taking the camera to the ladder, he crawled up into the top level of the barn which had a large barn door that went out on another level of land. On the other side of the barn, he set the camera up, pushed record, checked the front of it to make sure the infrared glowed red, and he then placed a digital audio recorder on the side of the camera with Velcro and pressed it to record.

He climbed back down the ladder and took out a second audio recorder and pressed record. He then put it up near the door with the camera and let it run.

Victoria came back to his side and, as he turned off the L.E.D. flashlight, he felt her hand reach for his in a comforting manner. To assure her, he squeezed it and she squeezed back. The barn returned to pitch black. There was no moon that evening and very little breeze. The inside of the barn was very quiet. You could hear a mouse move and, if he had, they would have recorded it in some manner. Hunter put his hand up in front of his eyes.

He could not see his hand as he brought it closer to his face.

"Ok. So now we are here looking for someone. Whoever is here, you might see the small devices with red lights around the barn. You can communicate with us by talking into them," intoned Hunter. "And we will be able to understand what you said when we play them back. You may see a lot of strange items here but there is nothing here to hurt you. These devices are merely scientific in nature. If you pass some of them, they may light up and then go out after you have passed. That is to help us determine where you are."

"We are here as investigators," started Victoria. "We are investigating the murder of Jacob Crouch, his daughter Eunice, her husband Henry White, and the family friend Moses Polley. All shot in their sleep by someone. No one, as yet, has been able to solve the crime. Even the Pinkertons could not solve it. My name is Victoria and I am a relative of the Crouch family. Jacob was a direct descendent from a person in the 1600's that I am a direct descendent of so I feel I have some vested interest in this case, trying to solve it and put all the speculation as to who did it to rest after all these years."

"My name is Hunter Ross and I, too, am an investigator. I found this case personally appalling and I am sorry, if Jacob is here, that it has taken so long for this to come to light."

The K2 meter lit up shortly in the back of the barn as he said that.

"If there is someone back there please come out to us or talk into the recorder back there. Tell us your name if you would, please. First and last name, if you can, just for the record. Jacob Crouch, if you are still here I am going to tell you right now I will get to the bottom of this case. It has been set aside and forgotten by law enforcement but I think there is still enough there with today's investigative science. We have to make more from the evidence than they did in those days."

Hunter walked slowly toward the back of the barn changing position so he could get a better view of the meters in the far back of the barn.

"Jacob, I hear you like to come out and feed the cows at night and check on them. Are you still doing that today? There are a lot of suspects in the case and I will be back with a whole team of experts on the anniversary of your death. I hope you can, at that time, help us. Anything you can say or do would be greatly appreciated."

Victoria could now feel a cold presence near her. She had taken readings in the barn with the digital thermometer and they had a base of forty five point six degrees. She flicked it on, moved it to her right and watched as the temperature went from forty one degrees to twenty nine point six degrees.

"Hunter, I have a cold spot next to me. Twenty nine point six degrees," she said in an alarming voice.

Hunter turned and moved back toward Victoria shooting picture after picture of her and the surrounding area. Finally, he stopped and looked down at the thermometer. It had risen back to 38 degrees and was slowly climbing from there. Victoria grabbed her small infrared camera to video the area and the battery was dead.

"Battery drain, too," she said in a nonchalant manner. She was a seasoned professional who had worked many cases with Hunter in the last two years. She reached in her pocket, pulled out a new battery and stuck the old one in another pocket.

"Well, I guess that means that someone was here and they seem to like you and your batteries," said Hunter smirking.

Victoria giggled and then flipped on the video recorder and started recording the barn floor to ceiling.

"So, if you helped us, that's good and I thank you. If you think you can escape as you have all these years, I am here to tell you that you can't. I will be back and back and back until we get the truth," said Hunter. With that they started breaking down the equipment except the cameras and audio recorders.

"Let's go take a look at this house," said Hunter taking Victoria's hand and walking up the slight incline toward the small house. On the back was an all-season porch of good size. He climbed through some debris and managed to unwedge the back door. They moved up into a small entryway which had stairs that went down into the basement and two steps up into the kitchen. Someone had been working at installing kitchen cabinets and nice new modest countertops. Hunter put the cases up on the countertops and stepped down into the living room. Off the living room to one side, he could see a new bathroom in progress and to the right of the living room was a sunken family room with fireplace that had an adjoining door to the garage.

"This is small but I guess it could be made cozy," said Victoria.

"Yeah, well, there is debris all over so be careful when we do the investigation out here next week. There might be nails sticking out of boards and things. Let's go up and investigate the upstairs," said Hunter

They moved up the steep stairs, all thirteen of them, and then turned at the top to see a small bedroom about ten by fifteen. Off to one side with two steps down was a ten by ten walk-in closet. The ceiling was hipped on both sides so you could not walk directly to the side of the room without stooping. The ceiling was done in tongue and groove hardwood that had been stained a soft color.

"Well, maybe you will get something in here and maybe not. We shall see. My guess, it is all too new to be of any help. More likely, find whatever is here attached to the land," said Hunter.

"But the story was that Jacob left the house to take care of the animals. So, what does that all mean if he is not in this house? Where does he come from?" asked Victoria.

"From his old house in his time crossing over into ours. But the thing is, if he is in ours how do the animals come to end up in this equation?" queried Hunter.

They went back down the stairs and out to the barn to dismantle the rest of the equipment. A small breeze had come up in the trees that were devoid of leaves and the limbs creaked and groaned at being moved by the wind. They loaded the car and headed back towards Marshall. Both were silent; stuck in their own thoughts. Thoughts about the case and how it all tied together; thoughts about the attack on Victoria in the cemetery; thoughts, and maybe concerns, to their reaction to one another in a moment when both had their guards down. For the first time since they met, something romantically had happened and they could not deny it to themselves or anyone else.

She looked over into Hunter's face from the side. His face had a lot of character in it not to mention that he was handsome from that side, even with the stubble from the day.

Hunter suddenly realized he was being scrutinized and quickly took his eyes off the road for a second to look into Victoria's soft eyes. She smiled a cute, small soft smile at him as her eyes danced and flickered in the changing shadows of light and dark passing through the night and the car.

"So, what is that look all about? You never have looked at me that way before," asked Hunter. He looked back at her as she smirked a little and shyly said, "It has been a long time since a man kissed me that way and, well, it can have an effect on a girl, you know."

Hunter looked ahead at the road and said, "It's been a long time since I kissed anyone that way, at least a week."

Victoria turned in surprise and punched him in the arm.

"What the fuck is that for?"

"Two-timing rat bastard, you know how I have felt for you for a long time. Bringing you your coffee every morning, tending to your business, and going out to all of these places at ungodly hours with you, did you not even have a hint that I had feelings for you?"

Hunter laughed and looked back at her and said, "Yeah, I suppose I did but I was not sure it was anything you wanted to pursue with the children and all. I was never quite sure where I stood."

"Let me tell you something, mister," and she broke off the sentence as they rolled down Main Street in Marshall.

The lights had not yet switched to yellow blinking lights as Hunter slowed in front of the book store. Just as the light began to turn green, Victoria grabbed her purse, leapt out of the Charger, ran around the back, across the street, and in front of a car waiting the other way. A man in the passenger seat yelled out, "Hey, baby!" as she jammed the key into the lock to the store. She put in the code to silence the alarm and then locked the door back up. She turned to the back and up the stairs to Hunter's apartment. There she again keyed in the alarm and it let her pass. Once inside, she reset the alarm, dropped her purse on a small stand at the front door, kicked off her shoes and moved across the room and into the kitchen where she poured herself a generous amount of Patrón into a glass.

Slowly sauntering across the large living room, she sipped at her Patrón and came to the big front windows. She pulled back the curtains and looked out on the street. The Charger was nowhere to be found. She liked the soft yellow light from the street lights below and how it lit up the buildings. The light splashed into the room like soft, romantic glow lighting up the area.

She heard the door downstairs in the back close and then heard his footsteps on the stairs as he ascended with some eagerness she ascertained in his step. Victoria sat down on the couch with one leg tucked under her and sipping on the Patrón as he came through the door. He stopped and set the alarm once again.

"So, what the hell was that all about?" yelled Hunter moving to turn on the lamp next to the door.

"No light" she said as he stopped in mid-movement. Slowly he moved toward her and stopped in front of her. He looked down into her face. Some of her dishwater blond hair covered her face on one side. She parted her lips slightly and smiled at him.

Standing to face him, she put down the Patrón and brought his face to hers kissing him long and passionately. His response was somewhat mild and, though there was some response on his part, it was not what she had expected.

She pulled away and slapped him hard. He closed his eyes and then opened them. She was staring daggers at him.

"For God sake, Hunter! Don't you feel anything for me at all? Not one sentiment? Here I am for the taking, throwing myself at you and no response! I can't do this after all this time with nothing I have to go on. Don't bother to take me home."

She turned and bolted for the door but a large hand caught her as she passed and he said, "Please, don't leave me!"

Victoria turned to look into his eyes. They had softened somewhat as if some guard had been taken down. He pulled her toward him and kissed her back with all the body language and more she had expected the first time. At the end of the kiss, he looked deep into her eyes and said "Ever!"

She again grabbed at him and they entwined for several kisses. Hunter was at the point now he knew he wanted her and he wanted her forever. The feelings he had kept under lock and key all those years let loose as his hands moved under the soft sweater and found the erect breasts. She raised her arms and he pulled the sweater off of her exposing her breasts nestled in the bra, one in and one out. He reached down and unfastened her jeans. They slid down and, as they hit the floor, he picked her up out of them and carried her off to the back and the bed.

She pulled at his shirt and hastily undid his belt. As they reached the bed his pants fell. He grabbed at her bra and pulled it off exposing her breasts as she lay back on the bed.

He was on her and as they rolled on the bed. One side then the other taking turns on top until they both recoiled and fell into a heap breathing hard. She had her face buried in his chest and could feel him inside of her. She had not been that aroused in years.

He pulled her up gently to him and kissed her softly all over as she arched and moved in time with him. They finally reached climax at the same time and once again they lay in a large heap on top of each other. She reached over to the nightstand and dialed in a number on the phone.

"Hello," crackled her mother's voice.

"Mom, this case is taking longer than I thought. Are you good for the night?"

"Yes, dear, I will stay with them and he is a keeper."

Victoria rose up in bed with Hunter still wrapped around her and said. "Ma! We are on a case."

"Yeah, well it took ya long enough. I did not think the two of you would ever get together. Now I can go to bed? And sleep well." With that her mother hung up. She looked at the receiver of the phone as if she expected some response from it. She was suddenly aware of his hand between her legs. She threw the receiver back on the floor and said, "Oh my God!"

They continued their love making for another hour and then fell asleep in one another's arms. Hunter awoke realizing that she was not at his side. He lay there smelling her scent that was strong still on the sheets. He finally arose to see where she had gone. He stopped and put on a pair of pajama bottoms. Walking out into the kitchen area, she was wrapped in a short Japanese Kimono that he had hanging in the closet from one of his overseas deployments to Asia.

She looked up at him as he came to her side. She had taken his laptop and turned it on capturing the wireless connection in the building. She had gone online and the light shone across the dark kitchen from the large screen.

"What's up, hon?" he asked softly caressing her shoulder. Pulling the Kimono back to her bare shoulder and slowly putting his lips on her shoulder, he licked and kissed at it.

"I woke up and decided to look on the 'net while I had a glass of iced tea. Do you want some? I want to showwwwww..." He had hit the right spot. She knew it and he did, too, by the inflection of her voice. He stopped what he was doing, rose, went to a cupboard and pulled out two tumblers and a bottle. He walked back across the room as she looked at his powerful chest and the muscle definition of his arms. She had dreamed of him many a lonely night but even her dreams were not this accurate or appealing.

Hunter set the tumblers down and poured a measure into each about half full. He then set the bottle off to the side. She could just make out the label in the light. It was an irregular-shaped bottle that did not narrow at the top but stopped and looked as if someone had put a spout in the top. The label had a small oval-shaped kind of black cloud and she could make out in the middle of it in white "GHOST".

"Ghost Vodka, baby, it is smooth," said Hunter. She picked up the glass and he toasted her clicking the glasses. "To us baby, ya tebya lyublyu," he said in Russian which means 'I love you'.

He sat down beside her and looked at the page she had up on the Internet. There in the middle was a large house and above it the words in bold large print said, "Even Pinkerton couldn't solve Crouch case."Below the house was the picture of four people. On the left stood Jacob Crouch with a heavy shock of hair and large untrimmed black beard that flowed down his front. His eyes seemed piercing.

Beside him was a comely woman, Eunice. Her head in the picture seemed large and out of proportion to her shoulders. Her face was that of one only a mother could love.

Beside Eunice was Henry White, her husband. He looked much younger than her and he appeared to be a fairly good-looking man for the time.

Beside Henry and the last picture on the bottom was that of Moses Polley. He was a rugged-looking man; handsome to a fault. He sported a large well-trimmed moustache. He seemed to look like a capable fellow and Hunter wondered how he had fallen prey in all of this.

"See, darlin', it's the Crouch House. Now we know what it looked like."

"Yeah, and it would be nice if we could come up with some kind of floor plan to show how it was laid out. If I remember, some things said that that boy Boles slept upstairs. Which meant the rest of them must have slept downstairs and Julia Reese had her own room in the back."

Hunter reached up, closed the top of the laptop down bringing the whole kitchen to complete dark. He grabbed Victoria, picked her up and carried her back to the bed as the kimono fell off of her. He unfastened his pajama bottoms and moved onto the bed beside her. She responded to his touch and soon they were lost in each other's arms.

Chapter 18

Morning rushed through the east window and she laid there for some time. Then, rolling over to meet Hunter, she realized he was not in the bed. Putting on the kimono she moved through the apartment but it was apparent he was nowhere to be found. She did find on the kitchen table a bowl and a box of cereal with a note on it, "Down in the office. Sorry, that is all I have here in the way of breakfast, Hunter!"

Pouring the cereal out into the bowl she sat and looked around at the space that was his. He was everywhere in here and she wondered if last night was a step into the future. She had known for years she was in love with him but it had never graduated to sex. She blushed slightly thinking of the night before. It had been more than spectacular sex; it was one-on-one bonding heart and soul sex. She wondered what he would be like the morning after. She grabbed her cell phone out of her purse and dialed out.

"Hello, Mom. Get in the car and come down to Hunter's apartment. And bring me some clothes to wear; my jeans and a nice top, underwear, etc. Yeah, Mom, it was a spectacular night just like a story about a prince and princess." She smiled at what she had just said and as she closed out the call she spun around in circles embracing herself with her own arms.

She showered quickly and her mother showed up soon after with clothes for her and an ear for details of the night before.

"Huh… I told you a long time ago just push him a little that was all he needed. I had to do that with your dad you know."

"All right, Mom, not sure I want details on all of that," admonished Victoria.

Victoria finished dressing, then kissed her mom goodbye and moved down the stairs to work. As she came in the door from the apartment, the girls were there doing the morning routine and it was not lost on them where Victoria obviously came from. Jemma raised an eyebrow. Cheryl had a look of surprise of which was so genuine she could not conceal it. Samantha had a puzzled look which quickly turned to an "Oh My God, you can't be serious" look.

"Good morning how is everyone this morning?" said Victoria looking from first one then to the other. Her intuition told her right away that they knew it must still be written all over her face.

"Hey, baby," said Hunter coming into the area with papers in his hand which he dropped down in front of Samantha. He turned to Victoria, pulled her to him and gave her a big kiss. She responded by putting her arms around his neck. He ended the kiss with a ringing phone in his ears. Samantha answered, "Hobbit's Nook. Why, yes, he is. May I say who is calling, please? Oh yes, I suppose. Someone for you; they won't say."

Hunter picked up the phone and said "Ross speaking."

"Mr. Ross, don't be too smug or smart. Stay away from the Crouch case if you know what is good for you. It could get rather painful." With that the caller hung up leaving Hunter holding the phone and processing what had just occurred. He the phone back to Samantha let go of Victoria and went back to the office without saying a word. He poured himself a cup of coffee and then sat down at his desk just staring out of the window. He tapped into his computer and tried to find anything remotely related to the Crouch case.

Victoria came into the office, sat at her desk and checked her e-mail. She ran some figures up for the day before checking out the amount of sales with receipts, etc. An hour went by when there was a second call for Hunter. Victoria answered.

"Hello. I am looking for Mr. Ross, the man who was in the paper about the ghost hunters in Spring Arbor?"

"Sure, just a moment," smiled Victoria.

"It's for you," she said.

"Hello!" said Hunter who had just come deep out of thought on text he was reading.

"Mr. Ross, I read about you in the paper yesterday," said the man as the phone rang again on the other line. "I have some information for you if you wish. First of all, let me apologize for the board. They should have let you do the investigation. There is absolutely no reason they should have not let you in but I have some information for you. If you want to find Jacob's grave, it is just inside the gate to the right of the burning bush. He is buried next to Ann. That was his wife. Also, I thought you might like to know that there was a woman several years ago who lived in Homer and she was writing a book on the Crouches but she never finished it to my knowledge. She got some threatening calls and it scared her. Went back to a name of Jessup; don't know if that means anything to you. Also, it was understood by the family that Judd had nothing to do with it. His preacher stated when he died that he believed that Judd was innocent. He was fully sure due to the fact that he spent the last day with Judd as he lay dying. He said that if he was guilty he knows Judd would have confessed. He knew he was dying that day and there was no reason not to do that to clear his soul. Judd was a very stout Christian and he would have cleared his soul. I hope you can figure this all out."

"I am sure we can and thank you for the information. I am sorry, I did not get your name?" said Hunter.

"That's not important, son, you just keep your head up."

"I have already been threatened once on the phone this morning. You would not know who that would have been, would you? Or can you tell me anything about Crouch descendants?"

"Well, there is on distant relative in California and another in Florida, but not sure how much they know. I really don't know why anyone would want to threaten you over this old case. Who would have anything to lose or gain?"

"Thank you very much. Uh… I did not catch your name?" Hunter tried again an old trick employed to get answers ask the same question twice from a different angle.

"Yep, did not give it to ya either, young man. Just be careful," was all the caller would say and he hung up as another phone rang in the background. Hunter put the phone receiver in front of his face and looked at it as if trying to see the face of the caller.

"We have no comment at this time, thank you!"

"Who was that?" he asked as she hung up the phone.

"A television station in Dothan, Alabama wanted to know if we would come down there for a live interview. When I said I did not think that we could they wanted to do a phone conversation with us."

"Alabama?" said Hunter in a shocked voice, as the phone rang, "What's next? Time Magazine?"

Victoria said politely no and hung up looking at Hunter she giggled and said, "Newspaper in Melbourne."

"Huh… now Florida," said Hunter

"No, Australia," laughed Victoria.

Hunter took his left hand and rubbed his chin thinking, "So now we are going viral with this stupid story. It is bringing us information and obviously notoriety, some of which we did not need.

The day continued on with the phone ringing intermittently.

As the afternoon went on Victoria asked Hunter for the keys to the Charger so she could go and pick up the children at school.

"Do you want me to come back?" she asked absent mindedly.

"Well, I don't know if I am going anywhere but it would be nice to see my car returned to me," he said in a pretend startled manner.

"Ok, I will bring it back later. Mom can follow me and then take me home when she goes home."

Hunter got up and poured out the old cold coffee in the pot and started a new batch.

"Staying up to work on things. Are you sure you don't want me to come back?" she asked.

"Want you always, to come back… nah… take care of the kids. They have not seen much of you and they need mom around, ya know."

She left and Hunter set himself to listen to Evps and look at pictures from the investigations they had done yesterday. He got up and poured himself a big coffee. He sat back down sipping his coffee and putting his mind back in to the 1880's near the time of the murder.

He summed up what he knew but before he could start Jemma Choun peaked in the door and said, "Do you want anything to eat? I am going down to Pastrami Joes for my supper before Cheryl leaves for the night."

"Yeah, sure," said Hunter as he rose from his chair and toward Jemma. He stopped, pulled out a twenty dollar bill and handed it to her, "I will take a Talk of The Town with mayo lettuce tomato, beef, turkey, salami, and some hot mustard."

Jemma moved to Victoria's desk and wrote down the order on a small piece of paper. "Nuttin' to drink?" she asked.

"Nah, I got coffee. Gonna be a long night of study."

Hunter leaned over to kiss her on the cheek and smudged her makeup. He could see quite clearly she had covered what appeared to be a black eye. She turned, smiled and he said, "Buy what you want out of that twenty."

Hunter returned to his desk but he was taken aback. What was the deal with the black eye and why had she tried so hard to hide it? The only conclusion he could come to was that someone had hit her and she did not want anybody to know that it happened. He shook his head and decided if she needed help she would ask and that he would not mess in where he was not wanted. He again went back to the case as he knew it and looked at all of the evidence they had garnered online from different reports on the Internet to newspaper online libraries. He knew that probably two men had broken into the Crouch home and shot everyone except for the housekeeper and the stable boy. He also had learned that in January Jacob's oldest daughter had died in her house alone after, as the sheriff had stated, being force-fed rat poison. He was not sure what that meant because several articles called it a suicide. Someone would not have to force-feed rat poison. They would simply eat it and lay down. What had the sheriff been trying to tell everyone? Of special interest to her death was the fact she was found naked in her bedroom in the middle of the day.

Next was one item he was real interested in. A man by the name of James Foy, a farmhand on the Crouch farm, two months after Susan Holcomb had been murdered had committed suicide. He had ended his life by shooting himself with a shotgun behind the barn.

Hunter sat back and sipped more coffee staring up at the ceiling. So, had he been involved romantically with Susan, they had a spat and he killed her to keep her quiet? Or was it the fact he knew who the killers were and he was extorting them for money to keep quiet until they decided he had to go? To lose a liability… maybe he was too mouthy? One small article said that Foy was a big drinker and as he got drunk he got real mouthy telling about things he should not have.

Then we have the case of Galen Brown. He was a detective sent here by the Governor to crack the case. He was pulled off the force in Battle Creek and assigned here by order of the Governor. He had been here for a week or more, as far as Hunter could tell, and he had been questioning Judd Crouch about the murders. He had left the Crouch farm for Horton; a few miles walking distance. As he neared the city, two men in a covered buggy pulled up and ask him if he was Detective Brown. He had said yes to it and they had shot-gunned him in the street leaving him to die. But the wound was not fatal and he swore to the sheriff that it was Judd Crouch.

Then, there was the small note that Henry Holcomb had been tried on perjury charges in connection with the trial of his brother Daniel Holcomb. He was found not guilty. Also the trial ended with a not guilty verdict on Daniel Holcomb and at that time they dropped the charges they had on Judd. Something smelled like fish here.

Hunter sat back and put the family in his mind. First the wife Ann dies in childbirth and Jacob cannot bear to have Judd, the cause he believes of his beloved wife's death. After five days he gives the child to Susan who had married Daniel Holcomb to raise as their own son. Judd was quite old, according to one source, before he realized Susan and Daniel were not his real parents.

"That might just unhinge a guy. To live that close to his real father and never a word said," thought Hunter. "Could be a reason to kill daddy."

He remembered something he had seen on an Internet site about two older brothers who were in Texas at the time. One of the brothers had died down there of typhoid. A concerned uncle got suspicious and had him exhumed. They found three bullet holes in him. Hunter thought and thought.

Was someone trying to cash in on the family fortune and, if so, who? Was it kill them all off and whoever is left standing is the winner of everything? Hunter remembered something about a ranch in Texas and looked through the files until he came to it. The article was short; saying that Captain Crouch was coming home for a week from the Texas ranch. It was rumored that Jacob Crouch owned a 330,000 acre ranch in Texas.

Hunter whistled to himself. Knowing his Western history, a ranch back in those days, if set up correctly, could have garnered some serious cash. Maybe der Captain vas skimming money from the top and daddy was tired of getting cheated. Maybe he sent Dayton, the younger of the two, to Texas to watch over his assets. Back in those days, a little money spread here and there would account for a murder being covered up. The captain had to shoot junior before junior shot off his mouth.

"Stranger things have happened," thought Hunter. He then remembered a buddy of his. He stopped and wrote down all the information he could find on Dayton Crouch. Picking up his cell phone he called an old friend from the days in the Marines, Captain Peter Vale, now an investigator in his own right with the Texas Rangers. The phone rang once, then twice, three times and a message came on the answering machine. "This is Captain Peter Vale of the Texas Rangers. If this is an emergency, please dial 911. If you wish to leave a message, please leave your name, phone number, and reason for the call. I will get back to you as soon as possible."

Hunter began to speak, "Pete, this is Colonel Ross. Old buddy, how are ya? I got something I need some help with and I thought you might be able to supply some information for me. There's at least a cold beer in it when I get there someday."

"Who are you kidding, Ross? You won't ever pay up as usual. I remember poker games you still owe me for," laughed a voice on the other end of the phone.

"Pete!?" Asked Hunter, surprised. "Don't feed me that shit as I remember I practically kept you for 18 months in Okinawa when you had to send all your money home to wifey number one. Remember, old pal, the hookers, etc.?"

"Well, if you do come down here maybe we could keep the hookers quiet."

Hunter laughed, "Still married and pussy whipped, I see."

"Nah… actually happily married and, yes, to the same girl. Got one going off to college this fall. My pocket book is not lookin' forward to that."

"God, not Julie? Shit, last time I saw her she was only about two foot tall and barely walking."

"You should see her now. A beautiful young lady; takes after her mother."

"Dang that is very beautiful. If you had not happened along when you did I would have married the General's daughter. You realize that, don't you?"

Pete laughed on the other end of the phone, "God, it's great to hear from you. Now you said you needed a favor from me. What is it, old buddy?"

"I am working on the ultimate of cold cases. It's a 127 year old unsolved multiple-murder shot in their sleep. Father, daughter who was 9 months pregnant at the time, her husband and a visitor that decided to stay overnight with them. Never been solved. Tori and I are gonna take a run at it."Hunter told the story about Dayton and when he died.

"I will get on that tomorrow. Should not take long to run that down. Might even have some notes somewhere on that. Give me a few days and I will let ya know."

"Great! Hey, thanks. You know, anytime with me. You need something, you only need to call. I will be there."

"Yeah, Hunter, I have always known that and, of course, the same goes for me."

"Well, buddy, you better get home to that wonderful wife. I mean life and say hi for me, will ya?"

"Sure thing, pal. Call ya back in a few days."

Hunter hung up the phone and realized it was getting late. Jemma had locked the front door and was in the process of bringing the cash drawers back to the office. He watched as she carried them in, put them in the open safe, closed the door, spun the combination lock and pressed down on the door lever to make sure it was secure.

"I'm going home, Hunter. You want anything else before I go?"

"No, sweetie. Did you hear from Victoria? I thought sure she would have been back by now with my car."

"Nope, not a word."

"Ok. Good night, dear, and I'll see ya in the morning."

"Goodnight," waved Jemma as she walked out of the office. Hunter reached for his cell phone, pressed in a number and a woman answered.

"Ellen," said Hunter recognizing her voice, "Is Victoria there?"

"No, hon. She just left to get you. Sorry, I was talking her ear off and the time got away from me. The kids are in bed so you don't have to rush back."

"Uh… er… yeah sure, Ellen. Have a good night."

Hunter hung up the phone, got up, turned off the office lights and made his way to the private stairs to his apartment. He locked the door behind him and set the code in the alarm system. Then he walked up the stairs to the little hallway that wound its way back towards the front of the building and the door to his apartment. Walking in, he shut the door and dropped his keys onto the stand at the front door. Kicking off his shoes, he moved to the far corner of the room, reached in a small refrigerator, grabbed some ice, dumped it into a glass and poured Maker's Mark over it till the glass was full. Walking to the windows, he looked out sipping his drink when he heard Victoria coming up the stairs. The lights in the room were low for no purpose other than Hunter craved the yellowish-orange glow of the street lights that reflected off of all the buildings downtown. He heard the door close behind him. He turned to confront Victoria to tease her about being late, to him it really did not matter but he would tease her all the same, when he stopped dead in his tracks and the mind ceased to exist.

"Wha…," was all he could get out of his mouth. There stood Victoria in a short plaid skirt with white knee socks and penny loafers. She had on a white button-down blouse that was almost too small for her. His body was taking over his mind and the body was quite evidently winning the battle.

She walked up to Hunter, took the Maker's Mark and downed it in one gulp. She smacked her lips looking up at him.

"Mom said she would stay with the kids one more night and I put them to bed and made sure they were asleep. I will get up early and wake them for school like nothing ever happened."

"Yeah? How you gonna 'splain dat outfit, Lucy?"

"I thought that maybe the headmaster might have to take in one of his students for the night to maybe punish her for being very, very, very bad. And he discovers that when she is bad she is very good. Hmmmm?" she purred in his ear.

She sat the glass down and in his best Jack Benny imitation he yelled, "Now cut that out!"

Standing on her tiptoes she whispered in his ear, "I also don't have any panties on."

With one fell swoop, Hunter picked her up and carried her back toward the bedroom as she laughed and cried.

"Oh, you beast! Let me go!"

Chapter 19

As Hunter sat at his desk the next morning, he was scouring the Internet for any type of article, clue or anything else he could find on a Crouch entry into Google. Victoria came and sat by his desk. She was reading the morning Detroit News and had positioned herself so that she was looking at Hunter. She sat right across from him. There was a small enough opening in the desk in front that she could place her foot underneath and rub the inside of his leg with her bare foot.

"Ok, babe, we need to get a team together. I think this is too big for just two of us with the business and everything. The first thing is go over and call Chandra Keene. Let's get her on board; it is a good time to test her psychic abilities. I would just like her read on all of this plus she knows how to set up all the equipment and Jemma can learn from her."

Chandra Keene was a noted psychic in the business and had been friends with Hunter for years. She had recently been spotlighted by shows on TV for helping detectives across the country solve cold case files with her intuitive readings.

"Jemma has quite a technical background. She does have a two year electronic degree."

"I think that would be good for her. Something is up and I don't know what it is," said Victoria.

"Yeah, I am going to have a talk with her soon. I think there is some domestic violence going on. I swore she had a black eye covered up with makeup yesterday," said Hunter.

"That's strange, because I saw several bruises on her arms the other day. They looked like someone had grabbed her by the arm and held her."

"So, you think Kyle is doing this to her?" asked Hunter.

"I don't know who else it could be. She is such a nice girl and does not really seem to have anyone else but him. She never talks about family."

Suddenly they heard a shriek from outside in the store area. Both jumped up and ran out to find Cheryl Treadway kneeling next to Jemma who had fallen off a ladder. She was awake but not coherent. Hunter picked her up, carried her back to the office and laid her down. In doing so, her sweater hiked up on her torso revealing bruises all over her mid-section and side.

"Get me some water and a washrag out of the rest room, will ya please?" asked Hunter. He took the wet washrag and wiped her face then made it into a nice compress for her head. What he had really done was wash the makeup off of her so as to show the black eye. He also could feel lumps on her skull.

"Jemma, are you all right?" asked Victoria.

"Yeah, I will be. Silly me just lost my balance and wham!" said Jemma.

"I want to know who is beating you, young lady, and I want to know now," said Hunter.

"I'm ok. Just been clumsy lately," said Jemma.

"Bull shit!" stated Hunter. "I think a lot of you, dear. You are like the daughter I never had and dad is pissed so I want to know who did this to you?"

Jemma shook her head as Hunter gave her a kiss on the forehead and squeezed her hand which made her grimace from pain.

"Kyle. He does not mean it. He gets to drinking and well… he goes off and sometimes he just does not know what he is doing."

"Ok, you just lay there and rest while I go out and get some cold compresses for your head. Maybe get some strong coffee in her and a few Tylenol would not hurt her disposition."

Hunter stood up and walked out of the book store and across the street to Jemma's walk up apartment.

He knocked on the door and Kyle answered with a smug grin on his face.

"Mr. Ross, what brings you here?" asked Kyle.

"Jemma's health. It seems she is suffering from a malady. I assume you know what I am talking about?"

"Ah, no man, but if she needs to be taken care of I am sure I can do that. She has a wild imagination you know."

"Yeah, very vivid. It seems to cause her body to be bruised and looks like it was battered all over."

Kyle laughed, "Well, she is really clumsy."

This was all Hunter could take. Grabbing the young blond boy by the hair, he pulled as hard as he could sending the boy head first into the wall across the hall from the door. Surprised and off balance, Kyle spun facing the downstairs door as Hunter put a foot in his back and sent him sprawling down the stairs. First head over heels and then rolling sideways, he landed in a heap at the bottom of the steps. He lay at the bottom not moving with one arm askew. Hunter knew immediately it was broken on the way down. There was a door at the bottom that went into the downstairs' business. It opened as an old man looked out.

"Goodness gracious! What in the world? Is the young man all right?" he asked.

"Yeah, he just had a clumsy moment like his girlfriend does and took a header down the stairs. You better call an ambulance."

Hunter reached into his back pocket and pulled out a handkerchief. He jammed it quickly in Kyle's mouth and then pulled on the broken arm as he tried to scream but could not. Sweat beaded up on his forehead.

"Now get this, asshole, you beat her again and they will never and I repeat never find your body. Not a threat, buddy, but a promise."

Kyle by this time was writhing in pain as Hunter dropped his arm and pulled out the handkerchief from his mouth. He stepped over and purposely landed with the heel of his shoe and all of his weight on the fingers of the good hand. As Kyle yelled Hunter could hear the bones snap.

He stepped outside as he heard the sirens coming. He leaned down to the young man again and said, "Ambulance is coming Kyle. I hope you mend well; I am sure Jemma will, but if there is any doubt in your mind let me know because we can have this talk again."

He stepped back to see Jemma running across from the store.

"Hunter, what happened?" she asked excitedly.

"I told him you fell off a ladder and, you know, I'll be darned if he did not miss the first step on the way down. You two have to be more careful on those stairs. Kyle already promised me that neither one of you would get hurt again." He smiled a nice warm smile at Jemma as she caught his drift. The attendants were there picking him up and moving him to the stretcher. The hospital was just one block away so he would receive immediate attention. A Marshall police officer came up to the scene.

"What happened?" he asked. "Did anyone see what happened?"

"Yeah, I did. His girlfriend here who lives with him works for me across the street. She had fallen and hit her head putting books up on a shelf. So, I came over to get him to come and take her home so she could rest for the afternoon. He got excited and ran out the door past me and missed the first step. Actually, I don't think he missed another one all the way down. I really expected to find him with a broken neck but I guess it is just his arm and a couple of fingers. Don't know about ribs or such."

"Yeah, so what is your name?" asked the young officer.

"Hunter Ross, sir, I am the proprietor of the Hobbit Nook across the street."

Jemma looked back at Hunter with wide eyes as she got on board the ambulance with Kyle. He finished his report with the officer and walked back across the street to a waiting Victoria.

She handed him a cup of coffee as he came through the door and followed him back to the office.

"What happened?" she asked closing the door to the sales room.

"I went to get Kyle to get Jemma and take her home for the day. He was showing me how she fell down the stairs herself and I'll be darned! It's a funny thing, the same thing happened to him! I told the super he needs to fix those stairs. They are really treacherous."

Victoria looked back at him with a suspicious look but did not challenge the story. She had a good idea how he had fallen down the steps and it probably had nothing to do with being clumsy.

"I called all the team and they will all, including the sergeant, meet us at the library in Jackson tomorrow morning."

"Great! It has been an interesting day to say the least."

The phone rang and Hunter answered it with, "Hobbit's Nook, how can I help you?"

"You and the woman, leave it alone or you will get hurt real bad. No more Crouch stories, mister."

"Why I am not only going to solve it; we are going to write a book about it, shove it down your throat, and dump it over your fat head, buster. By the way, I am armed and I do know how to use it, and I have. One more won't send me to hell any quicker."

Hunter hung up the phone as Victoria looked at him again in a quizzical manner, "Another one?"

"Yeah, I just seem to be a very popular person today."

Hunter sat down and thought about the events of the day and how they had turned out. He wondered, past someone just being a smart ass, why someone would still kill today over a murder that took place 127 years ago? The property was no longer in the family. Who could possibly loose out of all this rigmarole that they would go to the nth degree to hurt or kill someone? One call he could see as a prank; maybe some kids, etc., but three?

1883

Byron Crouch, along with Judd and Daniel Holcomb, all sat in the sheriff's office in Jackson discussing the case.

"So what you are telling me, sheriff, that before this proceeding starts that you may have to let the two main suspects go because of this writ of habeas corpus?" asked Byron.

"Yeah, that's what the court tells me. I have no evidence to hold them on. Maybe something will come out at the inquest to tell us that they did it but I have to admit to ya, I am not sure myself that they are guilty. Just a couple of really stupid people; simple in the mind at the wrong place at the wrong time. I reckon they weren't killed 'cause no one suspected they would be taken seriously at a trial as a witness. The woman's character would come into play and the boy, bein' black and all, with little or no education would and could be used against him as any kind of material witness," said the sheriff.

"Do we have any idea, since the papers are missing from the safe, who is gonna inherit what?" asked Judd.

"Well, the court can decide that if need be but my guess is that you, I and Susan can determine what goes where well enough. I got my ranch in Texas and it was free and clear so I am content with that really. I guess it depends on you and Susan. No Will. Who else could be involved with this? Maybe someone that owed him a lot of money? Nothing of great value was stolen, money left with jewels at the murder sight so it was not really a robbery. They took nothing but the papers as far as we are concerned," said Byron. "I guess it falls to you and Susan and if you want to leave some to Edith (Susan's and Daniel's daughter) then that is fine. I really do not want to move back up here and run this operation."

"Either way I got to get back to the farm and help Foy do some chores or he will be complaining for a week. I really don't like that guy around. Something about him and his bragging that I really don't like but he is one hell of a good hand," said Judd.

The three got up and left the office with the sheriff drinking coffee and pondering the case. He had been sitting there almost 10 minutes in the quiet of the room when the door opened back up and it was Daniel Holcomb.

"What's up, Dan?" asked Winney.

"I got to thinking with the others and maybe I will swear out a complaint for an arrest warrant against George Bolles and Julia Reese. Would you not be able to hold them then at that point?"

"I would," said the sheriff.

Daniel sat down at the desk and filled out the paper the sheriff had shoved in front of him.

"Jessup," yelled the sheriff as Daniel had finished the paper.

A short unkempt man came into the office next to the sheriff.

"This here is Harold Jessup. He is one of our jailers and he is here to witness the papers you have filled out," said Winney as he passed the papers to the man along with a quill pen for writing. Jessup signed his name as did the sheriff.

"I will run these over to the court and that will be enough to bind them over until at least after the inquest."

The door to the sheriff's office opened. Mr. Cutcheon and Mr. Park entered the office as Daniel Holcomb was leaving.

"Good morning, sheriff .Mr. Cutcheon and I not only wish to see our clients but we also wish to serve these papers of habeas corpus on behalf of our clients. You either charge them as the judge states here or you let them go," said Mr. Park.

"They will be charged. I just had an arrest warrant made out to serve to the judge to bind those two over for first degree murder," said the sheriff.

Both men stopped and Cutcheon grimaced somewhat. "Who would have made that out?" he asked.

"The man who just left. The son-in-law, Mr. Daniel Holcomb," said the sheriff.

"Why in the hell would the son-in-law be involved in this? Two brothers and a sister and it takes a son-in-law to come forward?" asked Park.

"Well, Mrs. Holcomb is not holding up too well and in poor health from all of this. I believe he is protecting her interests and possibly doing her wishes. You may have to ask her."

"So, when is the inquest starting?" asked Cutcheon.

"Tomorrow at ten AM sharp, gentlemen. The coroner is picking the jury panel as we speak," said the sheriff.

2010

It was only a few days now until the anniversary of the killings of the Crouch family and Hunter sat secluded at his kitchen table reading the inquest reports that they had dug up. There was none to find, of course, as in the trial transcripts but what the person who destroyed all of this did not realize was the power of the written word. The Jackson Citizen Patriot of the day had written down in reporting all of the testimony of the inquests and the trial giving us a glimpse back in time at the trial and a good idea of what was said by whom. The library in Jackson had all of these papers on file as microfilm. Hunter and his team had spent exhausting days combing through the old files, reading and saving to thumb drives the microfilm testimonies, as well as all of the news reports and accounts of the day. The following is the true account (in the words of a Jackson Citizen Patriot reporter) of the inquest into the murders of Jacob Crouch, Eunice and Henry White, to ascertain how they were killed and who may have killed them.

Chapter 20

THE INQUEST:

Julia Reese was called to the stand. The coroner as well as the impaneled jurors could ask questions of each witness as they desired. There was no counsel for defense or prosecution as there is in the trial, however the sheriff and the District Attorney were present and were free to ask questions of any witness.

"Mrs. Reese," asked the Coroner, "Could you tell us in your own words what transpired the morning of the murders, from your point of view?"

"Well, I sleep in a back room that is closed off by a door from the house. I usually get up early and try and get breakfast started while Mr. Crouch," she stopped at the mention of the name and hung her head a tear came from her eye as the coroner handed her his handkerchief. She thanked him and went on.

"Mr. Crouch and George Boles always got up and went out to look after the stock before breakfast. Mr. Crouch's motto was to take care of the animals and they will take care of you. So they would feed them and get them started out of the barn for the day and then come and have breakfast. This always gave me time to have it made and ready for them when they came in from the field."

"Did you hear George Boles get up and call for anyone?"

"No, sir, I did not but I might have still been back in my room at the time. Also, I did feel sleepy that morning like I was drugged and as soon as the people came to check I could swear there was the smell of chloroform in the house."

"Mrs. Reese, could you tell us how the bodies were laying when you first encountered them?"

"Well, I can't. I was just too frightened about the whole thing thinking I slept through it and I also could have been one of the victims. But the door to Mr. Polley's room was open as was the door to Mr. White's room and the door between the sitting room and parlor."

"Do you know where Mr. Crouch kept his money?"

"No, sir, I do not."

"To the best of your knowledge, did Mr. Polley have any money with him when he stopped for the night?"

"I do not know if he did or not, sir. If he did, he did not display any when I was in his presence."

"What time did Mr. Polley come to the house?"

"I can't rightly say but he was around the farm earlier in the day, he left and then returned at supper time."

"Was Mr. Polley drinking at all during the day or was he intoxicated that night?"

"No, he did not seem drunk to me and as far as I know he had some cider with us but it was fresh not hard as Mr. Crouch had instructed George Boles to fetch it and to make no mistake about which one he grabbed. We all had some fresh apples along with the cider."

"Why do you think that in all that commotion that went on George heard what he thought was gun shots and you did not?"

"I don't know, sir. Again, there was that smell in the house like sickness that morning but I don't rightly know unless it was chloroform."

"You are familiar then with the smell of chloroform?"

"No, I heard someone say that was what the smell was in the house. I have never smelled it before just going on what others said and the fact that I felt drugged that morning when I arose."

"Would you tell us about yourself, Mrs. Reese? For instance, you have a married name but you are not living with your husband, are you?"

"No, sir. I was married when I was 17 am now 22; left my current husband two years ago. We have a daughter who lives with him and I have a mother and step-father that lives near Sister Lakes in Van Buren County."

"Did you awake anytime during the night or hear a train pass?"

"No, sir. I did not awake which is unusual for me. Also did not hear any trains pass after 9 pm."

"Can you tell us more about that morning?"

"Yes, sir. I got up as usual, had kind of a headache, went to the kitchen and started some breakfast. Did not see George that morning and did not see his boots near the door where he usually takes them off. That is why I figured he and Mr. Crouch was already up and out and about. I started a fire in the stove and set to fixin' breakfast."

"So, George took his boots off that night. Do you know where he put them if they were not at the door?"

"No, sir, I do not."

"Did you happen to go up to George's room that morning of the murders?"

"Yes, sir. I tried my best to continue my routine and take care of everyone as if they were guests just like Mr. Crouch would have wanted me to. I went up to make George's bed as usual. It looked slept in as usual."

"What else did you notice, if anything, out of the ordinary?"

"No, sir, just George's chest in the closet. It had shirts and clothes folded on top of it so I took them and put them inside the chest."

"Was there anything else in that chest?"

"A few books, a slate and some chalk. That was about it."

"But the clothes were on top of the chest. You are sure?"

"Yes, sir."

"Have you talked with George about the murders since they happened?"

"No, sir."

"Do you know what George did the week before the murders?"

"Yes, sir, he worked on the farm everyday with or without Mr. Crouch and hung around close to the house. He fixed the fence out back by the rail stop and worked some shingles on the barn. He did go to Horton one afternoon driving hogs in for Mr. Crouch to market."

"Did George receive any letters or visits from anyone that week?"

"No, sir, no mail 'cause I collected that daily and I don't remember any visitors to see him, but…"she hesitated and the coroner could see she was tentative about something.

"Please, Mrs. Reese, if you have something that may be important, tell us."

"Well, it was the day before out in the back. I was getting some kindling when these three men walk right past the house towards the barn. One stopped and pointed to the house and then they disappeared across the field. I just thought at the time it was maybe some men looking for horses that ran away, that has happened before, but I really don't know who they were."

"Very good, Mrs. Reese. I guess that is all. Does anyone of the jury have any questions or any citizen in the crowd? Please, speak up now or we will dismiss this lady."

The court was silent and, having nothing further, Mrs. Reese was taken into custody by the deputies and taken back across the street to the jail.

"We would like to call Dr. W.A. Gibson to the stand, please."

Mr. Gibson stood with his hand on a Bible and was asked by the clerk, "Do you solemnly swear to tell the truth and nothing but the truth so help you God?"

"I do," answered the good doctor.

"Please be seated, Dr. Gibson," said the coroner.

"First of all, Dr. Gibson, in your autopsy and examination did you find any of the persons having been under the influence of chloroform?"

"No, sir, I did not. I did find some evidence of warmth beneath the bodies that indicated the time of death of somewhere between midnight and two A.M. Mrs. White's body was quite a bit warmer than the rest and my guess is she died at maybe around 6 A.M. that morning. The shot to her breast would have been the fatal one. There could have been as many as five shots and as few as three shots, but there is no way to really tell the trajectory of each round. She probably awoke when they shot her husband and the wounds in her arms were from a defensive posture that she took. The bullets could have gone through her arm and into her torso otherwise; she was, of course, nine months pregnant with child which could have been born almost any day."

"Now Mr. White was shot twice; once in the neck which appears to be the first shot and that was the shot that killed him."

"Mr. Polley was shot twice; the second shot to the head being fatal. Mr. Crouch was shot once in the back of the head as he lay asleep."

"Anything about the crime scene that you could tell us?"

"Well, it is possible that one man did all the shootings in the middle of the loud thunder that night. It would not have made that much noise if he chose to do it during the hardest part of the storm. It would have been over in about five minutes or less. Also, a lantern may have been used. A person asleep and lightly woken would not have been able to see and would have been bedazzled by the light for a few seconds giving the killer ample time to shoot and hit his target without much of a struggle."

"Would George Boles have been able to hear the shots upstairs?"

"We tried that one day on an experiment, and it might have been a dull thud to him at best; like someone falling on the floor. And you could not hear anything from Mrs. Reese's room even on a calm day with the door closed."

"Thank you, Dr. Gibson. If there are no other questions, you may step down."

No questions at that time were fielded. Arthur Van Gieson was called to the stand and given the oath.

"Mr. Van Gieson, it is known that you were at the house the morning of the murders with others in the area and before the sheriff had arrived. Can you tell us anything about what you observed?"

"Yes sir, I saw the bodies just as stated by the doctor. Also, just outside the house at the window which looked into the parlor, they found a rubber boot print in the mud. It was quite distinctive in the heel and tread area. A coarse tread."

"Was any other tracks found at that time to your knowledge?"

"Yes sir, about five rods west of the house we found another track going west toward the railroad. No others were found and it appeared to be made by a different boot which had fine tread."

"Thank you, Mr. Van Gieson. There being no other questions, sir, you may step down."

"Next we would like to call Thomas Courtney to the stand."

Thomas Courtney was a tall thin man in his thirties. He had blond hair and a pointy chin. He arose and moved to the stand. He still had his broad-brimmed hat on as the clerk, in disgust, reached up as he passed by jerking it from his head and handing it to him. Thomas took the oath and, holding his hat by the brim, took the stand.

"Mr. Courtney, please tell us what you know of the morning you came to the house."

"Well, sir, I was at ta house dat morning and saw them tracks he was talkin about; seen them bodies, too. I is of a mind ta think that the boot track at the house was a new boot. You could see dem nubbies and all in the mud 'cause it had hardly been worn it had. I alsos talks to dat colored boy 'bout what he saw. He tole me dat he jump in da chest quick and he stays in there with the cover down till morning come."

"Thank you, Mr. Courtney. I am sure there are no further questions and you may step down."

The man put his hat back on and moved off the stand. As the clerk rose he jerked the man's hat off his head again waving his fist at him as a threat. The crowd laughed and the coroner called for order.

"We would, at this time, like to call Ray Clement to the stand."

Mr. Clement stood an average-sized man with a bushy beard, in his mid-fifties and dressed in black pants, white shirt and black coat. He was given the oath.

"Mr. Clement, we are very anxious for you to tell us all you can remember that morning; you being one of the first ones in the house besides Mr. Boles to see the bodies and the crime scene."

"Well, sir, as I recollect we was outside doin' morning chores when that crazy colored boy with no shoes on comes a runnin' down the road. He was yellin' his head off 'Dey's all been killed!'He was at the bridge so I called to him to come back to my house and tell me what was wrong. He did and asked me if I had seen Whitey (meaning Henry White Eunice's husband). I said 'no, why?' and he says 'well then he is dead, too.' And I says 'what you mean?' and he says down at the farm Mr. Crouch and all them has had their throats cut."

"I said 'are you sure?' and he says 'yes sir. I calls dem names and no one's is answer'. So I went down to the house accompanied by George Hutchins and Henry Cronin. We rode up on horses, got off at the back door and went into the kitchen. Julia Reese was standing there making breakfast on the stove. She turned, looked at me and said 'good morning, Ray'. Well I said right off to her Julia, whose been killed?, She looked at me kind of funny and said 'why no one that I know of' in a very matter-of-fact manner."

"How did you find the house? In what shape was it in, ransacked?"

"No. Mr. White's door was closed and everything I could see except Moses Polley's room seemed in the right order."

"Did George Boles say anything to you about what might have happened that night?"

"Yeah, George told me he heard screams and pounding in the night. So I asked him 'why didn't you come down to investigate the sounds or jump out the window?' He said I would have hid just as he did if it was me and, well, I guess I don't know what I might have really done in that instance."

"The inquisition will be adjourned until Monday, December 3rd.

The newspaper stated, after the inquisition, that the testimony by Julia Reese was strong and compelling to the point that it appeared that they had nothing to do with the murders. Both were, however, remanded back to the sheriff's custody. The district attorney was interviewed and he said he was satisfied of their innocence but he was sure the colored boy Boles knew more than he was telling.

2010

Hunter was brought back to the present as his cell phone lit up. "Hello," he answered.

"Hunter, this is Pete Vale. Just getting back to you."

"Great, Pete! Have you got some scoop on this case for me?"

"Yeah, well, maybe but not all you want. First of all, there were two ranches and it appears that Jacob only had a nineteen thousand dollar investment in both of them far from owning 330,000 acres. The first ranch was in Seven Rivers, New Mexico. It was mainly a sheep ranch operation with some cattle. It does appear to have been somewhat successful but Byron knew there was money in cattle and when he got a chance he latched onto this ranch on Texas and moved there to run it. His brother, Dayton, stayed in New Mexico to run the Seven Rivers operation. They would ride back and forth between the two ranches; both of them keeping up on what the other brother was doing. Seems that Dayton idolized his brother. I think that Byron probably was very close to his brother. Dayton did, in fact, die from a gunshot wound to his head. It does not say in what little New Mexico records there were for the day whether it was self-inflicted or by someone else. He was buried in Seven Rivers on the ranch and for a while Byron continued to run both operations. He was very successful in cattle from Texas; probably making over a hundred grand a year for many years. He finally sold the ranch in Seven Rivers and, at that time, Dayton was exhumed and brought to Texas because Byron wanted him nearby. So, yes, the body was exhumed but not at the insistence of an uncle. I don't know how that rumor was started or the fact that he died of typhoid but it is not true - any of it. Byron had him exhumed. There is also a mention of the fact that Byron also had paid back the original investment plus interest to Jacob after Dayton's death. No special things going on from here that are sinister in any way toward Jacob. As a matter of fact, found an old article here in Texas that says Jacob had visited the ranch in Texas at Christmas of 1881. Sorry to poke holes in your story but it is what it is."

"Yeah well, thanks. Actually, that does help me sort out a lot of things that I did not know. The truth can be very enlightening. Thanks, Pete, for doing this for me."

"Sure, no problem, buddy. Anytime and if you need more just let me know. Will be glad to help in any way I can."

Hunter hung up the phone and regretted immediately that he had not asked for an e-mail from Pete. Almost as if on cue his computer e-mail lit up and it was a message from Pete giving him a report of all he just told him."

Hunter smiled and thought, "Good old Pete, reliable as the day is long."

December 3rd 1883 Results of ballistics test:

Sunday before, the date: December 2nd, Prosecuting Attorney Hewlett, Coroner Casey, accompanied by W. Roscoe Dodge fire arms specialist, and also in their company was William Maloney and John McDevit as impartial witnesses. A series of experiments were conducted at the Crouch farm by those mentioned to ascertain the volume of sounds put off by the shots made in the house during the murders. It was found that Mrs. Reeses' Room the sound was very low and could have been mistaken easily for something falling on the floor. From George Boles room it sounded more like the pounding of the hammer with the door closed; opened it could have been construed as gunfire. We also took into consideration the storms that night and the tremendous thunder that came with it and it is easy to see why the two really did not hear nor recognize the sounds as gunshots.

Continuation of the inquest:

"Mrs. Reese, we would like to recall you to the stand if we may?"

Mrs. Reese got up and started to swear but the clerk stopped her telling her that she had already sworn to the community and almighty God that she would tell the truth so there was really no need to say it again. She was reminded that she is still under oath and all penalties of lying to this court are still in place.

"Mrs. Reese, what time did you see or encounter George Boles the morning of the murders?"

"I think it was around 7 o'clock. He came behind the other men. He had nothing on his head and no shoes on, I do remember that."

"I see. Can you tell the court, did George ever own a pair of rubber work boots?"

"No, sir, I never saw that he did the whole time I worked there."

"Mrs. Reese, do you know a man by the name of Charles Parks?"

"Yes, sir, I do. He was in the employ of Mr. Crouch as a hired hand up until a week before the murders."

"Why was he discharged from his duties?"

"Sir, I really don't have any idea except that maybe he was not doing a good enough job."

"Where did Mr. Parks stay while working there? Did he have a room?"

"Yes, sort of, sir. He slept in the room with George Boles upstairs."

"Were you having an intimate relationship with Mr. Parks?"

"No, sir, I was never intimate with the man."

"You never shared a bed with Mr. Parks?"

"No, sir, I did not ever do that."

"Did you ever write him any letters?"

"No, sir, I did not ever send him any letters. I wrote one once but did not send it."

"Did you know a young boy named Freeman?"

"Yes, sir, I did. He was in Mr. Crouch's employment at one time but he was discharged for not doing his job. He was also discharged for talking nasty about me and Clara Smith."

"Did you and George Boles ever argue about anything? In other words, were you on good terms with George?"

"Yes, George and I got along real well we never had no trouble."

"Did George ever deliver a letter to Mr. Parks for you?"

"I did not write him a letter; only a note that
George delivered saying I would like to see him sometime."

"Did you send any other notes by George or anyone to anyone else while you were employed by Mr. Crouch?"

"I sent one with George once to Henry Brown, one of my previous employers, asking if there had been any mail dropped off there and, if so, it was ok for George to bring it to me."

"Do you at times use another name, Mrs. Reese?"

"Yes, at times I use my maiden name Julia McCann but usually I refer to myself as Mrs. Julia Reese, my husband's name."

"So you never used another name in any situation other than those two?"

"Well, yes sir. I requested once that my sister write to me in Jackson under the name Gertie Rivers. I did that so as my husband would not get the letters. I was not very happy at that point with my marriage."

"Do you own a pair of rubber boots?"

"Yes I do, sir; size 4 1/2."

"Recount for us one more time in greater detail what you were doing that morning from the time you walked into the kitchen."

"Yes, sir. I was putting wood in the stove for the fire so I could make breakfast thinking that George's boots were gone from the kitchen then he and Mr. Crouch must be out tending to the animals."

"I had not started the fire yet when men came riding up into the yard and got off their horses. I said good morning Ray in a surprised voice and he said to me who had been killed. I said nobody to my knowledge and he pushed past me with the other men following in behind to the alcove where Jacob slept. George, he came in behind them. No shoes on, no hat at all and he was looking rather sickly and his eyes they was as big as tea saucers. I said George what is going on and he just shook his head and went on with the men. I walked over to Mr. Crouch's bed under the stairs in the alcove and I saw him a lying there with some blood around his head. I could tell he was dead and the men went to the other rooms and looked," she sniffled as tears ran down her cheeks.

"I returned to the kitchen and just sat down for a while trying to let it all soak in. The fact I had slept through all those people being killed. George he came out to the kitchen and I realized he had put on a shirt and was putting on his boots. I don't know where he got them from. I can't tell you too much more. I was not scared but I am a very timid person and I tried to shut it all out till Mr. Judd he showed up and ask me if I could get some breakfast cooking for there were some there waiting for the sheriff that had not had theirs and he wanted to feed them for their kindness."

"Some people talked to me. Can't really say what they asked but I do remember crying some when the questions were asked."

"Were all the lamps put out before bedtime?"

"Yes, they are always put out. Mr. Crouch would not have it any other way."

"Were the doors locked?"

"No, sir, again Mr. Crouch he did not think the doors to the house should be barred. I ask Miss Eunice once if she was afraid not having them locked at night and she said no."

"Did anyone else visit the farm the day of the murder?"

"No sir, except of course Mr. Polley. And Mr. Holcomb, he and his brother Henry came around supper time to see if Mr. Crouch had any work for his brother. He was a good hand but Mr. Crouch told him no not much for him. Mr. White and George could handle all winter. He would, however, give him a job if he so wanted in the spring."

"How about the day before, Mrs. Reese, was there anyone strange there that day?"

"Well, not strange. There was a silver peddler; he came through late in the afternoon. Mr. Crouch he sometimes bought things from him and he told him he could stay for the night if he so wished and have supper with us. And he did and went on his way the next morning."

"Did Mr. Crouch buy anything from him?"

"Yes, he did but I don't know what it was. I just saw Mr. Crouch hand him the money. There was also a man there in the afternoon. Mr. Crouch greeted him as if he had known him for a long time and they talked some. I know he borrowed money from Mr. Crouch which a lot of people did. I saw Mr. Crouch outside counting it out to him. I don't know how much or who the man was. I had never seen him before."

"So all this money between two men changed hands and you never saw Mr. Crouch take any money from anyplace?"

"No, sir, I was busy with my own chores and did not know that he was doing anything of the sort; nor would it have been my place to watch. I am really not that kind of person to snoop much."

"Mr. Crouch knew this man well enough to lend him money but you, as an employee, have never seen him before. Does that not seem odd to you?"

"No, sir, I really don't know many people in the Spring Arbor Horton area. I came from Jackson and east towards Ann Arbor and I had only worked for Mr. Crouch for eight weeks prior to his murder."

"How much did Mr. Crouch pay you?"

"Two dollars a week and I only had a dollar in change when I came to work for him."

"Mrs. Reese, did you drink any of the cider that night and how much?"

"Well, I don't know the exact amount but I drank as much as anyone. I suppose no one consumed a large amount. I did have kind of a dull headache when I went to bed."

"Mrs. Reese, you had several jobs before Mr. Crouch took you in, is that correct?"

"Yes, sir, I guess they were several."

"Starting at the beginning of the year, could you tell the court where you lived and for whom you worked?"

"I lived with my brother-in-law, Mr. Hall, last February. I went there to a town called Unadilla, Michigan to work for a Mr. Webster. I left because my work did not suit them."

"Is it not true that you and Mrs. Webster got in a fight about you sleeping with her husband that she caught the two of you in bed?"

"No, sir, I did not sleep with her husband and yes, she struck me twice but not because I was in bed with her husband."

"Did you also not get a letter from your mother and sister telling you not to come back there because the community was incensed by something you did and you would, according to them, be tarred and feathered?"

"No, sir, I never received such letters."

"I have several letters here to that effect signed by your mother and sister addressed to you. Maybe they will refresh your memory?"

Julia took the letters looked at them but never really read them, "I am sorry but I have never seen these letters before in my life."

"Was is it not also true that you took your thirteen year old sister to a party and stripped her down and put her in bed with several different men?"

"No, sir, that is not true. I did no such thing. I would never do a thing like that."

At this point the District Attorney allowed Mrs. Reese to step down. He at that point read several letters from her mother to her talking about men she had slept with, known and homes she had broken up due to her promiscuousness. He then stated he had pursued this line of questioning to show that Mrs. Reese was of bad character.

"I would like to call Eliza Hammer to the stand."

She was sworn in and took her seat.

"You are the sister of Julia Reese, are you not?"

"Yes, sir, I am."

"Could you tell the court about the time you went to a party with your sister when you were just 13?"

"Yes sir, I went with Julia, Ed Durgin and Orr Gould."

"So what happened there at this party? Were there lots of men there?"

"Yes, sir, I got tired and Julia undressed me, put me in bed and left Ed Durgin there with me. He also undressed and got into bed with me and stayed there until about three in the morning. Julia came in several times to check on me; she knew Ed was in bed with me."

"Thank you, Eliza, you may step down."

"I wish to call to the stand Nelly Snyder."

Nelly was sworn and took her seat on the stand.

"Where are you employed, Ms Snyder?"

"I am in the employ of Mr. and Mrs. Daniel Holcomb."

"Were you working for them at the time of the tragedy?"

"Yes sir, I was. I am now living at home. I went there last Saturday at the bequest of my father and he wanted me to come home and help take care of them."

"So you were there the night of the murder, is that correct?"

"Yes sir, I went to bed about eight o'clock."

"You had your own room in the house, is that correct?"

"Yes sir, I slept in a room next to the boys. I knew Mr. Judd Crouch and James Foy. They stayed and worked on the farm; Mr. Foy was a hand."

"So you could hear that part of the house real well?"

"Yes, sir, I am a light sleeper most of the time. I remember that night I could hear them talking in the other room but I really did not pay much attention to what they were saying. I was very tired and drifted off to sleep with them in conversation."

"To your knowledge, did you hear anyone get up in the middle of the night?"

"No, sir, I did not."

"Did you sleep through the night?"

"Yes, sir, I did."

"Thank you, Miss Snyder, you may step down."

"The court would now like to call Judd Crouch to the stand."

The clerk stood and held out the Bible as Judd placed his hand on it. "Do you solemnly swear to tell the truth, the whole truth and nothing but the truth so help you God?"

Judd responded with a nod of his head and, "I do."

Judd was seated and the district attorney arose to question him.

"Mr. Crouch, would you tell the court how old you are?"

"I am twenty-four years old."

"How old were you when Mrs. Crouch, your mother, died?"

"Six days old, sir."

"And from that point on at six days of age you lived with Mr. and Mrs. Daniel Holcomb on their farm and have ever since, is that correct?"

"Yes, sir, I always thought and still do of them as mom and dad."

"At what age did you realize or were told that Jacob Crouch was your father?"

"Probably around the age of nine or ten."

"How have you gotten along with Jacob and your sister Eunice?"

"We have gotten along splendid. I have had no animosity toward my father and I dearly loved Eunice as anyone would an older sister. She was a fine person."

"I understand that you, at times, carry a revolver with you is that true?"

"Yes, mainly when I travel. I have a thirty two caliber and it is at home in my room at this moment."

"Can you tell me of anything strange or different the night of the murders?

"No sir, I went to bed early 'cause I was tired. I sleep with Andrew. I got up about nine P.M. and went downstairs to put out the cat that was making quite a ruckus. I then went back to sleep and stayed asleep until morning."

"When were you aware of the tragedy?"

"That morning from George Boles when he rode up to the house to tell us all; I immediately got my coat on and went directly to the house."

"Were you angry at the possibility of being cut out of your own father's Will?"

"No, I was not because I knew of no such thing as Jacob leaving the entire estate to Eunice and the unborn child. I was never really promised anything and really had not thought about who would get what when he died. I was just concentrating on helping my mom and dad run our farm."

"Thank you, Mr. Crouch that will be all."

"At this time the court would like to call Will Maloney."

"Mr. Maloney, you were taken along to the Crouch home when the test shots were fired, were you not? And, also, were told you would be a witness to those experiments made?"

"Yes, sir, that is correct."

"Would you please tell the court in your own words the results of those tests?"

"When the doors were closed to any of the rooms at the times of the shots fired it sounded as though a stick of wood had been pounded on the floor. But when opened there was the ring of a gunshot and it was unmistakable."

"Thank you, Mr. Maloney. The court would like to call Mr. Dodge to the stand, please."

Dodge was sworn in and took his seat.

"Mr. Dodge, are you not a expert in firearms and so considered not only by the court but by the state of Michigan and many police departments?"

"Yes, that is correct."

"You were asked and have testified to the shots that were fired during the Crouch murders, is that not correct?"

"Yes, sir, I have been on the stand before."

"We have heard testimony from several people, including the attending physician, that there was probably only one shooter. Do you concur with that?"

"No, sir, I do not. The amount of shots made between the four killings had to have been made by at least two men. One man could not have killed all of those people without waking the others and, as the autopsy states of Mrs. White, she did awake and tried to fend off the attackers due to the defensive wounds found on her body."

"So, this would be a true statement no matter which room the murder or murders would have commenced there spree?"

"That is correct."

"Thank you, Mr. Dodge, you may step down."

"The court would like to call Mr. James White."

James White was a tall man even for his time with long white beard. He was very thin in stature and had deep-set eyes. He had the look of a preacher that was to about preach fire and brimstone and just scare hell and the devil out of you.

"Mr. White, do you solemnly swear to tell the truth, the whole truth and nothing but the truth so help you God?"

"I shore do."

James White stepped up on the witness stand and sat down in the chair. The entire audience was silent with anticipation in what was to come next. James White was the father of the murdered husband, Henry White. He was a law-abiding God-fearing man who backed down from no one for nothing. He had worked hard all of his life to scrape out a meager existence. He thanked the Lord every day for his small existence and was quite pleased with what had been handed him in life. Mr. White and his family had, at the time, been quite verbal in their belief that this case could be settled if a reward were posted for information about the killers and the crime but the local trustees seemed reluctant to do so. Even the newspapers from the area had blasted and scolded the trustees for dragging their feet in this matter. Mr. White was quick to point out that he was furious at this situation. He had lost a son, a daughter-in-law, a grandchild and a old friend in Jacob Crouch for what seemed at the time to be a senseless murder. He wanted justice to be done if only in the form of a rope.

"Mr. White, can you tell the court of anyone to your knowledge that would have wanted to kill your son or any of the others?"

"Well, before Eunice and Henry were married, there was this man named Ayers whom Henry said he was afraid of as he had been lurking around Jacob's house and making threats. I saw a letter afterwards to Eunice from Mr. Ayers dated from the Crouch Ranch in Texas. In that letter, he begged forgiveness of Eunice for the way he acted when he saw the change coming. I think he was referring to the marriage of Eunice and Henry."

"Who was this Mr. Ayers and why or how did he know the Crouch family?"

"He came up here once with Captain Byron Crouch on business with Jacob and he came back several times saying he just liked the place. He would stay at times to work with Mr. Crouch. I think he kept coming back because he was kinda sweet on Eunice and when she and Henry fell in love and told everyone they was gonna get hitched well, that just set him off a mite and kinda unhinged him. He never came back after that to my knowledge."

"Can you think of anyone who would have wanted your son dead, Mr. White?"

"No, sir, I can't and I have studied on it quite a bit since we put him in the ground. He was a good boy; worked hard. Him and Jacob had a good relationship and he was devoted to Eunice and quite happy that they was gonna have a child."

"Did he ever say anything about him or Eunice or the child getting all the money and land from Jacob?"

"No, sir, I never ever heard of such a deal."

"Thank you, Mr. White, you may step down."

"The court will adjourn until nine o'clock Tuesday morning."

Chapter 21

As the court opened again the next morning, the court room was packed. Everyone wanted to hear the testimony so they could prove or disprove rumors that had been floating around town.

"The court would like to call Miss Edith Holcomb to the stand."

The swearing in process was done as Edith, a very pretty girl and the biological daughter of Daniel and Susan Holcomb, took the stand. She had dark hair that draped down almost to her shoulders in ringlets. She wore a full dress that was pink and white and flounced as she walked. The young boys in the front elbowed one another and grinned as she walked to the stand.

"Miss Holcomb, did you hear of your father, Daniel, or Jacob Crouch ever arguing about anything? Was there any bad blood between the two?"

"No, sir, to my knowledge the two never had harsh words. Mr. Crouch visited our family quite often; even coming down for meals."

"Was there any discussion ever about what would happen to Jacob's property once he died?"

"No, sir, not to my knowledge. Jacob was my grandpa and I loved him dearly. I never knew him to worry about such things. He was asked several times by the family to make up a Will but he always refused or just put it off."

"Has there, to your knowledge, been any talk of inheritance since the murders?"

"No, sir, not to my knowledge."

"You frequented your grandfather's place. What did you do there?"

"Oh, sometimes I would just visit and at times we would go down there and have meals. I would help Eunice around the house doing chores and the like. I would help grandpa sometimes with his bank accounts and business deals but Eunice always cast the interest on the loans he had made each month. She and I would always help him keep track of who paid and who did not."

"Did Jacob have a bank account?"

"Yes he did, but I really don't know much about that. Eunice and mother kept track of that."

"Where did Mr. Crouch keep his papers?"

"He kept a lot of them in the first and second drawer of the bureaus. The drawers were small and on the top. He also kept them in a box under the whatnot in the corner."

"Can you describe this box to the court?"

"It was small enough to fit under there out of plain sight. It was covered in blue satin."

"So someone not familiar with the house would not see its location or, for that matter, assign any importance to it from its looks?"

"Yes, it would look like any normal ladies' sewing box. If you would notice it, you would not think to pull it out and look inside of it. The box did, however, have a lock."

"Has this box been seen since the night of the murders?"

"No, sir, it has not."

"So, it is your opinion that Mr. Crouch kept papers in there and maybe some money?"

"The papers yes, but I am not sure about the money part. I never saw him take out or put any money in it."

The district attorney walked over to a small table off to one side of the bench. It was stacked with items. He picked up a purse and brought it to Edith.

"Do you recognize this purse, Miss Holcomb?"

"Yes, it belongs to Eunice."

"Where does she keep it usually?"

"It is almost always on the commode in her room."

"Did Eunice ever say what was in the small box under the whatnot?"

"She told me once that there was money kept in there but she did not say how much. I never seen her take the box or open it. Always grandpa did that."

"Thank you, Miss Holcomb, you may step down."

"The court would like to recall Judd Crouch."

"May I remind you, Mr. Crouch, that you are still considered under oath," stated the coroner.

"Yes, sir," said Judd.

"Mr. Crouch, uh Judd, do you know of anyone at either place, Holcomb's or Crouch's, that had or owned a thirty eight caliber?"

"No, sir, I am not aware of that nor have I ever owned one myself, sir."

"How much is your father's estate worth?"

"I have never been told by him nor do I have any idea at this time."

"How far is it from the Holcomb farm to the Crouch farm?"

"Well, it is two and one half miles by road or about two miles by the fields."

"What time did Mr. James Foy go to bed the night of the murders?"

"We both went to bed at the same time - just before nine o'clock. We both heard that damn cat wallerin' down in the kitchen and by the time I got up he had also. We chased it around for a few minutes before we were able to chase it out of the door. Then we both went back to bed. I can't speak for him but I did not get up the rest of the night and he was there the next morning when I got up."

"Did you ever make the remark that Jacob had not spoken to you in twelve years and you planned to not speak to him for the same amount of time?"

"No, sir, I have heard that rumor and none of it is true. I have spoken to my father Jacob often and actually went to his farm several times to take a meal with him and sit and talk about - things, politics, farming, stock, just general things."

"Thank you, Mr. Crouch, you may step down but you are not excused. We may have some other questions for you later."

Judd nodded his head in acceptance and moved back to his seat in the audience next to

Edith. She put her arm around him when he sat down and kissed him lightly on the cheek.

"The court would like to call James Foy to the stand."

James Foy was a hired hand of Daniel Holcomb's and he sometimes also worked with Jacob Crouch. He lived at Daniel's house. Mr. Foy was a tall man, maybe six feet tall, and about one hundred and ninety pounds. He was a tough man but also a very good worker and dedicated hand. He was a top hand in those days. He got special privileges and top pay from whomever he worked. Foy was also one to go out into town and brag about things as he got drunk. He was known as the town loud mouth.

"Mr. Foy, please tell the court about yourself if you please?"

"I am twenty nine years of age. Was born in Rome, New York. I have worked for Mr. Daniel Crouch since 21st of May this year. I live now with Judd Crouch in Jacob's house assisting with the running of that farm."

"Have there been any visitors to the farm since the tragedy?"

"A few ladies have come by to ask if there was anything that we needed such as food and to help around the house."

"Have you heard Judd say anything about Jacob while you have been there?"

"Well, he did say once that he thought Jacob was getting old and silly in his head and that he had scolded Judd a few times but he still liked Judd. Have never heard Judd speak ill feelings of him nor have I heard Mr. Crouch, when he was alive, speak ill of Judd."

"Has Judd ever said anything about his father's riches?"

"He said to me once that the farm was big and he thought meaning Judd that it could be good for wheat."

"Have you ever heard Judd say anything about Henry White?"

"No, sir, I think he and Mr. White got along real well. I believe that Judd liked him."

"Was there anything said, to your knowledge, about Eunice and Henry getting married?"

"No, nothing was said bad about them. Was at Mr. Crouch's farm several times while Henry and Eunice were in Texas. Never heard Mr. or Mrs. Holcomb say anything bad about Henry or that they was against the marriage. Judd said once that Henry was ok but he thought Eunice would have been better to have married Mr. O'Brien."

"Mr. Foy, have you seen either Mr. Holcomb or Mr. Judd Crouch with pistols?"

"Yes, sir, I have!"

"What kind of pistols do you remember them having and when? Lately?"

"Both of them had thirty two calibers.' I saw Judd cleaning them about three weeks ago on a Sunday afternoon. Then he took them out to practice with them."

"Do you own a pistol, Mr. Foy?"

"No, sir, I do not!"

"Have you ever seen a thirty eight caliber pistol at either place, Crouch's or Holcomb's?"

"No, sir, I has not!"

"What did you and Judd do the day before the murders in question?"

"Well Judd, he went into town. Stayed most of the day and I husked corn. Stopped around four PM and then Mr. Judd came home about dark. He took care of his own horse and me, I believe I was setting reading the Police Gazette. Then that evening Judd, the boys and myself we played some cards like Bungo Pedro. We all retired about nine PM. The cat got to yowlin' shortly after we went to bed, so I lit a small light and Judd… he grabbed it at the bottom of the stairs and put it out."

"Did you sleep through the night, Mr. Foy?"

"No, sir, I woke up in the middle of the night. The storm was blowin' hard."

"Are there any wheat fields between the Holcomb and Crouch farms?"

"I am not sure, sir, but I don't think there are any at this time."

"Tell us about the morning of the murder. What was going on at the Holcomb house?"

"Well, when Boles brought the news it greatly affected everyone, especially when the colored boy said that they was all dead and had their throats' cut. Judd, he was crying. Asking why such a thing or maybe how such a thing could happen and Boles escaped? Someone ask him what time it happened. Maybe it was Mr. Holcomb who asked. Anyway, Boles he tells them between midnight and one A.M. Says he was scared and he crawled into the chest and pulled the lid down till morning."

"You and Judd have been at the Crouch farm living ever since the murders is that correct?"

"Yes, and 'cause we don't know who did this we have been sleeping together first in Mr. Crouch's bed then in White's bed. Judd had me go to the Holcomb home and get us a few weapons so as if we had to we could defend ourselves. He told me if I found a blue box of shells that they was Mr. Daniels and I was to put them in the drawer and leave them there. I never came across them."

"Thank you, Mr. Foy, you may step down."

"The court would like to call Charles Andrews to the stand."

Charles Andrews was a boy the Holcomb's had taken in and he lived on the farm. He was thirteen years old at the time of the murders.

"Can you tell us about the night of the murders? Like where you slept, what time you went to bed, did you awake and, if so, what time was it?"

"Yes, sir. Mr. Judd, he went out about eight pm to take care of his horse for the night and we retired about nine PM. Woke up about one A.M. cause the wind was blowing hard. I slept with Jim and Judd, he slept with Fred. I don't know how they knew it was one AM but someone said it was."

"Thank you, Mr. Andrews, you may step down."

"The court would like to call Fred Lounsbury to the stand."

Fred Lounsbury was a 16 year old boy whom the Holcomb's had also taken in. He worked on the farm when needed.

"Mr. Lounsbury, in your own words, will you tell the court about the night of the murder?"

"Yes, sir, well we all went to bed around nine P.M. I awoke about one A.M. Judd, he was awake and he asked me if I had heard the rain and I said I did. We slept the rest of the night and in the morning all the clothes for Mr. Foy and Mr. Judd were at the same place as they were when we went to bed. Heard about the murder that morning. Mr. Judd, he had a nosebleed just after he got up that morning. I can remember him playing with the dog before breakfast."

"Do you know if anyone in the house has pistols or rubber boots?"

"I don't think anyone in the house has any rubber boots and I am not sure… there might be two pistols but could not tell you much about them."

"Thank you, Mr. Lounsbury, you may step down."

At this point the court was adjourned until one thirty for lunch. There again was a large crowd in the courtroom. The chief of police and his officers gave the ladies who attended seats down near the bar for their comfort. The chief of police must be commended on his ability along with the help of his men to keep everything and everyone in order.

Chapter 22

"The court would like to recall Mr. James White. The court would like to remind Mr. White that he is still under oath."

James White took the stand with a quizzical look on his face.

"I am sorry, Mr. White, but in reviewing testimony we have discovered a few more questions we would like to ask you and it is nothing against you nor do we think you are a suspect."

White nodded his head as if to say ok go on I'll play.

"Mr. White, can you tell the court if you ever borrowed money from Jacob Crouch?"

"Yes, I have. The last I borrowed was last winter since the marriage of Henry and Eunice."

"Were you able to repay it?"

"Yes."

"And how was the payment made?"

"I paid a note to Mr. Crouch and it always went in a big leather wallet. I am not sure if that was his or just something they kept money in."

"Did Mr. Crouch ever give any money to Eunice after she and Henry were married?"

"Yes, Mr. Crouch gave Eunice two thousand dollars some time ago to pay for her services of working around the house and keeping the farm books up to date."

"Was anyone else, like Captain Crouch or the Holcomb's, aware that he paid her this money?"

"I cannot answer that 'cause I really don't know. I do know Eunice gave it to Henry to pay on their farm or rather his own farm and I am sure that is what was done with it."

"Do you know if Captain Crouch was opposed to the marriage?"

"Yes, according to Henry, he came to me about it said that the Captain was very upset over it but for the life of him he could not understand why. Henry tried to break off the engagement but Eunice wrote him a letter insisting upon the marriage."

"She insisted, is that correct?"

"Yes, sir!"

"Was there any reason?"

"If'n there was, Henry he never told me. The next thing I know the weddin' is back on. I have no idea what she said to him in the letter or whatever happened to the letter."

"Would you say Henry was in bad shape financially?"

"No, sir, I would not. That is one thing that Jacob liked about him was the fact that he was a good prudent man and his farm always turned a profit at the end of the year. He did better at it than most of the family. It was kind of like it came natural to him; he knew how to make a buck without spendin' a buck. I think that is why Eunice was so attached to him 'cause she was pretty much the same way."

"To your knowledge, was any of Henry's property missing after the murders."

"Yeah, he had a pretty nice watch he bought from Daller had it many a year. He never parted with it. We looked high and low through their belongings and never found it. I also know Henry sold some hogs the day before and the buyer gave him fifty five dollars in cash and a check for three hundred. I don't know what happened to that money. Henry was not much of one to carry money on his person unless he was going to buy and or sell something in town."

"Where would he have kept it then?"

"Not really sure. Where he was living he had a box at home in his room where he stashed it most of the time but there was never more than fifty dollars in there at one time. He would take any extra money he had and pay things off and keep them up to date. That is just the way he was."

"Thank you, Mr. White, you may step down."

"The court would like to call Seymour Weis to the stand."A younger man of average build with a thick head of black hair and a protruding nose took the stand.

"Do you solemnly swear to tell the truth, the whole truth and nothing but the truth so help you God?"

"I do!"

"Please, take the stand."

"Mr. Weis, are you married?"

"Yes, sir, I am."

"To whom?"

"Julia Reese?"

"But your last name is not Reese. How can you explain that?"

"There was a problem at the time of our marriage and the name was translated incorrectly to the marriage license. We did not notice it till quite some time after we were married."

"And can you tell the court who performed this marriage?"

"Yes, sir, Squire Welling."

"Can you shed some light on the letters that the court has seen that she denied?"

"Yes, I got both of those letters out of the wood stove. I am sure she thought they were burned up."

"And, by marriage, you have a child with Mrs. Reese?"

"Yes, but when she left she said if she couldn't see the child she would take its life."

"How long ago did you part with her?"

"Two years ago Christmas."

"How would you describe your wife, Julia?"

"A woman of high temper and great determination."

"Thank you, Mr. Weis, you may step down."

"The court would like to call Mr. Byron L Crouch to the stand."

A tall man with a Texas broad-brimmed hat in hand stood. He wore a dark suit with a string tie and white shirt that showed ruffles that came out from under the coat sleeves. There was also a black vest. He had on pointy-toed black cowboy boots which showed stitching on the side of the tops in the forms of roses. He had broad shoulders, a large handlebar moustache and dark piercing eyes with a full head of hair. He walked with a swagger.

"Do you solemnly swear to tell the truth, the whole truth and nothing but the truth so help ya God?"

"I do," said the man with a commanding booming voice.

"For the court records, state your name and relationship to the deceased, please."

"Byron L. Crouch and I am the oldest son of Jacob Crouch."

"And where do you live, Mr. Crouch?"

"I live 50 miles outside San Antonio, Texas and have lived there since the end of the great war of emancipation."

"And what is it you do for a living, Mr. Crouch?"

"I am a cattle rancher, sir. I raise cattle on the ranch and, when they get fat, I send them to market."

"And are you or have you been partners in this business with anyone?"

"Yes, sir, my brother, Dayton, who is now deceased. He operated another ranch near Seven Rivers New Mexico, and my father Jacob helped put up the money for the ranches."

"How much do you estimate that your ranches are worth today?"

"Between nine hundred thousand and one million dollars."

With that detail, the court exploded with people talking and it came to a large roar as it was a surprise at the amount of holdings of Jacob Crouch, most in the Jackson area had no idea that the family was so wealthy.

"Order! Quiet in the court, please!" As the coroner smacked his gavel on the bench, "Order, Quiet please!" The crowd complied and it died down to a few small whispers.

"Why is your brother Dayton not here?"

"He died last spring about February."

"And what was the cause of death?"

"Typhoid. He died in Seven Rivers."

"I am sorry for your loss, sir," said the prosecuting attorney.

"So who now owns the ranch in Seven Rivers?"

"I do and my father sir. Dayton also left Jacob nineteen thousand dollars that had been collected as his part of a summer cattle drive to Dodge City, Kansas. I sent the money onto Jacob a few months ago as a settlement of the estate."

"How did you learn of the tragedy?"

"I was setting in the Menger Hotel in San Antonio eating breakfast when I saw it in the morning paper."

"So, you had no prior knowledge of the murder until you read it in the paper?"

"No, sir, I did not. I live exactly 53 miles southwest of San Antonio and there is a railstop there eight miles from my house. E.B. Holcomb said he sent me a telegram, but I never received it."

"Is that a common occurrence there?"

"Yes, sir, it is delivered to the station stop and then it sits until someone comes up to check the mail. Things are all the time getting mislaid and lost. It might be weeks before we got that direction. I really think the telegram is there now. I just left as it went to the ranch and it was not read so I was never informed. I could not at first believe it was true so I sent telegrams to Major VanAntwerp and W.D. Thompson. They returned my telegrams assuring me, sadly, that it was true. That was Friday evening and I left for Jackson that Sunday."

"When did you last see your father?"

"I saw my father last September just before I returned to Texas. I had been home to settle my brother's estate. There were no hard feelings between my father and myself over the ranches. The family has a habit of signed contracts for all business we do amongst each other and all was signed by my father and witnessed by Eunice. I have never left my father with a greater set of love and devotion as I did then, sir. All was fine between us."

"Were you opposed to the marriage?"

"Yes, sir, I was and told my sister so but she could not be dissuaded."

"Why were you against it?"

"No particular reason against Mr. White, I think he was a fine gentleman. I just did not think the two of them would fit together, different personalities and backgrounds, but I may have been wrong. Several others in the family also were against it."

"So you liked Mr. White?"

"Well, yes, but there was never any kind of bond between us like there should have been with brother-in-laws."

"What about the fact that he might be marrying your sister for money?"

"I did not care about that nor what my father left for anyone. I had my own space in Texas and never brought up the matter with Henry."

"Can you tell the court the value of your father's estate?"

"No, sir, I have not had the time to look at anything concerning that and I had no idea prior to this moment. He was to be paid thirty thousand dollars by my brother's estate as he was half-owner in Dayton's ranch. When a person dies intestate (without a Will) in the state of Texas then the property is automatically split 50-50 down the middle by the court and that would have been my father's share of the New Mexico Ranch"

"Had your father received his share from that deal?"

"I am not sure. Again, I would have to go over Eunice's books to see what has been paid in and what has not, I have no idea of the size of his bank account or if he had more than one."

"Then, Eunice did all of the bookwork and money matters for your father?"

"Yes, sir, if there was a payment due she knew it and would tell father, or if there were papers to be produced she would also do that."

"Did you know a Jon Ayers?"

"Yes, sir, I did."

"How long have you known Mr. Ayers?"

"Since shortly after the war. When I first arrived in Texas, I became good and fast friends with him. We had a lot in common and both loved ranching. That would have been around 1870."

"Do you know the whereabouts of Mr. Ayers now?"

"He may be in New Mexico at this time looking at some beef to buy."

"How about on the night of the murders, do you know where Mr. Ayers was?"

"I do indeed, sir. He was closing business deals and paying off debts from Dayton's ranch for me. He was, in fact on the night of the murder, on his way back to Texas from New Mexico."

"Do you know where the papers were kept in the house?"

"Yes sir, almost any paper Jacob wanted Eunice would always find it in the bureau drawer. The land papers and deeds were kept in a small box I think under the what-not in his room. That way it could always be handy to pick up in case of fire."

"Thank you, Captain Crouch, you may step down."

"Sir, if I may?" asked Captain Crouch.

"Yes Captain, you have something more to say?" asked the coroner.

"Yes, sir, if I may I would like to address the court on my family's behalf?"

"Please proceed by all means, Captain."

"Having arrived here on the scene of what must have been to the entire community a horrific crime, I was saddened to read all manner of text and hear much gossip about how my family was involved in this dastardly crime because we were hungry for the land and my father's fortune. I must tell you, I am now very sorry to be a son of Michigan with so many small-minded individuals that would not only take the name of a great citizen (my father) of their county but also his family and drag it through the mud for sensational purposes. I can assure you, no one in my family had anything to do with this for any reason. We all loved and respected my father and would have done no harm to him for money or land. As for Henry White, I did not object to him marrying Eunice on the grounds of financial background nor religious nor even his place in the community. I pointed out to Eunice and Henry separately on several occasions that they were not suited for one another in neither character nor disposition. I could have been wrong but I had nothing against Mr. White. I think in the end he saw what I was pointing out and at one point he even tried to break off the engagement to Eunice, only to be talked back into it by her in the form of several letters and poems. Eunice could be quite persuasive when there was something that she wanted. As for Mr. Ayers, I have, as you heard, known him for many years and he indeed loved everyone in our family. He did not have a family of his own and we adopted him into the family as well as he adopted us. He was just like a brother to myself and Dayton and well-liked by my father and Eunice. There was at no time any romantic notion between Mr. Ayers and Eunice. That is all I have at this time, sir."

"Thank you, Captain Crouch, for a message from the heart. Due to the lateness in the day, we will adjourn. I would like to take this opportunity to thank the jurors and their patience in this case. And for taking so much time out of their busy schedules and life so we may try and get to the bottom of the truth of this matter and bring to justice those who are responsible. I must also agree with Captain Crouch, that this was a very reprehensible crime and when the miscreants are found I can assure, along with the district attorney, they will be prosecuted to the fullest extent of the law. Due to some items in this case that the sheriff and the coroner's office would like answered, we will adjourn until next Tuesday at nine am.

Sheriff Winney left the proceedings quickly as did Coroner Casey and this was not missed by the crowd. They wondered what was up.

Winney walked through the office door to his desk and sat down, "Get me Bill Adams at once. I don't care if it's his day off or if he's eating or even in the dentist chair get him here now," bellowed Winney to another deputy who knew the tone and rushed to comply.

"Casey, you need to give an order of disinterment for Jacob Crouch's body so that it can be checked for possible drugs or poisons. I think, according to Doctor Gibson, that we can still get tests on the stomach and we cannot Eunice or Henry because they were embalmed."

"Yeah I concur, I will do that and we can get onto that immediately. I will get doctors Gibson and Wilson to accompany us and you can bring the undersheriff to witness the proceedings."

Bill Adams came through the door.

"Bill, you talked to people about this peddler that stayed the night before with the Crouches, did you not?"

"Yeah!"

"Well, do you have any idea where he is now?"

"Might be in Hillsdale area… as I understand he has a normal route that he follows."

"Do you think you could find him?"

"Yeah, I think so. No problem."

"Great, I have a set of questions I will write out for you to ask him and then you bring them back and answer them for the man to the court."

"Yeah, just let me go home and change shoes, kiss the wife and I will be on the next train south."

"Great, I will alert the sheriff of Hillsdale County that you are coming and if he knows this peddler not to place him under arrest, just detain him for the time being."

Adams left in hurry to start and hopefully complete his mission.

Chapter 23

December 11 1883

The council chamber was full that morning all in attendance as had been, when the proceeding was Jacob Crouch's body had been disinterred and his entire stomach removed. This was sent to the University of Michigan for analysis. A letter of a complete testing was sent to the council and it was read into the record for all to know.

In accordance with your request I report the results of a chemical analysis of a portion of a human body for poisons in the following statement to which I certify.

On December 7th 1883 at 11 ½ o'clock a.m. I received of P. Casey coroner of the county of Jackson a glass jar, securely closed and sealed with red sealing wax, and stated by him to contain a human stomach to be subjected by me to a rigid analysis for poisons, especially stupefying poisons. In this glass jar I found a stomach beginning to decompose weighing 2.832grams and which I proceeded to examine. The appearance of the stomach upon its inner coat was ordinary and normal and it contained only a small quantity of liquid common to the stomach without any undigested food. On a careful microscopial examination of the fluid contents and mucus membrane only ordinary and normal forms, such as common fat globules and epithelia were found. The one third of the stomach and its contents were reserved; one-third subjected to a systematic analysis for organic and alkaloidal poisons; and one-third subjected to a systematic analysis for metalloid poisons, so that all ordinary poisons were searched for. Both chemical and physiological tests for narcotic and somnolent poisons were applied with detailed faithfulness. In all results no poisons were found, and from my analysis I can testify that no poison known to ordinary chemical analysis as a poison of administration was present in the stomach and contents as I received them. From the time they were delivered to my study it was never out of sight of myself or my assistants for any point in time. The seal was intact when delivered as it had been sealed for delivery by the Jackson County Coroner. I also submit that I am a professor in good standing with the University of Michigan and head of the chemistry department therein. I also have been noted by the United States Chemists association as a person who is very familiar with poisons and a top scientist in my field. ALBERT B. PRESCOTT.

"The court at this time would like to recall Captain Crouch to the stand. We would remind the Captain he is still under oath. The jury and the coroner requested that at this time all witnesses to be called or that could be recalled were to be sequestered outside of the proceeding room until either called or further notice was given.

"Captain Crouch, it has been several days since our last hearing. Have you been able to ascertain the exact amount of your father's estate?"

"No, sir, I have not. Without all the papers, it will take some time to bring it all together to see what is owed to him and by him as well as what is owned."

"Have you or any of your family been arrested?"

"No sir, except for myself. I was arrested and detained during the war of great independence by southern soldiers who actually exchanged me and several others for southern prisoners."

"Have you, in the fit of anger, ever drawn a weapon against any member of your family?"

"I have never done such a thing, sir, and I must say I do not like this line of questioning."

"I am sorry, Captain Crouch, but in order to bring some order to all of the allegations that are floating about, we must ask these questions to allay any gossip that might be taken as truth so that we can ascertain the truth."

"I am sorry, sir. I do understand your plight."

"I also must make you aware, Captain Crouch, that you have the right not to answer any questions that you feel may be too personal for any reason and you do not have to disclose that reason to the council," said Coroner Casey.

"So, did you ever threaten to shoot your father or brother?"

"No, sir, I most certainly never did such a thing."

"What business were you engaged in that it took you until Sunday morning to leave San Antonio for Jackson?"

"You said I can refuse to say and I do refuse this, sir. It is my business. The dead must take care of the dead and the living take care of the living."

"How much is your obligations to your father in round figures?'

"Again, sir, I do at this time refuse to answer that question."

"Why? Is it that if you are so bent on catching your father's killers that you yourself have not offered a reward? Surely you have the means, do you not?"

"I have refused to offer a reward so that every jack-a-nape in the world won't come out of the woodwork to hunt them down, forcing them deeper into hiding, making it harder to find them in the long run. I have though, sir, spent quite a sum at the Pinkerton Detective Agency hiring detectives to help sort this all out and, undoubtedly, they have already been here and amongst the people in secrecy."

"There are rumors around, Captain, that you have told people in Texas that your father's estate may be worth well over two million dollars. Is that true?"

"No, sir, I have never said such a thing to anyone anywhere. As I said before, I am not sure of my father's holdings at this time."

"We understand that a person came to Texas with you and stopped in Chicago but did not accompany you here. Why was that?"

"My friends in Texas did not think I should make the journey alone. So a friend of mine, a Mr. Gilman, came with me and he stopped at Chicago for the Fat Cattle Show. I, of course, did not attend and came straight here. Had it not have been for the murders, I was planning on attending."

"When was the last time you saw Mr. Ayers?"

"At the ranch in New Mexico on October 18th of this year in the morning. I said good bye to him and proceeded to my ranch in Texas. I received a telegram from him the morning I learned of the murder from New Mexico saying he was coming to see me in Texas to discuss some business."

"What do you know of Moses Polley?"

"I know very little. I only met the man maybe three times and then for only a short while."

"How many heirs are there to the estate?"

"There are but only three. Myself, Judd, and, our sister Susan."

"Do you know how the land and money will be divided between you three?"

"I have no idea as to what goes to whom and, at this moment, I really don't care."

"So, you still decline on speculating on how much your father's estate would be?"

"I do not really decline, sir, I just do not know at this moment. Eunice kept all of father's books and those have been located and, of course, I do not have the slightest idea where the box went. There was nothing in there but land papers. All of the important papers and the notes that I owed my father have been found intact with other papers. The box that is missing had no such papers in it."

"Thank you, Captain Crouch, for answering these questions. You may step down."

"The court would like to recall Edith Holcomb to the stand.

Edith was the daughter of Daniel and Susan."

"Did your Aunt Eunice ever give you any jewelry?"

"No, she did not but she did give me a gold pen for my birthday."

"Did she ever express any fears to you?"

"It was funny, she told me a few weeks before her death that she believed she would not live long. I think she remembered her mother giving birth to Judd and that worried her that she may have a similar malady."

"Was she apprehensive of anyone or in fear of anyone?'

"No, she was very stoic like my grandfather. They were very similar; that is why they got along so well. She did tell me that she had encountered three low mean men in the kitchen one afternoon talking with Mr. Reese. She seemed upset about that.I think she and my mother spoke of it but not with me. She did ask mother if she would take her in after the baby was born because she did not want Mrs. Reese around the child."

"Thank you, Edith, you may step down."

"The court would like to recall Daniel Holcomb and, as we recall people, we again would remind them that they are under oath."

"Mr. Holcomb, can you tell us where you were the day of the tragedy?"

"I was home all day and all night. I never left the house. I was there when Judd left for Jackson and I was there when he returned."

"Do you remember what time you went to bed that night?"

"I believe it was around eight o'clock."

"Were Judd and Foy in the house at the time?'

"They were in the dining room playing cards with James and Fred, and I was in the front room reading."

"Where is your bedroom?"

"My wife and I occupy a bedroom in the northeast corner of the house of the upright."

"Did you awake during the night and, if so, do you know what time it was?"

"Yes, I heard a loud noise and went outside to investigate. It was a barn door that had come loose in the wind and it was flopping some. I secured the door and returned to bed. The house was quiet and I believe I heard the clock downstairs strike one as I returned to bed."

"Do you keep your doors locked at night?"

"Yes, I always do."

"Do you know how much Jacob's estate is worth?"

"I really cannot say. He had nine hundred acres here at about sixty dollars an acre, plus his cattle notes owed to him, etc. That is as close as I can come and it, of course, is not an exact figure. That does not include his holdings in Texas or New Mexico."

"Are you aware of any other heir or pretend heir?"

"No, sir, I am not. Outside of Susan Judd and Byron I know of none."

"When did you hear of the murders?"

"About seven thirty that morning. I heard it from George Boles. He said he heard a thump in the night. I asked him why he did not jump out the window and go for help but he said he was too scared and kept repeating over and over that their throats had been cut."

"Why is it that you did not employ any type of reward for the apprehension of the murderers?"

"Waited until Mr. Byron came home to see what he had to say and besides, at the time, the board of supervisors had not posted a reward either. I talked with Sheriff Winney about this when Byron came home and I became afraid as did Byron that it might cause the wrong person to be accused and hung for something they did not do. After talking with Captain Crouch, we decided to use the money to employ the Pinkertons to help the case along and it would be better used at that point."

"Has there ever been any harsh words between Judd and Jacob?"

"I have never heard Judd say anything bad about his father except that he thought that lately he was becoming childish."

"Do you know if Mr. Crouch left a Will?"

"I have heard him say many times that he did not believe in Wills so I would think that he did not. He did say that he would call us all together at some point and time and tell us all what we would get in the event of his death."

"Did he ever say anything about leaving everything to Eunice and her baby?"

"No, sir, I never heard that nor did I have any reason to believe that he would do such a thing. He did say to Captain Crouch and I that we should all share and share alike. And that the farm maybe should go to Judd. If there was anything that he needed to pay to anyone for their share that he should be allotted the time to do this."

"Do you own a pair of rubber boots?"

"Yes, shortly before the murder Judd bought me a pair of new boots at Gilson's."

"Does Judd own a pair of rubber boots?"

"No, sir, he has never owned a pair."

"Does Judd own a revolver?"

"No, sir, he does not. The only revolvers I know of him coming in contact with were the pair that he and Foy were cleaning some weeks before the murder."

"How did Judd take the news of the murders that morning?"

"He is not one to show a lot of emotion but it clearly bothered him. He never cries because of all the years of pain he had with his leg. He is a very emotionally well-kept individual."

"Have you worn those rubber boots since they were bought for you?"

"Yes, sir, I have."

"Sheriff Winney, would you send someone out to get those boots and bring them back for examination immediately?" ordered Casey.

"When did Judd and Foy move into the house?"

"The day after the murders. It was just easier for them to take care of the stock. They have been there ever since."

"Where was James Foy the morning that the news came of the deaths?"

"I believe he was in the barn taking care of the horses."

"Thank you, Mr. Holcomb, you may step down."

"The court would like to recall Julia Reese."

"Mrs. Reese, you stated to the sheriff in questioning that you got up after you went to bed. Can you tell the court why and when that was?"

"I got up to close my window because of the wind coming up and I knew it was going to rain and it might rain in. I think that maybe it was half past ten. I had not been to sleep yet at that time."

"Did Eunice say she was going to discharge you?"

"No, sir, she never said such a thing."

"Did she admonish you because of all the low characters you had hanging around you?"

"No, sir, she did not and I never had any low characters hanging around me; only Mr. Eastman came to call. I have to admit, I was kind of sweet on him and hoped that he might be sweet on me and might actually court me."

"So, did you ever go anywhere with Mr. Eastman?"

"Oh… yes, sir, we went riding once and he took me to a dance once."

"Did you ever talk to Mr. Eastman about Jacob?"

"No, but he did ask me if Mr. Crouch and Mr. White were pretty well off once. And I said I don't really know they have some money but I really don't know how much."

"Thank you, Mrs. Reese, you may step down."

"Mr. Casey, I would like to say something about the way I have been treated by Sheriff Winney and his men and the low tricks they have tried to play on me."

"Mrs. Reese, we are not here to ascertain how well you have been treated since your incarceration. We are here to determine who may have been responsible for the killings of the residents of the house that night. Please, now kindly step down or I shall have the bailiff remove you."

Mrs. Reese rebuffed, stepped down smarting somewhat from the scolding. She could not understand what she would have to do to get out of jail and the clutches of the sheriff.

"Ladies and gentlemen, the boots in question have been located at the Holcomb farm and brought here for inspection. Would Mr. Holcomb please come back to the stand?"

Daniel came to the stand and pulled on the boots. They were between a size 9 and 10.

"How much have you worn these boots since you got them Mr. Holcomb?"

"I would say some everyday."

"Do you know how much Captain Crouch owed his father at the time of his death?"

"Do not know for sure. I do know that he was to pay Jacob thirty six thousand dollars for his share in the ranch."

"Mr. Crouch then did not own the ranches in Texas?"

"No, that was a Spanish land grant that was bought by the Captain. I think Mr. Crouch gave him some of the money at the time. I know Mr. Crouch had three notes against Byron at the time. One of eighteen thousand, one of ten thousand and one around nine thousand. I think there was some twenty seven thousand acres in the land grant."

"Has Judd ever said he wanted to buy a pistol to your knowledge?"

"Yes, but it has been since the murders. He was wondering if he should have one for protection."

"When you got up and went to the horse barn that night to check on the banging door, did you check the stock to see if anyone had removed a horse?"

"No, sir, I did not but the next morning all was there and in ship-shape."

"Do you know why Byron opposed the marriage to Eunice?'

"Well, I finally pressed him to it and he did not think that Mr. White was up to her intellectual standards."

"That is all, Mr. Holcomb. You may step down but we will have to retain the boots in the care of the sheriff at this time."

"I would just like to say one thing if I may, Mr. Casey?"

"Yes, Daniel, please do."

"If there is anyone here who has the smallest inkling or idea of who may have done this, no matter how silly it may seem, please come forward and tell your story so that we may ferret out the real culprits and bring them to justice and closure for the family."

"With that said, ladies and gentlemen, this court will stand adjourned."

Sheriff Winney sat at his small desk in the middle of the county jail with his lamp on scrutinizing remarks made by people when interviewed about the murders. The door to the jail swung open and Detective Adams moved slowly across the room and stooped into the captain's chair next to the sheriff's desk. He let out a breath that bordered on exhaustion and exasperation.

"Well, did you find the peddler?"

"Yeah, I ask him all your questions and a few of my own but he really does not know much. Just hearsay from other folks that would not be admissible in court or relevant to the current coroner's trial."

"Shit, I had hoped being there the night before he could have added something that would give us a lead. What are we gonna do, Bill? This is going nowhere fast and we are running out of leads."

Bill Adams was a tall young detective and Winney knew he was maybe the best detective he had ever seen. Without a doubt he was one of the best men on his force. Adams sat there looking up at the ceiling. His blond hair was messed from the day as he looked up at the ceiling with an exasperated look on his face. He had been working on this case with little rest since the inception and now he was tired. He needed to go home, rest, get some sleep and recharge his mind. Even the simplest tasks had become hard for him to do.

"Adams, tomorrow I am going to put you in charge of the case as far as the detection goes. Take it to whatever ends you think it must be taken so as to ferret out the guilty parties. I will take care of the entire political end of it and inquiries from the outside such as newspapers. Refer them all to me and any political things that may come up by important people who do not like being shoved. This might be my last term after I step on some toes, but it seems we owe this to four murdered people. Spare no one and I will take the flack for it as well as the hit at the polls if it comes to that. I just want to make sure that, if we walk away because of an election, that we do it with our heads held high knowing we did not leave any stone unturned. I don't want at sixty years of age to still have a scrapbook about this and trying to solve it. You are my most capable detective so I put this in your hands. I have no other place to turn."

Adams looked over at his friend the sheriff, smiled and said," I, sir, shall endeavor to do my best. I fear now that there is a reward out we shall be overwhelmed by tips and amateur detectives."

"I will leave the undersheriff to take care of them. Meanwhile, you are to answer to no one but me unless you find out that I am a suspect."

"So, what about the woman and the darkey? You gonna keep them locked up?"

"Till the very end of all of this inquest, I am. I don't think either one had anything to do with it. She has had a hard life but I just don't see her staying around at the end of all of that and she sure did not gain any money out of it. I really don't think any of her friends had a hand in this 'cause they knew about certain things that outsiders would have not known about and they would not have left Boles alive to tell. Also, they would most likely have gone off to spend lots of money they gained from this and there are no reports within the state of strange people spending money beyond their means. Boles, of course, did not do it but I really think he knows more than he is telling. When we turn him loose, I want somebody on him day and night making a list of who he talks to where and for how long. I want to make sure he is not getting paid off by someone to keep his mouth shut. I really thought we could scare him into telling the truth but it appears not. His story about hiding in that chest was made up but why? He has stuck to it even though we have proved that he could not have been in the chest either physically or due to the fact all the clothes were still piled on top in the morning and the contents not emptied."

"Ok, so let's go home and sleep on this. The inquest is almost over. I am sure it will come to murder at the hands of person or persons unknown."

"Yeah, you are right," said Winney.

Chapter 24

2010

Hunter sat back and looked at the clock. It read one fifteen a.m. He yawned and stretched but was determined to finish the inquest. Rising, he went over to the sink, pulled down a Maker's Mark out of the cabinet and poured himself a stiff one straight up in a glass. He walked over to the window and thought about the case.

Why was George Boles so adamant that he got in that chest when all the evidence proved him wrong? Why not change his story or give one that would have been more plausible like 'I pulled the covers up over my head?' He stood in front of the living room window overlooking Main Street Marshall from his second floor apartment above his bookshop. The night was quiet; not many cars and the traffic lights now blinked on yellow all the time. The glow to the street from the lights was a yellowish-gold that gave the whole downtown area a serene look while still looking warm and inviting. He ran things over in his mind as he sipped at the drink.

"Julia Reese… she was quite the whore even in those days. Maybe even by today's standards. One thing was for sure, by taking that young thirteen year old girl to entertain men, stripping her and putting her in bed was not the act of a women who had loose morals, but of one who may also have had a cruel

streak and maybe stopped at nothing if she became vengeful.

The problem with Julia and George, separate or together they really had no motive but robbery and it is hard to fathom, even back then, that a woman and young boy would kill four people in cold blood for money when they could have easily stolen it and ran. Maybe, in those days, never to be caught if they actually ran far enough."

Hunter took a second drink from the glass nearly downing it all.

"Who else could or would have benefitted from the deaths? Judd… he got the farm but then some testimony had said that Jacob had planned to give it to him anyway. Byron… because he owed Jacob money he could not pay back. Daniel and his wife Susan… because if Jacob gave it all away then they would have nothing to fall back on. But if Judd inherited it, he would have more than kept them all of his life just as if they were his aging parents. Was Jacob really going to leave everything to Eunice and the child? Was this the rift in the family that caused the killings? Or had someone just followed Polley because he had a sizeable bank roll? But then they would not have known nor found the box under the what-not. That, also, is an enigma. Why take land papers that really did nothing to change anything because all of the papers would have been filed with the county and all property owners would have been recorded on the township tax record? Without those papers,

there was still many legal ways to claim property rights. No one had really taken over any property as of the murders. Well, maybe Judd, but he was asked to go live there with Foy and attend the cattle."

He had more questions now than answers. Where would all of this end? Moving back to the table with the dimly lit lamp, he sat down and finished off the Maker's Mark, picked up the pile of papers, his notepad and went back to reading the proceedings of the inquest. Most of the remaining inquest summonses for witnesses were not filled due to the fact of no show of the people in question. It seems that, in those days, if you did not show up for court when you were summoned then there was no cause for alarm and you actually must have gotten away with it.

Hunter read the rest of the few remaining testimonies and really nothing further came to notice. It was mostly hearsay that could or would not be used in a real court of law. Such as "I was told by John that he overheard Lem say that his neighbor talked to the Holcomb's and they had lots of trouble with the Crouch's."Finally, he got to the end of a long inquest and read the final verdict. The following is a transcription of the verdict that was printed in the Jackson Citizen Patriot as a formal verdict rendered by the coroner's jury.

Verdict

State Of Michigan ss

Jackson County

An inquisition, taken at Jackson, in said county and state, before P. Casey one of the coroners of said county, on the 22nd day of November, 1883, and subsequent days, on view of the bodies of Jacob D Crouch, Wm. Henry White. Eunice White, then lying dead on oaths of the jury whose names are hereunto subscribed, who being sworn to enquire on behalf of the people of this state when, in what manner and by what means the said deceased persons came to their death, upon their oaths do say that said Jacob D. Crouch, Wm. Henry White, and Eunice White, came to their death on the night of the 21st or the morning of the 22nd of November 1883 A.D. Sometime between the hours of 9 P.M. of the 21st and 7 A.M. the 22nd, by wounds from pistol shots, inflicted by the hands of some person or persons to this jury unknown.

Signed

Wm. Dilley,

Jesse Hurd,

James L. Thorn,

Daniel S. Peterson,

W.H.H. Snow,

H.M. Eddy,

Jurors.

The jury was dismissed by the coroner and then impaneled again for the case on the cause of death of Moses Polley. (I, as the author and investigator of this, cannot tell you exactly why they did this and not use all four deceased people in the first case. It was, as you shall read, very expedient.)

Two witnesses were sworn as a matter of form and the jury rendered a verdict in exactly the same words as above except that Moses Polley's name was inserted in place of the other three.

The Hon. S.M. Cutcheon rose to state that he spoke for the boy, Boles, as said legal representation and said there was certainly no shadow of evidence against him. And that the fact that the jury rendered its verdict without mention of indictment of Boles or Reese, that he petitions the court at this point to have both parties released and all charges dropped at this time in an immediate manner.

Prosecuting Attorney Hewlett said he would be perfectly willing to release these people since the jury did not mention them in an indictment. He was sorry for their time of incarceration and apologized for the District Attorney's office and the Sheriff's department having kept these people incarcerated for so long. He said he would make sure that they were released within the hour with no pending charges and all previous charges revoked.

Julia Reese and George Boles were released on their own and free of any encumbrances of the law less than an hour later.

Signed P.Casey, Coroner

1884 Jan 2nd

The Crouch tragedy had been over quite some time now and life still was not back to normal. Edith Holcomb, the young daughter and only living biological child of Daniel and Susan Holcomb, had returned home in late December of 1883 to help her mother who had become quite ill due to her being distraught over the murders. The morning of January second would become a morning that would be talked about for over one hundred years and what actually happened.

Edith, Judd and Daniel sat around the breakfast table that morning discussing normal matters of the day. Susan, feeling much better, was up and in control of the household as usual. She felt a bit strange but she seemed happy and was of better mind than before. It may have been that the new year brought promise with it and maybe a chance to start life anew by putting the catastrophe of November 1883 away from memory. Time, as the sage once said, does in fact heal all wounds.

"I am going into Jackson this morning to meet up with Byron at the Sheriff's office and talk about where the case is headed," said Daniel.

"I want to go into town, also," said Edith. "Mother, do accompany me. Judd can get the cutter hooked up and we can sleigh into town, do some shopping and pick up some food items we are in need of."

"Oh, my dear, that would be wonderful but not this morning. I just don't want to go out in the cold this morning. You and Judd go into town, have fun, buy some things and come back and tell me all about it," said Susan.

"Yeah, I can do that. Let me go get Foy and we can get it all hitched up," said Judd rising from his seat and searching near the back door for his work boots and coat.

Daniel stood up, took one last sip of coffee, and said, "Well, Foy should have my conveyance ready also." He walked over to Susan and, with a warm glow in his eyes, put his arms around her from the back as she moved back into the caress of his body.

"Now, mother, don't you over do. The boys are here if you need anything done. I should be back before dark. I do love you so very much," and with that he bent his head around and kissed her on the cheek. She smiled and raised a hand to caress his head. Daniel put on his hat, coat and boots and waved once more to Edith and Susan as he walked out of the door.

"Are you sure you are well enough for me to leave you alone, mother?"

"Yes, dear, I am perfectly fine and feel in very good spirits this morning. Now you run off with Judd and the two of you have a good time."

Edith put on her items of winter clothing and moved out the door to the sleigh. Two fine-spirited horses were up front and ready to move out so as to keep themselves warm by racing across the snow. Judd jumped down. He and Foy helped Edith up into the sleigh. Judd rushed to the other side, jumped up and in as Edith covered them both with a heavy horse blanket across their laps. With a "Ho!" and a slap of the reins from Judd, the horses moved up and out of the farmyard to the road and he made the turn toward Jackson. Some snow flew behind them from the blades as they whisked toward town. You could hear Edith laughing all the way.

Susan moved around in the kitchen cleaning up after the breakfast. She saw James Foy standing there looking back at the house and her. She thought that odd but waved her hand to him and he waved back and smiled. He then turned to the road and moved on up walking in the snow back to the Crouch farm to finish his morning chores. Susan, feeling a bit of indigestion coming on, turned to the two boys, Fred Lounsbury and Charles Andrews.

"I am going upstairs to lie down for a while. I do not wish to be disturbed for any reason. Please tell anyone who may inquire that I am indisposed and please call back at a later time," she smiled and rubbed the cheek of Fred who was nearest to her. He smiled back and nodded his head as if to signify that he understood.

Susan reached under the kitchen sink and came out with an old whiskey bottle that still had the cork in the top. It was clean and devoid of any label. She grabbed the pitcher pump on the counter and pumped water up from the cistern and filled the bottle. She then corked it. Taking off her apron, she wiped the outside of the bottle down to get rid of any moisture that was present. Turning, she walked across the kitchen and upstairs to the bedroom she and Daniel had shared for so many years. She opened the door, closed it and the snap of the lock by key was heard from inside as she bolted the door.

2010

Hunter was excited as he put all of his gear into a large metal case; checking each for fresh batteries. He put on his tactical vest and filled it with all of the equipment he would need at a critical moment during the investigation. Grabbing his case, he moved down the steps slowly to the outside door and then across the parking lot to his Charger. He opened the trunk, took out the 9mm pistol and placed it in a box in the trunk and locked it in the box. He then took off the tactical vest and laid it in the trunk on top of the case. The sun was setting fast in the west as he drove up to Victoria’s home.

Jemma came out of the door first followed by Victoria. They were both carrying cases and duffle bags that were then stowed into the trunk.

"Hey, sweetie," said Hunter grabbing Victoria by the waist as she closed the trunk. He pulled her close and they kissed for a moment as Jemma made her way into the back seat of the Charger. Victoria and Hunter jumped into their respective sides as she turned to her house and waved goodbye to the children who were looking out of the living room window.

The Charger roared east toward M-99, then south to Route 60 and on East to Spring Arbor. Stopping in town, Hunter pulled into the Mickey D's. They each ordered coffee; Hunter's with an espresso shot.

They continued on to Reynolds Road, turned south and sped on down the road. Hunter kept his eyes peeled for deer as it was nearing dusk. This was deer season in Michigan and no telling where one might spring out in front of you having been chased out of hiding by a hunter returning to his vehicle. As they neared Reynolds Cemetery, he slowed the car to a stop and they climbed out.

"This is past dusk, is it not?" asked Jemma pointing to a sign prohibiting anyone in the cemetery after dusk.

"Yeah, you are correct, my dear, but I talked with the Chief of Police for Spring

Arbor and, of course, our deputy friend and I am being allowed by them to set up some equipment here as long as I don't linger to do an investigation."

Hunter opened the gate and lugged in a case close to Susan Holcomb's grave site. He set a small device below it and turned it on. A small red light came on and it made a beep. They moved about the cemetery spreading electronic gadgets everywhere. A small car drove up into the church's corresponding parking lot just bordering the south side of the cemetery. Hunter walked around and shook a young man's hand as Victoria and Jemma stood outside the car sipping coffee. The night had started to turn cold as dampness came down to soak in with the cold air. It was wet out due to rain that day and the day before.

"Curt, glad you could make it. This is where I want you to set up and just let it roll keeping an eye on the cemetery and all my gadgets for me."

"Cool, dude. I got the Wi-Fi hooked so you can monitor all of the devices from the farm. It will give you read-outs to a printer every fifteen minutes if there is no event. Should an event trip one of your devices, then it will record until the event is finished and or five minutes have elapsed. Then it will go back into its hibernation mode of every fifteen minutes."

"Thanks, Curt, I appreciate this," said Hunter grabbing the laptop from the young man.

Victoria walked up and put her arm around Hunter as Jemma materialized next to her. She looked at the young man. He was about five foot six inches tall, slender build with a slightly round face with stubble and a goatee. He had on a tech jacket that said Motley Crue Crew. She smiled at him and lowered her head a little as he smiled back and turned his attention to her.

Hunter, sensing the chance meeting, said, "Curt, I would like you to meet an employee and friend of mine. This is Jemma Choun. Jemma, this is Curt Davis. He is with South Michigan Paranormal Services, a very good group. He is one of the co-founders."

"Very nice to meet you," smiled Curt extending his hand to her and she took it shaking it. She noticed that his hands were warm just like his brown eyes and she could feel it spread to her body warming her to the core.

"Well, Curt, do you need any help setting up here? The pastor said there was an outside receptacle if you needed power. I was not sure."

"No, I have batteries and I am gonna used mini DVD's for recording. Also, I have this setup so if you power up the laptop and click on the top icon that says 'picture maker' it will show you what I am looking at here and give you a good impression of what is going on. Also, it will be recorded into the laptop. You keep the laptop for now and download all of it to your computer and then I can come and pick it up."

"That would be great, and maybe we can have lunch?" asked Hunter.

"I was hoping that maybe Jemma here would do me the honor of having lunch with me. She is much better looking than you ever were."

Hunter laughed and tightened his grip around Victoria's waist as she leaned in to nuzzle him. "Well, I guess you got me there. You two can have the town to yourselves. Us old fogies will just heat up some soup and sit by the fire roasting our toes. You got my cell number if you need me or there is any kind of beef about you doing this and a few of my D & R cards. Those are gold with the sheriff and it will tell the chief in Spring Arbor who you are. Just tell them we have permission from the church."

"Will do and good luck," said Curt still looking at Jemma and smiling. She turned slightly, brushed her hair back and waved at him.

The Charger roared on down Horton Road to the site of the old Crouch Farm. The house that used to be there had burned in 1948. Just recently, there had been a new structure added. A two-story house, small with a nice back porch for all seasons. The old barn was there as well as some upgraded silos. You could see, off to the east of the property, where other small structures stood. The yard in the back was fairly expansive and there was a small tent set up with a roaring campfire as the owners of the property sat there with a group of friends. Hunter could smell the food from the fire as he stepped out. He grabbed his coffee and moved over toward the fire.

"Good evening, Mr. Ross," said Clark Stauffer rising from a lawn chair on the other side of the fire.

"Hello, Clark, and call me Hunter, please. Julia, nice to see you again," he waved at Clark's wife. He counted in his head and decided there were 15 people there.

"Ladies and gentlemen, this is Hunter Ross. He is a Forensic Paranormal Investigator and he is working on the Crouch Case trying to figure out who the killers were. He knows a lot about the story. I was hoping that he might enlighten us and tell us the story as he knows it."

Hunter started his story as another vehicle drove in the driveway and backed up to the Charger. The back hatch door opened up automatically and a slender brunette got out with long hair down past her waist.

"Hi, Chandra," said Jemma helping her pull out a work bench. They both started to unload and set up equipment. Jack Monroe and his friend Ed Dwyer, deputy, also drove into the parking area. They were off duty and had come to help out on their first investigation.

"Hey, ladies, where is the big cheese?"

"He is down by the campfire entertaining the owner's guests with Crouch stories," said Victoria coming up close to the table.

"You know where to set the cameras up," said Chandra to Jemma."Take these big strong police-like guys and let them string the cable and help you set up. I would appreciate it," Jemma smiled as both deputies surrounded her, picking up bags and gear for the cameras.

With that, Chandra pulled out a large DVR and a huge big-screen monitor 32 inches across. They hooked up the cables to the DVR and the monitor. Chandra opened up the laptop that Curt had given them and punched in commands. Then, pulling out another big screen monitor from her vehicle, she hooked it up and displays came alive. Chandra pulled out a converter, started her vehicle and plugged in a printer to the converter, placed paper in the tray and turned it on. Jemma, returning from having put the deputies to work, took a small generator out of the SUV and pulled it into a depression in a corn field next to the parking area. She then trekked up after a long heavy extension cord and plugged it into the generator. She gave the rope a pull and it kicked off, running smoothly and quietly. Walking back up, she was happy to have found the small swale as it did a good job of hiding the noise.

The monitor and DVR turned on and the night vision infrared cameras kicked on and lit up the dark yard as if it was mid-day on the monitor.

"Jack, camera three needs to be down and to the right some to catch the whole side of the house," she said into a small radio clipped to the shoulder epaulet on her jacket.

"K, hon, how is that?" returned Jack.

"Yep, we got it. Now for the big guy, we need to move him back. He is too close to the barn and turn him away from the fire. The other two seem to be ok. We shall see what Hunter thinks when he looks at this."

"What about sound recorders?" came a voice back on the radio.

"Oh, yeah, I got them here. They snap on the top of each camera and are 360 degree mics. Take the orange wire from the main feed that is not being used and plug in to the back of them."

Hunter was moving up from the campfire and flipped open his phone. He pressed a button, "Hey, Dave, how is it going? Everything is ok there?

"Yeah, no problems. Just sitting here scanning. I don't see anything on my end that shows any readings except what you had when you placed those recorders to start."

"Remember, the story is that late tonight Eunice will rise from her grave in Jackson and visit her father's grave here in the form of a mist. He is supposed to move up out of the grave to meet her, they embrace for a short time and then they return to their resting places."

"Yeah, well, I am sitting here waiting. Glad you are paying for this nonsense and not me. Like that is gonna happen."

"Ya never know it might and if it does not, I'd like to be able to prove to people by film that it did not happen."

Hunter walked over toward the vehicles and Jemma as Victoria and the two deputies came around the house.

"Did you want cameras in the house?" asked Victoria of Hunter while placing a hand in the middle of his back and moving her fingertips up and down.

"No, not this time at least. I think if there is going to be any action it will be outside of the house or in and near the barn area. The house itself is not of an era to contain anything and I am not sure looking at the inside of it with all the wallboard down in piles, etc. that it is safe to walk around in there. So, everybody, gather 'round, please."

Chapter 25

Hunter turned and then made a motion toward the fire. As Clark and Julia started up with two lawn chairs in hand, they were followed by two other people.

"Ok, we will split into two teams of three. We have two less-experienced people here tonight in Jack and Ed but they are investigators in their own right and I am glad they are here. I will lead one team and Victoria will lead the other. And on my team I will have Jemma and Jack. Hmm… Jack and Jemma went up the hill to fetch a pail… oh yeah, never mind… and, of course, that leaves Chandra and Ed to go with Victoria. My team will take the house and, like I said before, be careful in the house. We will not spend much time in there tonight. That leaves the barn for Victoria and her crew. Sweep your area good for EMF and then set up and do an EVP session. Then break it down into a hack box session. Do the hack in two different locations. Jack, you and Ed have audio recorders and a k-2 meter and you know how to use them. Any questions at all?"

They all looked at one another, shrugged their shoulders and, by that time, Clark and Julia had arrived.

"Ok, Victoria, you guys head to the barn. We will meet back here. Sweep it inside and out and don't go up top. Anybody. That floor is no good up in there."

Hunter turned to Julia and Clark.

"This is Sam and Betsy, friends of ours, and they wanted to watch with us. Is that ok?" asked Clark.

"Yeah, sure, the more the merrier. Another set of eyes is good. So, here is the layout of the farm on this monitor and the other monitor is of the cemetery at Reynolds Road. If you see anything, just use this walkie-talkie and give me a shout. Victoria or I will respond. Also, there are read-outs printing on devices here and at the cemetery. Don't worry about that. It is time and date stamped so we can use it with any other evidence that might occur at the time. Any questions from you folks?"

With no questions, Hunter moved with his group toward the house. He pulled out his Mel-meter and swept the area in front of him as he moved. He walked past the IR camera on the west side of the house, made an ape face into it and moved on by.

Dave was standing at the cemetery, sipping on the last bit of Mickey D's coffee he had, was approached by a young couple.

"Hi, what are you doing?" asked the man with a smile. He was a tall man with well-kept hair and a broad smile.

"Well, I am monitoring the cemetery for any paranormal occurrences such as electromagnetic fluctuations. Also, there are audio recorders set all over the area as well as motion monitors some with IR trip cameras; there are laser beams that disseminate into patterns in case something walks across it that can't be seen by the naked eye; and I am filming it all with this infrared camera at the same time."

"So, you think the ghosts will meet up out here as the tale says?" asked the lady. She was a bit shorter than the man; slim with long black hair and very red lipstick.

"We shall see. If it happens, we will be the first to know and we will have it up on YouTube by tomorrow night. That is for sure," smiled David.

"Well, we have not lived here long. Came from Ohio and we just thought we would stop and see for ourselves when we read the piece in the paper. Are you here by yourself?" asked the man.

"I am here alone; the rest of the team is down the road at the old Crouch property where the murders took place. They are hoping on the night of the anniversary something may come out to play and they will get some pics and EVPS."

"I am sorry… what are EVPS?" asked the woman.

"Electronic Voice Phenomenon. The audio recorder will, at times, pick up voices out of our hearing range digitally and then, when we replay them, they are presented back in an area where we can hear them. Some are plain, some are not so plain but it is good evidence especially when you can get direct answers to the questions you have asked," said David.

Two cars pulled off to the side of Reynolds Road. The occupants emerged and walked across the road to the fence of the cemetery. They stopped on the outside looking in and then started snapping pictures moving up and down the fence but not entering.

"I think we shall go do the same if you will excuse us," said the man.

"Sure, and have a good night folks," said David smiling and waving as they moved off to the front of the cemetery.

Victoria had walked to the back of the barn and was standing there near an old cobblestone wall. Chandra walked up next to her and said, "I can feel it. Can you?"

Victoria nodded her head and looked back at Ed. He was bringing up the rear, sweeping as he had been shown with the K-2 meter. The wall was over head high and had, at one time, been the back wall of the barn. Only half of the original barn was standing. The back half was gone except for the cobblestone walls. As he neared the last one-fourth of the length of the wall, his K-2 shot up all the way to orange, the highest reading it could show. He stopped and, holding it very gingerly, he looked at Victoria as if to say now what do I do?

Victoria pulled out her Mel-meter; a device used for checking EMF which is basically what the K-2 meter does but it has no scale for recording how much EMF is there. The Mel-meter has a scale and ranges can be reset into it to go very high if necessary.

"Point zero one," she said, "Now zero point 5, now one point two." She kept on moving and the meter suddenly went down. Chandra reached up with a large black marker and marked a stone in the wall where the EMF had radiated the highest.

"Maybe we can come back here in the daylight in a week or so and check this spot out."

All three stood snapping pictures with their cameras. Then they moved around the east side of the barn toward the door that opens into the old barn bottom itself. The inside of the barn on the bottom was supported with old post and beams - some looking like railroad ties. At some point in its use, the floor had been covered in concrete wall-to-wall and small pens had been made on both sides to house animals. The center was open to the top of the barn where one could have reached up with a fork and pulled down hay for feeding and straw for bedding.

Victoria stopped again as the K-2 meter went off in the doorway. She held up a hand holding Ed to the outside of the barn as it again went to orange. She again pulled out her Mel and got similar readings as before. She walked out of the barn toward the field to the east picking up EMF readings as she went. She stopped at the field for it was the property line but then followed it back to the barn and back inside again.

"I can sense something but I am not sure what and I am wondering if we have some ley lines to the east here that is giving us some readings?" quizzed Chandra.

"Hmm… that's a good question. I don't know nor do I know how to measure for them, do you?" asked Victoria.

"No, not really unless Hunter has an idea."

"We will ask him on break," said Victoria.

"What did we find, ladies?" asked Ed.

"It might be what is known as a ley line but we can't be sure. It is like a strong energy strip in the earth due to electromagnetic force from maybe the poles of the earth," said Chandra moving inside. As she started to move down the center of the barn to the back, a shadow crossed over in front of the back wall blotting out the small reflection of light that shown in from a window above. She instinctively raised her camera and snapped off a picture then looked in the back screen of the camera to see if she had gotten anything. There, on the bottom right, was a partial black splotch as if something had retreated from left to right. She put her audio recorder down on top of a fence rail for a pen and pulled out her Mel-meter.

"Is there anyone here who wishes to talk to us? We mean you no harm. If you step up and tell us your name or whisper it into one of the small red lights of the recorders we have set out, we may be able to hear what you have to say later."

"Can I take it that there was something that crossed the back wall of the barn then and that is why my entire body is goose flesh at this time?" asked Ed.

"Well, I thought I saw something. Did you, Victoria?" asked Chandra.

"No, I was fidgeting with my camera at the time and not looking up. I am sorry."

"Ed, just because we saw something blot out the light there could be some logical explanation for it and the goose flesh is quite common on your first investigation. It is from your mind cooking up things and making you feel that way. Just take a deep breath like in Zen, then concentrate."

"Yeah, I suppose you are right. I have seen Jacob several times out here. He loves this barn and his cow."

"Where is he when you have encountered him at night?" asked Victoria.

"I have seen him in the barn twice and thought maybe I saw him carrying a lantern from the house to the barn once. But in here he was over on the right side in that last large pen. There is a door, if you look closely, in the back corner of the pen and it leads outside."

"Please, we mean you no harm. We would just like to ask you some questions; understand what it is you do here on the farm. Are you a farmhand?" asked Victoria.

It was quiet in the barn and they thought they heard a noise at the right side inside the barn.

"If that was you, can you do that noise again or give us a sign of your presence? We would very much like to talk to you. Please, come forward," said Victoria.

Chandra moved ever-so-slightly to her left and up the center past Ed. She stopped in her tracks and looked to her right. "I know you are here. I can feel you. We can't see you as well as you might us, that is why we act so strange toward you. Please, come out of the dark corner and talk to us."

She stopped and bent her head down looking into the dark abyss between her and the floor. She could see in her mind the face of a bearded man with piercing eyes and frowning.

"I can see you fine now. My name is Chandra and what is your name? Are you, by any chance, Jacob Crouch?"

"Jacob, this is a very nice farm you have here. Please tell us all about it. I have to believe it is a hard job keeping this place in working order. Do you have any hands to help you in your daily tasks?"

Ed swallowed hard and looked first in Chandra's direction then in Victoria's. Satisfied that they had said there piece he decided he would try.

"Jacob? It's me Ed Dwyer. Deputy Ed Dwyer. You and I have met a few times over the years. I have brought these two nice ladies out to meet you. They would like to ask you a few questions; maybe talk to ya."

Chandra reached up to the post next to her that was supporting the upper floor. Using her knuckles she rapped on the post twice.

"Jacob, if you are here could you make a noise like that for me? Once for yes and twice for no. That way you don't have to talk if you don't want to."

From the back of the barn came a small knock.

"Thank you, Jacob. It is so nice to meet you. I am Chandra and the lady behind me is Victoria and, of course, you know Deputy Dwyer."

Another knock resounded from the back corner.

"Do you like it here on the farm, Jacob? I have to believe after all these years you have to know that you are dead and things are just not right, is that true?

Knock from the corner.

"That is good, Jacob. I am going to guess that maybe you don't know how you died? Is that true?"

Two knocks.

Ed Dwyer was incredulous. He was not sure what to make of this but it was almost for sure something intelligent making the noise in the corner. He strained to see in the darkness, trying to make out any movement or form.

Victoria looked towards Ed and said, "Ed, whatever you do don't shine your flashlight towards the corner. That will be the end of the communication if you do and you will see nothing."

Dwyer looked at her and shook his head in the semi-darkened barn. He turned off the flashlight at that point and put it in his pocket.

"Do you know you were murdered, Jacob?"

Knock from the far corner.

"Do you know who it was that murdered you?"

Two knock's from the back corner.

"Ah… well, that is why we are here. To find out, Jacob .Believe it or not, it has been 127 years since you died. The crime was never solved, Jacob, and that is why we are here. Victoria and Hunter, whom you will meet later, are special detectives. They work on unsolved cases sometimes with very good results. They are here to start the investigation with you. It would be nice if you found some way to communicate with Hunter when he comes down later."

"Jacob, hi. I'm Victoria. Did you know that three other people were killed with you that night?"

A knock came from the back of the barn.

"Then you know that Henry White, Eunice, and Moses Polley were killed the same night and time that you were shot and killed also in their sleep."

One knock from the back of the barn.

"Good, Jacob. Are you happy we are going to investigate this?"

One knock response.

"Thank you, Jacob, and maybe, if we can get this all out into the open and get it solved, people will leave you and your family in peace. My friend, Hunter, wants to put up a headstone for you. Would you be glad to have one?"

One knock response.

Chandra wondered in her head now if there was a response or if this was a mere coincidence. They had not been asking negative questions so she decided to try it out to see.

"Jacob, I am confused about the young boy who slept upstairs in your house. Of course, he was not harmed but I can't remember his first name was it Fred? Yeah… maybe Fred Boles?"

The barn was quiet and there was no response. Chandra shook her head. She was not sure now if it was an answer to questions or just a happenstance. Had they mind matrixed the whole thing?

"I am not sure of this being credible evidence, Victoria. I suggest we sweep the barn and let's try something else."

She turned to Ed who was transfixed by the whole ordeal and she grabbed his K-2 meter. She walked toward the back of the barn and set it on another rail. She passed her cell phone in front of it and the lights lit up on the front about halfway but not all orange. She pressed the direct connect button on the side and it beeped sending the K-2 meter all the way past orange to red.

"Yeah!" Came a voice out of the dark and Ed jumped almost out of his pants.

Chandra walked back to her position and keyed the phone again and said, "Sorry Hunter I was just making sure the K-2 was working properly."

"No problem," said the voice back on her phone. She stopped and turned now facing the back of the barn.

"Jacob, there is a small gray-like box I set up on the fence rail back there on the pen to the left. If you step up to it and run your hand over the front of it the lights should shine."

They waited no response.

"Jacob, why have you stopped communicating with us if that was you? In order for us to believe it, you will have to continue to communicate in some way."

Still no response. They stood there for a long time waiting for something to happen in the dark. Anything that would lead them to believe in the original session.

"So what do we do now?" asked Ed, finally cutting through the dark and the silence with his statement.

"Well, for whatever reason Jacob does not want to talk anymore and really we can't say why because we don't know why they come and go like this," said Victoria.

"Let's leave Jacob and company in peace and move on to another place, see what time it is and we may want to start up. The storm sounds soon," said Chandra.

The trio snapped a few pictures in the dark and then moved back to the door, exited the barn to the south moving out past the silo and up the incline. They headed towards the campfire on the right for some warmth.

As they moved out of the barn, a small pinpoint of light in the back pen grew till it formed a man. He was about six foot tall with brown hair parted on the left and combed neatly to the right. He had on a heavy wool flannel shirt and brown pants. He was scowling as he moved to the door watching the women go up the small hill.

"Damn cunts!" he whispered. He turned not noticing anything else except that the other entity had fled at his presence. Moving back past the first post on the right he did not notice the small audio recorder red light right next to him. He walked up to and then through the back wall disappearing into the night. An older man then reappeared in the corner. It was the spirit of Jacob. He looked carefully around and then moving toward the audio recorder that he saw he stopped in front. What was it they said? Talk into the red light and we will be able to hear you. Jacob leaned down and spoke into the red light and said, "Be careful of him. He is mad!"

Chapter 26

1884

Byron Crouch and Daniel Holcomb had spent the better part of the morning discussing the case with Sheriff Winney and his deputies. The gist of the conversation revolved around the continued use of the Pinkertons and if the reward should be increased. Daniel was against increasing the reward and Byron was for more Pinkerton involvement. They had left and had lunch with Edith and Judd; then went to the Hurd house where he spent the afternoon engaged with business.

He did, however, go back to the dinner to meet Beverly Snow an insurance agent who had all the insurance on the Holcomb's' and their properties.

"Hello, Daniel," said a woman walking up to his table.

Daniel stood and held the chair out for the woman. Her name was Beverly Snow. She was in her mid-thirties, quiet, petite with a thin face and a pointy chin. Her hair was a sandy blond and was up in a bun under a hat. Around her shoulders was a hooded cloak. The afternoon's weather had turned frightful and the snow was now falling consuming all in its wake.

"I am glad you could come. I was hoping that you received my message, Beverly. I do wish to try to transact some business with you," said Daniel smiling at her across the table.

"That is good for me then. What is it that I can do for you?"

A server came to the table. Daniel ordered hot tea for them with some scones and jelly on the side. The server complied and as they sat eating their food Daniel finally spoke up.

"Beverly, I did not want to bring this up at all but I feel I must. It is a time when things are not going well for me and I really can use some money. I did not want to do this too early and I know it will cast suspicion on me from all groups, but they have to understand it was done to help out my family and, well, now seems the time."

"Daniel, I can lend you some on the insurance policy if you like but I don't know if that will be enough to really help you. I would have to go back and recalculate the premiums."

"Loan me off of it. What kind of silly talk is that? Jacob is dead, damn it! I have paid on that insurance policy on him for over ten years. I should be getting the full amount from it and I must say I am not only surprised at you for not contacting me about this after his death, but I am beginning to wonder if you were going to bring it up at all."

Beverly stopped in mid-bite of a jelly-laden scone, put it down and wiped her mouth.

She chewed rather nervously and then said to Daniel, "Whatever are you talking about?"

"The policy that I took out on Jacob back in the 70's. He is dead and I am the beneficiary. I am entitled to that money!" he said leaning over the table now with a drawn brow and a frown on his face. She could see under his collar that the veins were now bulging in his neck and his face was starting to redden.

"But Daniel, there is no policy on Jacob, with you or anybody else as beneficiary, regardless of what Jacob may have told you. He did not believe in insurance policies. I could never get him to sign up for one. Why on earth would you have an idea otherwise?"

Daniel pounded his fist on the table making Beverly jump and the tea cups rattle. "I bought the damn policy on Jacob! Don't you remember? I have been paying on it all these years. Remember I came to you and told you to drop my policy and keep his, Jacob's, enforced several years ago."

This time it was Beverly's turn to be mad and she yelled back at him. "You dunce! You told me to drop Jacob's and keep yours in force and that is exactly what I did," her voice went almost to a whimper at the end realizing that one or both of them had made a mistake, a large mistake. She looked up at Daniel and all the color had now drained from his face. Even though it was January and cold, his brow was sweating profusely. He balled up his hands into fists as he shook all over. Again, he pounded the table once more.

"Bah!" he cried out realizing the implications of the statement she had just made. He jumped from his seat and moved to the window taking a napkin with him. He stared out into the street for a long time slowly wiping his brow of sweat.

Beverly sat there for the longest time wondering what she should do. Should she go over and comfort him or just leave him? And now she was curious about one thing, who really killed Jacob and was there a hidden motive that no one but herself knew? This frightened her and she was not sure if she was in danger if all that was coursing through her mind were true. She finally turned and moved toward Daniel. She put a hand on his shoulder. He turned his head away from her still breathing heavily. She dropped her head, turned and went out the door placing her hooded cloak on.

Daniel stared at her outside as she disappeared into the snowstorm. Finally he turned, dropped some money on the table and left. He moved across the street and down to the Hurd House. He stepped to the counter in the sitting area and rang the bell.

The clerk came out from a door just as Sheriff Winney came from the bar area. "Staying the night, Daniel? Gonna be quite a storm it looks like."

"Yes please, sir, a room. I am not feeling well and will not travel again until morning. I wish to merely go up, lay down and rest some. Please, make sure I am not disturbed."

"Bad news or something, Daniel?" asked the sheriff.

"No, it's just this business has me on edge and I need to just spend some time by myself, do some thinking and maybe some sleeping."

Winney patted him on the back as Daniel took the room key and moved away almost in a stupor. The sheriff watched as he moved away and rubbed his chin in deep thought. This morning he was in good spirits, anxious to end the investigation with arrests and to have lunch with Judd and his daughter. Now it looks as if he has lost his last friend. What would make a man turn so in such a short time?

The sheriff shrugged his shoulders and moved on over across the street. There he met Judd and Edith packing the Cutter for the return trip home.

"Seems Daniel is not feeling well. He just got a room at the Hurd house. I think something is ailing him. Maybe you should check on him before you go."

"I'll go see Judd; you finish loading the stuff," said Edith.

She moved across the street with a shawl up alongside of her face fending off the wind driven snow in the air. She walked into the Hurd house and up to the clerk. "My father has checked in - Daniel Holcomb. Can you tell me what room he is in?"

"One Twenty just down the hall and on the left, ma'am."

Edith turned, moved down the hall and knocked on the door.

"Go away! Leave me alone, please!" came her father's voice from inside.

"Father it is me Edith please let me in." She waited a few moments and the door lock snapped and it opened to reveal Daniel with his shoes off and the bed obviously had been laid upon.

"Father, are you ok?" she asked.

Daniel tried to cover his dismay and said. "Just a little tired. Thought I might spend the night here and come home in the morning. Just want to lay down and sleep, nothing more. Got a lot on my mind with everything going on and, well, it would be nice to have an evening of solitude."

She smiled at him and said, "Well, that is probably best for you. Go ahead. I shall tell mother you are fine and will be home tomorrow. Now get some, rest lock the door and sleep well," she said planting a kiss on his cheek. He smiled at the kiss. He truly loved his daughter and Susan. They were the center of his world. All he ever did was for them so they would have all they want and more.

The cutter slid along the country over drifts of snow lightly lifting the sleigh off the ground at times. This was a fun ride for Judd and Edith and they enjoying the snowfall against the bleak back drop of the winter woods and pastures of the area. Sledding up Horton Road, they arrived at Holcomb's farm. Judd steered the sleigh into the farm lot and up to the door in the back. Judd climbed down as Fred and Charles came out to help unload.

Judd then turned the sleigh and headed up the road to the Crouch farm telling Edith that he would send James Foy back for his horse and saddle in the barn.

Edith moved into the kitchen. She removed her boots, put on her shoes and took off her cloak. She turned to Fred and asked, "Where is mother?"

"In her room. She went up there saying she had a headache after you left. She locked the door and we have not seen her since."

Edith, finding this strange, turned and went to her mother's bedroom door.

"Mother, are you asleep?"

There was no response.

"Mother!" She knocked on the door this time with no response; all seemed quiet on the other side.

"Mother, it is me, Edith. Please let me in. I am home from shopping." No response. She turned to Fred and Charles who looked at her strangely.

"Are you sure she is in there? You are not putting up a trick on me now are you?"

"No, honest," said Fred. "She told us that if anybody came to inquire about her that we should say that she was indisposed, take their name and tell them she would get back to them at a later date. No one has been here but us. It has been quiet. I once came up and tried to rouse her but there was no sound; just wanted to see if she needed anything. I just said to Charlie here that it is very strange to have been so quiet all that time and then not at least acknowledge my presence at her door."

Edith turned to the door and this time banged much louder and longer than before so as to make sure she could be heard; even Fred banged after her. "Mother, please, unlock the door! You are scaring us!" There, of course, was no response.

Edith turned and moved out to see if Judd might still be there but the sleigh was gone. She did, however, see James Foy walking into the lot for Judd's horse. She quickly ran to the back door, threw it open and yelled, "Mr.

Foy! Could you please come in here for a moment?"

James Foy stopped in his tracks and moved back to the house smiling at Edith. He thought she was pretty and always had an eye for her. He stopped at the door and took his hat off smiling.

"Yes, Miss Edith, what may I do for you?"

"Oh, come in here, James, please and close the door. We are letting out the heat and the cold in."

"Whatever is the matter with you?" again quizzed James.

Edith grabbed his hand and pulled him along behind her rushing to her mother's bedroom door. "It's mother! She will not answer the door and it is locked. I am afraid that something bad has happened to her! Oh please, get the door open, James!"

James Foy stepped up to the door with his six foot, one hundred and ninety pound frame and knocked on the door.

"Mrs. Holcomb, this is James Foy, ma'am. If you are able, could you open the door or at least respond so Edith knows you are all right?" There was no answer. Foy turned, looked down the hall and then at Edith. "You are sure she is in there?"

"Yes, the boys say she locked herself in right after we left for town with instructions not to be disturbed."

"Are we not then disturbing her?"

"Well, you would at least think she would say I am not feeling well go away and leave me alone or come to the door and explain herself."

Foy turned again, sensing the problem now more acutely, he banged with his fist three times hard.

"Mrs. Holcomb, Susan, it is James Foy, ma'am, we are just concerned that you are ok. Can you please at least answer us, ma'am?" There came no response. This time Foy banged even harder, "Susan, please, open this door or I shall be forced to break it in."

No response came from behind the door. James moved back from the door, took one of his large muscular shoulders and made a run at the door pushing it inwards. He stopped inside the door seeing Susan Holcomb on the bed naked with a small sheet wrapped around her chest only. He then felt the rush of Edith pass him before he could turn and stop her.

"Mother!, cried Edith in anguish as she rushed to her side holding up the lifeless head. "Mother!"

James Foy moved beside Edith and felt for a pulse on Susan's neck. He did not find any and knew the coldness of the body meant death. Edith, now in tears, looked up at him and he shook his head no as she jumped into his arms and cried then nearly passed out herself. James picked her up and moved her to a chair in the room. He turned and covered the body up with a blanket as to hide the nakedness from anyone else that may enter the room.

"Charlie?" yelled Foy as Charles Andrews came flying into the room.

"Get a horse and go into Jackson. Find Mr. Holcomb and tell him Mrs. Holcomb is dead and he needs to come home."

"Yeah, right away!" yelled Charlie.

As he sped out of the room, James grabbed him from behind by the ear and pulled him back. "Snowy and icy out there, boy. Hurry but not too fast. Don't want to bury you or the damn horse, got it?"

"Yeah, James, I will be careful. I promise."

As Charlie ran out the door, Foy bellowed again. This time even Edith in her despair jumped. "Fred!" he yelled.

Fred Lounsberry came into the room quickly, "Yeah, James?" he said skidding to a halt in front of Foy.

"I want you to go up to the Crouch farm and get Mr. Judd. Tell him he has to come down here, that Susan has died and I need him here. Go now, boy, and hurry!"

With that, Fred sped out of the room. By this time, Charlie had caught up a horse and, with no saddle or bridle, he kicked it in the side and sped out of the farm onto Horton Road towards Jackson. He did not even realize that he forgot a hat, a coat and gloves. The news had unnerved him so he really did not take into consideration for the horse or the snow and ice. He finally reached Main Street in Jackson. Riding down, he stopped a man on the street, Hank Pearl, and asked him if he had seen Mr. Holcomb in town today. He said he thought he was in the Hurd House. Charlie pulled the horse's head around and made for the Hurd House. He jumped down and ran inside. There he found Daniel Holcomb just returned from the restaurant down the street and engaged in a conversation with Sheriff Winney.

"Dan, you got to come home now. It's awful, please!" yelled Charlie tugging on Daniel's coat sleeve.

Daniel Holcomb turned around, looked at Charlie and said, "Whatever is wrong, Charlie?"

"Mrs. Holcomb… she is dead. They found her dead in her room. You gotta come!"

Daniel took a moment for the impact of the message to sink in. He started to shake somewhat and sweat began to form on his brow as his smile faded and his face sagged. The blood drained out of his face. Sheriff Winney came to his side and held him up ushering him over to a chair in the waiting area. Byron Crouch came in and dusted himself off from the snowfall outside. He looked up in time to see the Sheriff help Daniel down and into a chair. Wondering what had happened to Daniel, he moved across the room bumping into some people and excusing himself as he made his way toward the sheriff and Daniel.

"Daniel, what on earth? Are you ok?" he asked arriving at the scene.

"Susan," was all he said as tears began to stream down his face and his body shook uncontrollably.

Byron looked to the Sheriff who said, hanging his head with a steady hand on Daniel's shoulder, "They have found your sister dead in her bedroom. I don't know any more than that."

Byron stood up straight and looked at Charlie. "Get the cutter down at the livery. Get them to hook it up and then bring it down here, if you please." He then looked over at the doorman and said, "Please, fetch a bottle of brandy so we can fortify Mr. Daniel for his trip home."

Chapter 27

2010

Hunter, Jack and Jemma headed to the front of the house. "Here, Jack, if you look in the front on the ground you can see where the original house sat by the slope away from it that is still left. We have prodded and probed and found numerous cobblestones suitable for foundation along this slope all the way around the present house."

Jack looked down and he could see what Hunter was talking about. "What you are saying is that the present house sits inside of the old house so to speak?"

"Yeah, that is correct or at least I think I have it correct. When we take a break after a while I will show you some pictures of the old house. Don't know when they were taken but there was electricity running in the back of the house. That large tree to the west of the house can be seen in that picture and we know it was here at the time of the fire. We have taken samples from the tree and found charring amongst the remains. Also, you can see in the daylight how the tree was damaged on one side the way the bark runs as if it was singed hot at one time."

"Where was the railroad?"

"We have found that to the west and north of the house. If you go down in that tree line to the east you will find the old bed and remains of what once was a stone wall. In the back of the house, further back than the camp fire, was a small rural rail stop that did not have a depot or anything. The farmers would get on the train here and go to Jackson and on to points east and north or south towards Ft. Wayne. I would have supposed there was also an area for them to load cattle if they wished and maybe even a small spur for loading and unloading of cattle cars, although the map of the railroad does not really show this."

The group now moved to the west of the present house and stopped in the yard between the house and the old tree.

"Was this tree around at the time of the killings?" asked Jemma.

"I am not sure, hon. It is hard to tell. We would have to do core samples all the way through and send it to Michigan State University to find out and, really, I am not into spending the money to see because it has nothing to do with the original crime with the exception of being there."

Jack turned on his K-2 meter and moved toward the tree looking for anything that might trigger it. Jemma moved to the side of the present house and set her recorder in the window sill facing outward.

Hunter turned on his recorder and set it on the ground on a stone pointing upward and north. Then he took a second one out and moved toward the back side, found another window and set up a recorder facing out. He took out a third recorder, turned it also to record and placed it on his arm with Velcro.

"Hello. I am Hunter Ross. With me is Jemma and Jack. Jack is a deputy for the Jackson County Sheriff's department. We are here to investigate a crime that happened in 1883 on this date, November 21st. Four people were killed in a house that used to stand here. They were Mr. Jacob Crouch, his daughter Eunice, her husband Henry White, and a traveler who had stopped to spend the night with them, Moses Polley. Did you know any of them?"

There was silence and then Jemma caught a small blip on her K-2 meter. She brought it to Hunter's attention as it jumped up and down barely giving a reading.

"Follow it and see if it is close or far away. Maybe you are picking up something strong from a different direction. Jack watch for cold spots," said Hunter now snapping pictures and handing Jack a temperature probe.

"So somewhere near the side of the existing house is where the man stood guard watching the killing inside?" asked Jemma.

"Yeah, you are maybe close to spot on. Can you feel the spot where he stood or in your mind with your eyes closed see what he saw?"

"I am not that developed yet mind-wise but maybe Chandra will be able to do that."

"If there is anyone here who would like to talk to us about the murders, please feel free to talk into the red lights. We would like to know your name and why you are here on this property."

"Do you know anything about the people who were killed here in 1883?" asked Jemma.

Jack walked up to Hunter and said, "I don't know what to ask. What should I do, or say, or maybe not say?"

"Well, Jack, there is a theory and, believe me, this field abounds with theories. Most of them have little to back them up but one is that you never know who is talking to you so we very seldom use any names for them. Let them tell you who they are. Suppose, for example, if I asked 'Is Shakespeare here?' you might get a yes answer. But is it really him or just a spirit on the other side who is taking a chance at being heard or to just talk? They will be anyone I want. You have to verify that is who you are talking to. So you need to think out your questions just like you would on a case you were investigating for the department."

"You mean, two people can play good cop bad cop?"

"Tori and I have done that many times with good results. Sometimes you need to rattle their cage on the other side; get their attention. Why should they talk to you? Because you are a nice guy or because you have something to say that they may take great umbrage? That is, don't go out and intimidate just for the sake of intimidating. If you say or promise something then you have to stick to it. I am out here, just like you, on patrol trying to get to the bottom of the problem by getting not people but spirits and the right spirits to talk to me. I can't run them in if they don't cooperate so I have to use great amounts of psychology to get them to answer."

"Sounds complicated."

"Really, it is not much different than what you do on a daily basis in your job. Just hang with us and listen. When you think the time is right and you have something pertinent to say, then blurt it out."

Victoria and her group came around the corner at the back of the house.

"How is it going?" she asked walking up to Hunter and planting a kiss on his cheek.

"I don't know if we have much yet but I think this side of the house bears some more investigation. Chandra, this is the place; near this window where the lookout stood and watched the killings that night. I would like if you could get a read on it and maybe come up with an exact a spot as you can."

Chandra bowed her head deep in thought, not really a trance, as she tried to see and feel what she could in her mind. She was not a medium nor had she ever channeled. She would, at times, just get feelings and impressions in her mind. Moving around some more, she tried to bring up any feeling and finally looked up at Hunter in exasperation. "I'm sorry, Hunter. I don't feel a thing here but in the barn I could feel quite a bit. I think we had some real good things going on in there."

"Well, we shall move to the barn this time and see what it is that we can get out of all of this," said Hunter.

"I think we will head over to the equipment to see how they are doing and if everything is running ok and then maybe take a peek inside the house," said Victoria.

Hunter lead the way down past the campfire and off into the barn. There he stopped and moved quietly in the dark. "Let's just sit quiet for a while and see if anything comes out to play. Jemma, you right here next to the first pen on the left. Jack, you over by the east door and I am going back into the dark as far as I can and watch forward."

As Hunter moved toward the very back interior of the bottom of the barn, he placed two audio recorders: one on the left and one on the right. He moved back to a pen gate, around the gate and set his third recorder up on the fence. He then leaned in on the gate and looked towards the front of the barn where he could make out Jemma and Jack. He could see Jack moving his K-2 around to no particular light signal and Jemma just leaned against the pen. As she listened, she closed her eyes to deprive her sense of sight to help enhance her other senses.

There was suddenly a click up in the forward manger next to where Jack stood at the east door.

"Was that you, Jack?" asked Hunter

"No, I was wondering what that was," said Jack.

"Ok buddy, first rule of investigating: don't wonder. When not sure, investigate just like you would if you were looking around for a fugitive in here. Take pics in that area quickly after the occurrence."

Jack's camera flashed several times in each direction of where he was standing. With each flash he said the word "Flash" preceding each picture thus alerting fellow investigators of the impending flash.

"If there was someone here who made that noise, can you make yourself known to us? We would like to just talk with you. That is why we are here. Want to get to know you very well and just talk; be sociable," said Hunter. There was silence.

"Why are you hiding? I can feel you. We mean you no harm. We would love to talk to you. What is keeping you back from us?" said Jemma.

"My name is Hunter, the young lady here is Jemma, and the gentleman over by the door is Jack. He is a deputy sheriff. He has been to this property a few times and, Jacob, you may have even spoken to him."

More silence ensued. No noise save a few errant voices from the camp fire outside and an occasional car moving up and down Horton Road. The night was clear, not a cloud in the sky, crisp and cool but inside the barn there was strange warmth generated about. Even though it was cool, it was still bearable and, of course, the barn did keep the night dampness off of you. The wind had ceased with the setting of the sun and all was quiet in the world.

"Is there anybody here that knows about the Crouch murders on this farm in 1883? If so, do you know who did this? Do you have any proof or can you tell us who it was and maybe why they did it? Was it just for land, money, the combination of the two? I can see no other reason in this case other than to kill for money," said Jack. Hunter looked at him, amused that he came out of his shell so well. He knew he would get the knack of this.

"Jacob, if you can hear me, I promise that I will find out who killed you. It may be too late for justice but at least the world will know if it was Judd or Daniel or someone else… maybe your son from Texas? I am gonna smear them all over the state and beyond. Any reputation they had will be destroyed. I am going to solve this; I swear to you, Jacob. Any help anyone can give me by talking into the red lights it would be appreciated."

With that they ended this session in the barn and moved back toward Victoria's group. They were in the process of setting up the boom box with auxiliary speakers so as to set the mood of the area as it was on that fateful night in 1883.

"Got it all set up, Tori?" asked Hunter.

"Yeah, they are putting the last speaker in the barn if it makes any sense to have anything there."

"You may have been right about the house. There really does not seem to be much action in there. I even tried the basement."

"There is a basement? Somehow that escaped me. That seems like a more logical place in the whole house to really get something. It is probably part of the old basement in some way shape or form."

"Well, maybe if we don't get it this time we can give it a try next time."

"Yeah, well, I am going to drive to the cemetery to see how Curt is doing on his watch there."

Hunter moved slowly back towards the car and then up to the TV screens. He stopped and scanned the printer updates and found nothing to report. He looked at Jonathan and Abigail and said, "How is it going, folks?"

"We have not seen anything but I think we have the hang of it. This is kind of exciting in a way. It is mesmerizing to say the least. You get locked into a camera angle and then you just sit and stare at it," said Abigail.

"I am going to head out to the cemetery to Mr. Davis and see how things are going there, I shall be back. Victoria is going to set up a type of investigative tool we call an era cue. In this case, she is going to try and duplicate the sound of the storm the night the murders happened. We find, at times, if you can play music or something of this nature that the spirit can identify with that they will come out and meet you. So when it starts, keep your eyes peeled for anything."

Hunter moved away quickly to the car and drove on back down Horton Road to the corner at the cemetery. As he drove up, he saw several cars along Reynolds Road parked and people standing at the fence looking and watching with some snapping pictures. There also were some cars at the church and a group around Curt. He drove over to the church and walked up to the crowd of girls around Curt. Pretty young girls, all giggling at almost every comment he made hanging on his every word.

"Looks as if a rescue is not needed, old boy," said Hunter smirking at the girls as he moved in close to Dave. Dave stood up straight as if he had been caught with his hand in the cookie jar.

"Everything is going well," said Dave.

"Yes, I can see that from here," said Hunter smirking again gazing at the girls. "Are these members of you fan club?" he asked.

"Uh… no, these girls are the Spring Arbor Cheerleaders and they came out here to bring me hot chocolate and cookies. Wasn't that nice of them?" said Dave clearing his throat.

Hunter looked with a wry smile upon the group of young pretty beaming faces. "Yes, very nice I must say," as one of the girls in the group giggled.

"Well, I can see you are in no distress and actually are keeping warm so I guess its back to the farm I go. I take it you really are very interested in staying here and doing further research on this rather broad subject?"

"Well, uh… er," stammered Dave.

"Say no more, old man. In the sake of science, we all must make sacrifices," with that Hunter leaned in close to his ear. "If you blow this, old man, I will cap your ass." He started to move away. "Thanks, ladies, for looking out after our colleague."

Jemma, Chandra and Victoria walked around sweeping the area with a K-2 meter, a MEL-meter and an audio recorder. The sounds of thunder and the crash of lightening was everywhere on the farm along with some background wind noises and rain pouring very hard. The three had reached the west side of the house near the old tree when there was a voice between Victoria and Jemma that said, "Chandra."

All three stopped because all three had heard it.

"Play back the audio, Chandra, and see if we picked that up. All three of us cannot be accused of hearing things at the same time."

They stood in the dark with the pseudo-raging storm all around them playing the recorder over and over. They even used headphones twice but could not pick up the voice they were all sure that they heard.

"Mark that spot, Chandra, and we will put it up on the studio next week to see if there is something in the background that we cannot hear."

Jack had come from around the house. He and Ed had been sitting with Jonathan and Abigail watching the cameras on the DVR screen.

"Hey, we may have had something on the camera over there facing you. It looked like a shadow of a person standing next to the old tree. He even looked like he had a broad brimmed hat on."

"Ah then…" Victoria was cut short by a flash over the trees to the west and large red lightning bolt but no thunder report. All four people ducked and then jumped.

"What the fuck was that?" asked Jack scared out of his wits."

Victoria pulled out her cell and direct-connected to Hunter.

"Yeah?" came back his reply.

"You still at the cemetery?" she asked.

"Yes, why?"

"We, all four of us, just saw what looked like a red bolt of lightning toward your direction and I was just wondering if you saw it or had an explanation for it?"

"Uh…that is no to both questions. Maybe it's time to put the vodka away, Tori, and get back to work!"

"Ha! Very funny, genius. You better get back here, buster. There is some strange shit goin' on."

"Be right there, my sweet!" At that reply, Victoria crinkled her nose and stuck her tongue out at the cell as she snapped it shut and put it back in its holder. The four were now standing at the table looking at the DVR. Chandra had stopped it momentarily and was in the process of rewinding it as Hunter pulled into the farm lot.

"What's up here?" he asked.

"Well, Jack and Ed were sitting here having coffee and thought they saw a shadow person over by the old tree at approximately the same time that Jemma, Chandra and myself were standing next to it and thought we heard a voice call out Chandra's name."

"Hmmm… that is interesting," said Hunter as he reached for the large thermos and poured a small cup of coffee in a Styrofoam cup.

"There, it went past!" shouted Ed as Chandra quickly hit the stop button. She went back and then started it frame-by-frame until they had the picture up and stopped. It was grainy that way and also a bit fuzzy but, true to their word, was a shadow standing next to a tree. Chandra was just to the right of the shadow with Victoria right beside her. The shadow had the height of a full grown man in respect to the women and, as Jack had pointed out it, did appear as though he had on a broad-brimmed hat.

"God, that is the holy grail! You hardly ever catch anything like that. Very good, you two, thanks for catching that! It shall be a piece we will talk about for many years to come, I am sure," said Hunter staring at the screen in a transfixed manner.

"Well, kids, reset the cameras and let's all go to the barn for a hack box session," said Hunter finally looking away from the object and taking a large swig of the coffee he had poured.

The group once more entered the barn and spread out as before. Hunter stood with Jack and Ed showing them what the hack box was.

"The theory is that if we play a radio on AM or FM we may be able to pick up voices of spirits who want to communicate with us. I know you say 'then what about voices on the radio contaminating the session' and you are correct. Here we have a small radio we bought from Radio Shack. It is equipped with a scanner. You take the radio apart when you get it and cut the number 10 pin. This allows the radio to continually scan without stopping on a station. So you really never get more than sounds from air programs, broken words, etc. If you do get words or sentences, then you know you have something trying to communicate with you."

Hunter stepped back from the group and again retired to the far end of the barn on the enclosed side.

"Ok, now I want everyone to get comfortable and just sit still in silence for a while. That will give anything that is here time to scope us out and maybe come to us to see what this is all about."

The barn fell silent. Each person could sense themselves and the others in the dark. Each one had checked out their bearings to assure themselves where everyone was. Their senses got tense in the dark, skin on the alert for cold, ears straining to hear anything that might designate a visitor. The only thing that could be heard was an occasional cough from the camp fire and the camp fire itself crackling.

Chapter 28

1884

Daniel Holcomb was loaded aboard the cutter for the ride back to the farm. Sheriff Winney sat in his office talking to Adams.

"I see they sent for their family doctor Williams," said Winney.

"Yeah, so do we investigate this under the circumstances of the other murders or do we just let it slide as if nothing else had happened?" asked Adams.

"That is a tough call. I am thinking that we need to get Casey (The Jackson County Medical Examiner and Coroner) to come out and at least take a look at the death scene to see if we can determine anything at all. You know, as soon as this gets out the press will be hounding us for information and I guess we just can't shrug our shoulders as elected officials. Besides, we don't know the cause of death and having an investigation to do nothing else but prove that she was or was not killed will help settle the populace down," said Winney.

"Ok, I will go alert Casey and meet you back here for the trip out," said Adams downing the last bit of coffee from his cup as he stepped out into the snowy evening.

People around the area of the Holcomb's, mostly friends of the family, descended on the farmhouse to wish everyone the best and give their condolences in the face of all the family had gone through at that point. This seemed to some like a cruel blow.

The sheriff and coroner arrived at the same time. They, together with the family doctor, decided to go over the death scene before the body was cleared out. Moving into the room was the bed to the right of center with a window on that wall. A small area carpet on the floor showed no sign of struggle in the room. Everything seemed to be in its place. Dr. Williams moved to the chamber pot beside the bed and looked in making note in a small book of the fact that it was empty. Casey touched the body having pulled the sheet back from over the head. He noted no signs of a physical altercation on the body. He also noted that it was cold and some rigor had set in. Winney went over to the window and picked up a very small brown bottle on the window sill. He examined it. He opened it and sniffed at it; there was a very small amount of liquid in the bottom. He noted that it had the name of a doctor from Kalamazoo on it and it was made out to Edith.

"What do you make of this?" he asked the Medical Examiner.

"Could be just what it says, it is medicine for nerves and sleep," he said.

"Wonder if she took too much or maybe just decided to take it all and go to sleep for good?" inquired Winney.

"Not sure, but we will take it with us for further examination. I will contact the doctor and ask him," said Casey.

"I had been treating her for a heart condition for some time. She had complained some of chest pains but her last checkup showed she was fine and I did not find anything abnormal in her blood pressure or heart rate at the time," said Dr. Williams.

Williams opened one eye of the corpse and looked in. All appeared normal: no signs of being strangled or any other wild emotion such as pain showed on the face. She actually seemed very peaceful. He wondered if she had lain down to sleep and just simply died of heart failure in her sleep.

"Let's talk to Andrews and Lounsberry," said Winney.

The boys were called to the hallway door and stood looking in at the body covered by the sheet.

"Ok, tell me all you know, boys," said the sheriff.

"She went up to her room and told us not to bother her," said Fred.

"She said if anyone came to the door asking for her to tell them she was not feeling well and to tell them she would talk with them some other day," said Charles.

"Did she say in what way she was not feeling well?" asked Dr. Williams.

"No, I don't think so. It is hard to remember her exact words - only the gist of what she was telling us," said Fred as Charles nodded his head in agreement.

"So, no one saw her after that, correct?" asked Winney.

"No, sir," they both answered.

"Did anyone come in the house? Any of the family, hired hands, anything like that during the time she was up here alone?" asked Winney.

"No, Miss Edith was the first to come home and raised a fuss when she came up here to get in and the door was locked from the inside," said Fred.

"Did you hear any unusual noises from up here?" asked Casey.

Both boys shook their heads no.

"Ok, that's all for now," said Winney as he looked out in the hall at Judd Crouch.

"Judd, where were you all the time this was going on?" asked the sheriff.

"Miss Edith and I went to town in the Holcomb's cutter. She had some shopping to do. We had lunch with her father, did the shopping and returned. I took the cutter back to my place and sent James Foy down here to fetch my horse I had ridden down in the morning. Fred came and alerted me of the find. Told me Edith was in an awful state and I had better come at once."

"Fine, would you please see if Miss Edith is in any condition to talk to us at all?" asked Casey.

Judd left and then returned with Edith, holding her up as she wept and stopped in the doorway. "She does not wish to enter and I suggest you quickly make any questions you have," said Judd nodding to Edith and inferring her mental state at the time.

"Miss Edith, I am sorry for this but I was hoping you could answer a few questions," said Winney.

Edith nodded her head yes as she held a handkerchief to her nose and mouth and tears streamed down her face.

"Tell us quickly what you found when you got home and then we will not bother you anymore tonight," said Casey recognizing that she was on the verge of a nervous breakdown and possibly fainting.

She sniffed as if to clear her nose and then said.

"I came in and called her name but she did not answer. So I came up here and found that her door was locked. I asked Charles and

Fred and they told me she had been up here all afternoon and had told them she did not want to be disturbed. So, I knocked again on her door. She did not answer and I knew there was something wrong so I went back out to see if Judd was still here to ask him what to do. I found James Foy walking past the house. I beckoned him to come in and told him what I had found and what should I do. So, he went upstairs to the room and called out mother's name several times finally telling her if she did not answer he was going to knock the door in. She did not answer and, well, he did knock the door in and we found her there," she started crying harder now.

Casey looked up at Judd and said, "That will be all. Thank you, Miss Edith, and I am sure Dr. Williams can give you something to make you more comfortable before he leaves."

"Well, what do you think?" asked Winney of the other two.

"She could have committed suicide. With that medication, the size of the bottle if full would have given her enough to do the job and she would have just gone to sleep and her heart would have stopped," said Casey.

"There are no signs of a struggle in the room or on the body of the corpse so we can rule out foul play, I believe," said Williams.

"Then there is the fact that the door was locked from the inside. I can't for the life of me figure out, unless you two have a theory, how someone could come in here, maybe force that stuff in the bottle down her throat, leave and lock the door from the inside. The only way out is the window. I looked at that and, by the looks, it has been frozen shut for some time," said Winney.

Casey looked at the body once more for any signs of a struggle and, as he turned her over to observe her back, he spotted a bottle of water in the bed with a cork in it. He picked up the bottle, pulled the cork and sniffed at the contents. The other two looked on at him gravely as he announced.

"Must be water."

Winney turned to the door looking at Judd once more and said, "Could we have a word with Mr. Holcomb, please."

Judd left and returned in a few minutes with Daniel Holcomb. They had once more righted the body and had covered it up so as Daniel would not have to look upon the body.

"Daniel, I know this is all very hard but could you give us a few minutes? We have some questions we would like to ask."

Daniel nodded his head and moved across the room. He sat down in a large captain's chair, "Proceed," he said in a muffled voice.

"How did your wife seem to you this morning when you left? I mean, was she in a good mood, talkative, you know?" asked Dr. Williams.

"She seemed better than she has been for quite some time. She was up early, fixed breakfast for all, somewhat talkative but smiling. I kissed her when I left and there was nothing unusual in any of it that I can remember."

"This seems strange to us, Daniel, but I have to ask… We found this in bed with her. Do you know what it is for or why she would have it there?" asked Winney holding up the bottle of water.

Daniel smiled a bit and said, "She always kept that in here. She used it for water. If she would become thirsty, she would drink from it. That way she would not have to go down in the kitchen if she was not feeling well to get a drink. She kept one up here all the time. It may be she refilled it and laid it on the bed when she came back up here this morning. That might explain why it was in the bed and not on the side stand next to the bed."

All three men then nodded in agreement that there really was nothing sinister about the bottle of water and it was just what it seemed to be.

"Daniel, as you may or may not know, she was naked in the bed with nothing but a lone sheet wrapped around her chest. Can you explain that?" asked Casey.

Daniel looked down at the floor for a moment and then raised his head with a fond comment.

"Yes, she at times would have chest pains and would warm the sheet and wrap that around her chest. It would ease the pain and discomfort quite well."

Williams and Casey both raised their eyebrows in a knowing look and starred at Winney with knowing looks.

"That's all, Daniel. Thank you for being available to us at this horrid time and you have my condolences, sir, as I am sure Sheriff Winney and Dr. Casey also give theirs. I will, if it is alright with you and the sheriff, take the body and do an autopsy of it for the family. I think the sheriff would like to have a good report on this to calm the community down in the light of the other murders. I am sure you can appreciate the rumors that will be flying around the state tomorrow perpetuated by some of the newspapers in the area. An autopsy by me, the family physician, will seem the correct course to most and it will ease the rumors I am sure. I believe I already know what killed your wife, but I will not comment on it at this time," said Dr. Williams.

Winney and Casey nodded in agreement with Williams.

"Very well, if you think that is the proper thing to do, Dr. Williams. By all means, you have my permission to proceed," said Daniel standing shaking hands with the men and leaving the room.

Casey turned to Williams and Winey. "Are you thinking what I'm thinking, doctor?"

"Yes, I am sure we now know what I am going to find!"

"Well then, could the two of you medical geniuses fill me in on what the hell is going on here?" asked Winney.

"She probably died of a heart attack. As I stated, she was having some heart trouble - especially in the light of all the stress she has been through in the past month and a half. The kicker was the sheet and I was not thinking of the reason she had that wrapped around her chest. She was having chest pains, hence the bottle of water and a warm sheet. 'Lock the door, lay down and all will be fine in a while' I am sure she thought. I think she may have relaxed, gone to sleep and her heart just stopped in her sleep. That is why she looks so peaceful," said Dr. Williams.

"Yes, I concur, sir. I think that is what you will find. I will, of course, be more than happy to lend you any aid or anything for the completion of this autopsy. Please, feel free to let me know if you need anything," said Casey.

Sheriff Winney now had a look of satisfaction on his face. He had known both

Williams and Casey for a long time and trusted their medical expertise like no one else. If they said that is what they would find then he would not bark up this tree anymore unless they find something different at autopsy.

"When the autopsy is over, we should convene a quick inquest. Maybe an afternoon is all that is needed to keep anything from being stirred up about this at a later date that may, for some reason, hurt the other case," said Winney.

Both Williams and Casey agreed.

Chapter 29

2010

The group had been quiet for some twenty minutes in the barn and had not heard anything out of the ordinary that an old sagging creaking barn would not have sounded like at that time of the night. Hunter checked his watch and it read 2 AM.

"We are here to investigate the foul murders of four innocent people who had no other crime in life other to be in the house the night someone wanted Jacob dead. Three people crept up on the house," the sound in the background, as if on cue, belched out the sound of thunder that was loud enough to make the barn shake.

"Guns in hand, you walked up to a door that you knew would be open. One of you had to get his balls off by sneaking around the house to watch it all play out inside the house. The other two drew their guns and walked through the door to the alcove where Jacob was sleeping. One raised a gun to Jacob's head and fired." Hunter then pressed a small audio recorder to play in his hand and the sound of a pistol being shot rang out across the farm. Again, as if on cue, on the sound system thunder once more rolled.

"Moses Polley stood up, came to the door to see what the noise was and, confused, you shot him."Another gun shot on the audio player. "Then you dragged him into the bedroom, threw him on the bed and shot him again." Another shot fired from the recorder.

"Now, you were in a panic and rushed into Henry and Eunice's room. Henry was up, leaning on one arm, trying to rub the sleep out of his eyes. You shot him," the sound of another shot on the recorder, "and he rolled out of bed where you shot him once more on the floor. His wife, 9 months pregnant, now realizing that there were gunshots in her room rose to see." Thunder rolled and the gun sounds on the recorder fired five times in quick succession. More thunder then all was still and quiet in the dark barn as an eerie feeling came over the occupants. It was like a swirling coldness that was almost out of control; first to one person then the next. Cameras flashed and a MEL-meter swept the darkness. Hunter moved and turned off all the sounds of thunder and guns. All were still now.

"Jacob, you have told me that you don't know who shot ya but I am betting that this special piece of shit is still here with us. Come on out, Daniel Holcomb. You were the watchdog in all this. Did you really get off watching Eunice shot so many times? Were you cheering outside hoping they would riddle the bodies even more? You don't fool me, Daniel, you are a piece of crap. Always will be. This is your chance, Daniel. Tell us you did not do this and we will look elsewhere, but I bet you can't. I am also willing to bet you still don't care."

"Ok, babe, start the hack box session, if you please."

Victoria moved over and plugged in two small speakers to the radio and turned them on. The radio jumped to life in the barn with the song One Tin Soldier. She pushed the button for scan and it began running up and down the AM dial without stopping. You could hear bits and pieces of words as it flashed by stations, once in a while a tune of maybe two notes and gone to a partial voice and back to tunes and then to blank as it hit sectors of no stations.

"Hi. I'm Victoria and these are my friends. We would just like to talk to you. We have come from some distance to try and make contact with you. Would you please tell us your name or introduce yourself to us?"

The radio kept on scanning without any voice discernable to the human ear.

"If you wish or it is easier, there are several small devices around the barn. If you want to communicate with us, speak into the little red lights on these devices and when we replay them we will be able to know what you said," instructed Hunter.

"We mean you no harm. We are investigators and there were some murders committed here one hundred and twenty seven years ago. We were wondering if you had heard of these and could tell us what you know of it?" asked Victoria.

"Something moving in here, Tori," said Chandra. "I can sense it. I think it is checking us out, going from person to person, so if anyone feels goose bumps just stand still. I sense no hostility from it."

"Got an image in your mind, Chandra?" asked Hunter.

"No, not really but I know it's here. It is like the image is being blocked maybe by something else."

Just then a K-2 meter lit up next to Jack and then went back to zero.

"God, you aren't kiddin' about those goose bumps, are ya?" said Jack.

"Can you tell us who you are or show me who you are? Give us a sign as to your presence like knocking on something," said Victoria.

"Jesus, now I can feel it back here," said Hunter straightening up and looking around in the dark. He quickly snapped a camera shot in two or three places.

"Fuck, don't do that, Hunter. You will chase it away," said Chandra. "Just let it investigate and then I think, when it is satisfied, it may communicate or even materialize for us."

Hunter frowned. He did not like standing there waiting for whatever was there to decide if he was chosen or not. He was pissed but held his tongue.

"Fred," came and audible voice on the radio.

"Fred, is that your name?" asked Victoria.

The radio skipped along and then there was, after about thirty seconds, a "Yes."

"Did you used to live here, Fred?" asked Chandra.

No reply to this question as the parts of voices skipped in and out in the night.

"Is there anyone else here with you, Fred?" asked Hunter.

"Yes!" came an almost immediate reply.

"How many are in here with you, Fred?" asked Victoria.

"Four!" came the reply.

"Why are you here, Fred?" asked Chandra.

"Hanged!" came the response.

"Who was hanged?" asked Hunter

There was no response to the question.

"Fred, can you make a noise like a knock on a wall or something so we will know where you are? We can't see you," said Hunter.

They waited for about a minute or more and there was no reply.

"Something else or someone else is here," said Chandra. "I think he may have chased Fred out."

"Who is here with us now?" asked Victoria.

"Quite frankly," came the reply on the radio.

"Whoa, dude its Clark-Fucking-Gable," said Chandra mocking it.

"Kiss it," came the reply. Then all was silent.

"Jacob Crouch, are you here with us?" asked Victoria after a while.

No response was heard above the radio. They continued on for some time but received no further response. Hunter wearily looked at his watch and it said 3:07 AM.

"Ok, folks, I think it's time to wrap it up. Let's gather all the equipment and then breakfast is on me at Denny's."

It took them almost forty five minutes to wrap up all the cables and stow the monitors and DVR equipment into Chandra's van. Hunter called to Curt who also wrapped up and came to the site to help finish up.

"Ok, everybody, let's see… it is Sunday… actually Monday morning… I would like to meet Thursday evening and set up at Chandra's to go over the evidence. Hopefully, all you law enforcement guys can come. We would enjoy the help. There is a massive amount of things to go through. How about 7 PM? I will send out for pizza and will also, for those of you who do not have her address, email it to you this week. In the meantime, if you want go ahead with your own recorders, check them out and if you find anything mark it, date it, so we can all listen to it Thursday. Curt, you can be in charge of your own material at the cemetery? If you find anything, let me or Tori know."

"Will do," said Curt heading back to his vehicle.

"I got one question, Chandra. What the fuck is up with this Clark Gable shit? How can a ghost from the 1800's possibly know who Clark Gable is?" asked Hunter.

"You got me, but who said we are talking to ghosts from the 1800's? We don't know who we are talking to. It could be from another dimension, another time, another place, even could be spirits who have only been dead a few years and impersonating who you want them to be. You know all this as well as I do," said Chandra.

"Yeah, I know. I guess I am really not asking a question as much as I am trying to roll this around in my mind to get a better grasp of it. I just don't understand it but, what the hell, none of us have the answers or we would not still be looking after all these years," said Hunter.

Chandra came up to him, planted a kiss on his cheek and said, "You know, hon, it's the ones who think they have the answers that scare and piss me off. Sorry, I did not mean to snap at you but that really pissed me off in there."

"So, later?" asked Hunter.

"Hell no! Some dude offered to buy me breakfast and by God I am going to collect," said Chandra with a smile.

They all climbed into their respective vehicles and moved away toward Jackson and breakfast.

As they pulled away, a dark shadow of an object stood near the side of the barn. It had a broad-brimmed hat and the appearance of hands in his pocket. Slowly a face emerged, that of a young man with brown hair and a smirk on his face as he watched the taillights fade.

Chapter 30

1884

Detective Adams and Sheriff Winney sat in the office alone talking out the case over breakfast and coffee.

"I talked to Casey this morning and he said Doc Williams has nothing to add from the autopsy that we did not already know," said Adams forking scrambled eggs into his mouth.

"They checked real thorough for poison and drugs in the body, right?' asked Winney.

"Yeah, sent it all out to University of Michigan and the results came back negative. They also said to tell ya that there was absolutely no sign of any kind of physical violence; no bruising, etc.," said Adams.

"Did Casey say what they planned to do about an inquest?"

"He said to tell you they would impanel a jury and do a routine inquest: ask a few questions of the boys, Edith, Daniel, and James Foy, maybe Judd. But he supposed it would show nothing that we don't already know and he would be able to wrap it all up in an hour or so."

"That is good. I will be glad to lay this one to rest and not have to worry about it with the other four, that is for sure," said Winney.

Adams wiped his mouth off and said, "You know, there was several paper reports that said you told the press she was force-fed rat poison and another intimated she was killed 'cause she knew who had killed the others. Oh, and the Detroit paper says she committed suicide."

"I wish these guys would get their damn stories straight and quit riling up the populace. I tell you, there is no good to come of it somehow, I am sure. Have you gotten any more leads than you had before on any of this?"

"Yeah, maybe a few. Seems like Daniel Holcomb went up to see his brother and bought a pistol while he was there. The clerk swears it was him when I showed them a picture of him. I asked Daniel about that and he said he bought it for a friend as a present. So I said to him 'Well tell me who the friend is and I will go take a look at it and scratch that off the list.' He says to me rather quickly 'Can't, cause I lost it on the way back from Lansing on the train.' I just looked at him with 'you don't expect me to believe this shit' written all over my face but he stuck to his story. I finally said 'Well, that was pretty damn convenient' and left him standing there. I never heard so much shit in my life and get this - they swear the gun was a thirty eight caliber."

"Good work! Keep them in mind and the names handy so we can call upon them if need be," said Winney. The sheriff looked at his detective and said, "So son, do we have anything on anybody as to who could have done this… motive, anything like that?"

"Right now it's tough. Maybe someone did follow Polley from the tavern that afternoon but it does not make sense that they would not have jumped him way before he got to Jacob's. Also, why did they steal the box of papers under the whatnot and leave cash and jewelry lying around all over the house, and never took Polley's money? That part does not add up. Right now, I can't and won't say much more even between you and me 'cause I don't want to wander off on a wild goose chase." With that Adams sat back coffee in hand staring at the floor. Winney lit his pipe and sat back in his chair stretching after a good meal. Both men sat there for some time silent and deep in thought.

"Have you ever thought of the fact that it could be Judd and Daniel out for some kind of revenge, or the money or the farm?" asked Winney blowing some smoke into the air.

"Yeah, but motive may not be as easy to prove. Lots of people had motive here in the county. Like a man said in the barber shop the other morning, almost everyone in the county had worked for Jacob once upon a time and ran afoul of his gruff nature. We would have to arrest a lot of people if motive was all we could bring," said Adams.

2010

The evening was cold and there was lots of snow in the air as it whitened the ground. Victoria and Hunter pulled up to Chandra's home, a nice two-story brick house in Albion. She lived there with her sister and nephew. Hunter came to the passenger side and opened the door for Victoria who stood up out of the car and kissed him on the cheek. Jemma then piled out of the back and said, "You two can get a room and spare the rest of us, old people acting like well… ewwww!" With that she walked away.

Hunter laughed and reached in the back pulling out an attaché case. He moved behind the women and up the snow-covered walk to a large green front door. Jemma jammed her finger into the doorbell as it rang inside. Chandra came to the door allowing them in.

"Jack and Ed are already down in the basement. I think we have everything set up and ready to go," said Chandra.

Turning to the right, they moved down a finished carpeted stairway to a carpeted floor below. There they were met by three doors: one on the left, one on the right and one straight ahead. Chandra opened the one straight ahead and it opened up into a room where all the monitors were set. There were large black leather office swivel chairs behind the table. Jack and Ed were at each end.

"We started without you guys. They are going over the DVRS and I got the mini-DVDs," she said.

Victoria and Jemma walked around the table to the center of the table and Hunter sat on one side next to Jack. Chandra settled in next to Ed and Jemma.

"Here, Jemma, you take these audio recorders and the digital stills on these chips. Victoria, you take these audios and the thermal camera footage. I'll take the rest of the mini-DVDs and what remains of the audio. Yell when you all get hungry. We will have some pizza delivered," said Hunter.

They all sat in silence in their own world of audio and video recordings. It had been about a half an hour when Ed spoke up, "Remember when Victoria, you and Chandra said that you heard a voice over by that tree call Chandra's name? You all, plug into the main and listen to this…"

The Tape:

Victoria: "That's the big old tree again."

Voice: "*Chandra*!!"

Chandra: "I swear I just heard a voice almost between us?"

Victoria: "Yeah, me too."

"That was cool! Good catch, Ed. Mark down the audio recorder and time on your log, if you would please, and we will cut that out at a later date and put it in an audio file," said Hunter.

The session went on for about another hour when Jack yelled out, "Oh my God! I got one gang. Listen to this!"

They all plugged their headsets into the main and Jack reran the tape. "These were in the barn. Remember when the voice told Chandra 'Quite frankly' and she made her reference to Clark Gable? Well, listen to the voice. I think this is outside the hack box."

Hack box: "Kiss it."

Different voice outside of hack box: "OOOH don't make him mad."

Second voice outside of hack box: "Let's go!"

"Hey, I think that second one is that of a woman. Very good catch, Jack. Mark it and let's go on some more. In about a half an hour I will call for the pizza."

"Ok," said Victoria, "Everybody gather around. I have something to show you. Remember when Jemma, Jack and Hunter were outside the house near the old tree? And Hunter, you said what was that and scanned around near the tree? Well, take a look at this, folks."

"Are you shittin' me? Holy crap, look at that, would ya? It has the heat signature right next to the tree and you can make out the broad-brimmed hat and all!" yelled Hunter jumping up and down. "We got someone watching and it was not one of us for sure. Look how it materializes, gets red-hot and then turns blue and disappears! Damn, Tori, play that one again, will ya?"

Hunter called for two large pizzas and the group sat around chatting about their finds.

"So, Jack, you and Ed hooked on this yet?" asked Hunter.

"I don't know about Ed but I am for sure," said Jack

"I will always want to do this now," said Ed.

"Well, Tori and I talked it over and the six of us make a great team so I think we should all stick together and become one under D & R - if that's ok with you two?" said Hunter.

Jack jumped up and said yes immediately high-fiving Ed.

"There is just one problem here. Jack has been a friend of mine for many years. We have stood shoulder-to-shoulder in the face of a lot of adversity; in rain, snow, cold, heat, awful accidents, blood and gore. Jack is on the fast-track to becoming an investigator with the department. He will be taking his test next year for detective sergeant and I want to see him succeed. I don't know how much time between work, study and school he will have, but I don't think he should stop what he is doing," said Ed.

"I agree, and we make no demands on anyone. If we need help, we ask. It's not a weekly thing and remember, Tori and I run a business, first and foremost. That is our livelihood and we will not lose it for adventure - at least at this time. We have spent five long, hard years building up the book business and have quite a collectible business online. It is the bread and butter of the operation buying and selling collectible books and it takes me some strange places, to say the least. So Jack you can come with us anytime you want, but this is not to get in the way of your education or advancement. And, of course, both of you have very important jobs for your community to fulfill so we can't expect you along all the time but your investigative expertise is a big plus to the operation."

The group talked a while about future events and things they would just like to investigate then went back to the evidence review. They broke up about midnight and all went their own separate ways except for Victoria and Hunter who returned to his apartment above the bookstore.

"Did you read all the content we had on Susan Holcomb's file?" said Victoria pouring a glass of Maker's Mark for Hunter.

He came out of the bedroom in sweatpants and a t-shirt. He stopped next to Victoria and nuzzled her on the nape of her neck; he knew that this drove her crazy.

"MMMMMMMM, you can do that all night if you want. I told mother that I may not be home till morning," she said softly to him.

Chapter 31

Hunter awoke to the smell of Victoria's hair which, in their slumbering embrace, had cascaded into his face. He looked up at the clock and it said 2:30. He rolled out of bed, pulled on his sweat pants and t-shirt and moved out to the table in the kitchen. He reached into the refrigerator and pulled out a Diet Mountain Dew. Sitting down at the table, he opened some file folders and began to read. He suddenly was aware of Victoria behind him in a Chicago Blackhawks Hockey jersey. She folded her arms around his neck and bent over pressing her breasts in his back. He arched his back at the feeling and smiled as he patted her on the hand. She walked over to the refrigerator and poured herself a glass of milk then sat down beside him.

"So, what is the verdict on the Susan Holcomb inquest?" she asked.

"I always thought that maybe she was killed somehow. Especially when I read that the sheriff was quoted as saying she was force-fed rat poison. But I found out quickly after reading all the reports from the paper, the quotes of the coroner and family doctor that was not true to begin with. She simply had gone to her room because she had chest pains and maybe some other symptoms that related to her heart. She did not commit suicide, which was another thought of mine. I thought that she knew Judd and Daniel did this and could not live with it. But according to the autopsy findings there was no sign of poison in her system or any type of drugs found. The little bottle on the windowsill was nerve medicine for her daughter prescribed by a doctor in Kalamazoo. According to the coroner, it was nearly empty. None of it was found at autopsy in her system. And the amount her daughter had taken was in accordance with the bottle being empty. It was merely a potion to help her sleep. There may not have been enough in the entire bottle to cause an overdose when it was full."

"Why was she naked at that time of the day in her room? Are you sure she was not waiting for someone or had entertained someone like that farmhand, James Foy? Didn't you say he was in the house to kick down the door of the bedroom? And a statement by Edith was that she did not know where he had come from or why he was there and thought at the time that was very strange," said Victoria.

"I did some research on that and it ties into the sheet wrapped around her chest. They did that back in those days to ease the pain of angina; chest pain. They would take the sheet, somehow warm it up, then wrap it around you and let the heat ease the symptoms of the heart which is exactly what she did. She went to her room, warmed up the sheet, and took the bottle full of water with her for drinking. (Daniel told the doctor she was in the habit of taking water with her when she would lie down to rest and it was always in that corked glass bottle). She then took off her dress, wrapped the sheet tightly around her bare chest and lay down across the bed hoping for some relief, which actually came in the form of a heart attack and death. She died in that position. She may not have known what hit her," said Hunter.

"Why was the door locked then from the inside?"

"Sheriff Winney thought that was the most suspicious of all. He could not figure how someone locked it from the inside and got out. The window was too small, no tracks in the snow under it, and there was no other door to the room. This bothered him for a while until Daniel, Judd, and Edith all told him that she had this thing about sleeping with the door locked. So, she naturally went upstairs deciding to wrap the sheet around her, take a nap and rest. She locked the door giving the two boys downstairs explicit instructions that she was not to be bothered by anyone who came asking about her."

"Wow! That was a lot to learn about all of that."

"Yeah, we have extensive information from the Jackson Citizen Patriot reporter who was present in the room during questioning and also at the small inquest they held. The verdict was correct as the family doctor had suspected that she died from heart failure due to natural causes. End of story."

"So, where do we go now?"

"Well, with the evidence we gathered this weekend, we need to go back for the inquest reports about James Foy's death and the causes. I read in one paper that he was shot-gunned behind the barn; another said he committed suicide behind the barn with a shotgun. Maybe he got too close to the truth and was killed to keep him quiet or he was black mailing someone about the truth of the matter. There is no way he is not connected to this. Whether he was killed by someone or he killed himself, it all goes directly back to the killings of Jacob and company. Maybe he was distraught over Susan's death. Maybe there was something going on there."

"I forgot to ask… why was Foy there anyways?"

"Oh, Judd explained that. He had taken the cutter he had which belonged back on Jacob's farm and left his horse in the barn that he had ridden that morning. He then asked Foy while he unhooked the cutter to go back and retrieve his horse for him. Foy was working for Judd at Jacob's farm at the time so that was how he appeared there. Edith actually saw him walking up the lane towards the barn and summoned him to come to the house. She then had him go upstairs with her and he could not get an answer so he finally kicked in the door."

"Ah, another mystery solved. Boy, this case takes some twists and turns. Are we still suspicious of Daniel and Judd and whoever their accomplice was?"

"Yeah, until something else comes along to tell me different I will still think that they had something to do with it. Probably all over the farm and money that Judd was not gonna inherit. It may be that Byron also had a hand in this. I read off to the side that he had vehemently resisted Eunice getting married to White but there is never any reason given except an offhand comment by a neighbor that said he believed her to be above him in station and all he was after was part of the farm."

"I think it was strange that Dayton got shot. There is no record of the incident nor any mention of whom or how or why he was shot. Don't know enough about them to know yet. My friend in the Rangers can't seem to run it down. When I mentioned it to Ed and Jack, they wanted to take a crack at it using their connections to federal lists that go way back. We shall see what they come up with. Any more questions, my dear?

"Yeah, would you carry me back to bed and ravish me one more time?" she said laughing and embracing his cheek with her left hand as she stared into his eyes.

Hunter jumped up as she rose and threw her over his right shoulder head first. "Dang, I see you are not wearing underwear as usual."

Victoria laughed and kicked but his grip was strong and he had that determined look in his eye that she loved as he plopped her down on the king-size bed. Reaching over, he turned off the bedside light. She could feel him removing the jersey from her body. She was not sure how he had done this but he was already naked. She giggled some more and then moaned in pleasure.

February 4 1884

William McCollum came through the door at the Crouch farm with Daniel Holcomb's brother, Henry. McCollum was an old friend and schoolmate of Judd's and, at the behest of Judd, came to stay with him for a while. Judd was afraid ever since the murders that someone would come for him next. He was so afraid that he was sharing the bed with hired man James Foy of whom, on a personal basis, he detested. His fear was so great that he did not want to be left alone at night. The two men had even brought pistols down from Daniel Holcomb's farm for protection. Judd now did not travel anywhere day or night without a pistol in his inside jacket pocket. James Foy came out into the kitchen where Henry's wife and his niece Edith were working on fixing some lunch for the men. Foy looked up quizzical at McCollum and said.

"Ain't you with Judd? I thought he left?"

"Yeah, but he said, seeing as how you were going to leave, that he wanted me to help Henry get the wheat ready for tomorrow's delivery."

"Just where did he go?" asked Foy.

"Said he was going into town to Bunnell's to get some new britches amongst other things he had to do," said Henry with a smile. "Why and where is you off to?" he asked.

"Just away. Don't you concern yourself with where, bub," said Foy wit han ugly-faced threatening gesture.

Henry backed off some. He knew Foy and knew him well. He was not to be taken lightly. But with recent events, he had kept some tabs on Foy's whereabouts and who he was talking to and why. This had begun to irritate Foy; he could see no use for a nursemaid. He was working for Judd now not Daniel and he would be damned if the little brother was going to jerk him around. He would do what he pleased.

Sensing some animosity and not knowing the pair, McCollum decided to poke Foy with a verbal stick to see if he squirmed. Maybe, somehow, it would become a good fight between Foy and Henry.

"Henry, was that you telling me this morning about the newspaper article from over Union City way about Foy here?"

"Not me, maybe somebody who came to buy wheat this morning but I ain't read no paper from Union City. Why? Where in the hell would I have gotten that from?" said Henry.

"Maybe not you… I know! It was Jeddediah Cross, that's who."

"What article you talking about, McCollum?" asked Foy.

"You know a guy named Major Easton? Guess he is the editor of the paper and the postmaster there in Union City. Seems he knows you says you used to live in Union City," said McCollum.

"You can't believe everything you hear. Right, Jim?" said Henry a bit nervous as Foy turned with a hard look on his face and his eyes narrowing.

"Just what did the Easton fella say?" asked Foy.

"Of course, I didn't read it but it was something about you being arrested in Union City a few years ago during a brawl of some sort. I guess Easton says if you were near the Crouch farm on the day of the murders then he, knowing your reputation, would make you the prime suspect."

Foy lunged toward McCollum but McCollum, stood quickly to meet the advance. Bill McCollum was a big man for the times (six feet two inches) that made him tower over most men. He had broad shoulders and very strong arms. Foy slid to a stop realizing that he was not a match in a brawl with this man.

"You just be careful what things you say unless you is damn sure they is true," said Foy backing down and examining all the faces in the room. He wanted to move away from the situation without losing his perception as a tough. All were quiet staring at him and waiting to see what was next. Foy had been in his share of fights in the Jackson area. He was known as a very good brawler and he also was a bit of a bully. When he started drinking, he got even meaner. Some people said that he had beaten a man to death with his fists in Chicago once but the story was never proven. Foy balled up his hands now, backed away from the kitchen and moved back to his bedroom. He dressed for the afternoon in some travelling clothes and then moved out the door. What he needed was a piece of tail and he knew the ladies that would be accommodating in Jackson. He moved out of the house and out to Horton Road. He started walking toward Jackson and it was not long before a wagon came along and gave him a ride. He knew where to go - down by the bars and near the railroad yards.

Chapter 32

In Jackson, James Foy moved down the street to a two-story gray house. Skirting the property, he walked down beside it to the back where there was a porch. No red light here but the place was frequented by railroad men looking for a good home-cooked meal and some female companionship. This was the house of the Murdock sisters, Helen and Louisa. The women had lived there now for many years. At first, they took in laundry from the men who worked on the rails. They even, at times, had a few borders but they found out that if they plied the right trade that it was quite profitable. Foy stepped up and knocked on the door. Louisa, a rather plump woman in a pale green dress with an apron, opened the door. She had lots of red hair piled high on her head and she also had plenty of makeup on so that her face was as pale as a pearl.

"James Foy, I do declare! We have not seen you in some time, darling. Why come on in! Helen has just baked up one of her famous apple pies and you may have a piece," she laughed. As Foy passed by she smacked him on the backside.

"What on earth? Why, James Foy! Well, this may promise to be a really good afternoon," said Helen coming out towards the parlor from the back kitchen. She was not quite as portly as her sister and her hair was a sandy blond that hung to her shoulders. James stopped and studied her. She was almost comical in her makeup; the lipstick was so red it actually appeared that her lips were on fire.

"Girls, I shore would like some of that pie I smell out yonder," said Foy.

"Might cost something, like a couple bucks, but I am sure we can come to an agreement," said Louisa with a smile on her face.

"Got change for a five?" he smiled.

Louisa grabbed an old cow bell on a hook near the back door. She opened the door, hung the bell on the outside, and started to giggle. She shut the door and snatched the five from Foy throwing it into a dresser drawer where she stood. Both women grabbed him each by an arm and almost drug him up the stairs laughing as they went. A door slammed shut at the top and you could hear Foy's laughter a block away. An hour went by as giggles, a few laughs and at least one splendid "OHHH" came from up the stairs. Finally the trio moved back down the stairs.

"Sure you won't stay a little, Jimmy?" chided Louisa.

"I gotta go, ladies. I have business to attend to, believe it or not, but I will be back. How about that piece of pie you offered me?" he asked.

Helen went to the kitchen table and cut into an apple pie. She removed a slice and Foy grabbed at it with one hand. He had one arm in the coat and another one out. As he went out the door he pulled on his coat switched hands with the pie and went down the steps. He turned and waved at the two women as he walked up past the house to the street and then north toward the railroad depot. Walking past the depot, he made a stop and checked the train schedule and then moved on down toward Bunnell's. He had finished his pie by that time and walked into the store. He looked around and then spotted Judd Crouch near a mirror trying on a smart black coat.

"Hey, Judd, can I have a minute with you?" asked Foy.

Judd turned around and made a smirk at Foy. He tolerated the man but really did not like him personally. Foy was maybe the best farmhand in the county, maybe several counties. He always commanded top-hand position and wages wherever he went. He had worked the many county area for some years now and was known by most of the major farmers who all, at one time or another, had used his services. The only problem Judd had with him was that he drank more than he should have and he was a blow-harded bully. Taking his arm and moving out toward the door he stopped and asked, "What is it?"

"I need some money. A little advance on the end of the week if you could, please?" asked Foy.

"I got five-fifty on me. If that ain't enough, I don't know what to tell ya," said Judd.

"That's enough. I gotta go to Athens to see a man over there on some business. I'll be back in the morning," said Foy.

"We got that wheat to load out tomorrow and I have to go into town and get that chestnut reshod. It was a lousy job last time, so I'm gonna have Gallagher do it. McCollum is going with me."

"How long is that galoot gonna stay around? I don't know if I cotton to him that much," said Foy irritated at the mention of the name.

"He's my friend and I will say when he goes. You just get along with him, will ya?" said Judd.

Foy raised one hand in disgust as he walked away from the doorway and back to the train station.

He went in and bought a ticket for Athens for the next westbound train. He realized that it would be stopping in 15 minutes.

Len Carsey a loud mouth in his own right and one to always have an argument with Foy, rounded the corner. He was followed by Trust Earwerthy, Pete O'Connel, Tate Davidson and Luke Mathy.

"Well, if it ain't Fearless Foy! Where you off to, son? And here is me hoping that ya might not return," said Carsey.

Detective Adams came out of the station and looked at the crowd. He knew this bunch, including Foy, and if they were up to no good it would be a good chance to run Foy in for some long-awaited questions that the sheriff had in relationship to the Crouch murders.

"Well, now," started Foy turning and seeing Adams and two more deputies coming down the street. He felt for the pistol in his pocket and it was not there. Checking his jacket he realized he must have dropped it at the Murdock girl's house. He never finished his sentence but busted through the group and down the street on a dead run. Coming to the house, he ran down the side and up on the back porch with a leap and a thud that caused Louisa to open the door back up again. "Why, lord, you back already James?" she laughed.

"Have you seen a gun? A pistol?" he asked

"Lord have mercy, no. Not such a thing around here now, mind you, why would you ask such a thing?"

"'Cause I dropped mine, I think," he stopped looked just off the porch to the right and there in the snow lay his .38 caliber pistol. He swooped down and picked it up. Then he bolted in the door as Helen came out of the kitchen to see who was there. He grabbed a kitchen towel off of Helen's shoulder and moved to the small dresser by the door. He wiped the pistol good to dry it off and then removed the bullets wiping them one at a time. He blew into the cylinder to make sure there was no snow obstructing it and then began reloading it. The women looked on with frightened looks on their faces. Foy picked up one of the bullets and held it up between his thumb and index finger so that it was at eye level to the women.

"This is just like the bullet and gun that killed the Crouches," he said with a smile finishing loading the gun.

He looked at the women. Helen had very little color in her face. Louisa eyes were very big as if they were about to burst. Suddenly, a dark sinister look came over Foy as he narrowed his eyebrows and looked at them.

"Of course, there is no reason to tell anyone of this conversation. Is there, ladies?"

Just then the train whistle sounded reminding him that he might miss the train. He tucked the pistol into the waistband of his trousers this time and turned, running out the door. He made a leap off of the porch, sprinted around the side of the house and up the street.

Helen went to the door and closed it. Snapping the latch, she turned and leaned against it looking back at Louisa.

"Oh my dear God, sister, what have we gotten ourselves into this time?" Louisa stood staring at Helen and the door. Slowly she lowered her head and leaned against the table with the palms of her hands flat on the table top.

Foy jumped for the platform just as the train was pulling up to the station.

Carsey came toward him and said, "No detectives around, lad, but they is interested in you I believe. Now tell me, where 'tis you are about there?"

"I am on my way to Athens to see about a position on a farm for next summer," said Foy.

"Ah, tis that. I would tink, me boy, that you would stay close to Judd and Daniel and maybe that cute daughter of Daniel's now that the missus is outta the way," winked Carsey with an elbow to Foy's side.

"Too much killing and death associated with that place. I am heading out the first chance I get and put that all behind me. I will take a small, quiet farm job to this anytime," said Foy.

"Tis I think you may want to be reading the Union City newspaper, boy-o, whilst you is making this ride," Carsey shoved a newspaper under Foy's arm and then walked on down the platform and out into the street.

Foy jumped on the train as the conductor called for all aboard. He sat down where there were two empty seats. He laid the newspaper down beside him on the empty seat as he gave his ticket to the conductor. The train pulled out and, mesmerized by the clickety-clack of the train on the tracks, Foy thought of very little staring out into space. The whistle sounded for the crossing ahead and snapped him out of his daze. He looked around the car. No one he knew right off hand. He decided that was good. He was not in a good mood for talking at this time. He reached down and grabbed the newspaper that Carsey had given him. Justice May Go Undone In Jackson."

"It has come to the attention of this newspaper that the recent events in Jackson to wit the murders at the Crouch farm that took place back in November are giving the local constabulary fits, for lack of evidence as to who may have had reason to carry out this crime. We here in Union City when examining the case find one person to us that is of interest that it seems has gone unnoticed and not questioned by the Sheriff. We in Union City know this man due to past disturbances that he has caused as a ruffian and bully and surely would be the person tied up in the fracas in Spring Arbor. We all know James Foy as a itinerant farm hand who while living amongst us for some time caused his share of trouble as far as resulting in him doing some short jail time. The numerous bar fights that he was in and also the brawl he started at the festival that summer which put several men under the doctor's direct care for quite some

time. Whenever there was any trouble afoot it was for a sure thing that James Foy was involved in it. To think then that this man of bad temper and worse character would be found to be working on a neighboring farm as well as the farm that the murders occurred is quite more than we could bear. Mr. Judd Crouch and Mr. Daniel Holcomb should beware this man and in my opinion be rid of him as soon as they can give him his walking papers. A bunch of detectives should sweat the truth from the blaggard, and make him tell what he knows and we think he may know quite a bit about the murders."

Foy put the paper down on the seat next to him. He could feel his face flushing. That man had no call to write that. Why, if that all gets out he will surely be sent to jail. He hated jail and it is one place that he did not want to ever be again in his life. He gritted his teeth and set his jaw as the whistle blew for a stop in Homer. Taking on passengers there the train proceeded west towards Tekonsha. The conductor came through the door announcing to everyone the next stop would be Tekonsha where the train would have a thirty minute layover for coal and water. The passengers were invited to stretch their legs at the station.

"So, they think I am trouble and a murderer," he said to himself, "We shall see tonight if they are still laughing." The train now was slowing for the Tekonsha stop .He got out, went across the street and had two drafts before getting back on the train. When he did, he sat down, reached to his inside pocket and pulled out a flask.

The train pulled away with the conductor calling, "Next stop - Union City!"

Chapter 33

Foy did not seem to know this Easton fellow but was sure he could find him at the paper. He knew just exactly where that would be. It was now dark outside, about 7 pm, as the train reached the Union City station and came to a halt. Foy got up to depart as the conductor said to him, "Just a short stop there, mister. Your destination is Athens."

"That's all right. I have decided that my business is right here in Union City so I won't be going on for the night. By the way, what time does the train come back by here tonight?"

"About 11 PM but it is a freight train and no room for passengers. Just a slow-moving freight that grabs the night mail at all the stops on the way to Ann Arbor," said the conductor waving to the engineer. Foy raised his hand in thanks and moved away from the train toward Broadway Street. He walked along briskly with the paper in his hand. He was going to shove this down Easton's throat and demand an apology. His character when he lived here was impeccable. He would show this high and mighty man and this stinking little community what it was to make James Foy angry. His face now was completely beet red as he moved faster and faster down the street; at times running into people with not so much as an 'excuse me'.

Major Tom Easton was the Editor in Chief of the Union City Register. He sat in his office in a wooden swivel chair reading some papers. He was a man of about 65 years in age. He came to Union City after the war and had worked there in many capacities since. He was even voted Mayor for a term. Easton was also the postmaster of the small town and the post office sat right on top of the railroad tracks. Mail was delivered from the east in the morning and the west in the afternoon. Mail sent out from there was picked up by a slow-moving freight each night around 11 pm.

Easton was partially bald with a protruding pot-belly. He put on his jacket, found his hat and he came out into the office to put on his big winter coat. A man and a woman sat in the office both engaged in writing something onto paper.

"Della, I left the two articles on my desk. They have been proofed and ready to be set in print. If you would be so kind as to take them to Jonathan for me, I would appreciate it. Also, Barton, do you have that story about the wheat price fall finished yet?"

The young man looked up and smiled, "Yes, Major, I am just finishing it now. It will be ready when Della takes your articles to Jonathan to be set in type."

"Very good. I am off to the post office for the rest of the night. You two, don't work too late now. Bright and early tomorrow morning, we go to press. We want to make sure there is not anything on the wires that needs to be stuck in at the last minute. Don't forget to check the wires before you close up and, if something big comes up, you will know where I am at," said Easton walking out the door, up the street toward the post office.

Foy walked into the paper office about ten minutes later demanding to see Major Easton. Della held him off telling him that the Major would not be back in until morning. Going to his house was out of the question as his wife needed peace and quiet due to an illness.

"Bah!" was all Foy said and walked out of the office onto the street and immediately spied his old watering hole in the middle of the village: Casey's. He walked across the street, bought a beer at the bar and stood there downing the first one right out. He slowed his pace after that as other men came in for the evening. Several knew Foy and they all sat down at a table to hear the Crouch stories from Foy of which he was more than happy to tell. The stories flowed almost as much as the beer as the men took turns buying rounds for Foy just to keep him telling one story after another. He talked about the habits of the family and his take on who might have killed them and why. He even told the story of how they were killed and in what order they were killed.

Across town, Major Easton worked away sorting out the day's mail for people in the morning. He had packages and two large stacks of letters and correspondence he had to go through hand-by-hand. Some had to be canceled; some just sorted to the proper route or box. About 10 PM, the back doorknob rattled and the deadbolt lock snapped open. Easton looked around his stack of letters to see his son-in-law, George Schuler, coming through the door. Easton laughed upon seeing the lad for he liked him just like a son that he never had.

"George, what brings you here this time of night?" asked the Major.

"Polly is not feeling well again and we had to send for the doctor. He is there now and would like a word with you. Maybe you could stay the rest of the night? I will close up for you here," said the young man taking off his derby hat and coat rolling up his sleeves. George Schuler was not only Major Easton's son-in-law, he was also the assistant postmaster.

"Oh, goodness! Thanks, lad, I surely am grateful for this. Oh my, Polly not doing well. I do hope there is something the doctor can do to ease her pain some. I hate so to see her lying there in pain like she is."

Polly Easton was wife to the Major. They had been married some thirty years. Last fall Polly had taken ill with chest congestion and seemed to only get weaker until she was remanded to bed for rest. She did, on occasion, have fevers in the night and took constant looking after. During the day and the evening, George and his wife (the Major's daughter) took turns looking after Polly while he was at work. NOTE: At the writing of this book it is unclear through all the research we had what was wrong with Polly.

"They are talking laudanum right now so I think you should get over there post-haste to make sure you are in on the discussions. Don't worry, I will lock up and set the mail bag out," said Schuler.

"Ah… very good, my boy, I shall hurry home. The bag is made up and sitting right over there in the corner. Mind ya, it is a heavy one tonight. Make sure you take the ladder out with you to hang it."

With that the Major darted out of his door and Schuler continued the assault on the pile of mail. At about 10:45 PM, George hung the bag near the tracks for the train to pick up. As he was climbing down the ladder a friend of his, James Cartwright, came upon him. Striking up a conversation, George said, "Let's head down for a nightcap before we go home. All I have to do is set up the office. It should only take a few minutes and then we can go."

"Right, George me boy, and the first one is on me," said James standing outside of the post office's back door waiting as George went back in.

Foy looked at the clock. It read 10:40 PM. He had been drinking profusely for quite some time now and, in his fogged brain, he remembered that according to some of his cronies Major Easton would be done at the post office at eleven PM. He would go up, wait for him outside the post office, and then catch the freight as it went on to the east.

He said his goodbyes to the friends and started up the street. He stopped under a street lamp just across the street from the post office and waited. He did not have long to wait. As he heard the whistle from the freight in the west, he heard the back door shut and two men come around the side. Realizing this was his chance and there were no witnesses. He pulled the pistol and opened fire on them when they got to the middle of the street. Schuler was hit and went down; James, with instinct, went down next to George. Foy had fired four times and, thinking he had gotten both of them, he took off on a dead run as the freight came by. He watched, waited and then he saw what he was looking for - an open door to a freight car. He jumped up grabbing a bar and pulled himself up and in. He was safe now and out of sight. No one would ever know who shot those two men and he would have taken care of that busybody editor once and for all.

The clickety-clack of the empty railroad car moving slowly to the east put Foy into a semi-sleep along with the effects of a night of drinking. He came to inside the car and had to think for a bit where he was He could feel the train slowing. His head hurt now from the drink. He crawled to the car door, opened it and looked out. He saw a sign on a depot that said "Homer". He sat there for a while thinking. He had shot two men and maybe killed them both. There was really no way that they could tie him into the killings. He was sure there were no witnesses but still, they might be checking trains at Jackson and he wanted no part of the railroad detectives or the sheriff's men. He hopped down out of the car and made his way up a small narrow street to what appeared to be Main Street. There he took the road walking east as a light cold rain began to fall. He pulled the collar of the coat up around his neck and his hat down tight over his head to keep the dampness out as best he could. His head was now banging as he walked. He felt sick and stopped twice to wretch along the side of the road. There was no traffic that time of night along the road.

Past farms houses and inns, he traveled in the rain as the night slowly turned into day with a gray sky in the east. He was almost back to the Crouch farm when he met his first person along Horton Road. The man said, "Hi." Foy neither shook his head nor acknowledged him. Instead, he hoped that if the man was asked later he would not be able to swear that it was Foy he met along the road.

Finally, he came to the farm. He could see a light inside and knew that Judd would be up. He went to the front door, fitted his key into the lock and walked in hanging his wet coat and hat by the fireplace.

"Jim, where the hell have you been all night?" asked Judd.

Not wanting to expose anything, he just said, "Out and about. Remember? I went to Athens."

"Ah, yeah. Did you take the position?" asked Judd.

"Not sure yet but I am cold to the bone. I am going down in the basement, tap me some hard cider to warm me and take off the chill blains."

With that he headed for the basement. The basement had a warm feeling to it that morning but chills ran up and down his spine. He reached a barrel, put a large tin cup under it and drew off the cider. He took a long drink from the cup and then leaned back against the wall thinking now of what he had done. He needed to clean the gun so there would not be any evidence of it recently being fired.

He was sure that he would not be in any trouble. Dead men tell no tales and his friends would not tell on him, of that he was sure. Easton, in his mind, would write no more tales of him. He drew two more cupfuls. Now, his head feeling better, he could almost eat something. Going back upstairs he went in, took off his wet clothes and hung them to dry. He then went out to the breakfast table where Jim McCollum sat enjoying his breakfast.

Foy eyed Jim as he sat down wanting no mouth from this man this morning. He was tougher than McCollum and he would stand him down today of all days. He had to clear his mind and think up a good story.

"Jimmy, coming in late aren't ya, lad?" asked McCollum

"What business is it of yours?" asked Foy as Henry Holcomb's wife sat a plate in front of him of eggs ham and potatoes. Foy grabbed at the coffee cup and almost downed the hot brew in one gulp.

"Just curious why you would be out so late. What kind of mayhem you were up to or got into? You look pretty rough this morning; must have been a pretty rough night. What the hell? Did you do sleep outside in the rain or just passed out in the rain?" laughed and taunted McCollum.

"Yeah, well, I had trouble in Union City last night. I knocked over two guys who started a fight with me. Shot them both maybe dead for all I know and then I came home."

Suddenly Foy now realized in his zeal to prove his toughness to McCollum he had just spilled the beans in front of witnesses.

Judd dropped his fork and looked at Foy.

"You shot two men? Maybe killed them?" he repeated.

"Yeah, they was fighting with me. Gonna beat the pulp outta me so I just pulled the gun and shot them. Then I ran; did not stick around to see if they lived or died. I was walking down a street, yeah that's it. Walking down a street after I had some beer with friends and these two yahoos think they is gonna knock me over the head and take my money. Well they got another thing coming if they think James Foy is gonna fall for that one."

"The sheriff will send men out to interview you. Better make sure you are sober and got your story together," said McCollum patting Foy on the shoulder as he walked by.

Foy furrowed his brow and thought on it for a while. He would have to be pretty quick for those guys if he was gonna get out of this.

"I'm gonna go lay down and catch some z's for a few hours," said Foy getting up to leave the kitchen.

"I am going back to Daniel's house. I will be back about noon with Edith. We will get you some dinner and clean up the house so, please, let me in when I come banging back at the door," said Henry's wife.

"Also, try and sober up some!" she said closing the door.

Foy lay down on the sofa and fell asleep immediately. He was awakened by Edith and Henry's wife knocking at the door to gain entry. Foy opened the door and she said to him, "Henry and them want you to come help them load wheat."

"Muh!" was all Foy said as he turned and went down the basement stairs to drink some more hard cider. He came back up after a few minutes, put on a warm coat, his Scottish cap and left from the kitchen headed towards the barn.

Henry's wife watched him go in fear. She had heard the others said that Foy had shot two men in Union City last night and, according to Henry, the sheriff would be around soon to question him. Her stomach churned at the thought of Foy being interrogated by the sheriff. She could not think of a worse thing to happen; she felt as though her very life was threatened. She knew that Henry would not say anything to Foy but she would have a say in it. She turned to go back to her household duties and saw the .38 lying on the table in the vestibule. She picked it up. It was the first time she had ever held a gun.

"Beastly thing can only do the devil's work," she thought as she laid it back down. Tears now began to run down her cheeks as she went in to help Edith make the bed.

Foy made his way into the barn. As soon as he did, the men stopped working and one said, "Hey Jim, I heared that you got in some trouble last night over ta Union City."

Foy waved his hand and said in his normal don't care bravado, "Ain't no never mind. I shot two fellers. They jumped me in the saloon and then came out on the street after me!"

"I reckon the sheriff is gonna take ya in, Jim, and ask ya a bunch of questions. I'd make sure I got my story straight if'n I was you," said another.

Foy raised his hand and said, "They will never put me in prison. I will blow my brains out first." He then disappeared outside and went back behind the barn for about five minutes. When he returned, he did not come back in the barn but instead went up to the house.

"Dang, he never did help us like Judd said he was 'posed ta," said one of the men.

"Git up there and tell him to get his lazy ass back down here and help or we is gonna be here all night at this rate," said another to Henry Holcomb.

Holcomb shook his head but realized this was a good moment to talk to Foy alone. He wanted to know what the truth was about last night and no hero stories. He just needed to know that Foy had not done something foolish to get himself in trouble with the law, which could be a disastrous problem. His heart quickened as he reached the kitchen. He heard a sharp crack and at first jumped wondering what it was and then proceeded inside to find Foy on the floor with a bullet in his head.

His wife and Edith came in from the vestibule into the kitchen. Edith gasped as she saw Foy prostrate on the floor. Henry looked up at his wife with quizzical eyes and she a look of horror to him. He recognized that the sight was too much for her to bear and said, "Edith, you get out of here. Take her. Go down to the barn and tell the men what happened. Foy committed suicide." Henry held his eyes on his wife's as if he was willing something and Edith finally pulled her away as she took in the last sentence Henry had said. "Tell them Foy committed suicide."

She rushed out of the house and to the barn yelling, "Come quick! Foy has committed suicide! He shot himself! Henry says do come at once! He is dead! He shot himself!"

The men went running to the house as Henry bent near the body. He saw the revolver between Foy's legs and he, at the same time, heard the men coming close to the house. Henry put the Scottish cap over the pistol and stood up as the men came in the house to see.

There James Foy lay in the corner of the kitchen on his back with both arms out at a ninety degree angle to his body. Blood pooled up under his head and now began to run toward the center of the room. His eyes were closed and the expression on his face was a peaceful one.

"Where is the gun?" asked one.

"Don't rightly know. Maybe underneath him but right now we got to leave everything as it is and somebody has to go to town to get the sheriff," said Henry.

Right then there was a knock at the door. Edith opened it and there, as if on cue, stood two deputies.

"Afternoon, ma'am, we would like to speak to James Foy if he is here, please."

Edith just shook her head and motioned in the deputies. "He is in the kitchen," she said matter-of-factly.

The deputies walked into the kitchen and stopped in their tracks as they viewed the ghastly site.

"What has happened here?" asked Patrick Ryan, deputy.

"Foy done shot himself in the head and he is deader than a doornail," said one farmer.

Frank Snyder, the other deputy, stooped over the body and felt for a pulse. He found none. He turned to Ryan and shook his head in the negative.

Ryan said, "Reckon you better git to the sheriff 'bout this and tell him he may want to bring the coroner with him. I will stay here and stand guard."

Snyder shook his head and ran out the door to the buggy they had brought to transport Foy back to town. He slapped at the horses. They leapt out of the farmyard eastward down Horton Road toward Jackson.

Chapter 34

Ryan turned to the crowd.

"Who found him?"

"I did," said Henry raising his hand.

"Ok, the rest of ya go about whatever it was you were doing before this but do not leave until the sheriff gets a statement from ya," said Ryan.

The men went back to their job in the barn and Edith and Annise Holcomb went into the parlor to sit and reflect gathering their nerves back.

"Now this is how you found him when you came in?" asked Ryan.

"Yeah, the gun is under the Scottish cap if you are wonderin'," said Henry.

Ryan reached down and lifted the cap. He saw the handgun then let the cap back down on it as it was.

"Who was the last one to talk to him, do you know?" asked Ryan.

"Well, it was me down at the barn. We had all heard about the incident in Union City last night. He was supposed to be down there loading wheat with us. He came down and we asked him. He claimed it was in self-defense; that two men had jumped him in a bar and then followed him out into the street where he shot them."

"He shot one, missed the other but, from what we have heard from Union City, I am guessing that the story may not be a correct one. He shot the assistant postmaster and a friend as they locked up the post office to head home," said Ryan.

Henry Holcomb just shook his head in disbelief, and with some welcomed relief that Foy had taken himself out.

2010

Hunter sat back in his office eating a sandwich that Victoria had brought for his lunch. The television on the wall blared CNN Headline News at Noon. A shadow crossed the door and he looked up to see Chandra standing with another woman.

"Hey big guy, are you about done putting on the feed bag? We got stuff to do."

"Yeah, just waiting for Victoria to come back. She went upstairs to get a hack box, a few recorders and a camera. I thought we would go to the cemetery first. I always like to stop at Susan Holcomb's grave to see if she has anything to say. I know in my heart she knows everything or she has the best idea of anyone in the world. I am just hoping that in death she will tell all she knows or send us on the right path."

"I brought along a friend of mine, Denise Krueger. She is an excellent paranormal investigator from Kalamazoo. She has helped me out countless times and has done some work with police in several states. She is also a member of a group in Kalamazoo."

"Nice to meet you, Denise," he said sticking out his hand.

He looked at her. She was cute, could be around 34 maybe 35, sandy-brown hair made up nice but her most outstanding attribute was that her smile lit up the room as she said "Hello!" in a cute coquettish voice. He guessed her to be around five foot tall and maybe 100 pounds.

"Well, it's nice to have you along. Has Chandra filled you in on our quest to solve this murder?" asked Hunter.

"Yeah, she has and it is really interesting. Thanks for having me along. I can't wait! Where are we going first?" she asked again with a smile.

Hunter laughed internally, "God, I gotta watch out for this one. She is a real charmer and a looker, and I'm in love with that smile." He heard a noise behind him and he turned to look. It was Victoria.

"Ah, Victoria! This is Denise Krueger, a friend of Chandra's. She is a paranormal investigator and would like to come along today to give us her impressions. Denise, this is my associate, Victoria."

Victoria smiled at the lady and immediately took a liking to her demeanor.

"Well, ladies, shall we proceed towards Spring Arbor?" asked Hunter.

"Yeah, I parked out back next to yours. They won't tow it or nothing, will they?" asked Chandra.

"No, here I got a pass for ya to use. Just put it in your glove box and put it on your mirror whenever we meet here to go out," said Hunter reaching into his desk drawer and pulling out a red and yellow tag to hang from the mirror. It said across the front and back in black letters, "Friend of Hobbit Nook Books!"

"Thanks, Hunter. Denise and I need to go and get our equipment out of the car. We will meet you out there," said Chandra leaving toward the back door with Denise close on her heels.

"She seems like a nice lady to me. I hope she can be of some help," said Victoria.

"She will be fine. I believe we may even talk her into joining us on the team if she is half as good as Chandra says she is and you never hear Chandra brag on anyone."

"Except you!" said Victoria pecking him with a kiss on the cheek, grabbing his hand, leading him out of the back door into the parking lot and the waiting women.

They all talked about the Crouch case as Hunter drove the Charger toward Reynolds Cemetery. Pulling up beside it, Denise got out and snapped some quick pictures in what seemed like aimless directions.

"Did ya see something?" smiled Hunter.

"No, more like felt. It was not bad or good but it was watching and waiting for us to show up I believe. I do have some empathic feelings. I kind of became aware of them after my second traumatic brain injury," said Denise grabbing her equipment out of her case. She had on a vest that had Velcro on it and her audio recorder velcroed to the vest. Ear buds came out of the recorder, looped around her neck and into her ears.

"So, you can listen real time as it records?" asked Hunter.

"Yeah, I just started using it a month ago and I have captured a few things. Sometimes you can go back and listen to it on the recorder right away," explained Denise.

"What are the bent rods for?" asked Hunter walking beside Denise into the cemetery as Victoria and Chandra split to the very south end for EMF reading along the power line fence.

"Those are my divining rods and I really have so good luck with them."

"How do they work?" asked Hunter.

"I can ask questions and the rods will cross for yes and open for no as I hold them in my hand," she took them out of her vest for Hunter to investigate.

The rods were made of brass. About a quarter of the way up the length it bent at a ninety degree angle. There were wooden handles that the rods went through and these you held in each closed hand.

"So, you have never been here before?" asked Hunter.

"No," answered Denise.

"And you can find Susan Holcomb's grave with those?" asked Hunter.

"Yes, I can sometimes but this time it would be easy as I have seen a picture of her grave on Find-A-Grave on the Internet. I am looking across the cemetery and can see the big Holcomb marker," she laughed.

Hunter looked around, thought for a moment and then said, "Ok, how about you find

Jacob Crouch's grave? It is not marked and it's not on Find-A-Grave."

"Ok," she responded with a nice smile and a perky but serious attitude.

She held the rods in front of her so that they were parallel to each other sticking straight out from her body. She tucked her upper arms into her sides along with her elbows and bent her forearms each hand holding a wooden piece that the rods transferred through the middle.

"Ok, Jacob Crouch, if you are here can you cross the rods for yes, please?" she asked.

Hunter looked around not sure what to make of this remarkable woman and, at the same time, wondering about the scientific veracity of these rods. There was no breeze. It had been a clear warm autumn day, unusually warm and little to no wind but the weather threatened. Clouds now had formed and blocked out the sunlight making it a gray afternoon. The rods failed to move. Denise scowled at them because she really wanted Hunter to see them work but she also knew that they did not always work on command.

"All we want to do is ask you some questions, Jacob. Please, if you are here, cross the rods for yes and open them for no," pleaded Denise.

The rods did not move so, taking a different tack, Denise went to another line of questioning.

"Well, if Jacob is not here is there anyone here?"

The rods crossed for yes.

"Thank you. Please return them to neutral," asked Denise as the rods moved back to parallel of each other.

"Are you a man?" she asked. She got no response.

"Are you a woman?" she asked and the rods moved across for a yes.

"Are you a relative of Jacob Crouch?" asked Hunter. The rods crossed for yes.

"Are you Su…" Hunter held up his hand and stopped Denise in mid word.

"I want to try something and then I will explain a theory of mine a little later," said Hunter.

Denise smiled an acquiescing smile as Hunter continued.

"Can you point the rods towards Jacob Crouch's grave?" asked Hunter. They were standing inside the front gate having not really completely entered the cemetery. The rods swung to the right and Denise moved to her right as the rods straightened. She walked slowly in the direction that the rods pointed and suddenly they swung left. She did a military left-face and continued slowly. She walked past a burning bush on the left and a small marker on the ground to the left. She then stopped in an open space between two markers. The one on the left was small and read simply across the top "Anna". The rods at this point crossed. She had a puzzled look on her face as she dropped her arms and looked at Hunter saying "There is nothing here. How can that be?"

"Oh to the contrary, my dear! You are standing right on top of Jacob Crouch's grave. That is his wife Anna next to you. The grave marker was stolen from here so many times that they stopped putting one up and left it unmarked so vandals could no longer find him. Those rods are amazing! I have never seen anything like it in my life! Let's go to the Holcomb plot and see if we can get in touch with Susan."He turned to see Chandra and Victoria also moving in the same direction.

Hunter stopped in front of a large marker that said "Holcomb". Just below the grave marker said: "Bert Holcomb born April 26, 1870 died May 3, 1874." Next to that, like on split tablets, was: "Susan M Holcomb wife of D.S. Holcomb, born February 21, 1839, death Jan 2, 1884". At the foot of the big marker were two smaller ones; one marked "Susan" and the other "Bert".

"She and Daniel had a child?" asked Denise.

"Actually two," said Chandra walking up to the markers. "As you can see, Bert died at age 4 from what appeared to be pneumonia. They then had a daughter, Edith, who married a Mr. Pease and lived until 1945."

"The reason I stopped you back there from asking a Susan to do your wishes is that anything could tell you it's Susan. But I wanted to be sure it was her without calling a name. Only she would know her father's grave," said Hunter to Denise.

"Yeah, I knew that. Just got a little carried away with the moment," said Denise smiling.

Each person set up an audio recorder in different positions and in different areas of the Holcomb plot. Denise kept her headphones on listening for real-time responses, also laid a recorder at the main headstone, and one more on Susan's small marker. The sky now was turning darker, not threatening, but it looked like it could rain. Hunter looked up and realized they could go on down to the Crouch barn when they were done and investigate there in the rain and fog that would probably follow.

"Susan Holcomb, are you here? Come up here and talk to me. We have to sort this all out and I know you have the answers," said Hunter leaning on the headstone. "Four people killed including your father and sister. How can you rest in peace and not tell us anything about it? You should be sad at all the conclusions that are being drawn by people of who did it. Was it Judd or Daniel? Susan, if they had nothing to do with it then I would think that you of all people would want to tell the truth but then silence can also speak volumes."

No answer was evident as Victoria looked at Denise and she shook her head.

"I can sense a woman crying very hard. She is sad. She wants to be left alone; left in peace," said Chandra.

"I told you I will not leave you alone until you tell me all you know about this murder, Susan. Only you can start us on the right path. This is your chance to tell the story to everyone. I can get it put in a book and published so then everyone will know the truth. Susan, I know it's painful but you have to stand up for what is right. Knowing who and why your father and sister were killed is the right thing to do. What about Eunice's unborn child? What did he ever do to deserve that? He never had a chance; killed before he could come into the world and for what? Land, money, meanness? What was the motive? Who was it, Susan? Now is the time to tell it all."

This time Hunter looked at Denise and again she gave him the no sign. Then she walked closer to the headstone and put her hand on the top.

"I know it's hard, Susan, but listen to Mr. Ross. He is here to help and he wants to solve this. There must be something that you can tell us. One word. Anything that can lead us in a direction. Something that you can tell us. I get the feeling that you hated Eunice. Why did you hate your sister?"

There was no response and then a small whisper in her headphones that made her raise her head and look at Hunter.

"Susan are you afraid of someone here? Tell me. I will set protection for you so they will not bother you. Please, come and talk to us, Susan. We really want to hear from you."

"Terrible can't talk!" came a voice in Denise's headphones. She looked up at the group and gave a thumbs up.

"Check the EMF!" she said to Chandra as she pulled out a MEL-meter and began sweeping the immediate area.

"Got some high readings toward the church," said Chandra as Victoria picked up her meter and headed in the direction of the church fence. Her meter spikes were up and down as if something was moving in and out but not sure what to do.

"Susan, thanks for talking with us. I am sorry about you losing your son. I can only imagine what that must have felt like. He was very young. What killed him?"

"Eunice!" came the reply. Denise looked up and said to Hunter.

"I got Eunice!"

"How did Eunice cause the death of your son, Susan?"

She then shook her head again at Hunter for no.

"Surely, that is not why she was killed. Did you not feel anything for her? And if she caused your son's death, maybe she felt bad about it and really did not know what to say to you. I think you should not take this beyond life with you. It is what happened and maybe she had very little to do with whatever might have been inevitable. Susan, I can't believe you wanted her dead. You might not have liked her and may have been jealous of her but to wish her dead and that of her unborn child? I can't believe you hated her that much which only leaves one conclusion, that you are protecting someone that was involved with this."

Denise jumped as her headphones crackled loud, her MEL-meter spiked out of range and then there was a cry of "No!"

"Leave her alone! You have no right to be here! Go! Leave her alone!" yelled Denise as she grasped the headstone and hugged it as if to give solace to Susan.

Towards the back of the cemetery on the north west side, Jacob Crouch and his wife Anna stood watching the confrontation.

"Blacky again. He may have some formidable foes this time. I hope Susan stands up to him. I have been trying to get her to do that for some time now," said Jacob.

"She will," said Anna.

Jacob left Anna's side and moved toward the Holcomb headstone. He stopped a few feet and watched as the black mass formed again for another attack. It moved quickly as Hunter moved back. Jacob decided for some reason the mass might be intimidated by Hunter but he was not sure why. He moved quickly to Chandra's side and whispered in her ear. "Blackie don't like Hunter. Sic Hunter on him and he will retreat."

Chandra stood there realizing by her MEL-meter that whenever the entity attacked, Hunter became upset and moved toward it that it retreated. She was not sure how she knew this.

"Hunter!" she called as the mass started to move toward Denise again. "Come here by me for a minute. I want to check something."

Hunter, now really mad at the intrusion and the attack on Denise, turned and moved toward the oncoming mass. He and Chandra could not see the mass. It was large, getting larger and it was a cold mass. An angry mass!

As Hunter advanced it slowed and diminished. Chandra took the MEL-meter and moved toward it unknowingly as it moved back with each step of Hunter's advance. Finally, with a small hiss that was inaudible to Chandra and Hunter, it disappeared seemingly somehow defeated.

"It went away, I think," said Chandra.

Denise went on talking to Susan who now had become braver at the sight of the retreating entity that she had feared for so long.

"Susan, who killed your father and sister?" asked Denise. A response was heard on her headphones.

"James!"

"Did Daniel have anything to do with this, Susan?"

"Yes."

"Who killed James Foy?" she asked.

"Denise," came the response.

"No, not me. Who really killed James Foy? Was it your husband?"

"No!"

"Judd?"

"No! Denise."

"You don't have to be afraid anymore, Susan. I have put crystals around your grave for protection. They will help you cope better now without intrusion from who or whatever that was. Are you saying my name because you want something?"

"No!"

"We need to know who else was there at the murders. Was Judd there?"

"No!"

"So, really… who killed James Foy?"

"Denise," came the voice.

"Ok, who else is here with us?" asked Denise. "Daniel Holcomb, are you here?"

"Yes!" came a voice.

"Did you kill Jacob and Eunice Daniel?"

"No!"

"But maybe you were there that night?" said Hunter now sharing a headphone with Denise.

"No!"

"For some reason I think you were there and you had those people killed. Were you the lookout, Daniel, for James and Judd?" asked Hunter.

"Brave people, you are!"

"Oh come on, you don't scare me. You can't even do your own dirty work, you spineless son of a bitch!" said Denise, "and I did not kill James Foy."

"You need therapy! What do I care? I'm dead," a slight laugh followed the confrontation and as quickly as the voices came they left.

Rain now started to fall in a light drizzle. It was dark now and they were illegal by still being in the cemetery after sunset.

"Okay, ladies, time to pack up. We got a lot and this was interesting. Let's head home for the evening but, Denise, I want your card before you leave. Chandra was right. You are a most excellent investigator. No walls, no fear, and a very sincere quest for the truth within you." Hunter patted her on the back and the award-winning smile was so great it almost chased the rain away to bring out the sun as it set in the west.

Chapter 33

THE INQUEST OF JAMES FOY:

Having found the inquest papers of James Foy, I am going to present that to you with all the information I found. I am not saying that there is not more. This is just all I could find and I believe it to be a complete enough a record for us to determine what they saw in those days.

The town of Jackson was in a tizzy over the death of James Foy. Headlines were that of several papers: Fearless Foy Commits Suicide, Two Men Shot in Union City Perpetrator then Takes Own Life. The Jackson Citizen wrote: Ferocious Foy-James Foy Murderously Shoots a Stranger at Union City. Did Foy Know of anything of the November 21st murders? (Untrue) Foy is Captured Commits Suicide, and the last headline is He Dies at Mansion-the House of Murder and now Suicide!

Foy did shoot a stranger - that much we know - because he thought he was shooting Major Easton for printing a nasty piece about him in the Union City Paper. Foy was never captured as the one headline suggests and as you will read in the inquest records that I am about to present. Also, there is a printed story out there from the day that mentions that two deputies were dispatched to the Crouch Farm to arrest Foy. When they looked in the window, they saw him asleep on a couch and decided not to disturb him. They then supposedly came back hours later to find him dead from an apparent self-inflicted gunshot wound. The sheriff did, in fact, send two deputies out to arrest Foy just as that chapter before states and it was the only time that anyone was sent out to arrest him. Sheriff Winney would have jumped at any chance to put Foy behind bars to try and sweat the truth out of him. He would not have left Foy to sleep nor would any of the deputies. In fact, Foy had a reputation as a fighter and a tough guy. Even though he was a bully he could back it up. I am sure the deputies would have loved to catch him asleep and been able to restrain him before he fully awakened.

You will also find newspaper clippings that say a deputy by the name of Schuler came to arrest Foy but, before he could subdue him, Foy drew a pistol and killed himself. The deputy supposedly watching as the blood gushed from his head. You will now find notes of interest as we progress towards the end from me, the author, on thoughts of certain incidents that may have actually contributed to the case. These will be made mid-paragraph in *italic.*

I do not have the first part of the inquest papers but I will start from where I do and go from there.

We will start on day two of the inquest, February 8, 1884.

Henry Holcomb was called to the stand and sworn.

"Mr. Holcomb, can you tell us where you were on the day of Foy's death?"

"Yes, I came to the Crouch Farm about 1 PM with my wife and Edith Holcomb. They had come to clean and I had come to clean wheat as Judd had instructed me to."

"Did you see James Foy about the property when you arrived?"

"No, sir. I let the women off at the house and drove straight to the granary."

"Do you know if they saw Mr. Foy?"

"Well, they went to the porch and knocked and no one came to the door to answer. Edith she looked in and saw Foy was sleeping it off on the lounge so they just commenced banging on the door harder and harder and finally they was able to wake him. It was not long after that he came to the barn and we spoke to him about the shooting of the night before in Union City. He made no reply to our questions and went behind the barn for a period of time. For what I do not know. He came back and then went straight to the house and I yelled at him. Hey come back here and help us do this wheat or we will be here all night. To which he never stopped nor replied."

"Is that when the deputies showed up?"

"No, but I heard the pistol go off in the house and went in and seen him on the floor with the cap between his feet that he was a wearin' that day. Not long after that, the deputies showed up in a buggy to arrest him. One stayed to question us and the other he high-tailed it for Jackson to get the sheriff and the Coroner."

"Is it true that after the Crouch inquest you sought out Julia Reese under an assumed name?"

"I did go looking for her but did not give my real name. I wanted to interview her 'cause I thought she knew more than she was letting on."

"So you were going to hire her?"

"Well, no, but I let on as if I did so as to get her alone and find out what she knew."

"And did you get to question her?"

"No sir, that preacher's wife… she wouldn't let me nowheres near Julia Reese telling me two days in a row that she did not feel good and she did not want to see me. She told me that when Julia was well they was gonna hire her as help for them around the house. 'Course I never believed any of that. They just wanted to keep me aways from her."

"Thank you, Mr. Holcomb. You may step down but stay until the proceedings are finished as we may discover we have more questions for you."

"We would, at this time, like to call Mathew Brown to the stand."

"Mr. Brown, do you swear to tell the truth, the whole truth and nothing but the truth so help you God?"

"I do!"

"Please be seated, Mr. Brown."

"Mr. Brown, were you at the Crouch Farm the day of the shooting?"

"Yes sir, I was there. Came just after noon; waited on Holcomb; tried to get Foy to come to the door but to no avail. Went to the granary to wait for Foy and Holcomb."

"I did not see Foy come out but heard him talking to Mr. Holcomb and I said tell him to get in here and help us and I heard Foy said he would. He went to the house with Mr. Holcomb and in a short time Henry's wife came back and said he was shot."

"So what happened next?"

"I went in and saw Foy on the floor on his back, hands spread straight out and the cap between his legs. He was dead for sure. I later seen part of the gun under the cap."

"Were you able to hear the shot fired from the barn?"

"No sir, I was not."

"Have you ever spoken to Foy about the Crouch murders?"

"No sir, I have not."

"Please step down, Mr. Brown, and also you are to stay until the proceedings are finished in the event we should have more questions for you."

"I would like to call Rev. Lemuel T. Frink to the stand."

"I am sorry, Reverend, but I do have to ask you to be sworn in."

"I am not offended in the least and it is your job and civic duty I believe," said Rev. Frink as he took the oath

"So did you receive a visit from a man calling himself Lane?"

"Yes sir, I did about a week after Julia Reese was released. Said he had read that he saw she was looking for employment and he was an old bachelor and kept two girls. Said he lived on section #5 of Liberty Township. I told him she did not want a place to work at this time or she could have had a dozen. He then thanked me politely and left."

"Did this Mr. Lane ever return?"

"Yes, he did."

"Is he in the courtroom here today, sir?"

"Yes, that man there in the front row, Mr. Henry Holcomb."

"Thank you, Reverend Frink, you may step down and we would like to call Mrs. Frink to the stand."

Mrs. Frink arose and moved across the room to the stand, took the oath smiled and settled in the witness chair.

"Mrs. Frink, can you tell us about Mr. Holcomb's second visit?"

"Yes, it was the very next day and I was in the parlor and answered the door. I told him right off I knew he was Henry Holcomb but he denied it stating that his name was Lane. I then related a circumstance from the church that reminded him that I knew he was Henry Holcomb and he started to stutter and hesitate. I told him he had no right to Julia and if anyone had rights to her services I did for all the room and board I had put up for her and still think that is true."

"Thank you, Mrs. Frink, you may step down."

At this point the author would like to point out that this seems a strange line of questioning and wonders what it had to do with the death of James Foy. Could it be that they suspected Henry Holcomb of killing Foy and were trying to base testimony on that fact? Nothing was written to substantiate this but this testimony shows that there must have been some inkling by the sheriff and the coroner that maybe Foy was killed to shut him up. One wonders if Henry Holcomb had not been recognized and Julia Reese left with him if she would have never been heard of again. Along with this, we must wonder what - if anything - that Henry thought she knew. She knew what maybe he did not want told."

"We now would like to call Mr. James White to the stand."

"Mr. White, do you solemnly swear to tell the truth, the whole truth and nothing but the truth so help you God?"

"I do!"

"Where were you on the day Foy was shot?"

"I went to the Crouch farm the morning that Foy was shot and saw the revolver on the table."

"Were you there again in the afternoon after the shooting?"

"I was. Saw the cap on the floor and the same revolver under the cap."

"Did they tell you anything about the revolver and why it was on the table that morning?"

"Yes sir, they said it was there to be cleaned."

"Thank you, Mr. White. You may step down."

"We would like to call Helen Murdock to the stand."

Helen Murdock was sworn and took her seat.

"Miss Murdock, did you know James Foy?"

"Yes sir, at one point he had brought laundry to us to clean and he was there about half past six on Monday evening."

There were some snickers in the court as the participants knew full well that the Murdock sisters had never done anyone's laundry but their own. Most of the people actually knew the trade plied by the women for the railroad men.

"Did you at that time have any conversation with him?"

"Yes sir, he told me about the Crouch murders and how it was queer that the sheriff did not look closer to home and that Helen you don't know what I know. He said he was on his way that night to Union City and had a job lined up maybe for next summer. He came back later looking for his pistol which he said he dropped and then found in the snow just off our back porch."

"Thank you, Miss Murdock. You may step down. We would like to call Louisa Murdock to the stand."

Helen's sister, Louisa, came to the stand, was sworn and took her seat.

"You heard your sister's testimony. Do you have anything to add?"

"Well, just that he came back to the house and found his revolver. Then he came in and took the bullets out of it, cleaned and wiped it off, and started to reload it. I think maybe I asked him if that was a .38 caliber and he said it was. Then he looked funny in the face and turned to us saying, as he held one cartridge in his hand, that was the same kind of bullet that killed the Crouches' and that poor woman. I mean, he could have knocked us to the floor with that remark. Scared us to death, he did. We went to the sheriff with it the next morning but they was already preparing to go out and arrest him for something."

"Thank you, Miss Murdock. You may step down."

"We would like to call Deputy Frank P. Snyder to the stand."

The deputy was sworn and took his seat.

"Deputy Snyder, you were at the Crouch Farm the day that Mr. Foy died. What can you tell us about what you found upon arrival?"

"I went with Deputy Ryan to the Crouch Farm with a warrant for Mr. Foy's arrest in connection with a murder that took place the night before in Union City. We arrived at approximately 1:50 P.M. We found Mr. Foy dead on the floor of the kitchen. I did not see the revolver at first but did see the cap on the floor between his feet. After that, I saw it under the cap and found it peculiar that it should have fallen in a way compared to how the body was laid out to end up as it did not only between his feet but also under his cap."

"Thank you, Deputy Snyder. We would now call Deputy Ryan to the stand."

Ryan took the oath and seated himself. He pulled out a small notebook from his inside jacket pocket so as to be able to answer any questions from his notes of the scene that day.

"Can you tell us what all you observed and reported on that afternoon upon arrival?"

"Yes sir, it is like Deputy Snyder said. We arrived at the farm at about 1:50 P.M. and found Mr. Foy dead in the kitchen, lying on his back, face up, arms spread out wide from his sides dead. I first saw the revolver at Mr. Foy's feet only after Mr. Henry Holcomb pointed it out to me beneath the watch cap.

"I could only ascertain, as I tried to reconstruct the occurrence, from the location of the revolver and the spread of the arms from his sides that it must have made some other action to place it where it was. The revolver itself was near the left heel and the right arm was stretched ninety degrees from the side of the body. One chamber was empty and it was a thirty caliber."

He was then asked to lie on the floor to show the court the position of the body using his own weapon as that of the one found to show where it lay in relationship to the body. He was asked if he thought the gun could have ended up where it was if Mr. Foy shot himself. He said that he would not rule it out. The assistant prosecutor then mumbled that the only way he could have shot himself like that was if he were bending over, head between his knees and tying his shoes at the same time. This gave the court room a small chuckle as the gavel, once again, quieted the crowd.

"Thank you, Deputy Ryan. You may step down. We would call Deputy Snyder to the stand please.

Deputy Snyder was recalled to the stand.

"Did you find the revolver right off when you found the body?"

"No."

"Please, elaborate on this if you can, Deputy Snyder."

"I did not see the revolver under the cap at the feet of the deceased until Mr. Henry

Holcomb pointed it out to me by raising the cap."

"So then the revolver looked to be in a position it should be?"

"No! I do not see how the revolver ended up in its location from the spread of the feet and the way the arms were spread out from the body. The scene really made no sense but yet, there it was. I suppose the revolver could have been dropped and it bounced or hit a boot or leg of the deceased and ended up where it was but I would say even at that the cap would have been unlikely to end up perfectly on top of the pistol hiding it as well as it was. The body laid on the floor just as Deputy Ryan had shown. The body had quite a bit of warmth to it so we guessed, from our experiences with dead bodies, that he may have been dead for maybe no more than seven minutes before we found the body."

"Thank you, Deputy Snyder. This Court stands adjourned until Saturday at ten A.M."

Chapter 35

Hunter put down the inquest report as a noise from out in the Book Nook had disturbed him. There was some laughter and then Cheryl Treadway leaned in against the doorway. Looking at Hunter, she said, "Well I don't know what you did but it must have been pretty bad to have two deputies show up to take you into custody," she giggled at the end as Ed Dwyer poked his head around the corner in uniform and Jack Monroe the other. The two men stepped in and Jack said to Ed, "I reckon we come to take you in. Marshal sent us and you is in a heap a trouble, boy!" Ed started laughing as Cheryl said; "Now boys, if you are not here to take him in you can handcuff me and take me anywhere!" The girls out in the store giggled and then laughed as Cheryl left the men to their own means.

Hunter shook his head and said, "Come on in, guys. I got something for you that may put us on our first real lead of the case. Sit down. You want a Coke or something? Got some in the fridge over there."

Ed and Jacked moved toward the black refrigerator, opened the door, and there it was, Coke and Mountain Dew was filled in the fridge.

"Throw me a Dew, boys," said Hunter as they closed the door.

The men sat down and Hunter began, "I am about halfway through transcripts of the Foy inquest. At least, all that I can dig up and it is a little bit of an eye opener. I can already tell you, without a shadow of doubt, that regardless of what some papers wrote in the day, Mr. Foy did not kill himself behind the barn with a shotgun nor did anyone else shotgun him behind the barn. Mr. Foy died in the kitchen of the Crouch house not far from the door to Mrs. Reese's room. Although I don't, at this time, think it significant enough to pursue as Mrs. Reese had long moved out by that time."

"So, what do you want us to do?" asked Jack.

"I want you guys to play CSI with this one. I am sure you are good at it and I am equally sure that you can get some help from people in your county involved in such things. I have for you two the entire inquests as it exists. From that I have sort of recreated the death as it seems to have happened. I have suspicions about this but you are the ones who will ultimately decide whether or not this was a suicide or murder. I can't see it as any other way. I think, as you go along in the testimony, after reading my account that you will see that there were things that came up that seemed to never be questioned by anyone. So, in short, I want you two to be the mock coroner in this case and read the transcripts. Do whatever else you can to prove, disprove, or whatever brings us as close to the truth as we can get. I don't think that they realized back then what they had and how close they may have come to solving the whole mess. If you need money for tests, transcripts, to hire people for opinions or testing - just get in touch with Victoria and she will issue money from the D&R account."

With that Hunter handed them each a huge file folder of information.

"When do we have to have all of this accomplished by?" asked Jack.

"Well, as soon as you can but don't rush through it. We want something that is provable to a complete of a certainty as we can with today's forensics. My guess is you are gonna enjoy this and make some very startling discoveries by using today's forensic techniques."

The three men talked for a while longer about other things of interest. Jack asked if Hunter could get him books for college next semester cheaper than he was buying them for. Hunter agreed to look into it. The meeting broke up as Victoria returned with coffee for her and Hunter from Mickey D's.

The author would note that we asked two ballistic people to really perform the exact same test and the results written into this fictional part are really the same results they came up with.

Hunter filled two storage boxes with manila folders full of items about the Crouch case and put them on top of his desk. He took a large swig of his coffee with an espresso shot and said to Victoria as he put the cup in the top box, "I'm going upstairs, hon, to work on this stuff. You can come up when you are done in here if you wish."

"Hmm… and how much work would you get done then at that point?" asked Victoria with a wry smile.

"Yeah, I suppose that is a good point but still, the offer is open. Of course, that can be really at anytime you want it to be," said Hunter smiling and picking up the boxes as he headed out the door to the back stairs of the office.

Hunter sat down in his twenty by thirty five foot living room on the hardwood floor. He had changed into an old Marine Corps t-shirt, a pair of rust-colored sweatpants and white socks. He poured himself a generous portion of Maker's Mark into a glass over ice and then filled the remaining void with Canada Dry ginger ale. He put the glass on a coffee table near where he sat, swirled the drink around with his finger, licked the finger and then commenced to lay out the files around him. He stopped as he got to the inquest file because he had found a newspaper item that had been copied by the library in Jackson for him about the case. It was called "Items of the Inquest". He stopped and read the article of the Jackson Citizen Daily dated Friday February 8 1884. It read as follows:

"When Judd Crouch was asked by Undertaker Delehanty what he was going to do in regard to

the burial of Foy, and whether or not he wanted to order a coffin for him, Mr. Crouch flatly refused with an oath.

"Julia Reese went to Dundee this morning on a few weeks visit to friends. A Citizen reporter read a letter that Mrs. Reese wrote to her sister Mrs. Benoni Hall, of Sister Lakes, Van Buren County, and its tone was such as it would seem no guilty person could write. She speaks in a feeling manner of the kindness of Rev. Mr. Frink and his family, with whom she has found a home.

The brazen and reckless display by Judd Crouch of a loaded 38 caliber revolver while on the witness stand has caused many to ask the question is there not a law in the state of Michigan against carrying dangerous weapons, especially in public assemblies. A statute was made and provided at one time to the effect, but it has been repealed and now all the provision is that a person carrying weapons may be put under bonds on the complaint of any person considering himself in the danger there from. The revolver, which was very properly taken possession of by Coroner Casey yesterday was returned to Mr. Crouch at the end of the proceeding.

Foy's body is still at Casey & Delahanty's undertaking rooms, remarkably well preserved. His brother, John Foy a merchant and ex-alderman of Rome, N.Y, was telegraphed to yesterday in regard to the disposition, but no answer has been received as yet. Foy's divorced wife, who is married again and lives *in Grand Rapids `but whose name we could not learn, came here yesterday, with the consent, as she said, of her present husband, gazed for a while on the inanimate form of him she once loved, and left a wreath of beautiful flowers to decorate his coffin when buried.*

Corner Casey, Sheriff Winney and Detective P.J. Ryan went to Union City today to pick up any information they can glean from Foy's statements while there, and the result will transpire upon the resumption of the inquest to-morrow.

It was rumored last evening that Daniel Holcomb's illness was caused by his taking poison, but we are assured that it is nothing but a slight indisposition caused by a severe cold."

Hunter sat back, sipped at his drink and mused at a few things. What was Judd so afraid of that would make him carry a loaded weapon into a court room? Funny that he would not bury the man he was living with. Sounds like there was no love lost there, he thought. He also wondered what kind of stories Mrs. Foy could have told of her husband. What was he like when he was younger? Why did they divorce? He shook his head and continued to sort more papers into proper piles.

AND THEN ALONG CAME BROWN...

Galen Brown was a young man formerly of Jonesville, Michigan and was employed at the time by the Battle Creek Police Department (although under what exact capacity it was never said). He made his way into the final mess of the Crouch case. The story goes as follows:

Mr. Brown, having spent almost a week in the Jackson area presenting himself as a police detective from Battle Creek Michigan, showed up one day in the sheriff's office. He stated he had been engaged by the Governor of Michigan as a detective and he believed in almost a week he would be able to solve the crime and return to Battle Creek. Of course the Newspapers picked up on this at the time. There was elation in the community, of a super detective sent by the Governor. He would surely be able to figure this case out and have it solved in very little time.

The following is an excerpt of what Detective Brown stated happened during a recent visit he claimed to make to the Crouch farm.

On a Friday afternoon February 8th 1884 Galen Brown supposedly had walked from his rooming house in Horton to the Crouch house knocked on the door and began asking Judd Crouch questions about the case. He had of course introduced himself as the famous detective Brown, the Governor's appointment to investigate the case. He asked many a question about the case but the actual conversation went to the grave with Judd and himself some years later. We can and will comment about a note that Mr. Brown supposedly found in the Crouch Home.

He noticed while engaged in conversation with Judd that a coat jacket hung on the back of a chair near where they held their conversation. He could not but notice a worn envelope sticking up out of the top pocket of the coat. Finally he feigned thirst and ask Judd if he could have some cider before he left. Judd agreed and went to the cellar to fetch some. As soon as he went down the stairs Detective Brown took out a letter addressed to Judd Crouch. In the letter there was a statement at the bottom that read "If that baby is born we will lose everything make sure it does not happen." It was signed Mathews and had a Texas address. He quickly folded the letter up and stuck it in his inside pocket. Judd returned they had cider and as it was getting late Detective Brown excused himself and left the house. According to Brown at the time no one was home that he saw or heard except for Judd.

Now as the story continues:

Detective Brown walked all the way to the outskirts of Horton on Horton Road and as he came close to the town a small two person black buggy with a canvas top pulled up in front of him. The driver was on the off side of the buggy at the time. The driver of the buggy asked, "Are you Detective Brown?"

To which Brown responded to yes and turned to face the side of the buggy. The man setting on the passenger side nearest him shoved a revolver out of the buggy and pulled the trigger striking Brown in the chest and knocking him to the ground. He says he may have passed out but when he regained his senses he found the strength to rise and stagger towards Horton for help. One story says he was found by a boy and a girl attending a Ball that night in Horton and another says it was two boys on the way to the ball, however this author noted in both versions one person was named Nell and if that was true I would expect in those days it was a boy and a girl.

Never-the-less they picked up Brown and drove him to a local house and summoned the doctor. The bullet had entered above his heart by three inches and lodged in clavicle. His father a most eminent surgeon in Michigan at the time who resided just south in Jonesville was sent for. Someone using the community phone called Jackson and alerted the sheriff's office who sent four men to Horton immediately to investigate. They Found Detective Brown able to tell them what had happened and when asked if he could identify the man who shot him he simply said "If I was an innocent bystander and had seen the whole thing play out I would have suspected by the looks of the man it was Judd Crouch. He also told them of the note and showed it to them from his jacket pocket. Under the signature on the letter three initials stood out B. L. C. The date was a week before the Crouch Murders. They assumed that the initials were that of Byron L Crouch.

Brown signed a complaint against Judd and deputies were dispatched to the Crouch Farm and Judd was arrested and taken to Jackson to Sheriff Winney.

Pretty much the story in a nutshell and really puts the blame on Judd because at the time of the statement given by Brown the deputies wrote it as a death statement thinking he would not live. Mr. Brown did live. Judd was questioned by the sheriff and released at 5 A.M. the next morning and the arrest warrant was withdrawn. The writer of this and of course Hunter Ross asked themselves why.

Mr. Ross and I puzzled over this for quite some time. I made a trip, quite by accident, to a Hillsdale, Michigan library and found some interesting articles about Mr. Brown. I also was able to dig up an investigative hearing into the shooting of Mr. Brown in the Jackson Patriot.

Hunter and I could not explain why the sheriff had let Judd go. Well, it seems the truth of the matter is that Judd had a house full of guests that Sunday afternoon and none of them remember a Mr. Brown attending. Furthermore, it seems that Judd never left the house according to the witnesses.

Brown had gone into great detail about the color of the horse and that it had a white streak on its nose just like the one in Judd's barn. Except, when the deputies looked at the horse, it was in remarkable condition and obviously never been out of the barn all day long. A buggy matching the description could also not be found.

Suspicious now, the sheriff did what most of us would have done to start with and found that the Governor did not send Detective Brown. Yes, he was on the police force in Battle Creek had been granted a short leave of absence. It was questionable if he had ever done any detective work for the Battle Creek police.

The coroner stated in his examination of Brown that the shot was from below the heart and not above according to the trajectory that it took. Even Detective Brown's own father doubted that the shot had come from an upper angle and told the sheriff so.

Upon examination of the .32 caliber pistol that Detective Brown carried, one chamber had been recently fired. Detective Brown had no explanation for this. The bullet found inside of him was that of a .32 caliber.

One other thing puzzled the sheriff; why in the hell would you write an anonymous note with a fictitious signature and then place your real initials on the bottom of the letter? He also wondered… if Judd had stopped him to get the letter back then once he shot him he would have stayed long enough to find the incriminating letter, remove it and making sure with one more shot that Brown was dead. There was no one on the road that evening and there was plenty of time to do all of this.

One other thing about the letter concerned him. If it was written by Byron to Judd then why would you keep this incriminating letter in the front pocket of your jacket for months and months after the fact? It would serve no purpose except to get you hanged.

According to the Hillsdale paper (of which I was not able to obtain a copy that day), the sheriff and district attorney for Jackson County paid a visit to Detective Brown. The District Attorney noted to the sheriff that being the son of a renowned surgeon, you might know just where to shoot yourself to make it look bad but not kill yourself. Upon greeting Mr. Brown, it was said in the paper that they persuaded him to drop all charges and for that there would also, in turn, be no other charges filed against Detective Brown. The sheriff then took possession of the letter. The paper believes that it was disposed in a proper manner which befitted it. Upon being ousted by this, Detective Brown did, in fact, drop all charges saying at last that he was not sure it was Judd in the buggy.

So we can scratch that story that really twisted things up on the Internet imagining that Detective Brown was attacked for what he had found out mucking up the real picture.

We were unable to find out what happened to Detective Brown after all of this. There are some newspaper articles but we cannot ascertain for certain that they are true as to the veracity of articles from these publications. We have found these particular publications to be no more than made up by story mongers of the press that have little or no validity.

Now onto the story:

Final Chapter:

This book will not cover the famous trial of Daniel Holcomb. He and Judd were arrested and charged with murder but it was decided that they would be tried separately. Daniel Holcomb's trial was first. I can tell you much of what happened in the trial is a rehash of actual events in this book. The judge, however, in our opinion was not very progressive. He tied the hands of the prosecution presenting evidence. He, at first, would not allow the boot tread testimony. The boot was an exact match to the one Daniel Holcomb had. The boots were new - less than two weeks old - and still had the nubs on the tread from the manufacturer.

Today, there would be irrefutable proof that the boot in question and the print in the mud were the same and could have been made by Daniel Holcomb that night. The boot was a special-made boot that only one store in the area carried: a Boston Boot. The store had only sold one pair all fall and that was to Daniel Holcomb.

Daniel's insistence with the insurance lady about collecting insurance on Jacob was not allowed; it was deemed prejudicial. But the truth of the matter is he was sickened when he found out that the insurance cancelled was that of Jacob's and not his own. At that time, he was at a low. His wife died, the insurance was no good, and he had very little of a way to claim the farm and money for himself which may have been his reason for masterminding such a crime.

One sidelight to the trial: strangely, two weeks into the trial, the prosecuting attorney keeled over during examination of a witness with a heart attack and died in the court room. A new prosecuting attorney was appointed and the judge refused to allow him time to study the case or catch up on any of the evidence he had to present. The old prosecutor died on Friday and trial resumed on Monday.

O.J. Simpson's lawyers could have learned a lot from the defense attorneys hired by Daniel. They argued each point against their client until it was foolish for the prosecutor to speak at all. If one did not object then the other would raise a question of law that would have to be studied by the judge. This had happened so many times that it was forgotten what had been covered and proven. The trial was attended by many people and newspaper reporters from as far away as Australia. All major newspapers in the United States sent men to report until there was not a room left to rent all the way to Ann Arbor. Seventy-five days of actual trial and far too much to sum up in this book. However, if there is interest in the trial of which I have transcripts, the book could be written and told just as it happened.

One last true gruesome detail of the actual trial was another murder in conjunction or at least in a way. A lady juror was shot and killed by her husband over her continued absence from home to fix his supper. Thus the death count due to the original tragedy is, Jacob, Eunice,(her unborn child), Henry White, Moses Polley, James Foy, Prosecuting Attorney, and a lady juror of who's name we do not know at this time. Seven deaths. Then there was Galen Brown self inflicted wound, and the two men Union City. We should also note the passing of Susan Holcomb was mostly likely speeded along by the stress she was under. So we end up with eight dead and two wounded in less than eleven months.

2011

"Victoria, did you order the pizza for tonight?" asked Hunter from behind his desk. Victoria walked into the room.

"Yes, all the tables are ready. We should be able to eat by five thirty and then begin our deliberations," smiled Victoria. She knew how important this case had become to Hunter.

"Good, then let me go upstairs and get all the files I have up there. You gather up all the thumb drives and CD's and we shall be ready to go."

The black Charger flew out of the parking lot and down the street off toward Chandra's house.

"Did she invite Denise to be with us?" asked Hunter his mind still racing trying to think if they had thought of everything.

"Yes, I already told you that this morning now calm down. Things will be ok. This will all play out. We will put the evidence together and come up with a plausible explanation as to who it was that committed the crimes. Jack and Ed said their forensic studies will cast some real good evidence toward the culprits and Chandra says she has a surprise for us that will also help Ed and Jack's evidence."

Finally, they pulled in amongst all the cars crammed into Chandra's driveway. Hunter carried his files like an attorney. Victoria moved along beside him with her arm hanging down holding his hand.

"Come on in," invited Chandra, "You are the last two to arrive. Downstairs with ya and the pizza is sitting out ready to be devoured."

After a few beers and some pizza, they all got around the table in chairs looking out at Hunter. There was Ed, Jack, David, Chandra, Denise, Jemma and Victoria. Hunter stood in front of them with a big dry erase board behind him.

"Well, we are all here to see if we can figure this mess out and I guess the best way is to start. I think, after looking over this case, instead of at the beginning we will start at the end. Or rather, with Galen Brown."

"I think you have all read my report but I will summarize. It is beyond a shadow of a doubt Detective Brown shot himself hoping to incriminate Judd and thus draw attention to the likelihood that Judd may have had something to do with the original murders. There was never any letter from a Mathews- just something that had been forged by Brown and planted somehow. No one would, for instance, carry such an incriminating letter around for almost five months in your front coat pocket. No one would sign the letter with a fictitious name and then put the real initials on the bottom. There was really no reason for the initials to be on the bottom except for the fact that Detective Brown put them there. My guess is Mr. Brown was not the sharpest pencil in the box and, by all accounts, was out to make a name for himself even at the cost of perjury.

"So Detective Brown, his fantastic story and accidental shooting of himself can be thrown out as a crank story that really has no bearing on solving this case whatsoever."

Everyone in the room shook their heads in agreement.

Hunter continued:

"So who killed Jacob and company? Was it the cattle baron son from Texas? The question is: what did he have to gain? And the answer is: nothing. The fact is, he was a very wealthy man in his own right. He had sent three good-sized herds up the trail in 1883. The ranch in New Mexico had sold and he had the nineteen thousand dollars they had borrowed from Jacob to pay back from the sale of the ranch in Seven Rivers, New Mexico. He actually brought the check prior to Jacob's death and had settled everything. He had no earthly reason, nor did he stand in the way, when Judd took over the day-to-day running of the farm. No, Byron L. Crouch did not have a reason to kill Jacob nor Eunice. He was in fact against the marriage between Eunice and Henry White but only because he feared her education and Henry's lack thereof would be a source of friction in the union.

Hunter moved back and forth as some, like Denise, took notes and others hung on his every word listening intently and trying to help sum this up.

"Why would someone want to kill him? What would they get out of it? Land and money? Who, in all of our knowledge of this case, do we know or have uncovered that might have actually killed Jacob and family? Only one name comes to my mind, it came to the mind of many back in those days and is talked about a lot. That name was none other than James Foy."

The room was silent as Denise raised her hand.

"I am new to this case. I have read everything that you have sent me but maybe tell me more about James Foy."

"You know I will. For all of you just a reminder, James Foy was the local bully. Especially when he had been drinking. He had a foul temper and many run-ins with the law. He was a great farmhand or foreman but he had two problems: women, and drink. They both kept him broke. He also would talk too much about things he should not after he got a snoot full. This he did without even thinking he was spilling the beans. There were some back then who may have suspected him but kept quiet about their suspicions until he was dead. That is how Foy got in this mess. He told way too many people about the murders, how they were committed and in great detail as to how the killers went about it. Today, it is easy to see he knew it too well not to have been there as it took place. The only way he could have known those things was if he had helped them take place."

Hunter stopped and looked across the room at Jack and Ed. He knew it was time for them to take the floor. He was not sure what they had but Ed said it would blow the case wide open.

"So, what we are going to do is something they never did back in those days. We are, just for arguments sake, going to take a good close look at the suicide of James Foy. Dissect it, talk about it, and go over the notes of the inquest I have given you. We are starting at the end of all the death and destruction that befell that household minus Mr. Brown and work our way backwards to the killings to see if they make any sense at all. To do this, I am going to turn the floor over to Ed and Jack who have done some very good modern-day forensic work using the notes from the inquest, the coroner's autopsy report, and notes from the investigating deputies that we uncovered in the Jackson Citizen Patriot. Gentlemen, if you please," said Hunter.

Ed started, "We took a look at what we knew was evidence from, like Hunter said, the reports. The one thing that people noted back then and stated the most in interviews was that the pistol was found in such a strange place. Why between his feet and why with his cap on top of it? What are the odds of him shooting himself, dropping the gun, his hat flying up in the air and landing on his gun? We smile now but the authorities did not seem the least bit concerned about that. One state official said of the coroner's inquest that: "Mr. Foy would have to of been bending over with his head between his legs tying his shoe and then shot himself to end up with the gun and the shot in the head as it appeared."

"On that note we agree," said Jack. "We spent a lot of time finding a thirty eight caliber pistol revolver that would have been of the day, eighteen eighty to be precise. We could not put the gun to our head three inches behind the right ear and still pull the trigger. First of all, why would you want to? When you could easily put it in your mouth or to your temple and get the same results? That shot behind the ear was exactly as Jacob was shot. This did not go unnoticed by us. We had any number of people try it and your hand is so cramped in that position you cannot pull the trigger without lifting it forward first," said Jack looking to Ed.

"To get some ballistic gel," started Ed, "and make some heads from it. We wanted to see what the penetrating power of a thirty eight caliber was in those days. The one thing that also puzzled us, and should have been a big tip-off even back then, was no powder burns to the cap, the hair or the scalp. Sticking that type of pistol to your head in those days would have scorched the hell out of everything. Consulting some ballistic experts, we put it to a test. We found the exact formula for powder in those days and made our own loads."

"Kids don't try this at home," intoned David.

All laughed and Ed went on, "We fired off almost twenty rounds in an attempt to see up-close what would happen and how far away we would have to be for the cap, hair and scalp not to get burned. Between twenty and twenty-four inches was the finding. Unless Mr. Foy was a freak, there is no way he could have held that gun that far back from his own head," finished Ed.

"So," continued Jack. "Now we are even more curious about the penetration of the bullet. It was found in the left side of the brain just past midpoint. We set up ballistic gel heads to simulate the shot to the head. Again, we loaded rounds into the revolver and fired at the heads from pointblank range up to two feet away. We found at pointblank range that the shot was through-and-through; always out the other side and with some range I might add. That gun stuck to the head and shot would have always produced an exit wound on the other side of the head. To get the bullet to midpoint, we had to make some more heads and fire at them from various ranges. As we got to about twenty inches away, the bullet would stop to the left side of the brain just past midpoint almost every time." Jack stopped and looked at Ed.

"So we have to conclude that Mr. Foy did not take his own life but was shot by an unknown person at this time," said Ed.

"Thanks, fellows, that leaves something for us to look into then," said Hunter starting to rise. Jack held up his hand and said.

"Hold on thar, partner. We gots more," he said smiling.

Ed started to talk, "We decided to look further into this and read all we could from the inquest, the on-the-spot statements taken, and we found a few peculiar things. For one, Henry Holcomb seemed to be really put out about the fact that Foy had maybe killed two men in Union City. He was afraid that the sheriff would get Foy behind bars and sweat a confession out of him about the night Jacob and family were killed. Why would that bother him so much? Maybe he was being protective of his brother but that seemed an unlikely reason to kill Foy. Really, Henry had his own farm and would not have been hurt by Daniel going off to jail. But wait, folks, there was three of them. The boot print outside the window exactly matched the boots that Daniel had. If he was there, and that today in court would have been conclusive evidence that he was, that means he did not do the killings. Two others would have had to. Was it Judd then? Did he really have a motive to want daddy dearest dead? The preacher said that Judd had a chance to recount his sins on the death bed but he never said a word before he died in front of friends, family and the preacher. It was also a well known fact that Judd wanted nothing to do with farming it was not his cup of tea and we suspect it may have been due to his crippled leg."

"Well," continued Jack, "We got two of the three. Who shot Foy then to shut him up? There were two women in the house as far as we can tell: Edith and Henry's wife. We actually looked up Henry and found that he and his wife had a small farm that was given to her of five acres. Not real easy to support a family on five acres, so that means Henry had to work and maybe take from his brother when times got hard. This meant that Jacob was paying to keep them both. Remember, there was another footprint found outside Jacob's house the morning of the murders. Someone had left a very distinct print jumping over the stone wall to the west of the house. When we found out that Henry lived near Horton and, if he had been there that night, he would have returned to the west by possibly jumping the stone fence to the west. No one back then seemed to think that the print by the stone wall meant anything. It was mentioned then dismissed and never brought up again."

Ed started, "The men at the barn, when questioned and asked the whereabouts of people prior to the shooting, brought up one point. That point was that Henry Holcomb went up to the house prior to Foy being found dead. Mrs. Holcomb came to the barn and told them that Foy had committed suicide. Did Henry have time to walk up the hill, grab the revolver off the table and shoot Foy then send his wife to the barn? The answer we came to after visiting the farm was: yes. There are almost three minutes that no one could account for Henry. Time enough to walk to the kitchen, grab the revolver off the table and shoot Foy in the head. Foy, remember, was in a most drunken state and still drinking. He may not have even known that Henry had entered the house." Ed turned to Jack.

"That's right and, as you all know, the deputies came quickly right behind the killing. Henry did not have time to get rid of the gun or place it in the right position so he dropped it between the legs of Foy and threw the cap on top of it as the farmhands came to look. One man asked where the pistol was in an interview and stated that Henry said he did not know but when the deputies got there he told the deputy where it was. So does that mean case is closed? Well, except we are cops and have had to investigate many a crime scene in our years and there is one more scenario that could have accounted for what happened. I said we looked up Henry's property deed and found that he and his wife did own the property outright. We also found out her name was Anise. I chuckled to myself at such a strange name for those days but Ed stopped me with a thought."

"Yeah, I got to thinking back on some of the remarkable material we got from the last investigation where Denise had a nice conversation in the cemetery with Henry Holcomb. When it was asked, as you remember, who killed James Foy the voice told you more than once that it was 'Denise.' Which you all laughed off and became a little irritated at the voice. But think back and listen as I play this tape again."

Ed switched on the recorder as a voice came on asking the question and getting the answer 'Denise'.

Jack stopped the recorder and said, "Maybe they were saying 'Anise'?"

This really took all in the room by surprise and Denise felt a cold chill go up her spine. She pulled her small jacket closer around her. Hunter stared at the duo for quite some time and smiled.

"Of course! It could have been Anise and maybe she did."

"She was already in the house," stated Jack. "She may have been in a tizzy over her husband going to jail. How would she survive on five acres on her own? It's not said if they had children or not. Maybe she went into the kitchen and asked Foy to give himself up and not say a word. Or maybe she wanted him to run and not be caught. In any event, she also could have easily in a state of mind grabbed the pistol - maybe having never shot one before - pointed it at his head and pulled the trigger. She more than likely would have had time to drop the gun in a moment of panic and it could have landed at the feet of Foy. Her husband comes in, sees what has happened and sums it up quick in his head. He knew he had to get her out of there so he told her to go and tell the men that Foy had committed suicide. As she and Edith did, he then covered up the gun thinking he could move it under the body later. He even mentioned to one of the men viewing the body before the deputies arrived that maybe the pistol was under the body. Which, in suicides, happens more than not? He then figured he would have time to put the gun under the body before the deputies got there. But about this time deputies are knocking on the door and now he is stuck with the pistol under the hat and then tells the deputy a few seconds later when asked that the pistol is under the cap."

"That means only one of two people could have killed James Foy," said Ed. "Either Henry

Holcomb or Edith Holcomb and both for the very same reason - to keep Henry out of jail. So now we have the killers of Jacob Crouch and family after all these years. Henry was obsessed with the crimes and he even tried to plant incriminating evidence on a man who was already in jail, a convicted felon who very well could have been believed to be the murder. Henry was actually tried for perjury but was found not guilty because of his brothers attorneys they were probably relentless at that trial also. Yes it is an even bet that Henry was the third one that night."

Hunter stood up smiling as he had already gone over this conclusion with Jack and Ed. They had done a remarkable job in proving it out almost beyond a shadow of a doubt.

"So, as it goes, to sum this up on the night in question: Henry Holcomb met Daniel and James Foy at the Crouch Farm. Daniel stood guard out front with Henry and James doing the shooting inside. Then Daniel and James went back to Daniel's house and to bed with a story James was putting the cat out and Daniel had to go outside and hook up a barn door blowing in the wind."

"What about Susan Holcomb?" asked Chandra.

"I will let Victoria tell ya all about her," said Hunter taking a seat again.

Victoria began, "There is more than one reference to Susan being in poor health and mental state over the vicious killings of her father and sister. I was not able to tell whether she knew or maybe surmised who had done it and that her husband had a hand in it. One thing was a fact, Daniel did love her very much and her death was nearly the end of him. He had planned this all out. They would kill Jacob and Eunice along with Henry White and then Judd and or Susan would inherit Jacob's farm and that would place it in his hands. No more scraping or bending to Jacob for money. He also had a life insurance policy on Jacob which would give him a nice, rich nest egg to work off of. With Judd in control of things, they could run both farms and get very rich. Two things he did not count on. One, that the life insurance had, in fact, been canceled by mistake a year before and two, that his wife would die leaving him with no way to inherit. Then, when Byron showed up with an interest of catching his father's killers, he felt he was losing the grip. He did lose it all and was still tried but not convicted for the killings. Susan simply died of heart disease probably exacerbated by all the stress she was under. Nothing in the inquest or the coroner's report show anything unnatural about the way she died. Also, it was proven that she had no poison in her body at the time of death by an autopsy performed the day after her death. This was just an untimely death at a strange time. When people found out she was locked in her bedroom dead, all sorts of wild stories started around the community until the press in some cities started believing the old biddies and their gossip therefore printing wild stories like she was force-fed rat poison."

Hunter stood up and looked at his watch. It was ten forty five PM. He looked at the group and asked if anyone had anymore to say.

"I also found no evidence at the cemetery the night of the anniversary," said David rising to tell all.

Denise asked if they could do one more investigation at the property to see if they got any more responses. She was anxious to try out her dousing rods on the farm.

"Yes, I will set up a time to do this and all who can or want to may come along. I will pass the time on to you once I have gotten the schedule made out. Now, we think tonight we have solved the murders of Jacob Crouch, Moses Polley, Eunice Crouch White and Henry White. After some deliberation and very fine work on the part of our team, I submit to you that they were killed by James Foy and Henry Holcomb while Daniel Holcomb stood guard. All of those who think this is correct, please raise your hand."

Everyone raised their hand and Hunter smiled.

"A bit melodramatic but I think that this is the best way to say we all agree. I think it's time to go home especially for Denise and David. They have the furthest to travel."

THE LAST INVESTIGATIONS:

There were two final investigations and I will not go through the first one only to highlight a few things. We had more rocks thrown at us in the barn as we baited them. On the way out I told Denise that I did not think we got any evidence tonight but upon listening to my recorder which I keep on all the way to my vehicle there was a small beautiful female voice on the audio recorder singing a song that really was beautiful but it was not audible enough to know what the words were. At the point that I said: "I don't think we got any evidence tonight" the voice intoned: "Poor Andru."

Later on at a second investigation inside the existing house, we were very lucky to pick up a voice on a recorder. This time I was with Dan Holroyd of SMP in Kalamazoo. What we heard that night was the same female voice I had heard down at the barn previously. The gist of the words were that she was confused, still nine months pregnant, could not find her husband or her father. I talked slowly to her and told her when she was ready to go where she would find her whole family. Maybe she should look for a light, a bright light, and move into it. That may clear up all of her confusion and I thought maybe put her poor restless soul at peace.

The last investigation there was with my colleague and best friend, Denise Gowen-Krueger. She, I and her daughter, Morgan who was 11 at the time, spent a rainy evening in the barn running tests with MEL-meters, taking different photos and videos, and asking questions with audio devices spread all over the bottom of the barn. We did get something that night that was unexpected. I had laid out the case as if I was a law enforcement investigator. I told them that I had contacted a professor of law, laid out the case that I had with all the facts and he told me that it would be an 88% chance of a conviction in today's court. I told them just before we left that they should have all been hung by their necks until dead. The night was very foggy with drizzle, very damp and cold. We had finished up and were leaving when Denise's daughter, Morgan, stopped in front of us and said, "Look at that!" To the right of us was a wall, a cement-parged wall, and water was running down the inside of the barn. It had made a perfect hanged-man rope and all on the wall as it ran down. Paranormal or just a coincidence? I will leave it up to you but the picture is on the back of the book. All of the years I have chased the paranormal I have never had anything like that happen to me before nor since. I can't explain it under any circumstances nor will I say it was the ghost's way of commenting to me one last time.

The End

To Erica
Thanks for the
Laugh Good Luck
With the New House
May your Life Be Filled
With Joy & Unbelievable Happiness
Some Day We Shall
Have That Late Night
Party

[illegible]

Made in the USA
Charleston, SC
11 December 2011